The Third Skull

A Paranormal Mystery Thriller

By Andrew M Stafford

Thank you to
DC Rob Callaway (Retired)
Beta Readers - Nigel Burrough, Claire Herbert, Sharon Newton and Philip Newton
Penny Rowe for proofreading
Ian CP Irvine for his advice and encouragement

For Kerry, Olivia, Sam, Mum and Sharon.
Especially for Dad.

Chapter 1

December 14th 1804

James Whitcombe's Field
Bristol

Alice Donaldson ran for her life, not only hers, but also the lives of Louisa and William Drake. The frozen ground cut through the soles of her cloth shoes and the sub-zero air of the winter afternoon burned her lungs as she gasped for breath. She mustn't stop, the dogs weren't far away.

The sun had almost set, giving her the upper hand over her pursuers. She knew James Whitcombe's farmland well and had played there as a child with her two brothers.

She struggled with the wooden handcart which bumped and rattled over the uneven field. If the children had been conscious they would be crying at the top of their voices as the cart jarred their bones whilst Alice navigated ruts and gullies.

The last time Alice had been here she had been eleven years old, and those had been happier times. Ten years had passed, and she hoped the small stone hut at the far end of the field would still be there. She needed somewhere to rest whilst she caught her breath and waited for the stitch to subside. The building would allow her a few minutes to recover and hide with the children from the approaching hounds. Their howling and barking was getting louder as they grew closer.

She staggered over the rise and the stone hut came into view, silhouetted by the setting sun casting a long shadow towards her. Adrenalin fuelled her as she made the two hundred yard dash to the dilapidated building as the children's limp bodies crashed from side to side. The pain in her chest was excruciating as she stumbled the final steps to the hut and pushed open the half rotten wooden door. Alice bundled the children in and laid them on the rough floor. She fought with the rusty hinges and closed the door.

She sat in silence and heard nothing but her pounding heart and the approaching hunt dogs. Alice prayed for a miracle that they wouldn't follow her scent to the hut. Her prayer was answered, the sound of the wailing hounds passed alongside the building, followed by a stampede of hooves and roar of angry voices. The dogs and the riders carried on to the west and away from James Whitcombe's field. Alice's breathing slowed and her heartbeat settled as she took a moment to compose herself. She pulled back a curtain covering the dirty window and watched the shady images of the riders disappear from view.

She turned her attention to the children who lay motionless on the floor. Alice struggled to see in the dimming light of the winter afternoon. As her eyes became accustomed to her surroundings she spotted tools and implements hanging from the wall. A length of rope hung from a hook on a wooden beam. Alice noticed a small shelf on which stood an oil lamp. After several attempts she coaxed a flame from the stubby wick, and the wavering flicker formed shadows that danced around the walls and the ceiling.

She turned to Louisa, the weakest of the siblings, and put her ear to her mouth to check whether the little girl was breathing. Nothing. Her limp body was warm and Alice searched for signs of life. She held the girl's body and cried. She woefully looked at William who lay beside her on the floor. Alice knew by the way his body slumped on the hard stone ground that he too was dead.

Hours of trekking through the countryside on a freezing December day dressed in their nightclothes and morning gowns had been more than their young bodies could endure and the final hour of being jostled and thrown around on the stolen handcart like rag dolls had been the final straw that had ended their young lives.

She lifted William from the floor, and held both children in her arms. Her tears flowed. She sobbed to herself, conscious she should not be heard, even at this time of overwhelming grief. Alice pulled the children closer as her tears rolled down her face and into their hair. After a few minutes she lay both children down, this time making them comfortable by resting them on straw which Alice found bundled in the corner. Even though they were dead she wanted them to lie as if they were sleeping.

Alice needed to think, and she needed to think fast. The children may be dead, but the secret they held must be kept from those from whom she was hiding them. They were as valuable in death as they'd been in life. She bent forward and ran her hand through William's thick blonde hair. Even in the dim light and through the fullness of his shock she could just make out the strange pattern embedded in the back of his head. She turned to Louisa, whose thicker and longer hair concealed her pattern. And even though it wasn't visible, Alice knew it was there.

Alice needed to find somewhere to lay the children to rest, and somewhere their remains could never be found. She sat with her back against the wall and concentrated, trying her hardest to block out the bodies on the floor. She remembered the dry well she used to throw stones into as a child. But where was it? In the past ten years her memory of the farmland was good, but not that good. She recalled the hawthorn tree that stood nearby. If she was able find the tree, then she could find the well. In their youth, Alice and her brothers climbed the tree countless times. She closed her eyes and recalled every bough and foot holding it offered. Alice grabbed the lamp, stood up and pulled her woollen shawl around her shoulders to keep away the biting cold. Outside, she saw how dark the field had become since the sun had set and that the low moon cast a faint light. The well wasn't far from James Whitcombe's dwelling which was a good country mile to the south. She made her way towards the farmhouse and hoped that her instinct and sense of direction would serve her well. She picked up pace and ignored the painful shards of stone beneath her feet. The lights of the farm came into view. It was hard to judge how far away they were, but she knew the well and the tree must be close.

With her heart in her mouth she ran towards the pale light of the farmhouse. The oil lamp offered a little glow as it swung in her hand, but not enough light for her to avoid a small gully underfoot. She lost her balance and fell upon the frozen soil. Alice rolled onto her back and cursed at the pain in her ankle.

"Please God, please help me," she muttered and lay on her back looking up at the black sky. The stars appeared like teardrops, looking upon her as if they were judging her. She rolled onto her side, reached for her ankle and rubbed the painful joint. She looked across the field and was drawn to the waxing moon low in the west. And then she saw it.

Silhouetted against the moon was the tree. The hawthorn tree she had climbed as a child. She recognised it instantly. After ten years of growth it looked the same. Alice limped towards it. She could make out spiny branches which looked like skeletal fingers pointing at her accusingly. She stopped for a breath and looked around to survey the field for the wall which surrounded the well. She strained her eyes in the darkness and with only the fading glow of the lamp Alice spotted it. She hobbled towards the small wall, not stopping until she had reached it. Alice placed the lamp atop the dry stone wall. She looked over and expected to see the metal grille covering the well head but she was taken aback to see nothing but soil and scrubby grass.

The thing's been covered over she thought to herself.

She climbed over the wall, lowered herself down and scraped at the soil. Frozen shards of stone pained her fingertips like paper cuts. After what felt like an eternity Alice had cleared enough soil to expose a timber beam. "Yes," she whispered and continued to scrape and scratch at the soil to expose more of the wood. She stopped to catch her breath, put the lamp on the ground and surveyed her work. "I'm getting nowhere fast," she exclaimed under her breath when she saw how little of the wood covering the well head had been uncovered. She got up and limped back to the building where the children lay.

She made her way back and thought about the events of the day.

The children awoke excitedly on their fifth birthday. Both had been expecting to be greeted by their father on their special day. But instead they saw Alice scurry into their room insisting they went with her and ask no questions. She'd told them they had to leave, and they had to leave straight away, with no time to dress or for breakfast. They were scared but believed

Alice when she told them they couldn't say a word and to come with her. They trusted her as she was the closest thing they'd had to a mother. Alice laced their boots, opened the door and fled the house holding the arm of each child as they tried to keep up with her.

"I'm cold," called Louisa.

"We mustn't stop," said Alice.

"What's happening, where are we going?" sobbed William.

"Please children, please keep moving. You need to trust me, I'll try to explain later."

It hadn't taken long for Alexander Drake to discover that the children were not in their beds and were nowhere to be found. He'd called for Alice, the girl who he'd employed for the past two years, but she'd also gone. After searching his grounds and outbuildings he mounted his horse and explored the surrounding area.

Drake cursed under his breath as he rode to the village. It was half past seven and morning was teetering on the edge of daylight. Condensation bellowed from his horse's mouth as its snorts and whinnies hit the wintery air. After fruitlessly banging on the door of every house he returned and by nine he'd assembled his gang to search for Louisa, William and Alice, the young nanny who he thought he could trust.

Alice and the children had a three hour head start and miraculously stayed ahead of Drake and his marauding gang.

It had been eleven hours since Alice left the house and now the children were dead. But if Alexander had got to them before they'd died, their fate in his hands would have resulted in something much worse.

Alice approached the hut and shuddered when she shone the lamp over the threshold. William and Louisa lay where she had left them. She was anxious that Drake may have found them.

She loaded the bodies onto the cart and went back to the hut. Scanning the dark room as the lamp threw a yellow insipid glow against the wall, she saw a shovel lying in the corner. Alice picked it up along with a length of iron bar that was lying next to it and tossed them out into the field. She heard the dull thud as they landed on the frozen ground. She grabbed the rope hanging from the wooden beam and looped it over her shoulder. She limped to the cart, threw in the shovel, bar and rope then made her way back to the well.

Within ten minutes she was at the well and went to work clearing the soil. Her hands were blistering as she scraped and dug the gritty earth. Soon, the timber plank covering the well head was exposed. She fell to her knees and scratched at the corner of the wood and struggled to lift it. Alice snatched the iron bar and used it to prise the plank. It was heavier than it looked and she cursed as she grappled with it, attempting to move it away from the well head. After several minutes the lump of wood was away from the entrance to the well and Alice propped it up against the wall. The lamp was fading, but was casting enough light for her see the well head was covered by the same iron grille which prevented inquisitive children and stray animals from falling into the shallow cavity when she was a girl. She used the iron bar to lever the grille from where it had lain for as long as she could remember. She hauled it onto its side and propped it against the wall alongside the plank.

Alice stopped to catch her breath. The temperature was below zero and she ignored the cold and pain from her cut and blistered hands as adrenaline charged blood raced through her veins.

She turned to the cart behind the wall and hung the lamp over the bodies. She picked up Louisa and held her close.

"I'm so sorry my darling," she whispered and hugged the little girl's body. "I am so, so sorry."

Gently holding Louisa in her arms, as if she was taking her to her room to place her in her bed, she carried the dead child over the wall and lay her next to the well. She took the rope and formed a loop at one end. Alice passed the looped end of the rope over Louisa's head and shoulders so the rope was under the girl's armpits. After pulling the rope tight around Louisa's chest, she bent forward and kissed her on her cheek and stroked her hair. "Please forgive me God," she whispered as she touched the girl's face.

She hauled Louisa to the well and lowered her, feet first, into the abyss. The lamp didn't cast enough light to show the depth of the well, but Alice knew it was no more than a fifteen foot drop. She remembered stories of children who had climbed into the well for a dare. The well had been a hiding place for children who'd run away from home, only to be found by James Whitcombe, who eventually covered it with the grille.

The rope juddered and Louisa's body jerked against the rocky shaft as Alice lowered her in. It slackened when Louisa came to rest at the bottom. Alice tied a loop in the other end of the rope and placed it around William. She had little time for farewells because Alexander Drake and his gang were likely to return at any moment. She kissed him on his head and lowered him alongside his sister. Wiping her dirty arm across her brow she looked into the dark hole and said two quiet prayers. One for the children and one for herself, again asking God for forgiveness.

Alice replaced the iron grille, hauled the heavy plank back into position and shovelled the soil over the wood and then pushed the hand cart back to the hut.

Alice returned to the building and fell to the floor. She was exhausted, scared and grief stricken but knew she'd done the right thing. Her muscles ached and her limbs hurt. The lamp faded and tiredness enveloped her as she sobbed until she fell into a deep sleep.

Chapter 2

Alice awoke to the sound of voices and whining dogs. She sat up and remembered where she was. The lamp had burnt out and inside the hut it was too dark to see. Light danced like fireflies between the cracks in the door as outside, a crowd of angry men jostled and shouted. Fear gripped her as the door flung open. Covering her eyes with the back of her hand to shield them from the bright lamps she shuffled backwards towards the wall.

"She's in here, tell Drake we've found her," shouted a short man holding a burning torch. A commotion ensued as the men hollered and jostled. A tall man pushed his way to the front and stood in the doorway. His eyes took a few seconds to adapt to the darkness, and when they did he saw Alice cowering in the corner. He stooped his tall frame as he entered.

"Hello Alice, I've been looking for you........ what have you done with my children?"

Alice said nothing. Her mouth was dry, and she trembled with fear. The clean shaven, dark-haired man knelt beside her and in a calm voice asked her again. "Alice, I need to know what you've done with William and Louisa. Please tell me where they are."

Alice felt weak and pathetic, but was determined not to be intimidated.

"They're not your children," replied Alice. Her voice wavering but confident.

He moved closer and put his mouth to Alice's ear. She could smell his cologne and feel the warmth of his breath against her face. Across his cheek was a scar which marred his handsome face.

"I will ask you one more time, so think before you answer. Where are they?"

Alice looked him in the eye as she summoned her mental strength to not be overpowered by his intimidation.

"I won't tell you. They're somewhere you'll never know. I may be young, but I'm not stupid. I know your secret and I know you're not their father."

"You know nothing!" he shouted as he rose to his feet. Drake stood over her and pushed loose strands of long dark hair away from his eyes, exposing the streak of grey which flashed across his temple.

"I know enough. And I've made sure you'll never see the children again."

Drake's temper got the better of him and he slapped her face with a leather riding glove. She flinched as the leather struck her skin. He grabbed her by her jaw, his strong hand squeezing as his nails dug into the sides of her face. He had no hesitation when it came to inflicting pain, but could tell by her air of confidence she wouldn't tell him what he needed to hear.

"Very well," said Drake. His calm voice returned and he released his grip from her face. She slumped back against the straw and saw the gold ring on his middle finger shimmering in the flame of the torch. She recognised the circular symbols etched onto the face of the ring. The same symbols she'd seen the evening before on the blue velvet cloth which adorned the circular table in the basement of Drake's home. Drake, and three other men who she didn't recognise, had sat around the table. On the table were two strange ornate wooden boxes. On the top of each box was a blue cushion. Both cushions had a pentagram etched on them. Alice had overheard their conversation and couldn't believe what she was hearing. She would have taken the children that night, but knew Drake would hear the commotion. She needed to wait until morning before he was awake.

Drake stood up, turned and walked towards the door.

The short man stood on the threshold with the burning torch in his hand.

"She's not going to talk," said Drake. "Mr. Morris, do your worst."

Drake walked away from the building to the sound of muffled screams as Joseph Morris kicked the defenceless but brave young girl. He grabbed an oil lamp hanging from the beam and smashed it to the ground beside her. Oil splashed across the floor and onto Alice's clothes. Morris looked upon her with a remorseless expression as he held the flaming torch.

"You should have told Mr. Drake where his children are," grunted Morris as the flame cast an orange glow upon his scarred and pitted face, casting shadows which made him look as if he was a gargoyle. Morris had more tattoos than teeth. The tattoos on his face were a throwback from his days working as a seaman.

Alice looked up at him and with a defiant stare she whispered her last words. "They're not his children."

Morris dropped the torch and took two steps back as the oil ignited and flames raced towards the helpless girl. Her skirt was an instant fireball as she writhed and screamed in agony. Her skin blistered as the flames engulfed her. Morris smiled and shielded his face from the heat. He took delight in watching Alice's thrashing body as she became consumed by the inferno. Within minutes she had succumbed to the flames and her cadaver crackled and hissed as the heat intensified.

Morris stepped outside and shivered as the icy night air hit him. Drake leant against the handcart and smoked his briar wood pipe.

"It is done," growled Morris and pulled his coat around him. He considered stepping back into the hut to warm himself by the flames which engulfed the building.

"Good work Joseph, let's go. There are things to be done."

"But the children? How are we going to succeed without them?"

"Don't worry Joseph, that's something which shouldn't concern you right now. I am prepared to wait as long as it takes. Patience, Mr. Morris, is a virtue. And patience is a quality I am lucky to have."

The caw of a raven could be heard as it soared high above the flames.

The two men climbed onto their horses and galloped towards the rest of the gang who watched from a distance with the dogs. After speaking with his men, Drake ordered them to go their separate ways and told Morris to get back to his boy, Mathias.

The thud of heavy hooves against the frozen ground disappeared into the night as the burning hut cast an eerie glow across the field.

Chapter 3

Two hundred years later

December 14th 2004

Finn Maynard woke to the niggling sound of his ring tone. It was a missed call from Sophie. Finn put the phone back in his pocket and gazed through the window. He thought of his wife and young daughter as he watched low cloud smudge the distant trees.

He fought to stay awake as the hypnotic lull of the train did its best to lure him back to sleep.

The day had been uneventful. He rubbed his eyes and glanced at Sally who looked as bored as he felt. He'd only agreed to attend the meeting as it meant a day away from the office and now he wished he'd stayed in Bristol. As far as work was concerned he wasn't an ambitious man. He did what he had to do to make sure he could provide for his family. His wife and daughter were his universe.

Fifteen minutes later the train slowed as it neared Temple Meads, but it was still travelling at a fair pace as it approached Stapleton Road Station. He rubbed his eyes again.

With no warning he jolted forward, banging his knees into the low table in front of him. A woman screamed as she fell in the walkway. The grinding of the wheels against the tracks whined like giant fingernails scraping along a blackboard. Sally swore as coffee spilled over her skirt.

The train shuddered to a standstill and for a few seconds no one spoke.

A guard ran along the platform followed by the driver. Doors opened and passengers stepped from the train to see what had happened. Finn stood up and offered his hand to the fallen woman as she struggled to her feet.

"What happened?" asked Sally.

Finn didn't reply. He hurried along the carriage, ignoring the dull pain in his knees. The door was open, and he looked along the platform before getting out. A crowd had gathered and were looking at something beneath the train. The guard was doing his best at ushering them away, but no one moved.

Finn stepped onto the platform and made his way towards the crowd. He knew why the train had stopped, but morbid curiosity was getting the better of him. He'd not seen a dead person before and wasn't sure if he wanted to, but something within was urging him to take a look.

A headless body lay beneath the train. Finn turned away and noticed a blood soaked paper bag further along the track behind the train. Holding his hand over his mouth he walked towards it. Behind him was an older man walking with a stick. The man with the stick stopped at the edge of the platform and looked at the bag and then glanced at Finn. The man looked at

Finn as if he was seeking approval for what he was going to do. Finn said nothing. The man knelt down and prodded the bag with his stick. The blood sodden bag ripped, revealing the head of an old man. One eye stared at Finn with a look which held pained secrets of generations. He was transfixed by what he saw. The eye looked at Finn as if it knew he'd be there to witness the suicide. Finn felt as if the whole thing had been staged just for him. The man with the walking stick turned away shaking his head, leaving Finn alone to gawp at the gruesome find.

The sound of sirens filled the air and broke the unnerving silence. Other than the guard, no one had spoken. The small crowd and the driver had been shocked into an uneasy hush.

Half an hour later Finn and the rest of the passengers were talking with police and providing statements.

First Great Western arranged for a bus to take the shocked passengers to Temple Meads Station. Finn sat next to Sally, and she noticed how pale he looked. He gripped her hand. When the bus arrived at the station the tired passengers were met by an official and after a brief talk they were allowed home.

Finn stood in the taxi queue with his laptop slung over his shoulder.

"I can drive you home if you like," offered Sally with a faint smile.

Finn didn't relish the thought of making small talk with a taxi driver and took her up on her offer. She had remained on the train and hadn't seen the man's body. Although she had been shaken by what happened, she wasn't as affected as Finn.

They walked to her car in the station car park and soon she was driving him home. The memory of the dead man's head plagued Finn as he watched the cars inch along the rush hour traffic.

"Why don't you call Sophie?" suggested Sally.

Finn didn't answer. He continued to stare at the traffic and was mesmerised by the tail lights ahead.

Sally turned into Finn's road and spotted Sophie on the pavement wedging a black bag into the rubbish bin. She parked the car, lowered the window and was going to speak, but Sophie spoke first.

"Sally, what are you doing here? Is everything OK?"

Sally put on the interior light and Sophie saw Finn sitting alongside her.

"Finn's shaken, we've had a crappy journey."

He opened the door and got out. Sophie could tell by his pained expression that things weren't good.

He walked to the flat, leaving Sally and Sophie outside.

"He's had a shock, well we both have, but it's affected Finn more than me."

Sophie looked at Sally without speaking.

"There was an incident. A man jumped in front of our train at Stapleton Road. He was decapitated."

Sophie covered her mouth with her hand.

"Finn saw everything. He's the one who found the head, it was about twenty yards from the body."

Sophie shuddered.

"Are you OK, do you want a stiff drink to calm your nerves?" asked Sophie.

"No, I'll be fine, I'd best be on my way, it's my son's birthday and I'm in a rush. I stayed on the carriage, so Finn's the one who needs a drink. A large scotch should do the trick."

Sophie hugged her and thanked her for bringing her husband home.

"I won't be surprised if he doesn't make it in tomorrow," said Sally as she walked to her car.

"Tomorrow's Saturday, thank God."

"Yeah, sorry, of course. Tell him I'll catch up with him in the office on Monday."

Sophie waved her off as she disappeared from view.

Finn was in the lounge. His coat was wrapped around his large frame and his scarf was around his neck. Sophie sat beside him and held his hand.

"Sally's told me what happened."

Finn didn't answer. He had become fixated by a cobweb swaying in the corner.

Sophie said nothing. She didn't know what to say. She took Sally's advice and poured him a scotch. He took the glass but didn't drink. Instead he held it in his shaking hand.

She'd seen him like this once before. The day he'd been told that his best friend Mark had been killed in a climbing accident. But this was different. When Mark died Finn had mixed emotions of utter shock and sadness. But now Sophie could sense something else. Mark's death effected both Finn and Sophie because he'd dated Sophie's sister Heather a few weeks before the accident.

She was going to speak but was interrupted by their daughter calling from her bedroom.

"Mummy, is daddy home?"

Sophie walked to Rosie's room, turned up the light and closed the door.

"Daddy's home, but he's a bit tired…….. so I think it's best he doesn't tell you a story tonight."

"But he promised."
"I know, he did. Be a good girl and I promise he'll read you a really super one tomorrow."
The three year old slumped on her pillow and looked miserable. Sophie kissed her on her head and tucked her hair behind her ears.
"Get to sleep now. I need to see Daddy."
Sophie closed the door and returned to the lounge. Finn hadn't moved, but he'd drank the scotch. And then he spoke.
"It was horrible."
He placed his glass on the table next to him, and rubbed his face. Sophie knelt beside him and looked into his eyes.
"The whole thing was.......," his quiet voice trailed off without finishing.
"Rosie wanted to see you, I told her you were too tired to read her a story."
He looked at her and for the first time since Sally brought him home she detected a faint glimmer of the man she'd married.
"No, I'll go and see her. It will do me good."
He went to her room and sat on the edge of her bed. She threw her arms around him.
"Daddy, Daddy."
He held her and nuzzled his face into her hair.
"Daddy, ouch! You're squeezing me."
He let go, and she sat next to him.
"I'm sorry Rosie. I've missed you and needed a big hug."
She kissed him on his face. He tucked her in, and went back to the lounge.

Sophie waited in the lounge.
"Do you want to talk?" asked Sophie as she undid the buttons on his coat.
He nodded. "And I could do with another drink."
Sophie draped his coat over the back of a chair and poured another scotch.
"He was staring at me," said Finn in his softly spoken voice as he blankly gazed ahead. "One eye was looking right at me."
He paused for a sip of scotch, grimacing as he gulped it too fast.
"I know it sounds stupid Sophie, but it was as if he knew me, as if he was waiting for me to find him....... and the expression on his face........ I'm sure he had a message for me."

Sophie had been desperate to see her husband. She had been bursting with excitement and couldn't wait to tell him her news. But now wasn't the right time. The euphoria had been overshadowed by what had happened on the train.

Or maybe she should tell him. Now might be a good time as it might distract from the horrible event of the day.

"I have something to tell you."

Finn looked at her with no expression.

"Huh, sorry what did you say?"

"I have some news."

"What news?"

"It's time we looked for somewhere else to live, somewhere bigger with more bedrooms."

She pulled the tester from her pocket and handed it to him.

"Look what it says," said Sophie as a smile lit her face.

Finn was distracted from his thoughts and looked at the positive result on the pregnancy tester.

"Wow, is this for real?"

She nodded.

"Are you sure, is this thing working properly?"

She nodded again.

A rush of colour returned to his face.

"It's the third test I've done today…. there's absolutely no doubt, I'm pregnant."

Finn stood up and threw his arms around her. He held her as the news sank in.

"This is brilliant news….. have you told anybody else?"

"No, I wanted to tell you first. I'll ring mum and dad in the morning."

Finn walked towards the hallway, stopped and turned to face her.

"This really is the best news I could have hoped for."

He processed the information. Thoughts of babies pinged around his tired mind as a smile spanned his face. But within minutes his positive thoughts were eclipsed by the bloody head in the paper bag and the staring eye.

Finn had no way of knowing how the events of the day would affect his future.

Chapter 4

"The selfish bastard........... the selfish, selfish bastard," said Henry Buxton as the news sank in.

"We need you to identify the body...... but we're sure it's your father. He was carrying his driving licence." said the police officer.

Henry nodded.

The officer informed Henry of the circumstances of his father's suicide, including the head. Henry trembled as he listened.

"We weren't very close. Since he moved into that house, we've grown apart."

Robert Buxton moved into his son's road three years earlier to be near his family. But since the day he set foot in the house he'd changed. He'd become distant and reclusive.

Henry was sixty-one and his father had been in his early eighties.

"Did he leave a note?" asked Henry.

"I understand there's an envelope, but I don't know of its contents." replied the officer.

Henry stood up and put on his coat.

"Are you sure you can do this?" asked Katherine.

"I don't think I have a choice," he replied as he buttoned his coat.

"Let me come with you..... please."

"No thank you, I'd prefer do this on my own."

Katherine squeezed her husband's hand as he turned to leave their house. She watched from the doorway as the police vehicle turned out of the road with Henry sitting in the rear of the car looking grey and sombre.

Just over an hour later Henry had identified his father's body and stood alone in a waiting room.

The officer entered the room and stood alongside him holding a plastic folder.

"I knew he was unhappy, even depressed, but I had no idea to what degree," said Henry in a monotone voice.

The officer was concerned by Henry's lack of emotion.

"You said he'd written a note, may I read it?"

The officer opened the folder in which was the contents of Robert Buxton's pockets. He handed him a white envelope and inside were three sheets of white A4 paper. On two of the sheets was a pattern and alongside each was a tick. The other sheet was blank. Each sheet of paper had been numbered in the upper left-hand corner. The two with a pattern and a tick were numbered one and two. The blank paper was numbered three.

"We expected to find a note in the envelope, but instead we found those," said the officer pointing to the papers.

"Is that everything, is there nothing else?" asked Henry.

The officer shook his head.

Henry looked at the two patterns. Both were similar, but not the same. They had been drawn by hand in red ink. They reminded him of pagan images he'd seen carved on ancient stones. He glanced at the blank page and turned his attention back to the patterns.

"Can I have these?"

Again, the officer shook his head.

"Sorry, not yet. After the autopsy you may take your father's belongings, including those."

"Autopsy? Why an autopsy? It was suicide."

"I'm sure it was, but we need to be sure there was no foul play."

Henry looked at the drawings. So similar, yet so different.

"If you don't mind, I want to go home," said Henry, handing the papers to the officer.

Henry stood by the gate of his house and watched the police car turn at the bottom of his road. He turned and looked at his father's house which was four doors away. It looked dark and uninviting. Henry had never liked the house, even before his father lived there.

The police car made its way up the road and slowed as it passed Henry.

"Are you going to be okay sir?" asked the officer.

"I'll be fine. Katherine's here, I won't be alone."

The officer nodded and pulled away.

Henry stared at his father's house and the old hawthorn tree in the garden.

Sadness crept up on him. "I'm an orphan."

He rubbed his face and whispered again, "I'm a bloody orphan."

Tears welled in his eyes as the enormity of the day's events sank in. But he couldn't cry.

The door opened, and he looked up to see Katherine. She walked along the path, met him at the gate and put her arms around him. She kissed him on the cheek and walked him to the house.

Katherine struggled to find the right words. She'd not been fond of her father-in-law and Henry knew it.

"Can I get you something?"

He shook his head. "No thank you. I'm going to go to bed. I need to be alone."

Henry lay on the bed. He felt he should be more affected by his father's death. He couldn't understand why he wasn't a total wreck.

I'll grieve when I'm ready he thought.

He blanked out the hideous memory of his father's headless body and instead his thoughts were consumed by the strange drawings. He wondered about the blank sheet. What did it mean?

Just after two am he sat bolt upright. Something awoke him. He'd heard nothing but something had brought him round from a heavy sleep. Henry looked to his left and saw Katherine sleeping beside him.

He climbed out of bed and walked to the window. Pulling back the curtain he saw it was snowing. He put on his trousers, walked downstairs and opened the front door. The snow was settling and there was an eerie silence. The street light by the gate illuminated the flakes as they danced in the breeze.

Henry slipped his shoes on, walked to the gate and looked towards Robert Buxton's house. An upstairs light was on. He was sure that there were no lights on when he returned with the police officer earlier. He'd remembered seeing the house and how dark and lonely it looked. He scurried back to his house, put on a thick jumper, grabbed the spare keys he kept for his father's house and cautiously made his way back along the slippery path. He stopped to look again at the house and saw that the upstairs light was off.

"What the......?" whispered Henry as condensation blew from his mouth.

He carefully walked along the pavement, his footsteps crunching the untouched snow. He stopped. Everything was quiet as fresh snow absorbed the sound. But it was too quiet. Even in the early hours of the morning he should be able to hear a distant car or motorbike.

The doors and windows were closed. There was no sign of a break in. He considered calling the police, but his curiosity was getting the better of him and he continued to make his way to the front door.

Although he wasn't a young man, Henry Buxton was in fine health, as strong as an ox and had no fear when it came to finding an intruder in his father's home.

He glanced at the hawthorn tree and noticed that the snow had not settled on it.

He turned the key, swung open the door and waited for his eyes to adjust to the darkness. He picked up one of his father's walking sticks which was in the hallway and held it tightly.

Quietly he moved around the house, ready to swipe the first moving thing he saw. The lounge and the dining room were empty, there was no one there. He turned the handle on the kitchen door, but it wouldn't open. *Damned thing* he thought as he tried to open it. The door had a habit of sticking and he'd promised his father he would fix it, but never did.

He tiptoed upstairs and put his head around the bathroom door. Empty. Both double bedrooms were empty. He saw his father's suit on a clothes hanger. The orange glow from the street light cast strange shadows and he could picture his father standing there with his expressionless face. Henry shuddered.

He turned his attention to the single room which his father had referred to as 'the study'. The study was the room where Henry had seen a light. With one hand he turned the handle whilst in the other he held the walking stick above his head. He was coiled and ready to swipe should someone move towards him.

He pushed the door ajar and heard a cry as something brushed pass his legs. He thrashed with the stick as Suzy, his father's cat, charged down the stairs and out through the cat flap. Henry sighed.

Pushing the door he stepped into the study. The room was small, and even in the dark he could tell it was empty. He reached for the switch and blinked as the light flickered on.

It took a second or two for Henry to understand what he was looking at.

"What the……..?"

Each wall was covered from top to bottom with A4 paper. He lowered the stick and looked around. He looked at the ceiling which was also completely covered. Henry estimated that there must be five hundred sheets or maybe more. There was a sequence to the papers. Each sheet was numbered one, two and three. On the sheets numbered one and two were drawings. Drawings like the ones he'd been shown by the police officer. Each sheet which had been numbered 'three' was blank. The sequences repeated over and over covering every inch of the walls and ceiling.

No two were the same. The patterns were similar, but none were matching. The sequence was the same. Two sheets with patterns, followed by a blank.

Beneath every pattern was a cross.

What had he been doing? thought Henry.

He was interrupted by a sound from downstairs. He tightened the grip on the walking stick, then relaxed as he remembered Suzy. His father's cat was looking for food. She couldn't have eaten since this morning.

He walked to the top of the stairs and saw her pushing against the bottom of the banister. Then he heard it again, and it definitely wasn't the cat. It was a voice. He'd heard a giggle. The giggle had a mischievous quality. He made his way down the stairs, tightly gripping the stick. The voice came from the kitchen. It was a child's voice. He stopped outside the kitchen with the stick ready to strike out. The giggling stopped. He pushed against the door with his shoulder. This time the door swung open, letting out a low drawn out creak. He turned on the light and saw the kitchen was empty.

He was tired, very very tired, but not so tired that he could have imagined the laugh of a child. It was distinct and playful.

He looked behind the door. No one. The entire house was empty. Henry frowned and rubbed his eyes as he tried to understand what was happening. He hadn't imagined seeing the upstairs light, it had definitely been on. He clearly remembered snowflakes lit by the glow from the window. And the child's voice? It had been so clear and sounded playful as if it had been teasing him.

Suzy trotted in and brushed against his leg. Her purr brought him back to reality.

"Come on little lady, you must be hungry," said Henry opening a sachet of cat food and emptying it into a bowl.

Suzy jumped up on her back legs and tried to paw the bowl as he bent forward to put it on the floor. She was starving.

Without warning the cat let out a dreadful howl as if someone stood on her tail. Henry dropped the bowl, spilling cat food across the floor. Suzy froze as she stared at the fridge. She looked at Henry and ran out of the kitchen. He sighed and bent forward to clean up the mess, and then he saw it scratched into the door of the fridge.

Buxton.

Join me in he

Henry scowled as he read the words out loud. "Join me in he." Was this a message written by his father just before he'd taken his life? It made no sense. And who on earth was 'he'?

He closed his eyes and shook. Suddenly he felt alone and scared. Then he heard it. A faint scratching noise coming from the fridge. He opened his eyes just in time to see the second of two small vertical lines being etched into the fridge door. The two lines finished the message.

Buxton
Join me in hell.

Chapter 5

May 2005

Sophie Maynard sat next to Rosie on the wall waiting for the estate agent to arrive. She looked at her watch and sighed.

"What the hell do these people get paid to do?" she grumbled impatiently and rubbed her bump.

"Give her five more minutes," said Heather, "I guess it's the traffic, it was a nightmare earlier."

The appointment was at one pm for Sophie to view 11a Whitcombe Fields Road, and now it was twenty past the hour. Her sister had driven because Sophie's car was in the garage.

"It's okay for you, you're not lugging this around with you," said Sophie looking at her bump.

"It's a nice looking house, but I wonder why they built it like that?" remarked Heather.

"Like what?"

"The entire road on this side are terraced houses, apart from this one."

Heather was right. Every building was terraced, apart from number 11a. The property stood halfway along the road and bang in the middle of two rows of terraced houses.

"Maybe the house before had been destroyed in the war, or by fire and was rebuilt as a detached home?" suggested Sophie.

"It wouldn't have been the war, these houses look as if they've been built in the sixties. 11a looks like an eighties house."

"You're right, the estate agent's blurb said it was constructed in eighty-four."

"It's funny it's not number 13?" added Heather.

Sophie shrugged her shoulders.

"Each house has a consecutive odd number, apart from that one. It's 11a, it should be number 13." said Heather, pointing to the number on the door.

"Perhaps they were superstitious."

A car swung around the corner and parked behind Heather's. A woman wearing a blue trouser suit got out holding a briefcase.

"I'm sorry I've kept you waiting," said June Croft, the estate agent, as she slammed the car door. "There's been an accident and the traffic's backed up to the main road."

Sophie attempted a smile. She was in no mood to be waiting for such a long time. It was a hot afternoon in May, which didn't mix well with being six months pregnant.

Croft fumbled as she looked for the key to the property.
"I've found it," she said as she placed the key in the lock.
As soon as she opened the door, Rosie charged passed and ran along the hallway.
"Slow down," called Sophie.
"She's OK, let her explore," said the estate agent with a smile.
"I love it mummy, can we have it?"
Sophie walked along the hall followed by Heather. The estate agent rambled away with her usual small talk and sales patter and was interrupted by Rosie running around upstairs.
They walked around downstairs, taking time to appreciate the spacious lounge and dining room, and were about to enter the kitchen when Rosie called from upstairs.
"Mummy, mummy come and see."
Sophie and Heather climbed the stairs with the estate agent trailing behind.
Rosie ran into the middle bedroom and excitedly skipped around.
"Can this be my room mummy, please can I have this one?"
Sophie smiled, "slow down Rosie….. we're just looking today, besides Daddy needs to see the house too."
"Please mummy…."
Heather bent down and cuddled the little girl who had a grumpy face.
They continued to look around the other bedrooms when the estate agent reminded them they'd not yet looked at the kitchen.
"Let's go back downstairs, you'll love the kitchen. It's in need of modernisation, but it's a good size."
Sophie huffed as she made her way down, her back was hurting and she felt uncomfortable.
The estate agent opened the kitchen door. Sophie looked around and nodded with approval.
Heather stepped into the kitchen and felt strange. Overcome with a grey feeling as if she had no purpose in life. The feeling intensified, and she became overwrought by a feeling of depression. The kitchen spun, and she held onto the wall. Sophie and the estate agent's voices became distant and were replaced by a buzzing sound. She stumbled out of the kitchen and found her way to the bottom of the stairs where she staggered and fell to the floor. The buzzing developed into something different. She put her hands over her ears, but couldn't block it out. She could hear barking, howling dogs. Heather shivered and became enveloped by the cold of a winter's day.
"Mummy, Auntie Heather's not very well," called Rosie.
Sophie came out of the kitchen to find Heather slumped on the bottom stair. The colour had drained from her face and her hands shook as she cupped them over her ears.

"Heather, Heather what is it?" called Sophie.

Heather didn't answer. She curled up and pressed her hands harder against her ears.

Sophie put her hand on her sister's shoulder and was shocked by the coldness of her skin.

"Heather, please..... you're scaring me..... can you hear me?"

Heather felt the warmth of her sister's hand on her shoulder and the sound of dogs stopped. She opened her eyes and looked around.

"What happened?" whispered Heather.

The estate agent pulled a bottle of mineral water from her briefcase.

"Give her a sip of this," she said, handing the bottle to Sophie.

Heather took a gulp and pulled herself up into a sitting position.

"Sorry, I don't know what came over me."

"It's hot in here, you should step outside," suggested the estate agent.

"I think I've seen enough of the house for now. I'll speak with my husband and will be in touch with you," said Sophie.

The estate agent locked the house. Heather felt better and Rosie ran around the garden.

"It's a steal. I don't think it will be on the market for much longer. We've had lots of viewings. Let me know if your husband wants to see it, and I suggest the sooner the better," said the estate agent. Her voice carried a hint of desperation.

She was right about the price. It was fifteen thousand below the market value.

"Why is it such a low price?" asked Sophie.

"They want a quick sale. There's no chain, so I recommend that if you're interested you put in an offer as soon as possible."

Sophie nodded.

"I guess the previous owners didn't have green fingers?" said Heather.

The garden was bare. There wasn't a flower, plant or even a weed. Apart from a tree in the middle of what usually would have been a lawn, there was no sign of plant life.

The estate agent shrugged her shoulders.

"Bread and cheese," said Heather.

Sophie looked at her.

"We used to call that tree bread and cheese when we were kids. Don't you remember?"

"Yes, you're right. It's a hawthorn tree. I remember you used to say we could eat the leaves."

"You can, they're good for you. Full of vitamin C," added Heather.

"I'm sorry to rush off, but I'm late for my next viewing," said the estate agent.

"Okay, no problem, I'll be in touch after I've spoken with my husband."

The estate agent hurried to her car and sped away.

"Are you feeling better?"

Heather nodded. "It's two o'clock and I've not eaten. I need carbs."

Sophie, Heather and Rosie drove away from the pretty cul de sac and headed for something to eat.

The road was quiet, and the air was still. The hawthorn tree shuddered as if a strong breeze whipped around the garden of number 11a Whitcombe Fields Road.

And then it stopped.

Chapter 6

St Michael on the Mount Without Church
St Michaels Hill, Bristol.

An old lady wandered through the derelict graveyard. Most of the tombstones surrendered to weeds and brambles.

Although it was a pleasant May afternoon, she wore a heavy black coat buttoned up to her neck. Her skin was fragile like pressed flowers. The sun beat upon her face, but she was as cold as chilled buttermilk soup.

The church of St Michael on the Mount Without had seen its congregation dwindle, it closed in the early eighties, and the graveyard hadn't seen a burial in over sixty years.

The lady made her way between the graves, stepping over those of sixteenth century Marian martyrs' who'd been executed at the top of the Hill.

She stopped at a non-descript gravestone. It was the only marker not overgrown with nettles. The lady had been tending the grave her entire adult life. Over the past seventy years few people had paid attention as she lovingly cleared away the ugly foliage which enveloped the other forgotten graves.

The mottled grey stone had been weathered by the elements. Lichen spread as if it were an angry yellow rash. The faded inscription gave no clue as to whom the grave belonged.

The lady knelt beside the grave. Her face contorted as her bones strived to support her weak and olden frame.

She took a bottle of water from her bag and with gnarled fingers slowly unscrewed the lid. She smiled as she poured water over the gravestone. The inscription became clearer as the water spread over the stone. The name of the deceased had worn away long ago. A tear formed as she read what remained of the dates upon the stone.

Born ----ber 1- --99
Died September 6 1839

She ran her skeletal fingers over the stone and knew time was drawing to an end. She lay next to the grave and faced the sky.

"This body is of no use now."

She turned to face the grave.

"Please don't worry. Soon there will be someone else to watch over and protect you."

A contented smile spanned her face as the body which had been the repository for her soul for the last ninety one years exhaled its final breath.

Chapter 7

Late July

"Okay, so in which box is the kettle?" asked Finn looking at the stack of packing crates scattered around the lounge of their new home.

Sophie picked up the clipboard and turned over the page.

"K3, you'll find it in crate K3."

"I love you," smiled Finn.

"No, you love tea. You find the kettle and the tea bags, and I'll get the milk from the cool box."

Moving into their new home had gone without a hitch. In fact, the whole process of buying their first house had gone well. It had helped that there hadn't been a property chain and the contract on their flat expired at just the right time.

Sophie was heavily pregnant and the due date was in less than three weeks. Finn had his work cut out for him and had taken two weeks annual leave. Every waking hour of every day would be required to get the house in order.

He sighed, looked at the crates and took a sip of tea. He was lost in thought and visualised what had to go where. Just the thought of lugging everything upstairs, assembling beds and wardrobes was making him weary.

Finn was interrupted by the sound of a screaming child, the thudding of feet and a loud disturbance from upstairs.

"Rosie!" shouted Finn. He jumped up and ran up the stairs, taking two steps at a time.

Her screams became louder and the thump of her footsteps echoed throughout the house.

"Daddy, mummy help!"

"It's okay Rosie, I'm coming."

Then everything was quiet.

Finn stopped on the landing. The bedroom and bathroom doors were shut.

"Where are you Rosie?"

"Help me daddy!"

Her voice came from the middle bedroom.

He threw open the door and found his daughter cowering in the corner with her hands over her face. Scattered around the bare floor were dozens of black feathers.

"Rosie!"

She looked up at her father and he saw her face was bleeding.

He picked her up and held her close. She was breathing heavily and shaking.

He looked at the feathers.

"What happened?"

Rosie didn't reply. She buried her head into her father's shoulder. He hugged her as she sobbed. Her sobs turned to tears and within seconds she was crying her heart out.

He carried her to the landing, closed the door and took her downstairs.

"What's happened?" asked Sophie.

"Shush," whispered Finn as he rocked Rosie.

"I want mummy," sobbed the little girl.

Sophie walked over to her daughter. Rosie lifted her head and looked at her mother. There were cuts on her forehead and cheek.

"How did you do this?" asked Sophie.

At first she couldn't answer. Her tears were getting the better of her. Sophie pulled a tissue from her pocket and dabbed the spots of blood on her face. Rosie flinched.

"The bird did it," said Rosie.

"The bird?"

"There's a nasty blackbird upstairs, and it hurt me."

"Where did it come from?" asked Sophie.

"Behind the door in the corner," sobbed Rosie.

"She must mean the airing cupboard," said Finn.

Finn passed Rosie to Sophie.

"There are black feathers scattered around the middle bedroom, I'll find the bird and let it out."

He grabbed a towel and went upstairs. He knew it must be somewhere in the middle bedroom because he had closed the door behind him. But he definitely hadn't seen it when he'd gone in to get Rosie.

It must have flown back into the airing cupboard thought Finn.

Carefully he opened the bedroom door and poked his head around, expecting to see the scared creature.

The room was empty, and the windows were closed. He noticed the cupboard door was ajar and there where feathers scattered outside. He crept over holding the towel ready to throw over the bird as soon as he saw it. Nervously, he opened the door and inside it was dark. His eyes acclimatised to the poor light, and he saw it was empty. Not even a feather. He shut the door and looked around the room. Apart from the scattering of feathers, the bedroom was empty.

"What the hell?"

All the upstairs rooms were empty.

He picked up a handful of feathers and went back downstairs

"Did you get it?" asked Sophie.

"It's not there," said Finn shaking his head.

He handed the feathers to Sophie.

"These are too big for a blackbird. Check out the size of this one," said Sophie holding a jet black feather which was as long as her forearm.

"Maybe it was a crow?" suggested Finn.

"Maybe, but this feather is huge."

"How big was the bird?" asked Sophie as she turned to Rosie who was sitting on the floor hugging her doll.

"This big," replied Rosie stretching her arm as high as she could. "I don't want to be here," she sobbed.

"It's okay poppet, it was just a bird that got in, and I bet he was more scared than you."

Finn wearily looked at his wife.

"To be honest, I'll struggle to get her bed put together by bedtime, it's five o'clock and I've not even started unpacking yet. Do you think your sister would let Rosie sleep at her place tonight? Especially after what happened with the bird."

"I'll call her, I'm sure she won't mind."

Rosie was happier when she was told she'd be sleeping at her Auntie Heather's house.

An hour later Heather was at the house and Rosie was pleased to see her auntie. Sophie told her about the bird and handed her the feathers.

"They're raven's feathers," said Heather as she examined them.

"A raven?" said Finn with a confused expression. "I thought it was from a crow."

"Ravens aren't as commonplace as crows, but look," she replied whilst holding a feather by its quill.

"Raven feathers are long, between 20 to 36 inches, smooth and angled. Crow feathers are shorter and are more blunted than a raven's. This isn't from a crow."

Finn shrugged his shoulders.

"You'd think we'd have heard a bird as big as a raven flapping around the house."

"I don't know, but I can you assure it's a raven feather."

"You've got to trust my sister, she's always been a bird brain," said Sophie with a half-smile.

Finn and Sophie waved to their daughter as Heather pulled away.

"Okay, I need to get a move on, I've got loads to do," said Finn closing the front door.

A little later he was assembling his daughter's bed in the middle room where the bird had been. The sun was at an angle and cast a warm glow across the bedroom. The light caught his eye, and he looked towards the window. And then he saw it. The ghostly imprint of a large bird on the glass. He placed the screwdriver on the floor, and walked over to examine it. He ran his finger over the pattern. His heart skipped a beat.

"Sophie, come up here."

"Do I have to? I'm busy and my back's aching."

"Please, take a look at this."

He heard his wife's heavy steps as she made her way upstairs. She blew out a huff when she reached the top step.

"This had better be worth it," she whispered as she entered the room.

"It's the bird that attacked Rosie," said Finn pointing to the imprint on the window.

"Don't be daft Finn, that bird crashed into the window from the outside, it's more likely it fell to the ground and died of shock."

Finn shook his head.

"Come over here."

Sophie walked up to the window and looked at Finn.

"What am I missing?" said Sophie shrugging her shoulders.

"Touch the window where the imprint is."

She ran her hand over the pattern of the bird and gasped as her finger smeared the grease which made the impression.

"It was on the inside, the bird was in this room and flew into the window."

"The question is," said Finn, "where the hell is it now?"

Chapter 8

Early August

Heather stood at the traffic lights at the bottom of St. Michaels Hill and looked at the steep incline.

"I'll never make it up that hill," said her father as he contemplated climbing one of the steepest roads in the city.

"If you gave up smoking it wouldn't be so much of an effort for you." huffed Heather. "Besides, I imagine a walk up that hill is a lot less than Sophie's had to deal with."

Heather, her father John and mother Grace were on their way to visit Sophie who had given birth to Jack the previous day. The maternity hospital car park was full and the only place Heather could park was on the main road at the bottom of the hill.

"Come on John, keep up," said Grace as the lights changed allowing them to cross the busy road.

"Mum, I don't think they'll allow you to take those into the ward," said Heather pointing to the large bouquet her mother was holding.

"Nonsense, don't be so daft, of course you can bring flowers."

"She's right. I read it in the Daily Mail. Something about them spreading germs and creating extra work for nurses," added John as he tried to keep up.

After walking fifty yards John stopped and held his chest.

"I'm knackered, I need to sit down."

"Dad, we're not even a quarter of the way….. you need to get into shape."

Grace pointed to a wooden bench outside a derelict church on the other side of the road.

They crossed over and climbed half a dozen steps which took them to a paved area outside the churchyard.

John sat on the bench and let out a sigh as he reached for his cigarettes.

"Dad, please put those things away, you'll not make it up the hill if you smoke one of those."

He huffed and put them back in his pocket.

"What am I going to do with these if I can't bring them in for Sophie?" said Grace admiring the flowers.

Heather looked at the derelict church and read the name on the faded sign.

"St Michael on the Mount Without. That's a strange name for a church."

"It's because it was built outside the city walls," explained her father.

"But why 'without'"?

"It means it's without walls,…… outside the city walls."

Heather nodded and walked over to railings and looked at the dishevelled graveyard.

"It's such a shame they let it get like this. I bet no one ever visits the dead in this place."

She turned to her mother sitting beside John on the bench.

"Mum, I know what you can do with those flowers."

She held out her hand and motioned for her mother to pass them.

"I'll put them in the graveyard, it could do with brightening up."

"No, you don't, I've paid sixteen pounds for these, and you're not dumping them in an old church."

"Why not? You can't take them into the hospital and if you take them home, they'll be dead in a day, you know what you and dad are like for looking after flowers. Dad's great in the garden, but you guys never remember to water the plants around the house."

Grace sighed and reluctantly handed them to her daughter.

Heather walked back to the graveyard and pushed the rusty gate. The place was so overgrown with weeds and nettles she could barely see the gravestones.

She looked to her left and there it was.

That's strange she thought as she made her way towards the only gravestone which was not overrun with brambles and weeds. The grass around the edge of the stone was neatly manicured. A few wild flowers bordered the ancient slab of rock.

The stone was so old most of the words had faded. Squinting her eyes to block the glare from the sun she saw dates which were partially legible. She knelt down for a closer look.

"Died September 6th 1839, I wonder how old you were?" she whispered.

She placed the flowers on the grave and ran her fingers over the faded writing.

As she touched the stone a voice echoed around the graveyard. It appeared to come from everywhere. She jumped up, looked around and saw no one other than her parents on the bench.

She ran to the gate and called to her parents.

"Did you say something?"

Her parents looked at her with blank expressions.

"Didn't you hear that voice?"

They shook their heads.

She went back to the stone, knelt down and touched it again. As she did an image of a face filled her mind. It was a man who appeared to be in his early forties. His face wore a pained expression. He looked up, gazed into her eyes and smiled.

Then she heard it again. This time the voice was loud and clear and it bounced from one corner of the churchyard to the other.

"Charles Samuel Nash."

Heather stood up and as soon as she removed her finger from the stone the reverberating voice ceased. She was shaking.

"What on earth…..?"

She was brought back to reality by her mother's voice.

"Come on Heather, your father's got his breath back. I'm desperate to meet my new grandson."

Heather frowned and walked to the gate.

She glanced towards the gravestone and shuddered as she thought about what had just happened.

Under her breath she said the name "Charles Samuel Nash."

She shivered as if the chill of a December day had crept over her skin.

Chapter 9

It had been a whirlwind of a fortnight for the Maynard family. The new house was nowhere near ready and Sophie's waters had broken five days earlier than expected.

Finn pulled up outside their house and took a long look at Jack alongside him in the baby seat. He ran his finger across the tiny boy's cheek and smiled as he watched his face screw up.

"He's perfect," said Finn in his gentle West Country accent.

Finn glanced at Sophie. She looked tired.

"How are you?"

"I'm very very happy and very very sleepy."

Finn opened the rear door for Sophie who groaned as she stepped out. He undid the baby seat, gently lifted it out and placed it on the pavement. Jack yawned and wriggled in his comfy baby carrier.

"Good afternoon."

Finn looked up to see a bald man in his mid-fifties. The man had been watching Finn from his garden. He crossed the road and shook his hand.

"My name's Kieran, pleased to meet you."

Finn smiled.

"It looks as if the two of you have had a busy time."

"You could say that," replied Finn gripping his neighbour's hand. "Sorry we've not introduced ourselves earlier, but as you say, we've been a bit busy since we've moved in."

"No problem. Wow, he's gorgeous," said Kieran looking at Jack.

A look of pride spanned Finn's face as the two men stood over the baby boy.

"This is Sophie," said Finn gesturing towards his wife.

Sophie smiled and Kieran saw the face of a tired new mother.

"I'd better let you get on with things…… If there's anything you need, just ask."

Finn thanked him and turned to Jack who was sleeping in the warmth of the August sun.

"Come over for a beer one night," called Kieran while walking back to his house.

"That sounds like a good idea," replied Finn as he lugged Sophie's overnight bag over his shoulder and bent down to pick up Jack.

Henry Buxton watched from his porch as Finn carried Jack with Sophie slowly walking behind.

He looked at Kieran and screwed his face with an air of disapproval.

By seven thirty Finn was slumped on the settee, hungry and tired. Jack slept in his Moses basket and Sophie was out for the count upstairs.

Rosie was at Heather's and the house was quiet.

His eyes began to close when he heard a knock.

He opened the door and saw Kieran holding a hot oven dish covered with silver foil.

"My wife's cooked far too much pasta, and we wondered if you and Sophie wanted some?"

Finn smiled and pulled back the silver foil. The food smelled good. He looked across the road and saw Kieran's wife waving from the door.

"You're a life saver," said Finn.

"Do you fancy a beer to go with it?" asked Kieran.

Finn contemplated the thought of a cold lager to wash down the pasta.

"I think you've just become my new best friend," replied Finn. "And bring one for yourself," he added.

The two new friends enjoyed the beer and Finn ate his half of the pasta. He put the rest in the fridge for Sophie for when she woke up.

They spoke quietly so as not to wake Jack, who occasionally made little whimpering sounds like a kitten.

They talked about their jobs. Kieran told Finn about his work as a software engineer and Finn briefly explained that he was a graphic designer.

"This isn't a bad old road, and we're a friendly bunch," said Kieran before taking a sip from his can.

Finn nodded and sat back in his chair.

"But I'd warn you to not pay too much attention to Ruth Jackson, the lady next door."

Finn raised an eyebrow.

"She's nice enough, but she loves to gossip. She's one of those women who thrive on other people's misfortunes. It's as if she's a harbinger of doom."

Kieran glanced at the floor and then back at Finn.

"I've probably said too much. All I'm saying is don't take too much notice of some of the things she says."

"What about the man who we bought this house from? I understand he lives in this road and our house belonged to his father."

Kieran nodded.

"That's what I'm trying to say. Just take what your neighbour says with a pinch of salt, and it's probably best not to get to know Henry Buxton too well either."

"Henry Buxton? Is that who I bought the house from?"

Kieran nodded again. "Yeah, he lives at number five."

Jack stirred and snuffled.

"Thanks for the food and beer, but I'd best be getting on with things. It looks like Jack's waking and he'll probably want feeding."

Kieran stood up to leave.

"Sorry the place is such a mess, I'm nowhere near finished unpacking. We moved in two weeks ago and I've still got loads of stuff to sort out," said Finn.

"Don't worry, we moved into this road over twenty years ago and we have things in the attic still in boxes."

Finn smiled.

"If you need a hand with lugging stuff up to your attic, let me know. I'd be more than happy to help."

"I might just do that," replied Finn shaking Kieran's hand.

Kieran crossed the road to his house where Linda, his wife, was waiting for him.

"Did you tell them?"

Kieran shook his head.

"No, but I'm sure it won't be long before they find out."

Chapter 10

Jack was crying. His tiny voice was getting louder and was interrupted by sharp inhales of breath.

Sophie rubbed her eyes and looked at the clock. Six fifteen. She sighed, stretched and yawned. Finn was next to her and out for the count. She looked at him with a pang of jealousy. She was desperate for more sleep. If she had her way, she'd stay in bed for a week.

She carried Jack downstairs and fed him whilst watching television. She struggled to keep her eyes open as Jack suckled.

After Jack had finished feeding, his little eyes closed, and he drifted back to sleep. It wasn't long before Sophie joined him and fell asleep in the chair, holding him tightly against her.

Just after seven she was woken by Finn clattering around the kitchen making breakfast.

"Morning sleepy head," said Finn as he brought Sophie toast and tea.

She smiled and placed Jack in his Moses basket.

"If you prefer there's pasta in the fridge from last night."

"You didn't cook did you?"

"No, our nice neighbour Kieran brought it. He stopped over for a chat. I didn't wake you, I didn't think you'd appreciate it."

Sophie nodded as she took a bite of toast.

"What did he have to say?" asked Sophie, wiping butter from the side of her face.

"Oh, you know this and that. He offered to help me get these boxes up to the loft."

"That's nice of him."

"He told me something we should know. He said we shouldn't pay too much attention to Ruth."

"Ruth, who's Ruth?"

"She's the lady next door. He said she's the street gossip. He reckons we should be careful of her."

"I'll try to remember that. I won't tell her any of our big secrets," said Sophie with a glint in her eye.

"Kieran also said we shouldn't get too involved with Henry Buxton. He's the guy from whom we bought this house. It belonged to his dad."

"What happened to Henry's dad?"

"Kieran didn't say, and I didn't ask. But from what I gather Ruth will be chomping at the bit to tell us any juicy gossip."

Finn cleared the dishes and returned to the lounge.

"I've got to pick up Rosie from your sister's at nine. It's a nice day, and I thought I'd walk instead of drive. I think Rosie would enjoy the walk."

"Okay, but be quick. I'm alone with a two-day-old tiddler."

Finn left the house at eight fifteen and made his way along Whitcombe Fields Road. It was a glorious August morning, and despite being early, the sun made him perspire. He stopped and took a minute to consider how lucky he was. He had a beautiful wife and daughter and was now father to an amazing little boy. Everything was falling into place.

From the corner of his eye he saw he was being observed by a figure behind a net curtain. He was standing outside number five, Henry Buxton's house. Finn tried not to stare and recalled what Kieran had told him the previous evening.

He turned onto the High Street and called into the newsagent for a magazine and as he left the shop he noticed something he'd not remembered seeing before.

Across the road was an antique shop. He stopped and looked. He'd driven along the road hundreds of times over the years and couldn't recall it being there.

It wasn't even eight thirty, and the shop was open.

The shopkeeper had hung a 'closing down' banner from the window.

Closing down? thought Finn. He crossed the road to take a closer look.

An old man was carefully wrapping ornaments in bubble wrap and placing them in boxes. Most of the display cases were empty. There were pictures hanging on the wall. He was drawn to a beautiful painting of a huge black bird soaring over a landscape of trees.

The old man moved towards the display and smiled at Finn through the window. He opened a display case which contained necklaces, rings and brooches.

Finn spotted a gold ring with two patterns etched onto its face. There was something familiar about the patterns. He became fascinated by the red circular symbols. He was mesmerised until he was distracted by the man tapping on the window. The shopkeeper gestured at Finn to enter the shop.

He pushed the door and heard the ping of a bell which rang as it opened. The place smelt musty and old. In the corner where the wall met the ceiling was a damp patch and the paint was flaking.

"I've lived around here for years and before today I've never noticed your shop," said Finn as he gazed around the half empty display cases.

"Better late than never," replied the old man.

"And now you're closing down?"

"Better never than late," said the old man with an air of sadness.

"How long have you had this shop?"

"Longer than I care to remember."
Finn looked at the ring in the display case.
"Do you like it?"
Finn didn't answer, he continued to admire the ring.
"Would you like a closer look?"
"Huh, um, sorry yes please."
The old man gave Finn the ring.
He took the ring from the shopkeeper in his right hand and instinctively pushed out the middle finger of his left hand. The ring slipped into place. Again, Finn fixed his eyes upon the patterns. He was drawn to them and as he studied the ring in the sunlight streaming through the window he sensed something deep inside urging him not to remove it.
The shopkeeper passed him a jeweller's loupe.
"Here, use this."
He looked through the eyeglass and saw that the two circular patterns were not engraved into the ring, they were tiny individual red stones which had been placed into grooves etched into the face of the ring.
"Wow, the workmanship is outstanding," said Finn as he examined the detail of the ring.
"Are those rubies?"
The shopkeeper nodded.
"Amazing!"
Reluctantly, Finn tried to slide the ring from his finger, but it wouldn't move. He tried again, but it was jammed behind the joint of his finger.
"It slid on easily enough, why won't it come off?"
"Let me help," said the shopkeeper. "Hold on young man, we need something to lubricate that finger, something to help slide that ring off."
The shopkeeper disappeared through a door and returned with a plastic bottle of washing up liquid.
"This should get it off for you," he said as he rubbed the soapy liquid into Finn's finger. "Have a go now."
Finn pulled at the ring, but it wouldn't move.
"It's stuck fast," said Finn, with a hint of panic in his voice.
"Just relax, panicking won't make it any easier."
Finn admired the ring, and the truth was, he didn't want to give it back. There was something about it that made him feel different. It was a feeling he'd not experienced before.
Finn Maynard wasn't a shy person, but he wasn't a man who stood out in a crowd. Throughout his life he'd been someone who was comfortable in the middle ground. Happy not to rock the boat unless he felt passionate about something. He was the sort of man that didn't go out of his way to make friends, but once he'd befriended someone, they'd soon discover how lucky they were to know him. Finn was a true gentleman.

But wearing the ring made him feel different. He felt assertive and more decisive.

"How much is it?" asked Finn.

"That's a good question, but I'm afraid I don't know. Wait there while I find my book."

The shopkeeper rummaged around boxes and crates looking for a book in which he'd noted the prices of his stock.

"I'm sorry sir, but I appear to have misplaced my little red price book."

"Can't you remember, or have a guess?"

The shopkeeper screwed his face as he tried to remember.

"I think it may have been a couple of hundred pounds, but I'm not sure."

Finn pulled his wallet from his pocket.

What am I thinking, this is madness thought Finn. I can't afford to spend money on a gold ring.

The shopkeeper noticed Finn had a credit card in his wallet.

"I'm afraid I can only take cash, I don't have one of those card machines to take your money."

"I don't have any cash on me, other than the change in my pocket."

Finn wished he'd never set foot in the shop.

Suddenly he became overcome with a sense of assertiveness.

I work hard for my money, and if I want this ring, I'm damn well going to buy it, he thought.

He glanced at the time and hadn't realised how late it was. It was nearly nine o'clock.

"Would you trust me?" said Finn.

The shopkeeper looked up.

"I need to collect my daughter, she's with my sister-in-law and she's expecting me."

He handed the shopkeeper his debit card.

"Will you take this for security, and after I've picked up my little girl and taken her home, I'll get cash and come back and pay you. I'll be back by midday at the latest."

The shopkeeper shook his head.

"I'm sorry, I'll be gone before then."

"Sorry, but I don't know what else to suggest, I can't get it off."

The shopkeeper stood in silence whilst he considered what to do.

His kind eyes smiled as he looked at Finn.

"I'll tell you what…….. you can have it…….. you don't have to pay me."

Finn looked at the man curiously.

"But you told me that you wanted two hundred pounds."

The shopkeeper shrugged his shoulders.

"Let me have your address, I'll send you the money." said Finn.

He shook his head.

"I've run this shop for over sixty years, and before me it was my father's and before him it was run by his father. That ring has been here as long as I can remember. I'm sure it was here when my grandfather was alive, and nobody has ever shown an interest in it. Until now that is."

Finn frowned.

"You've not found the ring, the ring's found you," smiled the shopkeeper.

"But I just can't take it."

"Yes you can. I'm an old man and no one will inherit this shop or any of this stuff when I'm gone. I don't need the money. Please take it, consider it a gift."

Finn turned the ring in the sunlight.

"It truly is a beautiful thing."

"Take it and do it before I change my mind."

A grandfather clock chimed in the corner.

"You had better get going, it's nine o'clock…….. your daughter will wonder where you are."

Finn sighed.

"Thank you, you're a kind and generous man. Tell me, what's your name?"

"Go, get your daughter, you don't need to know my name."

The shopkeeper gently nudged Finn towards the door.

"Go now, or you'll be late."

Finn shook his head. The shopkeeper had won. He smiled and left the shop. The man smiled and waved him on his way through the window.

From his shop the old man stared as he disappeared from view, then instead of a smile, he wore a sinister expression.

Finn was late. He'd promised Sophie he wouldn't leave her on her own for long while he picked Rosie up from Heather's.

He hurried around the corner and into Whitcombe Fields Road holding his daughter's hand.

Rosie was excited to meet her new brother, she couldn't stop asking questions about him. She'd seen him two days ago in the maternity hospital and she couldn't wait to see him again.

Finn stopped outside the house and searched for his keys. He took them from his pocket with his left hand and as he fumbled to find the key to the door he noticed that the gold ring had gone from his finger.

He put his hand back into his pocket and found it. It had slipped off. Finn was confused. He took the ring from his pocket and looked at it. He slipped it back onto his middle finger and saw how loose it was. It made no sense. A red mark remained just below his finger joint where it had been earlier.

"Daddy, I want to see Jack," called Rosie.

Finn snapped back to reality. He slipped it back into his pocket and opened the door.

Rosie rushed passed.

"Where's Jack, mummy I want to see Jack?"

"Shush Rosie, you'll wake him."

Sophie knelt to her daughter's level.

"We need to be very quiet, he's tired and has just got to sleep……. shall we see him?"

She nodded and followed her mother to the lounge.

Her face lit up when she saw him scrunched up and sleeping in his Moses basket.

"What do you think?" asked Sophie.

"I love him mummy. He's tiny."

Finn put his arms around his wife.

"I'm sorry I took so long, is everything okay?"

"Everything's fine, but what took you so long? I expected you to be back an hour ago. Did Heather keep you talking?"

Finn shook his head.

"I just took longer than I thought."

Sophie looked at him and sensed he wasn't telling the truth.

"Are you okay?"

Finn nodded.

"Everything's fine."

He stood over Jack and watched as he slept.

"Don't you dare wake him up," said Sophie.

She looked tired.

"Go upstairs and lie down, I'll take over," said Finn as he kissed her on the forehead.

"No, I'm okay, I'd prefer to keep busy. I'll collapse in a heap when I'm ready," she replied with a smile.

Finn turned to her and looked serious.

"Do you recall an antique shop on the High Street, opposite the newsagent?"

She shook her head.

"Neither do I, but it was there this morning."

He pulled the ring from his pocket and placed it in her hand.

"What's this?"

"It came from the antique shop."

Sophie examined it and looked at him with a churlish stare.

"Jesus, Finn, what were you thinking, how much did you pay for this? It's gold."

"I didn't pay for it. At first the shopkeeper said he wanted a couple of hundred, but in the end he let me have it."

After Finn had explained what had happened, Sophie blew out a long sigh and handed it back.

"Well, now you've removed it, you should return it."

"He said I could keep it," replied Finn as he snatched it back from her.

"Take it back to the shop. You never know he may have had a change of heart and want it back."

Sophie saw a look in her husband's eye which she didn't like.

"Did he only want two hundred pounds for it? Because if you ask me, it's worth a lot more."

He glanced at his watch.

"He said he would be closed and gone by now, I don't think it's worth it."

"Go now and hurry, he may still be there," snapped Sophie.

He knew she was right, he should return it.

"Okay," he sighed.

Finn jumped in the car and headed to the High Street.

He parked on the main road outside the newsagent and got out.

The antique shop across the road was boarded up and empty.

He looked at the dusty windows and the weathered door. Paint flaked on the window seals. The place looked old and tired. It was a mess, and looked different to how it had earlier that morning.

He went into the newsagent.

"Hi, can I ask you a quick question?"

The lady looked up and smiled.

"Do you know what time the antique shop closed this morning?"

"Antique shop?"

"Yes, the one opposite," said Finn as he pointed across the road.

The lady walked to the door.

"Where?"

"Directly opposite, right there."

The lady frowned.

"That's not an antique shop. The last time it was open it was a sandwich shop."

"Are you sure?"

The lady nodded.

Finn was going to explain what had happened earlier, but decided against it. He didn't want to run the risk of sounding insane.

He thanked her and stepped out of the shop.

Dodging the traffic he dashed over the road to take a closer look.

A rusty padlock secured the door. He turned his attention to the window and squinted as he peered into the darkness of the shop. Old newspapers and junk mail littered the floor. Against the back wall stood a refrigerator which had once dispensed drinks. He could see a peeling sticker showing a faded Coca-Cola logo.

With the palm of his hand he wiped away grime from the window.

He looked again and saw the same damp patch and flaking paint he'd seen earlier.

He took the ring from his pocket, looked at it and quickly put it back.

I must be going mad.

He glanced across the road and noticed he was being observed by the lady from the newsagent.

Finn shook his head and returned his attention to the interior of the shop.

And then he saw it.

He grabbed the ring and gripped it in his palm.

It was there, hanging from the wall, just where he'd seen it that morning.

He cleared more grime from the window to get a better view. The wooden frame was split, and the glass was thick with dust.

He trembled as he stared at the painting on the wall. There was no doubt in his mind.

It was the same landscape painting he'd seen that morning.

The painting in which a huge raven soared high above the trees.

Chapter 11

Mid-September

Over the weeks, the Maynard's adapted to their new arrival.

Jack was developing well. Sophie and Finn were back in the routine of caring for a baby. Rosie was four, and it seemed an age since she had been as tiny as Jack.

She had shown signs of jealousy, which her parents had expected. Finn made the effort to spend extra time with her.

He returned from paternity leave in August and found work a struggle. His mind was preoccupied with his family. He'd loved nothing more than spending time with his wife and children and was desperate to get home each night.

And there was something else which preoccupied him. The mystery of the ring and the antique shop.

He'd spoken to a few people and had trawled the internet for photographs of the High Street. None of those with whom he'd spoken had remembered the shop and the pictures he'd found weren't much help either.

If it wasn't for the gold ring which he kept in a box on his bedside table, he would have wondered whether he'd made the whole thing up.

Why had the thing been so difficult to take off, and why later in the day had it slid off as if it were two or three sizes too big? And what was the story behind the mystery shop?

It was a late Friday afternoon in September and the sun beat upon the tarmac.

Finn stepped out of the car, wiped his forehead and looked at his house.

I need to start work on that ugly garden he thought and slammed the door.

He liked the hawthorn tree which grew smack bang in the middle. He wanted to keep it, but Sophie insisted it should be chopped down. She had told him it was an eyesore.

Suddenly, he heard a lady's voice.

"Hello, I've not introduced myself."

Finn looked up to see his neighbour Ruth, the lady whom Kieran had told him to be wary. Finn recalled how he had described her. Kieran referred to her as a harbinger of doom.

Finn swallowed hard and walked over and offered his hand.

Ruth smiled and introduced herself. Finn didn't let on that he knew her name.

"I should have said hello earlier, but what with your new baby and things, I thought it best to let you settle in."

"Don't worry. Besides, we could have knocked on your door to say hello. I'm Finn, Finn Maynard"

Ruth nodded.

"So, how are things going?" asked Ruth.

Finn detected an air about the woman which caused him to distrust her. Maybe Kieran had been right when he warned him not to take too much notice of her.

"Things are good. We're settling in well thank you."

"What do you think of the road?"

"It's just what we wanted. A nice quiet cul de sac, it's great for the children."

Finn sensed awkwardness, but felt compelled to keep the conversation going.

"I'm considering what to do with this garden," said Finn.

"Good luck with that."

"Why?" asked Finn with a nonplussed expression.

"Nothing grows, other than that old tree. I've lived here since the late seventies, I was one of the first to move into these houses soon after they were built. In the years I've lived here, I've seen nothing grow...... everything dies."

Finn looked at his garden and then to Ruth's which had an abundance of roses and was a picture of colour.

"Do you have any idea why my house is detached? The others on this side are terraced."

Ruth shrugged her shoulders and turned away. He sensed she was hiding something.

"My house was built much later than the others wasn't it?"

"The builders finished in eighty-four, they started work in nineteen eighty."

"They took four years to build it?"

Ruth nodded.

"Why did they take so long?"

Ruth looked nervy.

"I'm sorry, I'm busy, I have to get back. We'll speak again soon."

He watched her disappear indoors.

Strange woman he thought to himself.

Finn opened his garden gate and walked over to the hawthorn. He scuffed the ground with his shoe. Ruth was right. There was nothing, not even a weed. He crouched down and ran his fingers through the arid soil. He pushed his forefinger in as far as he could. There should be moisture, but the soil was dry.

"Hey Alan Titchmarsh, what you doing?"
He looked up and saw Sophie holding Jack.
"I'm thinking about the garden, what we should do with it."
"God only knows when you'll find time for gardening?"
"Maybe not just yet, but it would be nice to have something popping up by the spring. Maybe daffodils or something."
"You can chop down that tree….. It's horrible,"
"Why? It has character."
"It's ugly….. get rid of it….. grow some nice flowers instead."
He huffed and followed her into the house.

Finn stepped into the lounge and saw Rosie engrossed by the television. She glanced up and saw her father.
"Daddy, you're home."
The little girl jumped up, ran across the room and threw her arms around him. He picked her up and spun her around.
"You're making me dizzy," she giggled.
He hugged her and put her down.
Rosie was excited to see her daddy and told him about her day. He knelt at her level and listened to what she had to say.
"Can I have a drink daddy?"
"Wait there, I'll get us both a nice cold drink."
He opened the fridge door and turned around to see Sophie stood behind him.
"So you've been speaking with our nosy neighbour."
"Yeah, Ruth said hello, and we had chat."
"What do you reckon, is she okay?"
"I think she's fine, but I'm sure she's hiding something."
"Like what?"
"If I knew, she wouldn't be hiding anything would she?"
"You know what I mean."
"She seemed a little reserved…… well actually a lot reserved. I asked her about this house and she went quiet. She made her excuses and went."
"About this house, what did you ask?"
"She told me about the garden. It seems no one has ever managed to plant anything that didn't die."
"Apart from that tree?"
Finn nodded.
"I asked whether she had any idea why this house stood on its own and was not part of the terrace…… and that was when she didn't want to talk any more, she clammed up and went in her house."
"Did she say anything?"

"No, not really. Oh, hang on, she did say it took four years to build this place."

"Four years, that's a long time isn't it?"

"That's what I thought. That was when she started being odd and went inside."

"Daddy, where's my drink."

"I'm coming Rosie."

Sophie wore a puzzled expression.

"Don't worry, it's fine," added Finn.

Sophie said nothing. She only nodded.

An hour later Finn read Rosie a bedtime story. Finn was about to turn to the last page when he noticed she'd fallen asleep. He kissed her on her head and tucked her in.

He was going to leave her room when he heard hushed voices coming from the road. The conversation sounded heated.

He pulled the curtain, looked out and saw Kieran and Ruth arguing. He strained to make out what they were saying. Even with the window open he couldn't hear. Every few seconds Ruth pointed towards his house.

He opened the window more and caught the end of their argument.

"Someone needs to tell them," said Ruth. Her hushed voice became louder.

"You do what you want, but leave me out of it. I want nothing to do with it, or them," replied Kieran.

They looked up when they heard Rosie's window creak and saw her curtain move.

Finn watched through the gap in the curtain as Kieran went back inside and Ruth strutted across the road.

Sophie was feeding Jack when he returned from Rosie's room.

"There's something going on," said Finn as he looked out of the window and across the road.

She looked at him without speaking.

"I'm not sure what it is. Maybe I'm being paranoid, but I reckon there's a conspiracy against us."

"A conspiracy, why?"

Finn explained what he'd seen and heard from his daughter's window.

"Why don't you speak with Kieran? He appears to be nice enough. Ask him what's happening and tell him to be honest with you."

Finn nodded.

He felt uncomfortable knocking on Kieran's door and asking what was happening. Instead he sat by the window overlooking Kieran's house on the off chance he came out.

"Oh for God's sake Finn, be a man please! Just ask him."

He didn't answer.

"Jack's sleeping. I'm taking him upstairs and I'm going to lie on the bed. You do whatever you want."

She felt tired and crabby and her husband's procrastination annoyed her.

Finn huffed air through his cheeks and continued to watch from the window.

He'd been sitting at the window seat for half an hour and become drowsy when he heard a clattering.

It was Kieran emptying bottles into the recycling crate and making a lot of noise about it.

Finn jumped up, grabbed his keys and left the house.

Kieran looked up and saw Finn marching across the road.

Uh-oh thought Kieran.

"Hi, we need to talk."

The colour drained from Kieran's face.

"And you know why. I heard you and Ruth earlier. What were you saying?"

"Okay, you'd better come in. I'll get you a beer. You may need it."

He followed Kieran and passed Linda in the hallway. She smiled, meekly said hello, and went upstairs. Finn sensed an atmosphere.

"Sit over there, I'll get you a drink."

Kieran returned from the kitchen with two ice cold cans and handed one to Finn.

"What can I tell you?" asked Kieran.

Finn held the beer and looked at the floor. He remembered the brief conversation he'd had with Ruth.

"You said that Ruth was the street gossip and someone I shouldn't take too seriously."

Kieran nodded.

"I spoke to her for the first time this morning. I'd expected to her to tell me all the juicy stuff, but she hardly spoke. We made small talk, and she appeared desperate to get back indoors."

He nodded again and sighed.

"She's changed. She likes to gossip and as I said before, she's our own harbinger of doom. But I reckon she's had enough," said Kieran.

"Enough of what?"

"Bad things."

"Sorry, you've lost me. I only asked about our house. Is there something bad about it?"

"She told me you asked about your house and why it's not terraced." said Kieran.

"I did. It seemed a simple enough question. Sophie and I wondered why."

"Okay, well the truth is, the building contractors refused to work on your plot of land."

"Why?"

"They refused."

"Is that it? They just refused?"

Kieran cleared his throat.

"That's right Finn."

"Kieran, I'm not a fool. What are you not telling me?"

An air of tension filled the room.

"You've started, you may as well tell me everything."

Kieran placed his beer on the floor and sat next to Finn.

"Okay, I'll tell you what I know, but it's not the kind of thing you'd have found in the estate agent's blurb when your house was for sale."

Finn perched on the edge of the settee and waited for Kieran to begin.

"Back in the nineteen seventies Newbold Housing had been granted permission to build on this land. Their intention was to build a row of fifteen terraced houses on your side of the road and detached houses on my side."

Kieran paused for a swig of beer and continued.

"Everything was going to plan until work commenced on the plot of land earmarked as number thirteen. Things began to go wrong. Some of the contractors brought in by Newbold Housing said they wouldn't work there. The contractors included a team of Spanish workers who refused point blank to build there. It wasn't clear what was wrong, I think there may have been a language barrier. The Spanish guys couldn't be understood."

"Were the Spanish workers sacked?" asked Finn.

"No, I understand that after heated words they upped tools and left."

Finn nodded.

"After the Spanish had gone, they were replaced by Brits. They didn't have a problem and began with the foundations. The day the excavator dug the foundations is when things went wrong. Something wasn't right with the pneumatics and the driver couldn't control it. I'm not sure of the full details, but the bucket on the digger swung round, hit a worker and killed him."

Finn gasped.

"Everything had to be put on hold and an investigation took place, and eventually work recommenced. But things continued to go wrong. Every builder who set foot on the plot became ill. I don't just mean they got sick and had to take a week off, I mean really sick. One had a stroke, two were diagnosed with terminal cancer, one attempted suicide and another became depressed and within a day he'd killed his wife."

"I guess it happened over a long time?" asked Finn.

"No, it happened within forty eight hours after work recommenced."

Finn rubbed his eyes and lowered his head.

Kieran continued.

"After what happened, Newbold decided not to build on the plot, but continued building the other houses. They needed to, they'd invested so much money. When the houses had been finished and were being sold, the buyers wondered why there was a gap the size of a house between eleven and fifteen. The lady in the sales office said something about building permission, or mines or some bullshit, but she didn't tell anyone what had really happened. Newbold told her not to mention it, in case it put people off buying the houses."

"So how come you know so much?"

"My father was a builder. He worked on these houses and he was there when it happened."

"Jeez!" exclaimed Finn. "What about my house, did Newbold change their mind?"

"No, they wouldn't touch the land, it gave them the heebeegeebees. Those who worked for Newbold were affected by what happened. Staff left and in the early eighties Newbold went out of business."

"Because of what had happened?"

Kieran shrugged his shoulders.

"So how did my house end up being built?"

"Newbold needed cash, they were getting into financial difficulty. They sold the land at a knock down price to a private builder who built your place."

"So he didn't have the same problems that Newbold faced?"

"Oh, he did. Building work started in nineteen eighty, but the house wasn't completed until nineteen eighty four. It wasn't quite as severe compared to what had happened to the contractors who had worked for Newbold, but still, there were big problems."

"What problems."

"A few of the builders Drake-Butler employed became ill, a few left, and there were fights. But eventually, your house was built. And there you have it. That's the story behind why your house is detached."

"Who's Drake-Butler?"

"Sorry?"

"Who's Drake-Butler? You just said the builders Drake-Butler employed became ill?"

"Oh yes, Drake-Butler, they bought the land and built your house."

Finn finished his beer and gazed at Kieran.

"It's an interesting tale, but I don't understand why you or Ruth wouldn't have wanted to tell me."

"Well, you have to admit, it's not the nicest thing to know about where you live."

"But that was over twenty years ago. It's old news."

Kieran sighed.

"Is there anything else?"

He shook his head.

"I don't wish to sound rude, but I have to be getting on with things."

Finn stood up to leave.

"Okay, thanks for the beer and thanks for telling me the creepy tale about my house," said Finn sarcastically.

"You may find it laughable now, but believe me, at the time people were scared."

Finn nodded.

"I'm sorry, it's just………"

"Sorry, I really need to get on," interrupted Kieran as he opened the front door.

Finn got the hint and left.

Kieran closed the door as Linda came downstairs.

"So you didn't tell him everything?" asked Linda with a solemn expression.

"No, not everything………. But I'm sure he'll find out in due course."

Chapter 12

A telephone rang in the study. The old man of the house made his way along the wood clad corridor, cursing as he walked.

"I'm coming God dammit, don't be so impatient."

He grabbed the phone from its cradle and growled as he spoke.

"Yes, what is it?"

"Mr. Butler it's me, I have news."

"Okay, it'd better be good Mr. Tempest."

"I think we've found our man."

"Are you sure?"

"I think so sir."

"I don't want to hear you say 'think so', I need to know for sure."

"Sorry sir, but I need to find out one more thing."

"What?"

"The final connection sir, I need to check the final link."

"Is that it? The final link. Is that all that needs to be confirmed?"

"Yes, sir."

"Okay, and don't forget, you can't ask him, he will need to tell you."

"I understand."

"Good. Don't call me again until it's done."

Gabriel Butler ended the call and looked out from the window. He was a patient man, but seventy-one years was a long time to wait. But if what he'd been told was true, then he wouldn't be waiting much longer.

Chapter 13

December

It had been a glorious summer and a mild autumn, but winter crept up almost unannounced and now the nights had become long and days were bitter.

Finn cranked the thermostat up a notch, returned to the settee and cuddled with Sophie.

Jack slept in his cot, safe and warm in his baby grow. Rosie was in the kitchen with her colouring book at the dining table.

"It's seven o'clock. One of us has to break the news to her soon," said Finn as he glanced at the clock.

"Let her have ten more minutes, she's happy," replied Sophie.

A few minutes later Rosie ran into the lounge excitedly waving her colouring book in her parents' faces.

"Look mummy, do you like what I've done?"

"That's wonderful darling, aren't you clever!"

Sophie passed the book to Finn.

Finn looked at the quality of her colouring. She'd barely gone beyond the lines. Normally crayon would be everywhere and her choice of colours were debatable. Red elephants, blue grass, yellow sea. But tonight's offering was excellent for a four year old.

"Wow Rosie, that's clever. Your colouring is really good."

Rosie sat next to her parents and looked pleased with herself.

"It's time for bed," said Finn with a down turned mouth.

"Can I do one more picture………. please?"

"Sorry Rosie, it's late, and if you don't go to bed now there won't be enough time for a story."

Rosie huffed and crossed her arms.

"But please………."

Finn shook his head.

"Give mummy a kiss and a cuddle and I'll get you ready."

After kisses and cuddles and cleaning of teeth, Finn was reading a bedtime story. Rosie was under her sheets as snug as a bug and holding on to Amy, her favourite pink teddy bear.

He read the last page and closed the book.

"Daddy, can I tell you something?"

Finn nodded.

"You know my colouring was really good tonight, and it was nice and tidy?"

"It was brilliant Rosie, you're getting good at colouring."
"But daddy, can I tell you how I did it so nice and tidy?"
"Go on, tell me how you did it so nice and tidy."
"The man helped me."
Finn smiled and brushed her hair away from her eyes.
"Which man was that darling?"
"The man in the kitchen."
"That's nice Rosie. Do you have a name for your friend in the kitchen?"
"No, I asked him, but he didn't say. He held my hand when I was colouring and made sure I didn't go over the lines."
Finn's face changed from one of amused to one of concern.
He remembered how exact her colouring had been. It was completely different to what she'd done earlier that day.
"Did the man speak?"
"He had a funny voice, I couldn't understand him. He held onto my hand. It hurt when he held it too tight. I told him to let go."
Finn frowned.
"Look daddy, my arm's still sore."
She pulled her arm out from under the sheet and showed him her wrist.
He held her hand and looked at her wrist. It was red.
"Does it still hurt?"
"A little, it's getting better now."
"Show me your other arm."
She pulled her other arm from beneath the sheet. Finn compared both wrists. Her left one was unmarked.
"He made me do a drawing, but it wasn't very good."
"In your colouring book?"
"Yes. I didn't show it to you because it was rubbish," giggled Rosie.
"What did the man look like?"
"I don't know."
"Didn't you see his face?"
Rosie shook her head.
"Daddy, I'm getting tired and want to go to sleep."
"Rosie, why didn't you see what he looked like."
"Because he had paper over his face."
"Paper, what do you mean paper?"
"He had paper over his face, so I didn't see what he looked like."
Finn thought about what his daughter had just told him.
"Was it newspaper, or drawing paper? What sort of paper was it?"
"Daddy, I want to go to sleep now, I'm too tired."
"Concentrate Rosie, what kind of paper?"

"I'm not sure, but it was like a sweetie bag, like the one from the corner shop when you let me choose my favourite sweets and the man in the shop puts them in a little white paper bag. It was that kind of paper, but really big."

Finn shuddered. "Rosie, are you saying that the man had a big paper bag over his face?"

She nodded.

"I'm tired and want to go to sleep."

Finn tucked her in again and kissed her on the head. After closing her door he stood outside her room and thought about their conversation. He shook his head and tiptoed downstairs, mindful not to wake Jack.

Sophie looked up as Finn entered the lounge.

"You were a long time."

Finn didn't answer. He picked up Rosie's colouring book and thumbed through. Every page of colouring was random, which was what he'd been used to seeing from his daughter. He turned to the page she'd been colouring that evening and compared it to what she'd done yesterday. There was no doubt about it, they were different.

He flipped through the book until he came to a page on which were two circular shapes drawn with red crayon.

The picture in the colouring book was of a tree in a field. Surrounding the tree were cows, chickens and pigs. Rosie had coloured nothing in. She'd only drawn the two circular patterns. Beneath each pattern was a tick.

Sophie watched as her husband flipped through the colouring book. He looked perplexed.

"Are you okay?"

Finn took no notice of his wife and went back to Rosie's room with the colouring book.

"Rosie, wake up."

She opened her eyes and smiled.

"I wasn't really asleep," she giggled.

Finn opened the colouring book to the page with the two red patterns and flattened it out on her bed.

"Is this the drawing you were telling me about?"

Rosie nodded.

"Why did you tick them?"

"I didn't, the man with paper on his face ticked them?"

He tucked her back under her sheets, kissed her and left the room.

Sophie heard him coming down the stairs. He didn't tiptoe as he normally did when the children were in bed. Instead he thundered down. He flung open the lounge door and stared at Sophie.

"I think someone's been in the house. Someone was in the kitchen with Rosie earlier."

Sophie frowned. "Why?"

"Because Rosie told me. At first I thought she'd made it up, now I'm not so sure."

Finn went to the kitchen. He pushed the door, but something was stopping it from opening. He tried again. Sophie stepped out from the lounge and stood behind him.

"Damned thing's jammed. It must be the cold making the wood expand," said Finn.

He pushed his shoulder against the door and it swung open. He switched on the light and saw it was empty. He walked to the back door and tried the handle.

"It's locked."

"Rosie must have been imagining him. She's probably created him in her head as someone to play with," said Sophie.

"Most children who have imaginary friends create children, or nice things like rabbits."

Finn pulled out a chair and gestured to Sophie to sit down. She sat at the kitchen table while he went to the lounge and returned with Rosie's colouring book.

He explained the conversation he'd had with his daughter and showed her the two red patterns Rosie had drawn.

Sophie shook her head.

"Finn, don't worry about it, she's created this man in her head. It's her imagination. She's a four year old girl, it's what they do."

"I know, I know, but it's her description, she said he had a paper bag……. it's just because it sounds like……. well you understand what I'm saying."

Sophie shook her head.

"What?"

"Never mind."

"I'm going back to the lounge," said Sophie as she stood up.

She left Finn to consider the strange events of the evening. His daughter's description of the man she'd seen in the kitchen bothered him. She'd said he'd had paper stuck to his face, like a big sweet bag.

He couldn't help thinking of that hideous day last December when he'd seen the body of the man who'd jumped in front of the train. The man whose head he'd found. The head in the bag.

Finn sat bolt upright in his chair. *That was last December*, he thought as he pulled his mobile from his pocket.

He searched his contacts and found the number he was looking for as he walked back to the lounge.

"Who are you calling?" asked Sophie.

Finn didn't answer, he was waiting for his call to be answered.

"Hi Sally, it's Finn."

"Hi mate how are you doing?"

Finn found it difficult to hear her, it sounded as if she was in a busy bar or a restaurant.

"I'm okay. I won't keep you long, it sounds like you're having fun."

"Yeah, we're having a great evening."

"I need to ask you a quick question. Remember that horrible train journey at the end of last year?"

"Of course I do. How could I ever forget?"

"Can you remember the date it happened?"

"Are you joking with me?" said Sally. Finn sensed an uneasy tone in her voice.

"I'm not joking, I know it was December, but I can't recall which day. I think I must have blocked it from my mind."

"You really don't know, do you?"

Finn grunted and shook his head at his phone.

"It was a year ago Finn, a year ago today."

Finn shuddered. "Are you sure?"

"Yes I'm sure. I will never forget, not for the rest of my days."

"Why?"

"Because it happened on Luke's twelfth birthday. We're out together now in Pizza Hut celebrating his thirteenth. That's why I'll never forget. It was December fourteenth two thousand and four."

Finn said nothing. He dropped the phone to the floor.

Sophie could hear Sally's voice crackling over the phone as it lay on the carpet.

"Finn, Finn. Is everything okay?"

Chapter 14

Heather lay in her bed deep in thought. She'd told nobody what happened in the graveyard last August, the day she'd visited Sophie in the maternity hospital. The memory of hearing the name echoing around the walls of the old church haunted her. She recalled it with crystal clarity.

'Charles Samuel Nash'.

She didn't know who Charles Nash was, but was sure he had a connection with the church at the bottom of St. Michaels Hill.

Another memory had returned from when she was young. Over the past few months she recalled memories of visiting her great grandmother Elizabeth in hospital during her final hours.

Being a devout Christian, Elizabeth had not been scared of dying. In fact, she'd embraced the knowledge that she would pass through a door and enter the Kingdom of Heaven. Elizabeth had a strong connection with those who'd passed over. She took comfort knowing that those to whom she'd been close and who'd passed before her were now in a place in which their souls continued to exist in happiness. Elizabeth had a reputation of being someone different to most. Many people knew of her gift of speaking with the dead, and friends and neighbours turned to her for assurance that their loved ones who'd passed away had found peace and contentment.

Elizabeth knew that Heather inherited the same gift which skipped two generations. Neither her daughter, nor her granddaughter showed any signs of sharing her abilities.

Elizabeth was extremely ill the last time she'd talked to Heather. Heather saw her a few hours before she'd died. Elizabeth needed to tell her of the gift she'd inherited.

Heather remembered sitting with her parents and sister at Elizabeth's bedside in Frenchay Hospital. Heather was only seven and the sight of her great grandmother with tubes attached to keep her alive scared her. Elizabeth was weak, but had enough strength to beckon Heather to move closer. Elizabeth gestured to Heather to come close enough for her to whisper in her ear. Heather was scared and nervously climbed upon the bed to listen to her great grandmother.

Elizabeth's feeble voice was barely above a whisper and Heather couldn't hear Elizabeth's words. Heather shrugged her shoulders and shook her head. Elizabeth beckoned her to move even closer, and whispered a second time. As she spoke she ran her finger over a small silver cross which hung from her neck. This time Heather heard Elizabeth's words and was scared by what she'd been told. She climbed from the bed, sat down and shivered as an icy chill made the soft hairs on her arms stand on end.

At the time what Elizabeth said meant nothing to her, but as she grew older and discovered more about Elizabeth she'd understood her great grandmother's final words.

Eighteen years later, Heather could still recall what she'd said.

"Heather, you are blessed with the veil of tears. Learn to use your gift wisely."

What is the veil of tears? She didn't understand. She'd asked her parents and grandparents what it meant, but no one wanted to discuss it. Whatever it was embarrassed her family, and became taboo and wasn't mentioned again.

Many years later Heather talked with families of those who'd known of Elizabeth's gift and things made sense. Heather had been told of stories of the 'crazy lady' who spoke with the dead. She'd been ridiculed by many. Elizabeth was considered a medium, clairvoyant, and psychic and in the nineteenth century little was known of clairvoyants, which was why she wasn't taken seriously.

In the eighteen years since her great grandmother died, Heather had no contact with the dead. But since the happening in the graveyard one or two things occurred.

In September she saw a vision of her boyfriend Mark, who'd been Finn's best friend. Mark had died in a climbing accident the year before. They had only dated for a few weeks, but had become very close. Heather insisted that Mark shouldn't go on the climbing holiday because she had a bad feeling. She'd woken in the early hours one humid September morning. Her sheets repeatedly came away from her bed and ended up on the floor as if someone was pulling at them. She got up to remake it and saw Mark sitting in the chair in the corner of her room. Mark said nothing, he only looked at her and smiled. Heather froze. And then she heard his voice. His mouth didn't move, he continued to look at her and smile.

"You were right. I should have listened to you Heather, and I should never have attempted to climb that mountain. But I want you to know I'm happy, but I would be happier with you."

It wasn't a dream, it definitely happened. Mark had spoken to her.

The following week, a similar thing happened. Again, she was awoken by something tugging at her bedsheets and this time it wasn't Mark, it was Elizabeth. She looked young, radiant and beautiful and nothing like Heather remembered her when she'd been alive. Just as when she saw Mark, her mouth didn't move, but her words rang as clear as a bell.

"Heather, you have been blessed with the veil of tears. Only a few have been chosen. Good is on your side. Believe in good, always believe in good."

Heather had been frightened when she'd seen Mark, but seeing Elizabeth made everything okay. Things made sense and the veil of tears didn't sound so worrying.

Heather had been chosen, and had been born with the gift of the veil of tears. The power invested in her was greater than the power given to Elizabeth. Skipping two generations made the strength of her yet unrefined skills immense.

Heather had been selected for a purpose. She'd been put on the earth because she'd been chosen for a task. A task so important it would affect the future of mankind.

Chapter 15

Finn had not slept well. He was sure he'd not had a wink of sleep. Sophie assured him he'd been sleeping for at least two hours. His snoring had kept her awake since four thirty.

"I can't help thinking about last night," said Finn as he lay on the bed and stared at the darkness of the room.

"Finn, listen to yourself, you sound ridiculous. It's something Rosie's invented. It's a coincidence and nothing more. She's created an imaginary friend. I admit, what she's made up is a little unusual, but she has an overactive imagination."

"She's not created a friend, she's created a ghost," replied Finn.

Jack cried. His voice sputtered over the baby monitor.

"You believe what you want, I'm going to see Jack."

Sophie turned on the bedside lamp, threw on her dressing gown and left Finn on his own to wallow in his thoughts.

Finn replayed the previous evening's events again in his mind. It had been on his mind all night, and he was thinking about it again. He'd never believed in the paranormal, but now he'd changed his mind. In the eleven hours of thinking of nothing else but what Rosie had told him, and not being able to come up with a plausible explanation, he'd concluded that his daughter had seen the ghost of the man who'd jumped in front of the train. And, Sally had confirmed that the suicide happened a year to the day. That couldn't be coincidence.

Finn thought about the head in the bag and the way the dead man's eye stared at him. He remembered how it looked at him as if it knew Finn would be there to witness the suicide.

Slowly, he made his way down to the kitchen and made coffee.

He handed a mug to Sophie who thought how old he looked. He was only twenty-nine, but it was as if he'd aged overnight. She noticed a wisp of grey hair on his temple. He looked more like thirty-nine.

"Please don't worry about last night, I'm sure it was nothing."

Finn ignored her, cupped his hands around the mug and looked across the road to the light in Kieran's window. He was sure his neighbour wasn't telling him everything about their house.

He was brought out of his thoughts by the sound of Rosie scurrying down the stairs.

"Can I have something to eat, please?"

Finn stood up, and turned to his daughter.

"How are you poppet?"

"Hungry daddy."

"I mean after last night. Does your arm still hurt?"

Rosie shook her head.

"My arm?"

"Yes, is it better now?"

Rosie skipped to the kitchen as Sophie threw a glance at Finn. He followed her to the kitchen and poured cereal into a bowl.

"Last night you told me about a man in the kitchen with paper on his face and he'd helped you colour a picture."

Rosie shook her head as she sat at the kitchen table, swinging her feet and eating her breakfast. Finn asked her again, but she ignored him.

He went to the lounge, and returned with the colouring book. He opened it to the page with the two red circular drawings.

"You told me the man made you draw this."

"No one made me draw it, I did it myself."

He turned to the neatly coloured picture.

"You told me the man in the kitchen helped you with this."

She shook her head. "I did that."

Finn dropped the book on the table and blew air from his cheeks in frustration.

"Rosie, last night you said there was man in the kitchen who had paper on his face. You told me he hurt your arm when he helped you draw."

Finn was agitated. He looked at her right wrist as she ate her breakfast. He took the spoon from her hand and held her arm.

"Can you remember how you did this?" asked Finn pointing to the red mark on her wrist which was barely visible. Rosie shook her head, grabbed the spoon from the table and continued eating.

Rosie put the spoon in the bowl and looked at her father. A tear welled in her eye.

"I promised the man I wouldn't talk about him."

"The man with the paper on his face?"

Rosie nodded.

"Did you see him again?"

Rosie looked at the table.

"Rosie, you need to tell me. Did you see the man again?"

"I'm not telling you. I promised that I wouldn't tell you about him anymore. He made me promise."

"Okay Rosie, don't worry. Don't be upset."

He left her on her own to finish her breakfast, went to the lounge and looked out across the road. Outside it was still dark and he saw Kieran getting into his car. He was going to march across the road and speak with him but decided against it. Kieran drove away and their eyes met as his car passed Finn's window.

Sophie stood behind him and put her arms around him.

"I heard you talking to Rosie. I heard what she said."
Finn nodded.
"I'll sort this out. I need to find out what Kieran's not telling me."
Sophie nodded and kissed him on his neck.
"You'd better get a move on, you'll be late for work."
Finn sighed and made his way to the bathroom to have a wash and shave.
Sophie considered what Rosie had told Finn. She had to admit that it was strange that it had happened a year since the suicide.
Unlike Finn, Sophie had always believed in spirits and ghosts and pondered what had happened. Maybe Rosie had seen something last night. If it wasn't a ghost of someone who had thrown himself in front of the train, then maybe it was a ghost of another person who'd lived in their house before them.

Later that morning, after Finn had left for work and she'd dropped Rosie at reception class, Sophie was strapping Jack into the car and was ready to go shopping, when she saw Ruth walking along the road towards her house. In the months they'd lived there Sophie had hardly said two words to her neighbour. Other than Kieran, they'd spoken to almost nobody in the street. It was as if everyone was trying to avoid them. Even making eye contact was difficult.
As Ruth approached her house Sophie took time to adjust Jack's straps. She wanted to time it so she shut the car door just as Ruth got to her gate.
"Hi Ruth, cold morning isn't it?"
Ruth nodded. Sophie sensed an awkward conversation was about to take place, but was determined to speak with her. She came right out with it.
"Can I ask you something?"
"I'm busy, can we speak later?"
"No, Ruth if you don't mind I'd prefer to talk with you now. I promise I won't keep you. Jack's in the car, and we're in a hurry so it won't take long."
Ruth sighed and turned to face her.
"Okay, how can I help?"
"What happened to the man who lived here before us?"
Ruth looked apprehensive and ran her fingers across the top of her garden gate.
"I don't know what happened, he was an old man, and I presume he died of old age."
Sophie was sure Ruth wasn't telling the truth.
"Did you know him?"
Ruth shook her head. "Not very well, he wasn't much of a talker."
"Did he die in the house, or in hospital?"
"Sorry Sophie, I'm not sure what happened....... he just died."

Ruth was a goddamn awful liar.

"So you live next door to a man for God knows how many years, he dies and no one told you what happened, and you didn't bother to ask?"

Ruth said nothing.

"I don't mean to sound rude, but we were told you're the gossip of the street. If that's true, surely you would be the first to find out what happened."

"I don't take kindly to being called a gossip."

"I'm sorry Ruth, but I don't give a crap what you think. There's something about our house that's being kept from us, and I'd like to know what it is."

Sophie watched as Ruth shivered. She turned her back, grabbed a tissue from her pocket and dabbed her eyes. Sophie waited for Ruth to say something. The silence forced Ruth to speak. She turned around, cleared her throat, faced Sophie and with tears in her eyes spoke.

"Robert Buxton was a fine man, he was a gentleman. He didn't deserve to die the way he did."

A neighbour walking her dog passed them on the other side of the road. Ruth lowered her head. Sophie waited for the dog walker to pass by and then whispered to Ruth.

"Robert Buxton, was that his name? How did he die?"

"Sorry, I don't want to talk about it, please leave me alone."

"Ruth, it's important. Something happened in our house last night and I need to know what happened to Robert Buxton."

"What happened?" asked Ruth, her ears pricking up.

"Rosie saw a man in the kitchen, and her description of him was, ... well, let's just say it was strange."

"Did he speak with her?"

"Rosie said it was difficult to understand him, she said he had paper stuck to his face."

Ruth shuddered again.

"Robert Buxton died in the same way as the others who lived there before him." said Ruth.

"What others?"

"You're the fourth family to move to this house. Before you there was Robert Buxton. He bought the house with his wife in nineteen ninety five to be near his son Henry who lives at number five. Robert lived here the longest."

"We know of Henry Buxton and we know that we live in his father's house."

"Before Robert there was Emma and David, they lived here for six years and before them there was Shaun and Janet. They didn't last long."

"You said Robert Buxton died in the same way as the others who lived here before him, what do you mean?"

Ruth cried, blew her nose and cleared her throat.

"Shaun and Janet were lovely. They were a young couple, and this was their first house. Janet was pregnant and everything was great. Then something happened. I don't know why, but things went wrong."

Sophie waited while Ruth composed herself.

"They disappeared. Nobody had seen them in weeks. It was on the news, you may remember."

Sophie shook her head.

"They were found in their car."

"Who found them?"

"Police divers. The divers found them strapped in their seats at the bottom of a lake."

"Which lake?"

"Bitterwell Lake. There were tyre marks on the bank. Shaun had driven into the lake, killed himself, Janet and their unborn child."

Sophie gasped as condensation blew from her mouth.

"What about Emily and David?"

"It was Emma and David. Emma died. She had been ill, shortly after, David took his life. He couldn't get over her death. He was a very sad man."

"And Robert Buxton killed himself too didn't he."

Ruth nodded.

"Robert was a lovely man, as I said, a real gentleman, but he changed. Towards the end something happened to him. He fell out with Henry and became a recluse. He hardly left the house, and when he did, he didn't speak. We used to be good friends. He was a good neighbour."

"Ruth, did Robert kill himself in front of a train?"

She looked at Sophie and nodded.

"He died a year ago yesterday didn't he?"

Ruth nodded again.

"Ruth, my husband was on the train that killed Robert."

Ruth couldn't talk any longer. She shut her gate and hurried up the garden path. She turned to Sophie and looked at her through teary red eyes.

"Please get out of that house. Don't let it happen to you. Please move out as soon as you can."

She slammed the door and left Sophie standing on the pavement in disbelief.

Chapter 16

It was early evening and Finn listened as Sophie recalled the conversation she'd had earlier that day with Ruth. When she'd finished, he stood up, poured a scotch and gazed out of the window.

"So we've bought the house of the man whose head I found on the tracks," said Finn before taking a large gulp of whisky.

Sophie nodded.

"And everyone who has lived here has committed Hara-kiri?" he added.

"According to Ruth, yes."

"How do you feel about that?" asked Finn.

"To be honest, it scares me. We've two small children. If there is anything odd about this place we should 'up sticks' and get out before it happens to us."

"I think I may have overreacted after what Rosie said last night. We shouldn't do anything rash. I'm sure whatever caused Robert Buxton to kill himself would have nothing to do with the families who lived here before him."

"But don't you think it's a strange coincidence when you consider what Kieran told you, about the issues with building on this plot?"

"That's it. It's a coincidence and nothing else."

"So do you think Rosie saw Robert Buxton last night?"

Finn took his time to answer. He looked at Sophie and nodded.

"I think she did. But I can't see what harm a ghost can do."

"But according to Rosie the ghost held on to her, he made that red mark appear on her wrist."

Finn didn't have an answer. But he was sure about one thing. He wouldn't be intimidated into moving out of his own home. It would take more than a spectre to make him leave. He could see Sophie was nervous. She had a strong spiritual belief and Ruth's stories were affecting her.

He put the scotch on the table and hugged her.

"Now listen, everything will be fine...... but if I'm wrong, I promise we'll get out of here. If you bump into a man with his head under his arm, let him be. He won't hurt us."

Sophie didn't find her husband's remark funny.

"I'll tell you what I'll do though. I'll knock on Kieran's door tonight and ask him why he didn't care to mention the suicides when we had our little chat."

"He probably didn't want to overload you with any more scary stories about our house."

"Maybe you're right. But I'd like to speak with him again. I'll find out whether there's anything else he didn't mention."

After Finn had cleared the dishes from the evening meal and taken Rosie to bed he noticed Kieran's car was in his drive.

He hurried downstairs, grabbed his keys and told Sophie he was off to visit Kieran.

"Good luck!" said Sophie as he left the house.

Kieran opened the door and greeted Finn with his usual smile.

"Hi, can we talk?"

Kieran beckoned Finn and pointed to the lounge.

"Take a seat, I'll get you a beer."

"No Thanks, I won't have a drink."

"No beers? This must be important."

"Well, yeah, I guess. Why didn't you tell me about Robert Buxton?"

"Do you know what happened to him?"

"I do now. Sophie spoke with Ruth and she told her what happened, and what happened to the others who lived in our house before him."

"What did Ruth tell Sophie about Buxton?"

"Ruth didn't tell her what happened to Robert, Sophie knew. Ruth confirmed what we'd worked out for ourselves."

"So did Ruth *actually* say how Robert Buxton died?"

"What does it matter Kieran? No she didn't say how he died, but her body language gave it away. I've just said Sophie and I know what happened to him."

"Okay Finn, you tell me. How did he die?"

Finn was irritated. Kieran appeared to be playing a game with him. Finn wasn't in the mood to be messed around.

"Robert Buxton threw himself in front of a train at Stapleton Road Station. He killed himself a year ago yesterday. And I was on the train."

Finn expected a different reaction from Kieran. There was no 'oh my God'! or 'you gotta be joking!'. Finn wasn't sure he didn't detect a faint smile from Kieran.

"Robert Buxton's head was taken clean off by the train. I saw it, I was there."

"That sounds awful. It must have been a terrible shock for you….. are you sure you don't want that beer?"

"No thank you. You should have told me about the suicides. I reckon there're a few things you've not told me."

"To be honest Finn, I was worried I'd give you a case of information overload. I told you enough last time. I didn't consider it the right time to bring up the suicides."

Finn shrugged his shoulders.

"I wish you'd told me. I could've taken it."

"How's your wife taking the news?"

"She's not happy, she reckons we should move out."

"She's not taking it well. Give her time, she'll get used to it."

Finn nodded and looked nonplussed.

"Kieran, if we're to continue being friends, and I hope we will, you need to be honest with me. You need to tell me everything."

Kieran nodded.

"I will, but you need to see it from my point of view. It was difficult for me to tell you the odd things that have happened."

"Okay, I'd better be getting back to Sophie."

Kieran walked him to the door and bid him farewell.

The telephone rang in Gabriel Butler's study.

"Yes, who is this?"

"It's me. You're in business."

"Are you sure?"

"He confirmed the final link sir. He told me he was on the train and he found Buxton's head. They've definitely connected. He's the one."

"Good work. So now we sit back and wait."

"Yes sir. Mr, Butler, may I ask you something? Can I be paid now?"

"You will Mr. Tempest, you will."

Chapter 17

1st January 2006

Normality had returned to the Maynard's household. Rosie hadn't mentioned the man she'd seen in the kitchen and the last two weeks had been busy. Christmas Day had come and gone and Rosie had been excited beyond belief. Jack was too young to understand, but was happy to be part of it.

Sophie loved New Year's Day but Finn wasn't so keen. Sophie considered it a blank canvas to start over again and to achieve more than she'd done in the past twelve months. Finn was different. New Year made him low, all he wanted was to stay in bed. The run up to Christmas and the excitement was yanked away from beneath his feet leaving him in a short-lived void of gloom.

His melancholy outlook didn't last more than a few hours as luckily for him he'd been roped into a tradition that Sophie's family repeated every New Year's Day since she and her sister could remember. Sophie's parents insisted on a first of January family walk, no matter what the weather. This year Heather had suggested a drive to Sand Bay, along the coast from Weston-Super-Mare. The beach was quiet with a mix of pebbles, sand and when the tide was out, a gloopy clay that Rosie loved to stomp through wearing her Peppa Pig wellington boots.

Finn parked alongside Heather's car just behind the beach. The morning was mild, but the breeze from the Bristol Channel made him shudder as he got out of the car. Heather and her parents had arrived ten minutes earlier and were sitting on a large upturned tree stump. John and Grace shared a flask of coffee.

"Happy New Year!" called Finn as he, Sophie and Rosie made their way towards the stump. Jack was jostling from side to side in a baby back carrier as Finn struggled to keep his balance after tripping over a rock.

Rosie ran ahead and made a beeline for the beach with her bucket and spade.

"Bless her, she's so full of life," remarked John as he reached for his cigarettes.

"Dad!" called Sophie and Heather in unison. He stopped, grimaced and put the packet back.

"Why do you want to smoke here? It's so nice, you'll spoil it with your stinking fag ends," said Sophie.

"He promised that this year he'd stick to his resolution and give up," added Grace with a look of disgust.

"Shall we?" said Heather as she stood up and gestured towards the beach.

The five adults walked along the beach, stopping every now and again to pick up shells and small fossils scattered here and there.

"I want to take two or three of these rocks and a few pieces of driftwood, they'd be nice in the garden," said John.

"You're not supposed to dad. It's against the law," said Heather.

"Don't be wet girl, we can take what we want."

"She's right, there was a story in the paper. A woman who took pebbles to decorate her garden and she had a police warning," added Grace.

John grunted and moved a piece of driftwood with his foot.

"At least you can grow things in your garden dad. Our garden is incapable of sustaining plant life."

"I wanted to talk to you about that. Your front garden's bare. I'll come round and help if you want," suggested John.

Finn threw a glance at Sophie.

"Mummy, daddy, look what I've found," called Rosie as she excitedly pointed to the ground.

The adults trudged towards her and she was poking a large rock with her spade.

"It looks like a man's head."

John and Grace screwed up their faces as they tried to work out what Rosie could see in the rock.

"Sorry Rosie, I can't make it out," said Grace.

"Look nanny. Two eyes, a nose and a funny mouth," said Rosie using her spade to point out which bits of the rock were which.

"She's right," said Heather. "I can see it now."

One by one the adults agreed that the rock looked like a head, and if they used their imagination they could just make out eyes, nose and a mouth.

"Can I take it home?" asked Rosie.

"Sorry, you're not allowed. It's against the law," said John.

"Aww, granddad, it's only a rock."

"Why do you want that great big thing?" asked Sophie.

"I'd paint eyes and a mouth and everything on it. I'd give it a nice happy smiley face."

"Okay, I'll put it behind that big piece of driftwood over there, and we'll pick it up on the way back, it's too big to carry with us now."

"So it's okay for Rosie to take stuff from the beach, but not me?" huffed John.

Nobody answered.

On the way back to the car park, Heather retrieved Rosie's rock from behind the driftwood and cradled it in her arms. It was the size of a rugby ball and was a fair old weight. She was exhausted by the time she got to her car and was happy to drop it into the boot.

"Can I paint it when we get home please mummy?"

"I might be too busy to help you with it when we get back. I've got to cook a nice meal for everyone."

"Please please please please mummy," pleaded Rosie.

"I'll help you paint it," said Heather.

"You don't have to Heather, you'll end up covered in poster paint and you'll be stuck with her all afternoon."

"To be honest I'd prefer to do that than listen to dad moaning."

Sophie smiled. "It's your choice. As long as you don't mind. Rosie will enjoy that."

By early afternoon everyone was shoehorned into Finn and Sophie's dining room and were tucking into a New Year's Day meal.

"When can we paint Charlie?" asked Rosie.

"Charlie?" said Heather.

"I'll call him Charlie, he looks like a Charlie," said Rosie as a carrot fell from her mouth.

"Okay, when we've cleared away the dishes you and Auntie Heather can paint Charlie on the kitchen table. But only if you finish your food."

"Okayyyyyy mummy," agreed Rosie as she drew out her words with a sigh.

"That meal was amazing Sophie. You and Finn relax and your father and I will tidy everything up," said Grace.

John said nothing as Grace threw him a glance.

After the dishes were washed, the adults watched a film. Sophie fed Jack and Heather covered the kitchen table with newspaper to stop paint from splattering and spoiling the wood. Finn sat in the corner of the lounge and unboxed a laptop given to him as Christmas present by Sophie.

"Finn, do you mind getting that rock from the car so Heather and Rosie can paint it," asked Sophie.

Finn lugged it from the boot of the car and placed it on the table and then continued to set up his new computer.

Heather and Rosie spent the next hour working on the face. In fairness, Rosie had done most of the painting. Heather was doing her best to keep things tidy.

When Rosie had finished, Heather was impressed by what she'd done.

"That's amazing, you're clever, and he's scary looking."

"I know, he's supposed to be a skeleton man."

Rosie had sketched eyes, an indication where the nose would be, and a big mouth. She'd painted them with black poster paint. When the paint had dried she took her gel pens and drew and coloured individual teeth. Around the circumference of eye sockets she used the gel pens to make a dotted pattern. When she'd finished she sat back in her chair and admired her work.

"Wow, Rosie that's brilliant," said Heather.

"It's Charlie, the skeleton man."

She picked it up and looked at it.

"It's brilliant, you'll be an artist when you grow up."

"Show it to mummy and daddy."

Heather checked the paint had dried and carried it to the lounge to show the adults. Rosie was pleased with herself as Sophie, Finn and her grandparents made a big fuss and told her how clever she was.

"Okay young lady, you need to wash your hands and face, get that paint off and then it's time for bed," said Finn.

"But daddy……. "

"No arguments, it's late and time for bed."

"Can I take Charlie to bed?"

"If you like."

Rosie kissed her family goodnight and Finn carried her to her bedroom. He read her a story and was going to turn out the light when she sat up in bed.

"Daddy, you didn't bring Charlie with you, please can you get him."

Finn sighed, went downstairs and returned with the stone head.

"Put it on the floor, next to my light."

Finn placed Charlie next to Rosie's nightlight, kissed her and closed her door.

In the darkness of her bedroom Charlie's face was illuminated by the faint orange glow of her nightlight. She didn't like it. It looked as if he was staring at her with his big black eyes and shiny teeth.

"Daddy daddy, take him away, he's scaring me….. I don't like him."

Rosie's voice filtered through the ceiling. The adults looked at each other and raised their eyebrows.

"That didn't last long." said Finn.

He traipsed back to her room.

"Take it away daddy, I don't want him anymore. He's frightening me."

"Okay, don't worry, I'll take him downstairs."

"No daddy, put him in the bin I don't want him. Throw him away."

"You don't mean that, he's good."

"He's a skeleton man daddy, make him go away."

"Okay, okay I'll take him away, you won't see him again."

Finn brought it downstairs and put it in the lounge.

"What's wrong with her?" asked Sophie.

"It's this, it's scaring her. She doesn't want it any more. She asked me to get rid of it."

“No, don’t throw him away, he's so good. I’ll have him,” said Heather.

Finn passed it to Heather who placed it on her lap and stared at the eerie face.

As the evening continued the conversation died down. Everyone was feeling sleepy. Grace looked at John who’d nodded off.

Heather became mesmerised by Charlie and felt warmth emanating from the stone. Charlie’s big dark eyes pulled her in. The voices in the room faded. As she continued to be drawn in by the stone skull, she could see her great grandmother’s face superimposed over Charlie’s. Elizabeth appeared youthful as she looked at her great granddaughter. And then she spoke.

“Heather, Keep Charlie safe. You'll need each other.”

She held the stone head and rocked from side to side whilst looking deep into its eyes. The vision of Elizabeth had faded, but still, she was engrossed by what she saw. Then she heard another voice.

“Heather, …… I said it's time to go home……. your father’s asleep in the chair and I need to get back and feed the cat.”

Heather sat up and saw Grace standing with her coat on and her handbag by her side.

“Are you okay? You were a million miles away,” said Grace.

“Sorry mum, I must have dozed for a minute or two.”

John woke up after several attempts by Grace to bring him out of his brandy induced slumber.

Grace and John followed Heather to her car. John carried the painted stone head in a carrier bag. He turned and looked at the hawthorn tree and the barren soil.

“You’ve got to let me help with this garden. You two have the worst green fingers I’ve ever known.”

“Goodnight Dad, Happy New Year to you too!” said Sophie as she closed the door.

From his window Henry Buxton watched Sophie and Finn wave their visitors away. He looked at Heather and saw something in her that reminded him of his mother at a time when she’d been happy and before she’d moved into ‘that house’ with his father.

Henry was concerned for the Maynard family, and from what he’d recently discovered about his father, he had every right to be.

Chapter 18

It had been just over two weeks since Gabriel Butler received the call from Kieran Tempest.

Butler was a patient man and had been waiting his whole life for what was going to happen. Although he'd been waiting a lifetime, the last couple of weeks seemed a long time, and he was losing patience.

The legacy which had been passed to him could only be fulfilled when all of the links had been tied. And according to Tempest, Finn Maynard was the final link, the final connection.

He was definitely 'the one'.

Chapter 19

Henry Buxton spent the last few months researching the families who lived at number 11a before his mother and father.

In the beginning, he put the recent history of death and suicide down to bad luck. But he'd discovered something that made him change his mind.

He became overwhelmed by an enormous sense of guilt for selling his father's house. If he'd known back then what he knew now, he would never have sold it. No wonder the estate agent found it difficult to sell the house. Except for the Maynard family, every potential buyer turned the place down without a decent explanation. Although one young family said they'd decided against it as the 'vibes weren't quite right'. Looking back he understood what they meant. Henry agreed to lower the price by twenty thousand below the market value.

He was relieved when he'd sold the house as he'd debts to settle and could clear his mortgage. Now he wished for the debts to return and the house to stand empty if it meant the chain of events wouldn't continue.

After Robert Buxton died, many things needed to be dealt with by Henry as he was the only surviving family member. His spare bedroom became full of paperwork which came from his father's house and he'd meticulously gone through everything.

Two months ago he'd found the receipt.

Henry was going to screw it up when he recognised a name and address scribbled in his father's writing on the receipt which was over twenty years old. It was dated nineteenth of March nineteen ninety-three, which was two years before his father moved into Whitcombe Fields Road. Robert had sold his car and written a receipt for seven hundred pounds in cash. He'd used a duplicate book and kept a copy for his records. The man who'd bought the car was David Gosling.

Henry remembered his father selling his Vauxhall Astra to a man who collected it from his house.

Robert's scrawling handwriting confirmed that he'd received payment from David Gosling, 11a Whitcombe Fields Road, Bristol.

Henry couldn't believe the coincidence. Robert Buxton sold his car to a man who'd lived in the house which Robert would be next to own. Henry cast his memory back to just after he moved to the road and remembered an Astra. At the time he hadn't realised it had been owned by his father.

He'd remembered Ruth gossiping about the circumstances of David Gosling's death. She'd said he'd committed suicide after the death of his wife and that he'd died of carbon monoxide poisoning. He'd attached a hosepipe to the exhaust of his car.

It didn't taken Henry long to do an internet search and soon he'd found a news report of Gosling's suicide. He was discovered on an industrial estate in a red Vauxhall Astra.

He had killed himself in the car purchased from Robert Buxton.

Henry couldn't believe the connection and it bothered him for weeks. Two suicides, the house and the car.

Henry recalled a vague story he'd heard of the first family to live in the house and that they'd also met a horrific death. Henry hadn't lived in Whitcombe Fields Road at the time and so wasn't sure what happened to Shaun and Janet Morrison, the couple who'd lived in the house before David and his wife. But after speaking with a few of the older neighbours he discovered that Shaun drove his car into Bitterwell Lake, with his wife strapped in beside him. Police divers had found Shaun and Janet.

Lily Johnson had lived in Whitcombe Fields Road longer than anyone else. Although in her nineties, her memory was exceptional.

Henry called to her house and asked her what she remembered of the death of the Morrison couple. What Lily recalled floored Henry.

Lily told Henry that the team of divers who'd searched Bitterwell Lake included David Gosling. David, a professional diver, worked for the police and was the diver who'd located the car. He'd seen Shaun and Janet's bloated bodies strapped into the front seats of the Ford Cortina.

When he purchased 11a, just as Robert Buxton, he'd no idea of the connection between him and the other owners.

Henry didn't know that Finn had been on the train which killed his father. The only neighbours who were aware of this were Kieran, his wife and Finn's next door neighbour Ruth. None of them had any intention of telling Henry.

Henry's imagination was working overtime. He was concerned for the young family. Would the sequence of suicides continue? He deliberated whether he should speak with them. But would they take him seriously or consider him a foolish old man?

He'd told no one what he'd discovered, not even Katherine, his wife.

He sat on the bed in the spare room and opened the box file. The file which contained the strange paperwork that his father left after his death. Five hundred and eighty eight sheets of A4 paper. Five hundred and eighty five which covered the walls and ceiling of Robert Buxton's study, and the three which were on him the day he hurled himself in front of the train.

He held the three sheets, which the police had kept until the autopsy. He'd been thinking of the strange patterns since he'd discovered the link between his father and David Gosling, and Gosling's link with Shaun and Janet Morrison.

Was this another link in the horrific chain of events and should he tell Finn Maynard what he'd discovered?

Henry Buxton didn't know what to do.

Chapter 20

Mid-February

"Hello, what's your name?"
"William, my name's William, you're Rosie aren't you?"
"Yes. Do you want to draw a picture with me? I'll draw my baby brother Jack."
"I can watch, but I can't draw."
"Why not? Everyone can draw."
"I can't."
"Why not, can't you even draw a face?"
"I can't hold a pencil, look at this."
"Is that magic?"
"I don't think so."
"Put your hand out and I'll put the pencil in your hand, then you can draw with me."
"You can try."
"That is magic, it fell right through your hand."
"I don't think it's magic."

Rosie watched with amazement as the pencil dropped through the little boy's hand. She wasn't scared, just baffled by what she saw.
"Where do you live?"
"I'm not sure, here I think."
"What, in my house?"
"I think so. I enjoy watching you draw and play."
"Have you been in my kitchen before?"
"Lots of times, but until today you've never talked to me?"
"That's because I've never seen you before, silly."
Rosie smiled. William didn't, he looked sad.
"Don't you have friends to play with?" asked Rosie.
"No, but I play with my sister, she's called Louisa."
"Where is she?"
"She's shy, she doesn't like to come out."
"I'd like to play with her, tell her to come along next time."

Sophie was in the lounge tidying up and could hear Rosie chatting away in the kitchen. She put down a stack of newspapers to be recycled, popped her head around the kitchen door and saw her daughter playing on her own and talking to herself.

"How old are you?"
"That's funny, I'm five too. How old is Louisa?"
"She's the same age as you? You must be twins."

"Hello Rosie, who are you talking to?" asked Sophie.
"Mummy, meet William, he's my new friend."
Sophie smiled.
"That's nice. What are you doing?"
"I'm drawing and he's watching."
"Why doesn't William draw a picture?"
"Don't be silly mummy, he can't pick up a pencil. I have to draw a picture for him."
Sophie smiled again.
"Okay sweetheart, I'm going back to the lounge to do some tidying. Call me if you need me."

Sophie sniffed the air. There was a strong odour which reminded her of rain as it hit the ground after a hot spell of weather.
She grinned and returned to her chores. She was happy that Rosie had made up a 'normal' imaginary friend and wasn't talking to the strange man with paper on his face she'd told Finn about.
Sophie's concerns that they'd been visited by the ghost of Robert Buxton had subsided and looking back to when it had happened in December she realised how stupid she and Finn had been, even though it happened on the anniversary of Buxton's death. She carried on with what she was doing and let Rosie continue to spend time with her new imaginary friend.

"That was my mummy," said Rosie.
"You're lucky to have a mummy."
"Everyone has a mummy and a daddy, why haven't you got a mummy?"
"I don't know. Me and Louisa had a nanny who looked after us. She was nice."
"What, like a granny?"
"No, she wasn't as old as that, she was our nanny that my father got to take care of us."
"Where is your nanny now?"

William shrugged his shoulders.

"Does your daddy look after you on his own?"

William shrugged again.

"Who looks after you, who gives you food and toys?"

"I don't want to talk anymore, let's do drawing…….. I'll tell you what to draw."

"Okay, that sounds fun, let's do that."

Fifteen minutes later Rosie had covered every inch of her sheet of paper with the most detailed drawing imaginable from a five year old. She turned to show it to William, but he wasn't there.

"William, William where are you?"

She looked under the kitchen table, behind the door and in the tall cupboard where the canned food was kept. He was nowhere. Rosie was sad. She'd liked playing with William.

Sophie walked into the kitchen.

"Are you okay darling?"

"William's gone away."

"Don't worry, I'm sure he'll be back."

Sophie looked at the picture her daughter had just finished.

"Wow, what a lot of drawings all on one page, that's brilliant."

"I did it with William, he told me what to draw."

Sophie sat next to Rosie and asked her what was going on in the picture.

"The big house at the top is where William and Louisa used to live. It's a big big house. William said his daddy had lots of money."

"Who's Louisa?"

"Oh, she's William's sister, she's five and William's five too. But Louisa won't play. William says she's too shy."

"That's a pity. What else is in your drawing?"

"Well, so that's the big house where William and his sister used to live, and those are the trees his garden."

"What's that?" asked Sophie pointing to what looked like a wheel barrow, or a cart with handles.

"That's William and Louisa being pushed along in a cart thing."

"Who's pushing them, is that William's daddy?"

"No, silly, that's a lady called Alice, and she was like their mummy, but he called her nanny,"

Sophie became intrigued by what Rosie had created with her imaginary friend.

"And what are those behind the lady pushing the cart, are they farm animals?"

"No, they're dogs and they're chasing after Alice."

"Why are they doing that?"

"I don't know. William didn't tell me."

Sophie squinted her eyes, and she looked at all the other little detailed pictures that Rosie had crammed onto the sheet.

"What's happening there?" asked Sophie pointing to the top right hand corner.

"I'm not sure. William said it's a well, like in ding dong bell, pussy's in the well."

"Is that the pussy in the well?" asked Sophie, pointing to what she thought was an arm.

"No, it's William and Louisa. He said Alice put them there."

Sophie shuddered, she wasn't sure if she liked the direction the picture was taking.

"What's that tree by the well?"

"Oh, that's the one in our garden, you know, the bread and cheese tree in the front. William said it was by the well."

The picture had been drawn in black pencil, apart from the bottom right where there was a colour section in red, yellow and orange.

"What's the colourful bit at the bottom, it looks like a bonfire."

"It's not a bonfire. It's an old building that got set on fire."

"What kind of building, a house?"

"I don't think so, William didn't say. But that's where Alice is."

"You mean Alice is in the building and it's on fire."

"Yes, and she dies in the fire."

Sophie snatched the paper from the table.

"Rosie, that's horrible, I don't want you ever to draw anything like this again."

"But it was William who made me do it."

"Don't tell lies, you did this."

Rosie cried,

"Why don't you believe me? It's true."

"Because William's made up, he's in your imagination."

Rosie slumped in her chair, crossed her arms and looked miserable. She got down, left the kitchen and stomped upstairs to her room.

Sophie let Rosie have a tantrum. She'd talk to her in a few minutes after she'd calmed down.

She looked at the drawing again. There was so much happening. Rosie had drawn nothing like it before. She wasn't happy that her daughter had ideas in her head of people burning in a fire, or being thrown in a well.

The burning building drew her attention, and the way Rosie had mixed her colours to create the flame effect. She had to admit, it was a brilliant piece of work for someone so young.

Above the burning building Sophie noticed a bird soaring just beyond the flames.

Either side of the building were two large round balls of fire drawn in red. She stared at them, they were familiar, but couldn't remember why.

Sophie huffed. Maybe she shouldn't have shouted at Rosie and been so harsh on her. She checked on Jack, who was sleeping in his pushchair in the lounge, and then went up to see Rosie. She pushed her door open to find her lying on her bed looking at a comic.

"Are you okay?"

Rosie nodded, but didn't look up. Sophie sat next to her and ran her fingers through her daughter's hair.

"I'm sorry I shouted."

Rosie continued to read her comic and didn't speak.

"It was just that the drawing you made up was scary, that's all...... I'm sorry."

"But I didn't make it up, it was William's idea, he told me what to draw."

"I know, that's okay. Hopefully next time William will ask you to draw something nice."

Finn returned home late after a long and drawn out meeting. It was a dark and wet evening in late February. Sophie pulled a dried up meal from the oven which had been keeping warm for two hours.

"I'll say goodnight to the children before I eat," said Finn.

"They're both sleeping, Rosie went to bed early, she was in a mood," said Sophie as she put the hot plate on the table.

"Sorry, if I'd known you'd be back as late as this, I would have cooked later for you."

"Don't worry, this'll do just fine," said Finn, as he moved the food around the plate with his fork.

"What's the matter with Rosie, why's she in a mood?"

"Oh, nothing, I had a word with her over something she'd drawn, it was my fault, and I shouldn't have said anything."

"About what?"

"It was nothing, she drew a picture, and it was, ... well, a little unusual for her, It wasn't the style of drawing she would usually come up with."

"Unusual? In what way?"

"It was graphic, a lady burning in a fire and being chased by dogs, children being put in a well....... I don't know, it was horrible, and I snapped at her."

Finn pushed back in his chair and listened to Sophie.

"That's not her normal thing is it? But to be honest, it makes a change from her attempts at fluffy animals and rainbows," said Finn, with half a smile.

"I'm serious, you should see it, I don't think you'll find it so funny."

Sophie went to the lounge, returned with the drawing and placed it in front of Finn on the kitchen table.

"Whoa! I see what you mean, that's creepy."

"She's got a new imaginary friend. She said he told her to draw it."

Sophie continued to tell Finn what all the different elements of the picture were. He grimaced when she pointed to the children in the well and the burning lady.

"Oh, and that's supposed to be the hawthorn tree in the front garden," added Sophie as she gestured to the tree next to the well.

"And she said her imaginary friend told her to draw this?"

"Yes, she said his name's William."

Finn looked at the burning building and the two balls of fire. Sophie saw his expression change. He slid the dinner plate across the table, stood up and disappeared to the lounge. Sophie could hear him huffing and puffing as he searched for something.

"What are you looking for?" she called from the kitchen. Finn didn't answer. He returned a few minutes later with the colouring book Rosie had last used in December, on the evening she'd told Finn about the man with the paper on his face. He stood in the kitchen doorway, thumbed through the book and stopped three quarters of the way through.

He examined the page and frowned.

"What is it?" asked Sophie.

He lay the colouring book on the table, flattened it out with his hand and placed the drawing Rosie had done alongside.

"What do you see?" said Finn.

Sophie shook her head.

"Look at colouring book then look at the burning building."

She examined the picture in the colouring book. It was a tree in a field with farm animals. She had coloured nothing, but above the tree she'd drawn two circular patterns in red crayon and beneath each one was a tick. She looked back to the burning building and then she saw it.

"Those two red patterns, they're the same." said Sophie.

"I know. Rosie told me the man with paper on his face made her draw them, and now she's saying her imaginary friend William made her draw the picture in the other book. Where's she getting this stuff from?" said Finn.

"Her imagination and nowhere else," said Sophie as she closed the colouring book and slid the picture beneath it.

"Since we've moved here, her imagination is coming up with strange things," added Finn.

He closed his eyes and concentrated.

"Do you want a beer?" asked Sophie.

Finn put his fingers over his lips to shush her. She watched in an awkward silence as he rocked back and forth and focussed his mind. He jumped up, grabbed the drawing book and paper and headed upstairs. He went to their bedroom and sat on the edge of the bed by his bedside table.

On the table was a wooden box. In it were odds and ends. He opened the box and took out the gold ring. The ring the old shopkeeper gave him last summer from the antique shop that had never existed. He looked at the patterns on the ring and then to his daughter's drawings. Finn reached over to Sophie's side of the bed and grabbed the reading glasses from her table and held a lens up to the ring. He examined the two patterns made from tiny rubies which were placed in circular grooves etched into the face of the ring. His attention switched from the ring, to the drawing she'd done that day and then to what she'd drawn in December. He lay back on the bed and sighed. There was no doubt. The patterns were identical.

He studied the ring again and slipped it onto his finger and just like when he had tried it on in the shop, it slid on. But this time it wasn't sloppy and loose as it had become later that day. It was a perfect fit. And just like in the shop he suddenly felt assertive and decisive. He became overcome with an air of confidence like never before. Finn played with the ring and moved it up and down his finger. He attempted to remove it, but it was stuck behind the joint of his finger. He resisted the urge to take it off and lay on the bed as a look of contentment spread across his face.

Finn casually strolled back to the lounge and dropped Rosie's drawing book and picture on the settee.

"Be a love and get me that beer," asked Finn.

Sophie put her arms around his shoulder and kissed the back of his neck.

"What's the magic word?"

"Just get me that beer."

Sophie took her arms from him and was taken aback by what he'd just said. She dismissed it and assumed it was because of his late evening in the office, tiredness and maybe the strange drawing Rosie had done.

She headed to the kitchen and returned with the beer.

"Take off the top and put the bottle by the fire," said Finn.

Sophie warily removed the lid and placed the beer on the mantelpiece. She noticed the gold ring on his middle finger.

"You're wearing that ring, the one I told you to take back."

"Oh, I forgot to tell you, I went back to the shop, but it had closed. It was boarded up, and the owner had gone," replied Finn as he inspected the ring. "I like it," he added.

"I think it looks garish, it's tasteless, not your style."

"Really? I think it's classy. Maybe it's time for me to have an image change."

"You're talking as if you're heading for a midlife crisis," joked Sophie.

Finn turned to her, and said nothing. She saw a glint in his eye that made her uneasy.

He got up, grabbed the beer and slouched on the settee. She watched as he ran his finger over the face of the ring.

"Haven't you got things to be getting on with?" snapped Finn as he held the bottle to his mouth.

She couldn't believe what he just said. He'd never spoken to her like that in his life.

"Are you okay Finn?"

Finn felt in control and ambitious, as though he'd found new direction. He was no longer content just being a father and husband. Now he wanted more, much more.

"Am I okay?" said Finn.

He took another mouthful of beer and looked at her with a mischievous glint in his eye.

"I've never been better in my entire life."

Chapter 21

Gabriel Butler enjoyed the warmth of his log fire. He turned the pages of his newspaper and settled in his leather armchair.

The lights were low, allowing the orange flames to cast a comforting glow which illuminated his wood clad study, giving him enough light to read the paper. He reached for his brandy and took a sip.

He was interrupted by a dull thud. Butler replaced the brandy glass on the table beside him and lay the newspaper on the carpet.

On the floor behind his chair was a large book which had fallen from the bookcase. He walked over to where it landed. The book lay open, and he watched as the draught from the fire caused the pages to flutter. He bent down to pick it up and was startled as the book slammed shut on his hand. He turned the book over and looked at the cover and saw that it was a copy of the King James Bible. He opened it to where it had slammed shut and saw the page had ripped. The rip had torn through 1 Peter 5:8. The writing was too small to read in the low light so he walked to the dimmer and turned up the lights. Butler frowned as he straightened the ripped page and aligned the words. Then he smiled as he read the verse in a hushed whisper.

"Be sober, be vigilant; because your adversary the devil, as a roaring lion, walketh about, seeking whom he may devour."

Butler replaced the Bible from where it had fallen, reached for a Carlito Fuente cigar and took a lighter from beside the brandy. He inhaled the sweet smoke and looked from his window at the cold February evening.

He took the phone from the cradle, punched in a pre-set number and waited whilst it rang.

"Mr. Tempest, this is Gabriel. Your work is finished and I will arrange for the agreed one million seven hundred and fifty thousand to credit your account by close of business tomorrow."

He paused as he listened to Kieran's reaction.

"That's correct. You and Linda are free to go wherever you please. Thank you for what you've done and for keeping your side of the bargain. I appreciate that living where you have for the past twenty-two years has not been easy, but I hope the money you will receive will compensate for the inconveniences I have bestowed upon you."

Butler ended the call and replaced the phone on its cradle.

From the window of his study he could see the rooftops in Whitcombe Fields Road, just over a quarter of a mile away. Directly in his line of sight was the ridge of 11a, the only detached building in the row.

The hairs on his neck stood up as he contemplated what was going to happen.

Chapter 22

Late February

Charlie stared at Heather from the book shelf as she lay on her bed. His dark hollow eyes and manic grin were accentuated by the glow of the streetlight as it shone through the gap in the curtains. She'd become obsessed with the stone face painted by her niece ever since she'd heard her great grandmother's voice on New Year's Day. She'd been told to keep him safe and they would need each other. Heather didn't know what the message had meant, but was sure it was important.

Tiredness got the better of her and soon she was in a deep sleep and experiencing the most vivid dream.

Heather lay next to the tombstone in the graveyard of St Michael on the Mount Without. The same stone where she'd heard the strange voice the previous summer. Wearing only her pyjamas she shivered in the damp chill of the late February night. She sat up and ran her fingers over the dates which were only just legible.

Born ----ber 1- --99
Died September 6 1839

Alongside the grave lay a beautiful bouquet wrapped and tied with a blue bow. The flowers had a small white envelope attached. She took the envelope, removed a card and in the dim light read the words.

'To Sophie and Finn, congratulations and thanks for giving us a grandson, love mum and dad x x'

It was the flowers that her mother intended to take to the maternity hospital.

She looked at Charlie staring at her from a polythene bag next to the tombstone and placed the flowers in the bag next to the painted stone head.

She sat on the damp ground and looked at the gravestone.

"You've found me," said a voice coming from the stone head.

"Who's there?" called Heather looking around the dimly lit graveyard.

"My name is Charles Nash, and this place is where I rest."

Heather was afraid, alone and cold. The voice frightened her.

"Charlie," whispered Heather.

"That's right Heather. I'm Charles. I'd like to introduce you to an important person, who cared for me for a long time. Look over your shoulder."

Heather strained her neck to see a frail lady dressed in a heavy winter coat. She had a soft kind smile and tired eyes.

"Hello Heather. Don't be scared, I won't harm you."

Heather was beyond scared.

"What do you want with me?"

"You are an important person and have been chosen for something very special." said the frail voiced old lady.

"I knew your Great Grandmother Elizabeth." added the woman.

Heather sat up and backed away from her.

"What's going on?"

"I can't stay for long, but you must listen and believe what I say. You've been chosen, and Elizabeth has helped with making the choice. Your Great Grandmother has passed a special gift on to you. You have the gift of the veil of tears. You have the ability to speak with the dead. Charles Nash needs you and you must be here for him as I have over the years. My time has come and gone, and now it's your turn."

"What do you mean, my turn?" said Heather as she shivered in the night air.

"You will find out. Soon, things will make sense. Please be here for Charles."

Heather looked at the gravestone and wondered whether this was happening. She turned to the old lady, but she had gone. Instead stood a tall man in a high visibility jacket.

"Excuse me, are you okay?" asked the man.

Before Heather answered, he spoke on a radio and called for an ambulance. He slipped off his police jacket and put it over Heather to keep her warm.

"It's a bit cold to be out in your pyjamas isn't it?"

Heather was confused. The police officer knelt next to her.

"What's your name and where do you live?"

Heather told him her name and where she lived. She found it difficult to speak because she was shivering.

"I've called for an ambulance, it will be here soon."

The sound of sirens approached and within a few minutes the ambulance arrived. A paramedic helped her aboard and rushed her to nearby Frenchay Hospital. The officer sat with her and watched the paramedic attend to her. The ambulance sped through the night and within minutes pulled up outside Accident and Emergency.

"She has hypothermia," said the paramedic as hospital staff wheeled her into the warmth of the hospital.

Heather couldn't comprehend what was happening. Medics were scurrying along the corridor and staff were busying around her covering her in warm blankets to increase her body temperature.

The police officer waited with her until she could speak.

"So Heather, now you're warm and safe I want you to tell me what you were doing?"

Heather shook her head.

"I'm not sure. One minute I was at home in bed, and the next thing I remember is being in the graveyard."

"So you don't know how you got there?"

Heather didn't answer and took a sip of tea.

"Did you drive?"

She shook her head again.

The officer sensed her confusion.

"Is there anyone I can call? I think the hospital will be sending you home soon."

"Yes, you can call my sister Sophie. I'm sure she'll be happy to take me home."

Heather placed the tea beside her and turned to the officer. His face became a blur and the surrounding sounds faded as she slipped out of consciousness.

Heather woke to the sound of the seven o'clock alarm. She looked around her bedroom and thought of the dream. Stretching and yawning she sat up and perched on the edge of her bed. She made her way to the bathroom and ran the shower. She slipped off her pyjamas and stepped under the warm water which cascaded over her tired body and made her more alert. The water made her skin tingle and she let it flow over her short brown hair.

She noticed the colour of the water as it ran from her body. It was filthy brown. She looked at her legs and saw the remains of soil on her feet. She shut off the water and stepped out of the shower. She sat on the bathroom chair and examined her feet. Even after briefly being in the shower they were dirty. Bits of grass were between her toes and there was dirt beneath her nails.

"How did that get there?" she whispered as she removed the soil and grass with a damp flannel. Heather didn't bother to continue showering and instead went back to the bedroom to get dressed.

She looked at the bookshelf. The head was gone. She stood motionless halfway through buttoning her blouse.

"Where have you gone Charlie?" she muttered under her breath.

Things were becoming surreal. The dirt on her feet and now Charlie had disappeared. He was definitely there the night before, she remembered him staring at her with his toothy grin.

She made her way to the kitchen of her ground floor flat and saw something in the hallway by the coat stand. It was Charlie, and he was lying on his side and facing the wall in a polythene bag. Alongside him were the decayed remains of stems wrapped in a faded blue bow. She removed them from the bag and saw a weathered envelope. The ink on the front had faded, and the envelope was open. Heather removed the small card from the envelope. She squinted her eyes and read the faded writing and as she did she said the words out loud.

"To Sophie and Finn, congratulations and thanks for giving us a grandson, love mum and dad."

Heather shuddered as she tried to comprehend what had happened during the night.

She bent forward to pick the head from the bag. Warmth emanated from the stone. She was going to pick it up, but stopped as a voice echoed along the hallway.

"Heather, it's Charles Nash. We need to talk."

Chapter 23

Early March

Sophie glanced at her husband as he took a sip of coffee and turned the page of the morning paper. He'd become different and developed a short fuse which would turn into a nasty temper. Normally he wore his hair short with a little turn up at the front, which Sophie often referred to as his 'Tintin' haircut, but he'd been letting his hair grow and looked scruffy.

"You could do with a trip to the barbers' young man," said Sophie jokingly.

"Pardon?"

"Your hair's getting long, you need it cut."

Finn put down the coffee, folded the newspaper, stood up and walked out of the kitchen.

He went upstairs to the bathroom to have a wash. Finn glanced at his reflection, saw how long his hair had become and how the grey strands over his temple were more prominent. He smiled approvingly, took his razor from the cabinet and covered his face with shaving foam.

"Shit!" he cursed.

The blade nicked his skin and blood mixed with the foam on his face. He watched blood run down his cheek. He touched the cut with his finger and spread blood across the side of his face. Something about it fascinated him. He grabbed a pair of tweezers from the cabinet and picked away at the razor until he bent one of the fine blades out of place. It was protruding upwards above the others and was deadly sharp. He took the blade to his cheek and pressed it hard against his skin. With his eyes closed he dug the cold sharp metal into the side of his face, then gradually and precisely dragged the blade which tore through his skin so deeply it almost cut through to the inside of his mouth.

Blood gushed from the deep wound. It ran down his neck, onto his chest and to his stomach.

Finn watched his reflection as the right-hand side of his face became a crimson mess.

A few seconds later he was brought out of the dreamlike state by the burning pain from the cut. He came to his senses, grabbed a towel and howled in agony. The blood wouldn't stop, it kept coming. He howled again.

Sophie could hear him from downstairs and came crashing up the stairs. She swung open the bathroom door.

"Finn, what the fuck have you done?"

He pushed the sodden towel against his face and couldn't talk. Sophie took a step closer, pulled the towel from his cheek and gasped when she saw the cut which started at the base of his cheek bone and ran in a straight line to the side of his mouth. She grabbed another towel and pushed it against the cut to stop the blood pouring from his face.

"I'll get help, wait there."

She ran downstairs, out of the house and banged on Kieran's door. It was ten past seven and Kieran opened the door wearing his dressing gown.

"Finn's hurt, I need to get him to hospital, could you and Linda keep an eye on the children while I drive him?"

"Shit, Sophie. What's happened?"

"I'm not sure how he's done it, but he's got a long cut on the side of his face. It's deep, and bleeding heavily. He needs stitches."

She noticed a look in Kieran's eye, as if he wasn't surprised.

"Linda's not here, she's at her mother's, and I'm not the best person to look after your children. Why don't I drive Finn to the hospital? I can get him there in ten minutes."

Sophie agreed and Kieran went back inside and got dressed.

Kieran made his way to Frenchay Accident and Emergency. The same hospital Heather dreamt about.

In the car a one sided conversation took place. Finn held towels against the side of his face and Kieran did the talking.

"It feels good doesn't it? I mean that cut on your face. I expect you feel as if you're a new man….. a real man."

Finn looked at Kieran as he concentrated on driving whilst talking. Kieran looked down and caught site of the gold ring on Finn's finger. He smiled.

"I expect things may appear confusing right now. Don't fight these new feelings, go with the flow."

The searing pain caused Finn to shudder and was made worse by Kieran driving over a pothole in the road. But Finn wasn't bothered by the pain. In fact he found it comforting, as if cutting his face had been an achievement, a minor victory.

"Linda and I may be moving out soon. We don't want to be around to find out what happens next," added Kieran as he looked at Finn and winked.

Finn said nothing. What Kieran told him didn't bother him. In fact he felt excited.

Two hours later Finn was back at home with ten stitches in the side of his face. Sophie had cleaned the bathroom, taken Rosie to school and was feeding Jack.

"What on earth happened?"

Finn shook his head and looked at his reflection in the mirror in the corner of the lounge.

"It was an accident."

It was difficult to understand what he was saying as he could hardly open his mouth.

He went upstairs and changed into his work clothes. He stood in front of the long mirror in the bedroom as he did the buttons on his shirt. The ring caught his attention as it reflected. He looked at his scar and then the ring. Although the pain was still burning, he felt good. He felt more confident than he'd ever done in his life.

Sophie finished feeding Jack as Finn strolled into the lounge, with his jacket flung over his shoulder.

"Where are you going?" asked Sophie.

"To work. I've got a busy day and I'm late," replied Finn in a muffled voice.

"You can't go in today, you've lost a hell of a lot of blood."

Finn shook his head, grabbed his keys and left the house without saying goodbye.

He made his way through the mid-morning traffic. He'd called the office as he pulled out of his road to explain why he was running late. He'd never used his phone whilst driving. He used to abhor drivers who used their phones, but today he didn't care.

By ten he'd arrived at the office. Sally baulked when she saw the stitches and dressing on his face.

"Bloody hell Finn, you should be at home mate."

"I'm fine, don't make a fuss. I've got lots to do."

He'd being growing tired of Sally. Until recently they'd been best friends in the office and worked well together.

When Finn had taken paternity leave last summer, Sally picked up a lot of his work, including securing the deal on the Rusling account.

Finn dealt with Rusling Ltd when they first approached SOS Graphics with a view to them designing their winter collection catalogue. He'd done the majority of the ground work, but was away from work when Jack arrived. Sally took over, completed the agreement and won the contract. The deal was about to be lost, but due to shrewd negotiating by Sally, she earned SOS Graphics a quarter million pound contract.

SOS paid a healthy bonus to any designer who closed a deal, providing they also worked on the contract.

Sally had been working on the Rusling account and was doing a fine job. Finn had been happy for Sally to take the bonus because she'd worked hard to win the contract. He knew that had he been in Sally's position, Rusling Ltd could have gone with SOS's rivals. SOS had lost several contracts to their competitors Graphic Solutions Ltd over the past few years.

But now Finn resented that Sally was earning extra money and wished it was him who was receiving the bonus. Although she'd got the contract, It had been Finn who'd put in months of work wooing Rusling.

Finn took it upon himself to inspect her work. He had to admit it was good, but there were stupid errors here and there and he noticed that a few of her decisions in her designs were flawed.

He had a meeting booked with his boss, Ian Tomlinson, in which amongst other things, he intended to discuss Sally's progress with the Rusling account. At eleven o'clock he knocked on Tomlinson's door.

"Christ Finn, should you be in today? You look awful. How did you do that?" said Tomlinson when Finn stepped into his office.

"It looks worse than it really is."

"But what happened?"

"A mishap with a razor, don't worry I'm fine."

In a muffled voice, Finn told Tomlinson of the issues he had with Sally's work and that he was worried that Rusling won't be happy with the quality of her graphics.

"This is a big contract Ian and we can't afford to fuck up."

Tomlinson was taken aback. It was the first time he'd heard Finn speak in this manner. He was a talented designer, but he was a quiet and amenable man who was seen, but not often heard.

"What are you suggesting?" asked Tomlinson.

"That you let me take over the Rusling account, before Sally does any more damage."

"Okay Finn. Let me think it over, I'll speak with Sally."

Finn nodded with a smirk on his face.

"And there's another thing."

Tomlinson looked up from his laptop.

"I think we should expand our market."

"Expand our market? In what way?"

"I think we should get new accounts from overseas, and in particular the United States."

It was as if Finn had become a different person and Tomlinson was intrigued.

"I've been putting out feelers in the States for years and it's a hard country to break into."

"With no disrespect Ian, I reckon you've been taking the wrong approach. I've been looking into it and I think I've found a way in."

Tomlinson sat upright and focussed on Finn. There was a look of determination in Finn he'd never seen before and he liked it.

"Okay, I don't have the time to discuss this right now, but I'm interested in knowing what you have in mind," said Tomlinson as he stood up and put his jacket on.

"But you understand that if you go chasing overseas accounts you'll be spending time out of the country."

Finn nodded.

"How about Sophie, she'll be left on her own with the children, do you think she'll be okay about it?"

"Don't worry about her, she'll be fine."

Finn returned home just after seven. He'd been getting home later over the last week and Sophie was suspicious. Normally he'd left the office as the clock hit five and was always home before six. His wife and children were his number one focus and work was just a means to an end. But she'd sensed something different about him. He'd changed.

"How was your day? I didn't think you'd be in the office so late, especially after this morning."

"That's why I stayed late. I didn't get in until ten and had loads to catch up on. Are there any beers?"

"Yeah, in the fridge."

"Be a darling and get me one," said Finn as he slumped in a chair.

"Why don't you go upstairs and say goodnight to Rosie, she stayed up hoping to see you before she went to bed. She was tired and couldn't stay up any longer, but she might still be awake."

"Nah! I won't bother, I expect she's asleep."

Sophie went to the fridge, grabbed a beer, took off the top and handed it to Finn. He didn't say thank you. She huffed, sat down and watched Finn slug his beer. His hair was long, and he had dressing on his face to protect the cut. He looked a mess.

"What happened in the bathroom, how did you cut yourself?"

"A shaving accident. Okay!"

The tone of his voice suggested that she shouldn't ask again. He dropped the empty beer bottle to the floor which rolled under the chair, stood up and announced he was off to have a shower.

"Keep that dressing dry," called Sophie as he left the room. He didn't answer.

Finn took a quick shower and strolled naked across the landing to the bedroom. He caught sight of himself in the full length mirror and didn't like what he saw. He was a stone and a half over-weight with a paunch. Finn pushed out his chest and pulled his belly in with his hands.

"You need to get your sorry ass to the gym. You're disgusting," said Finn looking at his reflection.

He examined the ring and ran his finger over the two red patterns. He smiled. Things were going to change. He'd had enough of doing things for others. He'd become bored with providing for his family with nothing left over for him. After his meeting with Ian Tomlinson he was sure he was going to bring in a lot more money. Money he intended to spend on himself.

Sophie was watching the soaps when Finn marched into the lounge and grabbed the car keys from the mantelpiece.

"Where are you going?"

"The gym."

"You don't belong to a gym."

"Not yet. Wouldn't you prefer to be married to someone with a fitter body than this? I've let myself go I need to tone up……… do you have a problem with that?"

He threw the keys up and snatched them back from the air, winked at his wife and left the house.

"What's happening to you?" whispered Sophie as she watched Finn slam the car door and drive away.

Chapter 24

The following day Sophie was in the house alone with the children. It was Saturday morning and Finn had an appointment with the nurse at 9am to change the dressing and inspect the cut on his face.

He'd enrolled at the gym and was planning to go every evening.

Rosie sat at the kitchen table with a blank drawing book, a new pack of crayons and her favourite fluffy toys.

"Hello."

Rosie looked up to see William again.

"Have you come to play?"

William nodded.

"I wanted my sister to come and see you, but she didn't want to."

"Why not? We could play together."

"Louisa's shy."

"Does she have any toys?"

William shook his head.

They played for a while. Rosie picked up a pencil and paper, and William asked her to draw a picture of fields, a church and a wood full of green trees. In the sky Rosie drew an aeroplane.

"What's that?" asked William pointing to the plane.

"It's an airplane, silly."

William looked at her with a blank expression.

"What's an airplane?"

"You know, you go up in the air and fly to your holiday."

William looked confused.

"Why do you always wear those funny clothes?" asked Rosie.

"These are my bedclothes, they're the only ones I have."

"Do you wear them all of the time?"

"I'm not sure, I can't remember what I have on when I'm not with you. It's a shame I can't get Louisa to come with me, she'd enjoy playing with us."

"She can have one of my toys if she likes," said Rosie pointing to her collection of teddy bears and dogs on the table in front of her.

William smiled. "Can I take that pink one for her? She'd like it."

"Oh, but the pink bear's Amy, and she's my favourite. Take another one instead."

Rosie looked at William. He looked sad.

"Okay, take the pink one, I've got lots of others. But tell her to keep it safe and don't lose it."

William smiled. "Thank you. This will make her happy. I must get back to her…. goodbye."

Rosie looked up to say goodbye but William had gone. She closed her drawing book, put the crayons back in the box and scooped up her toys. She saw that the pink bear had gone.

I hope she likes it thought Rosie as she climbed from the chair and walked to the lounge.

"Have you finished drawing?" asked Sophie.

"I've finished drawing and I've put my crayons in the box."

Sophie cuddled her daughter as Rosie clung on to her soft toys.

"William played with me again this morning."

"Did he, what did you play?" asked Sophie with a serious tone.

"We drew, do you want to see what we did?"

Sophie nodded as her daughter dropped her toys, ran to the kitchen and returned with the drawing book opened to the picture she'd just drawn.

Sophie was happy to see her picture was a nice one. No sign of burning houses, or children thrown into wells. It was a nice picture with a church and fields. There was what appeared to be aeroplane above the trees.

"Is that a plane?" asked Sophie.

"Yes, but I don't think he's ever seen one before."

Sophie smiled.

"He's got a sister called Louisa, but she's too shy to play."

"That's a pity. At least you've got William to play with," said Sophie in a humouring tone.

"I like William, but he's very sad."

"Why do you think he's sad?"

Rosie shook her head.

"So, what's your friend like?" asked Sophie as she moved a strand of hair from her daughter's forehead.

"He's got dark hair, and he wears funny clothes."

"What style of clothes?"

"He told me they are his bedclothes. But they're nothing like my pyjamas. He wears what Wee Willie Winkie does," giggled Rosie.

"Does he have candle?" said Sophie with a smile.

"Don't be silly mummy, its light in our kitchen…. He doesn't need one."

Sophie sniffed the air. There was a strong odour coming from the kitchen. She walked along the hall and stopped by the door. It was a damp smell, but not something nasty that one would associate with a damp house. It was as if fresh rain had soaked the ground after a dry spell. She'd smelt it once before in the house. She racked her brains as she tried to recall when and where. Then she remembered. It had been in the kitchen, the last time Rosie had mentioned playing with William.

Rosie placed her toys on the carpet and played a game with them.

"What are you playing?" asked Sophie as she walked back to the lounge.
"Schools mummy. I'm making sure everyone's here."
"Where's Amy, your favourite pink one? Isn't she at school today?"
"I don't have her anymore. I let William have her to give to Louisa."
"That was nice of you."
"I said that Louisa had to keep her safe and not to lose her."
Sophie smiled as she played along with Rosie's game.

The front door opened.
"Daddy's home!" shouted Rosie, just as Jack stirred in his cot.
Finn stepped into the hall and Rosie threw her arms around his legs.
"Is your face better daddy?" said Rosie looking at the fresh dressing.
"Of course it's not better, but don't worry I'll survive."
"I love you daddy."
Sophie watched at how distant Finn was from his daughter. He didn't pick her up to cuddle her, which was something he always did. Instead he carried on along the hallway which gave Rosie no choice other to let go of her father's legs.
He entered the lounge and looked at her toys.
"Rosie, pick up your things, and if you want to play you can do it in your bedroom."
Rosie did as he said and one by one picked up her toys.
"Daddy, I saw William again today. He was in the kitchen again."
Finn's ears pricked up.
"Oh did you? What did you play?"
"We drew again. Shall I show you?"
Finn nodded. He remembered the drawing she did with her imaginary friend last time. He recalled the two circular patterns identical to the two on his ring.
Rosie showed him the picture. Finn looked at it with a blank expression.
"Do you like it daddy?"
"It's okay I suppose, you've done better."
Rosie looked disappointed.
"I mean it's not as good as the other one you did with William. Where's the picture with the well?"
Rosie ran to her toy box and rustled through her old drawing books then returned to him holding a crumpled and dog-eared drawing pad. She sat beside him on the floor and turned each page one by one until she found the drawing he wanted to see.
"There!" she said as she handed it to him.
Finn became intrigued by what she'd drawn.
He pointed to the person pushing the handcart.

"Who's this?"
"That's Alice, and she's pushing William and his sister in the trolley thing. She's being chased by dogs…… look," replied Rosie pointing to the stick animals behind the Alice.
"And who is in the well?"
"That's William and his sister again. See the tree by the well? That's the one in our garden. The one Auntie Heather calls Bread and Cheese."
"It's called Hawthorn, Rosie, not Bread and Cheese."
"But that's what Auntie Heather said it was."
Finn ignored her comment and pointed to the burning building.
"Tell me about this again."
"I don't know. It's just a building on fire. Mummy told me off for drawing it. Alice, the lady, is in there."
"And who is Alice?"
"William told me she is his nanny, but not like a nanny I have, a different one that his daddy paid to look after him and his sister."
Finn nodded and flinched as the pain from the cut shot through his face.
"This is a superb drawing. Don't listen to mummy, she shouldn't have told you off……. can I keep this picture?"
Rosie nodded and smiled.
"Listen my sweetheart. If you play with William again and I'm in the house, come and tell me. I'd love to say hello to him…... I may have a few questions for him."

Sophie gestured to Finn that she wanted to speak with him, and away from Rosie. She nodded towards the kitchen as she rocked Jack in her arms.
Finn followed her and shut the door to the kitchen.
"Is everything okay Finn?"
"Sure, everything's just fine. Things couldn't be better," he replied as he rubbed the dressing on his cheek.
Sophie shook her head and let out a sigh.
"It's just that you've become distant, as if you've gone off me, I don't think you love me anymore."
"As I said, everything's fine."
"You're not interested in our children, you've stopped reading Rosie her bedtime story….. you're different."
Finn raised his eyebrows.
"And the way you look? Why on earth are you growing your hair so long? It doesn't suit you. It's as if you're going through a midlife crisis and you're not even thirty."
"I thought I'd have an overhaul, sort myself out. You should be happy that I'm taking pride in my appearance."

"Pride? Pride? You look like a bloody pirate."

Finn smirked.

"Why have you enrolled in the gym?"

"As I said, I'm having an overhaul."

"I'll tell you what I think you're having, I think you're having a bloody affair."

Sophie's raised voice caused Jack to cry. She rocked him in her arms and kissed his head.

Finn just shook his head.

"You say you're working late, you've always done your best to avoid working late and now you're in the office every night."

"I've decided to put in extra hours. I've been talking with Tomlinson and I may get contracts from overseas. If I do there'll be a lot of money involved, and I doubt whether you'll be shouting and accusing me of having an affair then."

"I'm not shouting, I'm just asking what's going on. Anyway, this is the first you've told me about overseas contracts. Will you be going away?"

"Maybe, for a few days."

"And you didn't think to speak with me about it?"

"No, I didn't think it's any of your concern."

There was a frosty atmosphere during the weekend. Sophie was finding it hard to be around her husband. Usually a weekend in the Maynard household would be fun. They would take the children somewhere nice and if there was enough money in the bank they would splash out on a Sunday lunch. This weekend Finn kept himself to himself and was happy to spend hours in the bedroom doing sit-ups and push ups. He had become obsessed with his body.

On Sunday evening Sophie tucked Rosie into bed and read her a story.

"Where's Amy, your pink bear? You always take her to bed."

"I told you mummy, I gave Amy to William so he could give her to Louisa."

"I know that's what you told me darling, but where is she? Nanny Grace bought her for you and she'd be sad if you've lost her."

"She's not lost, she's with Louisa."

"But Louisa and William are your made up friends."

"No mummy, they're real…. not made up."

"Rosie, please. I know what will happen, you'll come in to see me when it's late at night asking for Amy, so please tell me where she is now, I'll get her and tuck her in with you."

"Mummy, don't get angry with me. I don't have her anymore. William took her. Amy's with Louisa now."

Sophie had to bite her lip to stop herself from losing her temper. Things had become very stressful, and she was finding it hard to hold things together. She knew Grace would be devastated if Rosie had lost that pink bear. Grace had written on the label. 'To Rosie, my favourite granddaughter'.

After she'd kissed Rosie goodnight she went to the lounge to find Finn with his feet up, watching the television and drinking beer from a bottle.

"Finn. There's a kitchen full of dishes to be cleared away. Could you give me a hand please?"

"Relax, do them tomorrow when I'm at work."

She sighed and went to the kitchen and tidied up alone. She had no intention of asking for help a second time.

Half an hour later she returned with a mug of tea to find Finn sitting in the same place, watching the television and drinking from the same bottle.

"Have you seen Amy around anywhere?" asked Sophie.

"Amy?" replied Finn clinging to the bottle.

"You know, the pink bear mum bought Rosie."

Finn shook his head.

"She goes everywhere with her and she never goes to bed without her, but hasn't wanted Amy last night or tonight. I'm worried she's lost her."

"Maybe she has," said Finn in a nonchalant tone of voice whilst shrugging his shoulders.

"She told me she gave Amy to William, you know her new made up friend. The funny thing is I can't find that pink bear anywhere, it's like she's just vanished."

Finn put down his bottle and sat upright.

"She gave the bear to William?" he asked with curiosity.

"Rosie told me her imaginary friend has a sister called Louisa and she let him take the bear for her."

"William has a sister called Louisa?" said Finn pushing his hands through his hair.

"Finn, why are you so excited? She's misplaced the bear that's all."

Finn didn't know why he had become so interested in Rosie's made up friend, but she said William had a sister called Louisa and this was making something stir deep inside. His mind connected the names. He remembered Rosie had mentioned a nanny called Alice. The names sounded so familiar

William and Louisa he thought to himself. *William, Louisa and Alice.*

Sophie watched as Finn ran his finger over the patterns on the gold ring, then looked towards the window and mutter to himself.

"William, Louisa, Alice."

Chapter 25

Late March

Three weeks earlier the stone head had spoken to Heather. She'd heard the words as clear as a bell as they echoed along the hallway of her flat.

She recalled the words.

'Heather, I am Charles Nash. We need to talk.'

It was the voice of a middle aged man with a slight Bristolian accent.

She was doubting her sanity, especially after the strange dream in the graveyard and finding soil over her feet the following morning. Not to mention the rotten bouquet with the handwritten note from her mother.

Was she in the churchyard that night? If so, how did she get there and how could she have made it home?

The dream was vivid. Heather recalled the police officer who found her and was with her at the hospital. She contemplated calling Frenchay Hospital accident and emergency to enquire whether anyone matching her description was admitted that night. She dismissed the idea and considered how stupid she was.

It was late in the afternoon. Heather wandered around her flat, attending to menial tasks to take her mind off things. But no matter how hard she tried, she couldn't think of anything else.

She thought of the visions of great grandmother Elizabeth and Mark, her boyfriend who'd died in the climbing accident. The visions were over six months ago. She'd told no one of what happened because she wanted no one to think she was crazy.

She knew that she'd been blessed with the veil of tears of which Elizabeth told her. Maybe Charles Nash *was* trying to contact her. Who was Nash and what did he need? The old lady in the dream said he needed her.

Heather didn't like nor understand what was happening. She was alone and needed someone to turn to. The only person was Elizabeth. Elizabeth told her on New Year's Day to look after Charlie and keep him safe because they needed each other.

None of it made sense. What's happening? she thought to herself.

The voices she'd heard always reached out to her. Now it was *her turn* to reach out. She needed Elizabeth but didn't know how to reach her.

Heather had never been a religious person and couldn't remember the last time she'd prayed. If Charles Nash, Mark and Elizabeth had all spoken from beyond the grave then maybe there was a God. A God who would listen to her, even though she'd hardly ever attended church. She knew Elizabeth had been religious and devoted her life to God and maybe this was why she had the gift of the veil of tears. But Heather was different. She considered herself an average person who lived day by day with no great plan in her life.

But perhaps she *should* pray.

She knelt on the floor in her small lounge, put her hands together and looked towards the ceiling. She closed her eyes and began.

"Dear God. It's rare you hear from me, actually I can't remember the last time I said a prayer. But something strange is happening. I need to speak with my Great Grandmother Elizabeth….."

Heather cried and held her hand over her mouth. She wiped her tears, composed herself and tried again.

"……. Sorry God….. I'm not very good at this. If you could ask Elizabeth to contact me, I would be so very grateful."

She opened her eyes and looked around. Heather felt stupid. Stupid for praying and stupid for asking for such a ridiculous thing. But she hoped her prayer would be answered.

Heather moped around the flat. She expected to open a door and find Elizabeth, or to hear her voice emanating from somewhere.

"This is fucking ridiculous!" shouted Heather as she considered what was going through her mind.

"There's no need to curse young lady."

Heather spun around and saw a beautiful lady in the hallway. She recognised Elizabeth, but not as the lady she'd remembered as a child, but as she had looked in her late twenties. Heather was rooted to the spot and couldn't speak. Her eyes were transfixed on the vision. Elizabeth's hair was tied in a bun and she was neatly attired in a white dress.

"Hello Heather, a little bird said you wanted to speak with me."

Was this happening? Was it really happening? Had someone listened to her prayer? Heather opened her mouth but her throat was too dry for her to form any words.

"Take your time Heather. There's no rush," said Elizabeth.

Heather closed her eyes, rubbed them with the palms of her hands and then looked again. Elizabeth was still standing in front of her. She wasn't translucent or vague, she was as real as everything else she could see around her. She even cast a shadow.

Heather took a step closer and reached out her hand.

"Don't get too close."

Heather took two steps back and lowered her arm.

"It takes an awful lot of energy for me to stand in front of you. If you get too close your skin will blister."

Heather felt heat emanating from Elizabeth. There was an overpowering smell which reminded her of rain hitting parched soil. Like the smell of ozone. This made the whole thing real and she was certain she wasn't having another strange dream like the one she had a few weeks ago. This time she took no chances. She went to the bathroom, ran the cold tap and threw water over her face. She placed her hands on the edge of the sink and stared at her reflection in the bathroom mirror. This was real. There was Elizabeth staring, watching her in the mirror. She had followed her and was standing in the doorway of the bathroom.

Heather had so many questions, but found it hard to speak. The vision she saw before her proved that existence continued after death. Should she ask her about God, or about Heaven? She was in awe. After a few seconds Heather spoke.

"Hello."

Her voice was weak and shaky.

"Hello Heather. You better sit down. Follow me."

Elizabeth turned around and walked along the hall. Heather followed. She watched Elizabeth's feet as she made her way to the lounge. Her black shoes left an impression on the carpet, just as a living person's would. Elizabeth entered the lounge and stood by the table. Heather sat on the floor and looked up at her.

"I can't stay for long. The energy it takes to stand here is immense so I need to get to the point."

Heather stood up, moved to an armchair and mentally prepared to talk with a ghost.

"The gift you've been given, which I've always referred to as the veil of tears, is strong with you. I was lucky to have been blessed with it and it comforted me when I spoke with those who'd passed over…,"
Elizabeth paused and Heather noticed a tear in her eye. "I gained comfort speaking with those who died, and like me, passed to the other side."

Heather said nothing. She couldn't believe what was happening to be real.

"You have been given a gift to do something special. I thought I was special to speak with the dead, but the reason you've been chosen is to do something which will affect many."

At last Heather spoke.

"What have I been chosen to do?"

Elizabeth looked troubled and shook her head.

"That's something which I can't tell you."

"Why not?"

"It's complicated, but you have to believe me…… I can't tell you. You'll learn what to do. There is nothing you can do to stop what will happen. It *will* happen."

Heather was scared.

"You will be strong and have faith."

"Who is Charles Nash?"

"Charles was a man who was very important. He holds a secret which remains with him after death. You will be his protector."

"What do you mean, protector? He's been dead since 1839."

"Sorry Heather, I've said too much….. but you will find out."

"What about the lady in the graveyard, the one I saw in my dream?"

"That was no dream Heather, the lady's name is Hermione."

"Hermione? You mean I really was there, I was in the graveyard?"

"Again, it's very difficult to explain and I have little time. But what occurred was something we refer to as 'a happening'."

"A happening?"

"Yes, it's the midpoint between a dream and reality."

Heather didn't know what to say.

"You will speak with Charles. I know not when, but you will. I'm here to give you some advice, something to make things easier for you."

Heather listened intently.

"You need a channel. Something that works for you which makes it easier for you to speak with the dead. Only in your case its Charles Nash you need to speak with and nobody else."

"A channel?" asked Heather.

"Yes, think of it as a telephone. Something which will help you communicate with somebody far away. You may remember, I wore a silver cross around my neck which a close friend gave me."

Heather remembered the cross. She remembered it around Elizabeth's neck the night she died.

"The cross I wore allowed me to speak with the dead. You too have a channel and it's with you here…. and I believe you know what it is."

Heather looked around the lounge. She couldn't think. She had no special pendant or locket as Elizabeth did when she was alive.

"I can't think what you mean, what kind of channel? There's nothing I can…….. "

Heather's voice trailed off as something occurred to her. She stood up and left the room. Seconds later she returned carrying the stone head.

"Is this it?"

Elizabeth had gone. All that remained was a faint smell of ozone. She put the head down and walked to where Elizabeth had stood. The air was warm, and crackled with static electricity.

"Elizabeth, are you still here?" called Heather as she walked to the hallway.

She called one more time and accepted that Elizabeth had returned to where she came.

There were questions Heather wanted to ask. She didn't get an answer to her question about Hermione. And what on earth did she mean by her being Charles Nash's protector?

Her mouth was dry, and she needed a glass of water. Filling a glass in the kitchen she saw how much her hand was shaking. The shock of what just happened registered. Heather gulped back the water and her entire body from head to toe shuddered. She went to her room and lay on the bed. She couldn't stop shaking.

A few minutes later the shaking subsided. She considered what just happened and tried to stay calm. She knew something important was going to happen, but she'd no idea what. Elizabeth wasn't giving much away. It was as if she was playing a game with her, as if she was teasing her with snippets of information which meant nothing.

She'd told nobody of the strange things that happened. She was a sensitive woman and worried that people would consider her crazy. But after what she'd witnessed she needed to speak with someone. There was only one person she could call, and that was her sister.

She reached for her phone and called Sophie.

With her head on the pillow she held the phone to her ear and waited for her sister to pick up.

"Sophie, it's Heather. I need to talk with you, but not on the phone, we need to meet. I've just had a visitor ……….. and you won't believe who it was."

Chapter 26

1st April

The tension in the small office of SOS Graphics was unbearable. Finn and Sally shared the same workspace and were just feet apart. Sally looked from her computer and watched him work on his project. She couldn't believe what her boss Ian Tomlinson had told her.

You sneaky smarmy bastard thought Sally trying not to show her emotions.

Finn looked up and smiled. It wasn't a friendly smile, but one of satisfaction as if he'd achieved something and had got one over on her.

Just before lunch Tomlinson asked to see her for an unplanned 'one to one' meeting. Sally didn't know what he wanted, but unplanned meetings were not usually good news. She expected to be loaded with another project with her workload already at breaking point, or to be asked to reschedule her holiday to accommodate a new contract. But when Tomlinson told her she was off the Rusling account and Finn Maynard was to take over she couldn't believe it.

"But why, I don't understand?"

"Sorry Sally, I've been looking at your work and it's not to the required standard."

"With due respect Ian, I disagree. Show me what is *so* wrong with my work you're passing it to Finn."

Tomlinson sighed, brought up the files and turned his laptop to face her. He ran through the list of things that Finn had brought to his attention.

"This is work in progress. You know that. I wouldn't hand it to Rusling like this."

Tomlinson could see her frustration and felt awkward, but had to agree with Finn that her work was under par.

"I worked hard to close that deal when Finn was on leave and I want to be the one who finishes it, not him."

"Sorry Sally, the decision's made. Finn's asked to take over the account and I've agreed."

"Sorry, did you say Finn asked to take it over, is this his idea?"

"He brought your oversights to my attention and yes, he asked to take the account back."

She was on the verge of tears.

"He wants it back? He wasn't working on it in the first place."

"To be fair Sally, it was Finn's contract. He agreed that you should close the deal whilst he was on paternity leave. But now things are different. I agree that Finn should finish the work. The thing is, Rusling Ltd is a big deal and if they're happy with our work there could be more contracts. SOS need this business and I don't want to jeopardise things."

Sally felt like handing in her notice there and then. She couldn't believe Finn had done such a thing.

"I understand things may be awkward between you, but things will settle back to the way they were. Besides, you won't be spending much time together. In the next few weeks Finn will be leaving for the States."

"The States, you mean the USA?" asked Sally in a bewildered tone.

"He's planning to fly to Washington. He's been speaking with a company over there and he's close to getting us a hell of a good contract. It could make us an awful lot of money."

Sally didn't understand. This just wasn't Finn. It was as if he'd become a different person. Before, he couldn't care less about work and did it because he had to. He was a talented graphic designer, but his heart had never been in it. He'd even joked about it. Work was a means to an end, and the end to which it was a means was the wellbeing of his wife and young family.

After the meeting Sally spent her lunch break pacing along the High Street. She was livid.

When she'd returned to the office she was still fuming. She didn't know what to say. She walked in, closed the door and stared at him. He didn't notice her. He was engrossed in his work.

She had seen changes in his appearance over the last few weeks. He'd let his hair grow. It was long enough for a ponytail. She knew he'd enrolled in a gym and had been going every night. His once flabby body was trimming up nicely. He wore a tight T-shirt which showed his muscles which were toning up. She'd never been attracted to him, but these recent changes appealed to her. Except for the awful gash on his face. Nobody knew what happened. When asked, he only referred to an accident whilst shaving.

But if Sally found him more aesthetically pleasing, now she disliked him as a person.

She could no longer stay quiet. She looked up from her computer, pushed her dark hair back and confronted him.

"I assumed we were friends?"

Finn said nothing. He carried on working at his computer.

"Can we at least talk about things?"

"What's there to discuss?" replied Finn.

"Well, why did you decide to shaft me?"

"Shaft you?" laughed Finn, "That's an unfortunate turn of phrase."

"You know what I mean, why didn't you speak with me first?"

"There was nothing to talk about. It's simple, your work isn't good enough."

Finn remained calm and collected whilst Sally became close to tears.

"Things are going to change around here. I'm going to turn this half-baked, two bit design company into a force to be reckoned with."

"Listen to yourself, recently you didn't give a shit about your job, now you're talking as if you own the company."

Finn glanced across the desk with a wry smile.

"You're planning on taking over SOS aren't you?"

"Tomlinson's getting old, he's out of touch. We need someone with original ideas. A fresh approach is what's needed……….. and I am the man to deliver the goods."

Sally was going to speak when she heard tapping. She looked up and saw a huge black bird on the window ledge rapping at the glass with its beak.

"What the hell is that?" shouted Sally.

Finn stood up and walked to the window.

"The raven," he whispered as he stared at the massive black bird.

With outstretched wings it cocked its head and looked at Finn. It opened its beak and made a low, gurgling croak.

Finn turned the latch and slid open the window.

"What are you're doing?" said Sally in a raised, but hushed tone. The bird scared her, but she didn't want to alarm it.

He didn't reply, instead he put his arm out. The bird hopped along the ledge, croaked and jumped onto Finn's forearm. The bird's talons dug into his skin. Finn didn't flinch and brought the bird into the office.

"Get that thing out," said Sally as she backed against the wall.

Finn stroked the birds head and it flapped its wings.

"My God, you're beautiful," whispered Finn as he admired the bird's plumage.

He recalled the bird in his daughter's room the day they moved into their house.

"I know you. You've been following me haven't you?"

The raven croaked.

"Man, you're something else."

The raven jumped along his outstretched arm and nuzzled its beak into Finn's neck. He smirked as the bird croaked and gurgled.

Sally was nervous. She hated birds at the best of times and the situation scared her. She stood motionless with her back pressed against a rank of filing cabinets.

The raven stopped and faced Sally. It cocked its head to one side and looked at her. It squawked and made clicking noises, which sounded like a pig. The bird jumped from Finn's arm, hopped across a desk and on to the cabinet next to Sally. It continued to squawk and make odd grunting sounds.

"I don't think it likes you," said Finn with a smirk.

Without provocation and with its wings raised, it hopped alongside Sally and became agitated. She put her hands over her face and peered between her fingers.

"Make it go away."

"Sally, calm down, it's only a bird," laughed Finn.

She screamed as it picked and pecked at her long dark hair.

"Get it the fuck away from me, please."

Sally screeched, the raven squawked and Finn laughed.

"He's playing with you."

"Do something, please."

Finn wandered over and put out his arm. He pursed his lips and made a chirping sound. The raven stopped picking at Sally's hair, stood stock-still and looked at Finn. It squawked and clucked, then hopped away from Sally and back onto Finn's arm.

"He's fine, he won't hurt you," said Finn. He stroked the back of the bird's neck then kissed it on its head. The raven clucked.

"He's friendly, come over and stroke him."

The door slammed and Finn looked up. Sally fled the office, and ran down the stairs. He strolled to the window with the raven clinging to his arm. From the first floor he watched her run across the road to the carpark. Her hair was a mess and she had speckles of blood on her white blouse.

He turned to the bird and stroked the feathers on its neck.

"I think you've visited me for a reason haven't you big fella?"

The bird squawked and clucked, hopped from his arm and onto the window sill. It stretched its wings and flew away from the office.

Finn watched as it circled the air before disappearing to the east.

"I won't be surprised if we see each other again," he whispered before sliding the window shut.

Chapter 27

Sophie fed Jack as Heather placed their order. She worried about what was happening with her family. Finn had become a different man during the past few months. His character had taken a complete U-turn. Had he been the way he was now when they'd first met, she would have had no interest in him whatsoever. Although she had to admit since he'd been going to gym every evening his body looked fantastic.

She was worried about her sister. They had a brief conversation on the telephone and she knew that Heather had been shaken by whatever happened.

Heather approached their table, balancing two coffees and millionaire shortbread on a tray. She looked tired and older than she should for twenty-six. Heather was five years younger than Sophie, but despite the age gap, the two of them had always been close.

Heather placed the tray on the table and passed a mug to her sister.

No one spoke for a few moments and Heather watched Sophie feed Jack from his baby bottle. Sophie wiped milk away from his mouth and cuddled him as he smiled and gurgled.

"He's growing fast. How old is he?"

"He'll be nine months next week."

"Jeepers Sophie, where's that time gone?"

Sophie smiled. "What did you want to talk about?"

Heather shuffled in her chair, not sure where to begin.

"Okay, forgive me for sounding cranky, but strange things have been happening."

"What things?"

"Hear me out, and don't judge me. I'm not making this up."

Heather took a swig of coffee, a bite of cake, cleared her throat and began.

"What do you remember about our great grandmother, Elizabeth?"

"She was lovely, and from what I remember special in her own way," said Sophie with a smile.

"Do you recall the stories of her speaking with the dead?"

"Yeah, mum and gran weren't too impressed. I think our family were considered nutters for a while."

Heather smiled and sipped her coffee.

"But do you remember the things she did, you know speaking with the dead?"

"No, because mum and gran didn't want to discuss it."

"That's the same as I remember."

Heather became crotchety.

"What's on your mind?" asked Sophie as she placed Jack in his pram.

"Do you remember the night she passed away, the time we all visited her in hospital?"

Sophie nodded.

"She said something, just before she died."

Sophie didn't speak, she stared at her sister expectantly.

"Although I was young, I can remember what she said as if it was this morning."

"What did she say?"

Heather paused before speaking and then looked her sister in the eye. "She said that I'm blessed with the veil of tears and I should learn to use my gift wisely."

"So is that supposed to mean you can speak with the dead?"

Heather nodded.

"Things are happening, I'm scared."

Her sister held out her hand and gripped her palm with her fingers.

Heather explained what happened the other night when Elizabeth had appeared in her flat.

"And that's not all," added Heather…. "I've been hearing voices of other dead people."

Sophie wasn't sure what to say. She had an open mind, but found it hard to believe what her sister was saying was true.

"How did she look, was she like a ghost?"

"Don't take the piss Sophie!"

"I'm not, I'm serious, and I want to know what happened."

Heather explained in detail how Elizabeth appeared as a young woman, not the frail lady she'd been in her later years.

"And what about these other dead people?"

"There's a grave in the churchyard at the bottom of St. Michaels Hill, do you know the church?"

"Yes, it's boarded up, been shut a long time."

"I was in the graveyard on the morning mum, dad and I visited you when you had Jack."

"Why were you there?"

"That's not important. But I was drawn to a grave. It's old, I mean really old. It's so old you can barely make out the inscription."

Heather was shaking. Sophie couldn't help but be sceptical about what Heather was telling her, but she could tell she was sincere. Either Elizabeth had appeared, or Heather had created it in her mind and believed it to be real.

"When I touched the gravestone I heard a man's voice."

"What did he say?"

"A name, the voice said a name - Charles Samuel Nash."

"Does Charles Samuel Nash mean anything to you?"

“Not at first. But since then other stuff’s been happening and the name ‘Charles Nash’ has surfaced a few times.”

Heather stood up. Tears welled in her eyes.

“I need fresh air.”

Sophie watched her sister step outside and light a cigarette. She'd given up smoking three years ago, but the recent happenings had frayed her nerves and yesterday she’d resorted to buying a packet of twenty. There were only three left.

She dropped the cigarette butt on the kerb and walked back into the coffee shop.

“Do you want another coffee? I’ll pay,” asked Sophie.

Heather nodded and smiled.

When Sophie returned to their table Heather looked brighter and could force a more convincing smile.

“Are you okay to carry on? I’m all ears……. Tell me about this Charles character.”

“Okay, but this is just as strange as seeing Elizabeth. Do you remember on New Year’s Day, when we went to the beach and Rosie picked that rock up?”

Sophie nodded.

“And do you remember I helped her paint it? We put eyes, nose and a mouth on it.”

“She named the stone Charlie, and it scared her. You’ve got it now, haven’t you?”

Heather nodded

“That stone head speaks and Elizabeth said that we needed each other and that I should keep it safe,” she paused, “and there’s another thing, the stone is always warm to the touch, as if it’s alive.”

“What did the stone head say?” asked Sophie, trying her hardest not to sound patronising.

“That we needed to talk, and it was Charles Nash’s voice…... the one who is buried in that old graveyard.”

Sophie said nothing. After Heather finished there was an awkward silence.

“It’s not that I don’t believe you, but it sounds very unreal.”

Heather nodded. She couldn’t blame her sister for doubting her. She would have done the same if the tables were turned.

“Is there anything tangible? Anything physical which proves these things have happened?”

“I’m not making this stuff up. I needed to speak with someone about what’s been happening and I needed to tell you,” said Heather in an agitated voice as she reached for her cigarettes.

Sophie apologised and watched Heather take another cigarette from the box.

“There is something, there's a smell.”

"A smell, when, what kind of smell?"

"When I saw Elizabeth. Do you know that smell when the rain hits the ground for the first time in ages, it's like a seaside smell?"

"The smell of a ghost?" said Sophie, who instantly regretted the remark.

Heather glared at her.

Sophie nodded. "It's a lovely smell."

Suddenly, Sophie stopped in her tracks

"This smell. Is it a smell like ozone?"

Heather nodded, "Yes, I guess so, it reminds me of being by the seaside, but it's more like fresh rain."

"Is it strong?"

"It was quite pungent….. why?"

Sophie didn't answer. She cast her mind back to when Rosie played in the kitchen with her imaginary friend William. She remembered a strong odour and how similar it was to fresh rain.

She reached out her hand and touched Heather's shoulder.

"Don't worry. I believe you."

Chapter 28

During the past six months, things had gone from bad to worse in the Maynard house.

Finn's obsession with work became all-consuming. He'd visited the United States four times since April and spent less and less time with his family. Sophie was distraught. She couldn't understand how her husband could have changed so much. He'd become a self-centred, work oriented bully and was teetering on the edge of being psychopathic.

He'd gained seven new accounts for SOS Graphics and all of them were North American companies.

Things were changing at SOS, and his boss, Ian Tomlinson, had employed two new designers to keep up with the customers Finn had attained.

But there was one account he'd not been able to close. He was desperate to get Goldman Inc. on board. A contract with Washington based Goldman would be worth almost two million dollars.

It was early October and soon he would return to the USA to nail the deal and sign the contracts. And when he had, he would ask Tomlinson for a share in the company.

Finn Maynard's plan was to take over SOS and turn the company into a force to be reckoned with.

Chapter 29

Mid October

A white hire van was parked outside Kieran Tempest's house. Ruth stood by her gate and watched as he and Linda hurriedly loaded belongings into the back of the van.

It had been over six months since Butler had transferred one million seven hundred and fifty thousand pounds into Kieran's bank account. He'd wanted to move house right away, but Linda had been reluctant to rush into a new property just for the sake of it.

At the end of September they'd found a five-bedroom house in Abbots Leigh on the outskirts of Bristol. They hadn't put their house on the market as money wasn't an issue.

Kieran had been getting bad vibes over the past few weeks and was itching to get out of Whitcombe Fields Road. Although he had never completely understood why Butler had been so interested in what went on in number 11a, he was aware the man's intentions weren't entirely wholesome and he'd prefer that he and Linda were out as soon as possible.

"Going somewhere?" called Ruth from her garden.

The couple ignored her and continued to load the van.

"I said, are you going somewhere?" repeated Ruth in a louder voice.

"What does it look like?" snapped Linda.

"I didn't even know your house was for sale."

"Believe it or not Ruth, there're a fair number of things in life you don't know."

Ruth tried not to look offended.

"Have I upset you?"

"It's always about you Ruth isn't it! Just for once this has nothing to do with you."

"If you know what's good for you, you should plan on getting out of the road too," said Linda. Kieran shot her a glance of disapproval.

"What was that supposed to mean?"

"Nothing Ruth, my wife's getting a bit cranky."

Ruth strolled across the road and looked in the van. She saw a bed, two cabinets, a TV and several cardboard boxes.

"If you're moving out, you'll need a bigger van."

"Don't worry Ruth, we're only taking the essentials."

Ruth was confused. She'd seen no 'For Sale' sign and she'd heard nothing of the Tempest's plan to move. Usually, there wasn't much that Ruth Jackson didn't know. She was surprised to find out they were moving. She was more surprised they'd kept the whole thing a secret. And it had been a small miracle that Kieran and Linda had managed to keep their new found wealth a secret from their over-inquisitive neighbour.

"What's happening with the stuff you're leaving behind?"

"That's not our problem," snapped Kieran, "If you don't mind, we've things to be getting on with."

Good riddance thought Ruth as she shook her head and crossed the road back to her house.

Kieran and Linda struggled to carry their settee into the garden.

"Put it down, I need a rest," snapped Linda whilst grappling her end of the sofa.

"There's no time, come on pull yourself together," said Kieran in an urgent tone of voice.

"Just two minutes please," pleaded his wife.

"Okay, okay two minutes," said Kieran as he sat beside her on the three seat settee.

They took a few minutes to catch their breath and Kieran saw a bird circling above the road. He watched as it swooped and soared back above the rooftops.

"Shit!" he whispered as the large black bird turned and headed back towards Whitcombe Fields Road.

It landed on the roof of Henry Buxton's house where it appeared to be surveying the surroundings. Kieran became agitated.

"What is it?" asked Linda.

Kieran didn't answer. He fixed his eyes upon the bird, waiting for its next move.

The bird hopped along the roof tops of the terraced houses until it perched at the end of Ruth's house. It looked down and cocked its head. The raven spread its wings and flew from the roof and landed on the hawthorn tree in Finn and Sophie's barren and empty garden. It stretched it wings and squawked as it hopped from branch to branch.

"Shit, there's no time, we've got to go!" shouted Kieran.

"Tell me Kieran, what is it?" pleaded Linda.

"It's the bird, the raven, things are gonna happen sooner than I thought……… get in the van."

"But what about the settee and the other stuff?"

"Forget it, let's get out of here."

Kieran scared Linda. She wasn't sure what was making him so nervous or why the bird had upset him so much.

Kieran slammed and locked the back doors of the transit and climbed in. In the rush he dropped the keys and frantically searched beneath the seat. He cursed beneath his breath as they were just out of reach. He grappled beneath the seat until he felt the plastic key fob. He snatched the keys, rammed them into the ignition, fired up the engine and left Whitcombe Fields Road for the last time.

Ruth watched from her window as the van sped away. She was confused. She looked at their house and saw they'd left the front door open and an expensive settee in their front garden. She could hear the screech of the van's wheels as it headed for the main road.

"What on earth is happening in this road?" muttered Ruth under her breath.

What would occur during the next few weeks would make Ruth Jackson wish she'd never set foot in Whitcombe Fields Road herself.

Chapter 30

The hot bath eased Finn's aching muscles. The candle on the window ledge cast a warm glow which shimmered as it reflected in his aftershave decanter.

Earlier that evening he'd had a marathon of a workout at the gym. Fitness and obsessing over his physique had become his passion. He was pushing himself further each day. Others in the gym were amazed by his transformation since he became a member. He was the quiet one who rarely spoke to anyone and lost himself in his training regime.

A late night bath was something he looked forward to. It was the perfect antidote to counteract a busy day in the office and an hour in the gym. Taking a bath gave him time to reflect. It was important to look back and consider his achievements. He used the time to think about his work plan for the following day.

Work had become his other obsession. Where before he would achieve the bare minimum, now he'd become committed. Ian, his boss, couldn't believe the transformation. Finn had come up with fantastic ideas, not only in graphic design, but also how to market SOS Graphics. He'd gained new customers and there were more on the horizon. It was all down to him. It started with his insistence to take back the Rusling account from Sally, and now there was no stopping him. His negotiations with Goldman Inc. in the States were going well, and he was planning on flying to Washington in December.

He couldn't understand why before now he never had the urge to work hard and play hard. Before now, he focussed on his family and nothing else. Every penny he'd earned he spent on them and he never considered himself as important. Now things were different. He was the important one.

Rosie loved her father dearly, but couldn't understand why he didn't play with her anymore. She used to enjoy piggy back rides, hide and seek and kisses and cuddles. Lately he'd shown little interest in her.

He lay in the bath and tried to pinpoint when the changes had happened. He looked at his finger and admired the gold ring he'd not taken off for months. The two red patterns fascinated him ever since he'd spotted the thing in the mysterious antique shop the previous year. He felt there was some kind of connection between the ring and the new Finn Maynard.

The warmth of the water and the flicker of the candle made him drowsy. Through half opened eyes he watched the flame as it danced and shimmied. The flicker grew until it became a bright flame. Finn slid into an upright position as the flame increased. He got out of the bath and slipped a dressing gown over his wet body. He grabbed the candle which was now burning ferociously and was about to throw it into the bath to extinguish it, when everything changed.

The candle had become a burning torch and in the corner he could see a young woman slumped against the wall. She looked terrified. Finn was calm. What he saw didn't worry him. He moved towards the girl and knelt in front of her. The girl looked at him with an air of confidence despite her obvious fear. And then she spoke in a wavering but assured voice.

"They're not your children."

He cocked his head to one side and tried to comprehend what was happening when a booming man's voice came from behind him.

"This will be my final time of asking. Think before you answer. What have you done with my children?"

Finn turned around, but there was no one there. He turned back. The girl's face reflected a look of true terror mixed with hard gritted determination.

"I won't tell you. They're somewhere you'll never know. I may be young, but I'm not stupid. I know your secret and I know you're not their father."

Finn stood up and opened his mouth to speak, and as he did, a voice came from within which was beyond his control and reverberated around the bathroom.

"You know nothing!"

It was the same booming voice he'd heard seconds earlier.

"I know enough to make sure you never see those children again," replied the woman.

The door flew open and Finn turned to see Sophie standing in the doorway with a thunderous expression across her face.

"Finn, what the bloody hell are you doing? It's gone midnight and you're waking the children."

Finn was confused. His dressing gown was loosely thrown over his wet body and in his hand was the candle. He looked to the girl, but she wasn't there.

Jack cried in his room.

"I don't know what's happening to you, but you're wrenching this family apart."

He put the candle down and followed her to Jack's room.

"What did you hear?" asked Finn.

"You, waking the children! Now get out of my way, Jack needs me."

"*Seriously*, what did you hear?"

"It's late Finn, I haven't time for this stupid game."

He grabbed her arm and pulled her towards him. Sophie stared at him and saw a look of confusion.

"I'm not playing a game, something happened and I need to know what you heard."

She broke free of his grip and rubbed her arm.

"Don't you ever lay a finger on me again."
"I need to know what I said."
Sophie sighed.
"You said I've done something with Rosie and Jack."
"I didn't say that," snapped Finn.
"No? Well then to whom were you referring when I heard you shout 'What have you done with my children'?"
He found it difficult to work out what the hell was happening.
"You said 'this will be my final time of asking. Think before you answer. What have you done with my children?' Who the hell were you talking to? There's no one else here," said Sophie in an angry whisper.
He stood in silence and thought about what she'd just said. 'What have you done with my children?'
Eventually he spoke.
"I wasn't talking to you."
"No? Well who were you talking to?"
He stared into the distance and considered what happened.
"I think I was speaking to Alice."
"Alice?"
"Her name is Alice Donaldson."
Sophie was having a hard time dealing with her husband's strange behaviour and had become less tolerant of his ways.
"Finn, please tell me who Alice Donaldson is, and don't lie."
He turned to her, and she saw sincerity in his face.
"Alice Donaldson? I've absolutely no idea."

Chapter 31

In the well

“Please come with me, she’ll be there soon.”
“Can’t I stay? I feel safe here.”
“But Rosie would love to see you……., she’s nice.”
“You can go, I’ll stay here. But don’t be long.”
“I won’t, I’ll just say hello and play for a little bit.”
“William? Can you ask Rosie if I can have another toy?”

Chapter 32

Breakfast at the Maynard's' was clouded with the familiar air of awkwardness which Sophie had come to expect over the past six months. She glanced at Finn who hugged his mug of tea. The scar on his cheek had healed well and she couldn't help feeling more attracted to him. More so than she'd ever done since she'd known him. At the same time as being attracted to him physically she was repelled by him emotionally. He'd become an arrogant, self-centred bastard who seemed to care for no one other than himself.

"Have you worked out who the mysterious Alice is?"

Finn looked up from his mug.

"Pardon?"

"Alice, last night in the bathroom? Have you worked out who she is?"

He vaguely shook his head and looked at his alienated wife.

"They weren't her children."

"No? Well I guess that makes everything okay then," replied Sophie sarcastically taking her cereal bowl to the sink.

She rinsed the dish and looked at the back garden. She wondered why no flowers and plants thrived there, or in the front garden. Everything everywhere was dead, other than that ugly hawthorn tree.

"Kieran and Linda have gone," said Sophie, placing the bowl on the side to dry.

"Gone where?"

"I don't know. I overheard Ruth talking with their next door neighbour. They took off unannounced. Apparently they left most of their things."

Finn was going to speak but Sophie interrupted him.

"What's that?" she said as she walked across the kitchen sniffing the air.

"What?"

Just as he spoke he picked up the faint scent.

"A damp smell, where's it coming from?" asked Finn.

"I'm not sure, but I've smelt it before."

The door flew open and Rosie entered the kitchen.

"Jack's awake, he's crying."

"Okay darling, I'll see him in a minute," said her mother.

"It's getting stronger," said Finn.

He was right. It was an odour that Sophie had noticed before. She was trying to think where she'd been last time she'd smelt it.

"It's William," shouted Rosie as she ran across the kitchen.

Finn looked up.

"It's her imaginary friend," whispered Sophie.

Finn nodded and viewed his daughter with interest as she happily chatted to thin air.

Rosie smiled at William.

"You've got your bedclothes on again."

"I'm always wearing them."

William looked around the kitchen.

"Who's that man?" asked William whilst pointing at Finn.

"Oh, that's my daddy."

"He looks like my father. He's got a scar like that on his face."

"Come and say 'hello'," said Rosie and walked towards her father.

William was nervous and stayed where he was.

"Come on silly, he won't hurt you," pleaded Rosie.

"He looks too much like my father. He might shout like mine does."

"Okay, stay where you are."

"Your mother looks nice."

Rosie smiled. "I love my mummy……. Shall we draw a picture?"

Finn and Sophie watched Rosie grab her drawing pad and pencils and make space on the kitchen table.

William stood alongside Rosie as she turned to a clean page in her book.

"Why don't you draw my sister cuddling the pink bear you gave her?"

Rosie smiled and worked on the picture as William described Louisa.

Suddenly it occurred to Sophie where she'd smelled it before. It had been where she was now. In the kitchen.

She thought back to her conversation with Heather. She'd mentioned the same thing when she'd seen the vision of her great grandmother, Elizabeth.

Sophie contemplated what Heather said and Finn was in a world of thought.

He became agitated and stood up.

"Rosie, is your friend William the same boy who helped you draw the picture with the burning building?"

Rosie nodded and worked on her drawing of Louisa.

"And he's the little boy who had a nanny called Alice?"

She nodded again.

William looked concerned.

"Why is he asking so many questions? And how does he know Alice?"

"I told him about Alice. I showed him the picture we did. You remember, the one with the burning building."

Finn and Sophie listened to Rosie's side of the conversation.

Rosie's conversation bothered Sophie. It didn't sound like a normal conversation a child would have with a made up friend, it was as if there *really* was someone talking with her.

Finn pondered over last night in the bathroom, and the vision of the mysterious girl. Why did he think she was called Alice? The name Alice was so familiar to him. He remembered how the name had struck a chord when Rosie had told him of the three characters in the picture she'd drawn with the burning building and the well.

William, Louisa and Alice he thought to himself.

Sophie was busy piecing together the significance of what Heather had told her of the visions of Elizabeth and the odour. She was linking it to what was happening with Rosie and her imaginary friend William.

Finn strolled over to his daughter.

He lowered himself to her level as she worked on her picture.

"Who are you drawing?"

"It's William's sister, do you think it's good?"

Finn didn't comment, he wasn't interested in how good Rosie could draw.

"Is William's sister called Louisa?"

Rosie nodded and continued with her picture.

"William and Louisa were taken care of by a lady called Alice weren't they?"

She nodded again.

William noticed the ring on Finn's finger and became nervy.

"Rosie, I must go, I need to look after Louisa."

"William, don't go, I haven't finished my drawing for you."

"Make him stay!" exclaimed Finn in a raised voice.

"I can't daddy……. William, my daddy says he wants you to stay."

William took a step back and Finn looked into space trying to locate where William could be.

Sophie watched cautiously, she was intrigued as to why Finn had become so interested in someone who was part of their daughter's imagination.

"I can't see your friend. Where is he?"

"He's stood next to me silly, why can't you see him?"

"Because I can't," snapped Finn. "Is he on your left or your right?"

"I don't know."

"Is he on the side you hold your pencil?"

She nodded.

William backed away as Finn moved to the other side of Rosie. William nervously watched Finn trying to work out where he stood. It reminded him of playing 'blind man's bluff' with Alice and Louisa, but a far more sinister version. Finn scared him.

Finn raised his arm and waived his hand through the air. His hand made contact with the space occupied by William. The ring on his middle finger passed through William's head.

As Finn waved his hand he noticed the surrounding temperature was warmer than anywhere else in the kitchen.

William was frightened when Finn's hand passed through his head space.
He waved his hand again, this time a little faster. The warmth increased and as it did, a faint image of a small boy appeared.
Finn fleetingly stopped when he saw the eerie vision.
He continued to wave his hand, this time with more urgency and haste. William appeared again. The faster Finn moved his hand, the clearer William became.
Sophie watched with her hand over her mouth. "My God," she whispered into her palm.
"What are you doing daddy? You're hurting my friend."
Finn took half a pace closer to the vision and waved his hand frantically as if he was fanning the embers of a dying fire. The more he waved his hand the clearer William became.
Sophie looked in amazement at the image of the little boy standing in her kitchen. He wore dour cotton bedclothes and appeared to be four or five years old. The expression his face reflected was one of fear peppered with the emotion of sadness. His hair was blond and thick, and he reminded her of a character from a Dickens' book.
Finn's arm ached, he slowed the waving motion and William faded. He dropped his arm to his side and William disappeared from view.
When Finn had been laboriously waving his hand, William had been rooted to the spot, but as soon as Finn stopped, William stepped back and occupied a different space in the kitchen.
"I need to go," said William.
"You've scared him away daddy, that's not nice."
Finn ignored Rosie. He turned to Sophie whose face was ashen.
"Did you see that?"
Sophie nodded without saying a word.
She knelt to her daughter's level and held her hand. Rosie felt her mother's hand shake.
"Did daddy and I see William, the boy who helps you draw?"
Rosie nodded. "Yes and daddy scared him away."
"And he knows Alice?" added Finn.
She didn't answer, instead she scowled at her father.
"Rosie, please could you go to your bedroom and play!"
"I don't want to, can I stay here?"
Jack cried again in his room.
"Come up and see Jack with me, and after that please play in your room for five minutes while I talk with daddy?"
"Go with your mother," said Finn with a stern look.
His look was enough to warn her not to argue and she went upstairs, trailing behind her mother.

Finn was alone in the lounge. All was quiet other than the sound of Sophie talking to Jack upstairs.

Part of Finn was staggered beyond belief by what he'd seen, but another part of him accepted what happened without question.

He turned to his daughter's drawing books and found the picture with the burning building and the children in the well.

He scrutinised the picture and tried to work out what it meant. Now he was sure that William was more than an imaginary friend the drawing took on a different meaning.

He recalled what Rosie said when she'd explained the drawing.

In the top left was the house where William and Louisa lived. In the lower middle section was a sketch of William and Louisa being pushed in a barrow by Alice while she was chased by dogs. In the top right section were two children in a well who were William and Louisa. The bottom right was a blazing building in which Alice appeared to be burning alive. Near the well was a hawthorn tree. Rosie said it was the same tree which grew in their garden, the tree which Rosie liked to call Bread and Cheese.

Out of the flames were the patterns. He looked at his ring and then back to Rosie's drawing.

The hairs on his neck stood on end as the significance of the drawing dawned on him. His hands shook as he held it in his grip. The sketch was a montage of the death of William and his sister who ended up being dumped in a well. But why the hawthorn tree? The same hawthorn he could see from the window of the lounge, less than thirty feet away. And the patterns? She knew of the patterns on the ring. But it wasn't Rosie who knew, it had been William. Something William said to her made her draw those patterns.

He cast his mind back to the picture she drew when she'd said the man with paper stuck to his face visited her. The same patterns were on that picture.

At last he understood what was happening. And as he did, his whole body became a shuddering mass of fear. His daughter was connecting with things he didn't understand.

Over the past few months Finn Maynard had changed. His confidence had soared. He'd become more dynamic and was making lifestyle choices he never would have made before. But now, as he sat gripping his daughter's drawing, he felt scared and lost. He needed someone to whom he could turn for guidance. He needed help.

Over his shoulder he heard a voice. The same booming voice he'd heard in the bathroom.

"Maynard you little shit. For once in your life be a man. Face what's happening. Because if you're scared now, just wait for what we've got in store for you."

Chapter 33

The black 1964 Rolls Royce Silver Cloud purred as it slowly made its way along Whitcombe Fields Road.

Ruth Jackson twitched behind her net curtain as the car pulled into Kieran Tempest's driveway. She squinted her eyes to see who was driving. The classic car waited with the engine running for five minutes. Ruth was distraught with curiosity.

A distinguished looking man in his early seventies wearing a Panama hat got out and walked to the boot. He popped it open and took out three cardboard boxes. One by one he laid them by the front door. He reached across the back seat of the car and removed a large grocery bag. Ruth strained and made out a box of tea bags and a carton of milk protruding from the bag. He carried it to the house, rummaged in his pockets and pulled out a set of keys, with which he opened the door.

Ruth was desperate to know what on earth was happening. If it had been a new neighbour moving in after buying the house, she'd be over in a flash to introduce herself and welcome them to the neighbourhood. But this was different. She knew that Kieran and Linda left under unusual circumstances and she couldn't just storm across the road as she normally would do.

Maybe if I go out to the garden he might introduce himself, thought Ruth.

Ruth went to the kitchen, pulled a half full black bag of rubbish from the bin and took it outside as an excuse to go out to her garden. She lifted the lid of her black wheelie bin and made as much noise as possible, ramming it in with the other black bags of landfill waste.

She looked over to the house, the cardboard boxes were still there. Peering through the leaves of her hydrangea she saw the man step out and pick up a box. Ruth noisily hauled the wheelie bin forward and clattered it along her garden path to make such a commotion that the stranger would have little choice other than to look in her direction. Her plan worked. He glanced at her, smiled, tipped his hat whilst carrying the box with one arm and continued back to the house. She needed to know who he was, or at least his name. The wheelie bin plan worked to a certain degree. At least the man acknowledged her. If he was as true a gentleman as he appeared to be, then his chivalrous side would urge him to help her, if she gave the impression she needed assistance.

The man stepped out of the house again and reached for the second cardboard box. Thinking on her feet, Ruth slipped off her wedding ring and let it drop into wheelie bin.

"Oh no!" exclaimed Ruth, bending forward into the bin as far as she could without falling in.

"For heaven's sake!" she cursed in a louder voice.

The man looked up and watched Ruth clattering around her garden, leaning into her bin and muttering to herself.

"Are you okay over there?" called the man with an accent befitting the clothes he wore and the car he drove.

Ruth looked up and smiled.

"I'm sorry, I appear to have got myself into a fix."

He put the box down and made his way towards Ruth and stopped at her gate.

"Whatever is the matter, can I help?"

"It's my wedding ring, it must have slipped off, and it's fallen to the bottom of the bin. I can't reach it."

"That will never do," said the man removing his hat, "May I help you?"

He handed Ruth his hat and leaned into the bin.

"Yes, I can see it. It's right at the bottom."

As hard as he tried he couldn't reach it.

"Pass me that bamboo cane over there."

Ruth pulled the stick from a flower pot and passed it to the man who used it to reach the ring and hook it out of the bin. He slid it from the cane and let it drop into his palm. He handed it to Ruth and smiled a charming smile. His charisma captivated her.

"Your husband wouldn't be very impressed if you'd lost your beautiful wedding ring."

Ruth blushed. "Oh, I'm not married, I mean I'm not anymore…….. my husband passed away several years ago."

"Is that a fact?"

Ruth's blushing face glowed like a beacon as the man offered his hand.

"My name's Gabriel, Gabriel Butler and I'm very pleased to make your acquaintance."

Chapter 34

"We've got to get out. This house is jinxed, it's haunted," said Sophie pacing up and down the lounge.

Finn shook his head.

"Listen to yourself, you're crazy. We're not going anywhere and that's final."

"But how can you say that? You've seen it for yourself. This place has ghosts, and not just William, there's the man with paper stuck to his face who Rosie saw...... and now, I for one, believe her."

"But what can they do to us? They're spirits, ...just echoes of a former life. They can't harm us."

"What if those harmless echoes were connected with the suicides?"

Finn shook his head.

"And hasn't it occurred to you as odd that you were on the train which killed Robert Buxton?"

"Coincidence, nothing more than coincidence!" huffed Finn.

"Listen to yourself..... we must get out. We've young children, let's go before the same thing happens to one of us."

Sophie shuddered with anger at her husband's obstinacy.

She turned to him after taking a few seconds to compose herself and calm down.

"And isn't it odd you've completely changed?"

"I've not changed," grunted Finn, knowing full well to what Sophie was referring.

"You're different. You look different, and you are different. You're nothing like the man I married. Something's happening to you, and if you can't see it, then you're blind."

At that moment, Rosie walked into the lounge hugging a teddy bear.

"Stop shouting."

Sophie looked over to see her daughter standing in the doorway with tears in her eyes.

"I don't want to move from this house. I like it here."

"It's okay, no one's moving, we're all staying here in this house," said Finn as he walked over and hugged Rosie whilst glaring at Sophie.

Sophie knelt to her daughter's level and held her hand. Finn took a step back.

"Remember Amy, your pink bear...... your favourite one?"

Rosie nodded.

"Tell me again, where is she now?"

"I've told you."

"Yes darling, but I'd like you to remind me, I'm not sure if I can remember where she went."

"You do silly," smirked Rosie.
"Just say it again please," asked Sophie. The tone of her voice developed an air of impatience which scared Rosie.
"Okay, I gave her to William, and he took Amy to give to Louisa."
"Is Amy with Louisa now?"
Rosie nodded. "Are you angry with me because I gave her away?"
"No, not at all. It was nice of you to give Amy to William's sister."
Rosie smiled.
"Does William ever tell you where he lives, where he goes when he's not playing with you?"
Rosie shook her head.
"Rosie, I may have heard Jack, would you mind being an angel and go in to see him? Make sure he's okay. I want to talk with daddy for a couple of minutes."
Rosie seemed happier. She skipped out of the lounge and up the stairs.
"So you don't believe these spirits can harm us and they're just echoes of a former life? Well I think they're more than that," said Sophie.
"Why?" asked Finn with a frown.
"Because there's physical interaction. Rosie gave that bear to William so he could give it to his sister. There's no sign of Amy anywhere. I've searched this house from top to bottom. Mum bought her that bear, and she'd be upset if it was lost, that's why I've searched everywhere for it."
"Do you really believe a ghost has taken Rosie's bear?"
"Yes I do, and we should get out. Whatever's here does physical things. And I'm certain it drove those who lived here before us to their deaths."
Finn stood up, shook his head and walked to the kitchen, leaving Sophie in the lounge.
He knew she was right. There was something in the house. They'd both seen the little boy and Rosie had been speaking to him. Finn couldn't disagree. There had to be a connection with what was happening and the suicides. He recalled the vision of the girl in the bathroom. He knew she had a link to William and Louisa.
But Finn couldn't help thinking about the bigger picture. He recalled the voice that told him to 'be a man' and prepare for something big. The words echoed in his mind. '*Face what's happening. Because if you're scared now, just you wait for what I've got in store for you*'.
But Finn wasn't afraid. Instead he was intrigued. He knew that he was part of something important.
When he'd seen William in the kitchen he'd been scared. The old Finn Maynard had briefly returned, but now he'd overcome his short-lived anxiety and was ready to embrace whatever was about to happen.
This was why he had no intention of leaving 11a Whitcombe Fields Road.

Chapter 35

Heather knelt by the grave of Charles Nash. She felt compelled to be there. It had become untidy since the last time she'd seen it and she wanted to make it look nice for him. As far as she was aware the grave received no visitors, and it was a shame to let it become overgrown like the other graves which surrounded his.

There was another reason for being there. She was desperate to speak with Charles. Since the visitation from Elizabeth she'd been expecting a message from the mysterious dead person. Elizabeth suggested that Heather needed something to make communicating with Nash easier. When she was alive, Elizabeth focussed on a silver cross around her neck when communicating with the dead. She'd suggested there was something in Heather's flat which she could use to channel her energies and speak with him. The only thing Heather could think of was the stone head painted by her niece which she named Charlie. Since Charlie had been around strange and eerie things had happened. Heather's nerves juddered as she recalled with clarity the strange dream in the graveyard and how she'd woken up in her bedroom with her feet caked in damp soil. She mentally placed the unnerving memory in a box, closed the lid and continued to pull at the weeds around the edge of the gravestone.

After an hour of tidying and placing potted plants around the grave she sat back and admired her work. She reached into her backpack and pulled out a bottle of mineral water. It wasn't a warm day, but toiling over Nash's plot had caused her to break into a sweat.

She put the bottle back in the bag and then unzipped the main section and removed the stone head.

Heather hoped that by bringing it to Nash's grave the chances of speaking with him would be better, as this was the first place she'd become aware of him and had heard his words bouncing around the churchyard.

She'd been afraid when she'd first heard his voice. But since then, and since the morning she'd heard him at her flat when his booming voice filled her hallway saying they needed to talk, Heather's fears had subsided. Maybe it was speaking with Elizabeth which had calmed her. Elizabeth had certainly prepared Heather for the strange things happening to her.

She needed to know what was happening.

It was late in the afternoon. Heather strolled around the small graveyard, to make sure she was alone and returned to Nash's gravestone. She lifted the head and placed it at the top of the stone. She knew which way Nash lay as Christian burials always faced to the east.

Sitting crossed legged on the grave stone, she placed her hands on top of the stone head and closed her eyes. A gentle breeze blew from the bottom of the hill. Heather heard the bushes rustle, pulled her jacket around her neck and concentrated on what she had come here to do. The sound of the breeze moving the bushes died away as she blocked out the surrounding noises. And then she spoke.

"Charles, it's Heather."

Nothing happened.

"Charles, I'm Heather, I understand you need to speak with me, can you hear me?"

Silence prevailed.

"Charles I understand there's something important you need me to do for you. Please speak with me. I'm ready to talk."

She opened her eyes. A noise from behind, made her jump.

A cat rustled through bushes. She sighed and swore under her breath.

"I'm wasting my bloody time," she muttered and placed the head back into the bag.

"I thought Elizabeth told you not to curse?"

She looked up to see a man standing over her. He had short blond hair with a hint of a curl. He was a few pounds overweight and wore a dark navy blue tailcoat, white leather breeches and black shoes.

He looked at her and smiled.

"Don't worry," he said in a reassuring tone, "I didn't always dress as smart as this, it's what they buried me in."

Heather sat on the gravestone with one hand covering her mouth. She was speechless. Even after speaking with Elizabeth, sitting at the feet of a dead person left her dumbstruck.

Something was putting her at ease. Whether it was due to seeing Elizabeth, she didn't know. But the cold chill of fear she felt when the man stood over her had lifted and now she was immersed in the warmth of love and sincerity.

"Hello, I'm Charles, and you must be Heather."

She nodded and attempted to smile.

"You're real …… you really are real!"

She looked at his feet, lifted her head and took in the full vision of the man in the nineteenth century garb until her eyes met with his.

"You're a real live ghost!"

"Well that's one way of putting it," laughed Nash.

She climbed to her feet and took a step closer.

"Don't do that."

Heather stopped and took a step back.

"Remember what Elizabeth told you. It takes an awful lot of energy for a spirit to become visible and if you get too close you'll burn."

An intense heat eminated from the vision.

"You won't see me for long, but I hope you'll hear from me again. I wanted to stand before you, so you know who I am."

Heather nodded and listened.

"And forget that nonsense about needing a channel to speak with me. The only thing you require is belief. Belief because I'm real."

Heather listened to the crackle of static as he raised his hand.

"Elizabeth was right. You have been chosen for something special. You are here to protect me. You will be my protector."

At last Heather found her voice.

"To protect you? But to protect you from what?"

"From the worst possible evil anyone could imagine."

Heather didn't understand what Nash meant.

"The unfortunate thing is, I can't tell you, but you will learn, you will adapt, you will become strong and you will become clever. You will need to keep your wits about you and you will always look over your shoulder. Learn to trust no one, especially those close to you."

"Those close to me? But why can't you tell me? I don't understand," pleaded Heather.

"Because, it is the way of things."

"And what if I refuse?"

Nash looked at her with sombre expression.

"Heather, you have no choice. The wheels are in motion, they cannot be stopped."

Heather said nothing, her silence urged Nash to continue.

"Your belief in me, and your belief you are strong enough to see this thing through to the end will allow you to succeed. Good will overcome evil."

Heather was going to speak when the cat leapt from the undergrowth. It arched its back and hissed at the apparition. Without warning it launched itself at Nash. The instant it contacted the space occupied by Nash it recoiled and screeched. Cowering, it stood behind Heather before running back into the undergrowth.

Heather turned to Nash, but he had gone. The air crackled with static electricity and smelt of burnt cat fur mixed with the familiar smell of fresh rain she'd noticed when Elizabeth had visited her.

"Charles, where are you? Can you hear me?"

Silence.

"Charles, I have so many more questions, where are you?"

She looked around the graveyard but he had gone. Apart than the lingering odour, there was nothing to suggest Charles Samuel Nash had ever been there.

Chapter 36

Finn sat in the kitchen alone pouring over Rosie's drawings. He didn't know what he was looking for, but he hoped to find a connection which would give him a clue to what was happening in his world.

Finn opened Rosie's colouring book to the picture of the two red circular patterns she'd drawn on the anniversary of Robert Buxton's death. The evening she said she'd seen the man with paper stuck to his face.

He also had the detailed picture she'd drawn under the guidance of William. Both pictures had the same red circular patterns, which matched his ring, but he was looking for something else. He was certain there must be something else to explain the strange things that had been happening in his house.

William and his sister were dead because of what was depicted in the picture William helped her draw. William had described the circumstances of his death.

He pushed back his chair and considered what Ruth Jackson told Sophie about those who'd previously lived in his house. Moreover he thought of those who'd died who'd lived here.

Before Kieran upped sticks and left with Linda, he'd told Finn that it would be best to keep away from Henry Buxton. But maybe a visit to Buxton would find a missing link, and help Finn work out what was happening.

Finn strolled into the lounge and looked at himself in the mirror. He couldn't help checking out the 'new Finn' whenever he passed one. He'd never been a vain person, but since he'd been working out at the gym and grown his hair, he liked the appearance of the person he'd become. He took a step closer and ran his finger along the scar on his cheek. It had healed well, and he thought it added to his 'new look'.

Sophie and the children were out. He went back to the kitchen, grabbed a beer from the fridge and returned to the lounge. From the window he looked at the mysterious hawthorn. The only thing that ever thrived in his front garden. He took a swig of beer and stared at the tree.

Finn became struck by a thought. He returned to the kitchen and grabbed Rosie's drawing with the children in the well. He took the picture to the lounge and compared her drawing of the tree to the hawthorn outside the window. From the lounge it was clear how precise her sketch was. Although childlike, the picture captured its detail. The trunk of the tree split into two sections eighteen inches from the ground. The section veering to the left split in two and grew in separate directions. She'd included a few of the major lower branches before colouring the foliage which covered the rest of the tree's skeleton. He'd not noticed the level of detail until today. William must have told her how to draw it. Rosie's picture gave the impression that the well was near the tree. Finn considered the significance of the tree and its relationship to the well. One of the major branches in her picture pointed towards the well. He could see what looked like the same branch on the tree in the garden which pointed towards the house, toward the kitchen.

No! thought Finn.

He turned around and paced to the kitchen counting his steps as he walked. Nineteen paces from the window of the lounge to the kitchen table. Plus another three from the tree to the wall of the house, he estimated that the tree must be twenty two paces from the kitchen. He looked at Rosie's drawing and using the stick-like sketches of the two children in the well to judge an idea of scale, he considered twenty two paces to be a likely distance from the tree to the well.

Finn stamped his foot on the kitchen floor and listened. He wasn't sure what he was listening for, but he stamped again. He dragged the kitchen table to one side and continued to stamp his feet where the table had been.

Finn was certain that the well was beneath the kitchen. He knelt down, bent forward and put his ear to the ground.

Finn sat up and paused for reflection.

Am I going mad?

He dragged the table back and sat down.

He recalled what Rosie said about William. He only ever appeared in the kitchen. He shook his head and took another gulp of beer.

He looked at the clock. Sophie wouldn't be back for at least another hour.

"Time to pay a visit to Mr. Buxton," said Finn to himself before finishing the last swig of beer.

Henry Buxton heard a sharp rap at his door, pulled back the net curtain and saw Finn at the door.

Finn rapped again. He turned his head to his left and spotted Henry behind the net curtain.

Buxton apprehensively made his way along the hall and opened up.

"Can I help you?" asked Henry hiding behind the door.

Finn didn't know what to say. He couldn't launch into the story of being on the train which ended Henry's father's life, but essentially that was his reason for being there.

"Hello Mr. Buxton, I expect you know who I am. My name is Finn Maynard and I bought your father's house from you."

"I know who you are. What do you want?" replied Henry in a standoffish tone.

"Do you mind if I come in? I've something I wish to ask."

"I'm busy at the moment, can you call back later?"

"I'd prefer to speak with you now," said Finn. His tone carried an air of urgency which Henry found difficult to ignore.

Henry sighed, which made it obvious he wanted nothing to do with Finn.

"Please Mr. Buxton, I promise I'll be quick."

Henry clung to the door. Eventually he nodded and Finn entered the house.

He followed Henry into the house and Henry directed him to the dining room.

They sat facing each other across a wooden dinner table. Finn looked around the room. The layout was different to his house. Henry's kitchen overlooked the front of the house and his lounge was at the rear.

Henry said nothing. An air of tension filled the room which Finn found unnerving.

"I'd like to ask about your father."

Henry didn't speak. He stared back at Finn with empty eyes.

"I understand this may make you uncomfortable Mr. Buxton, but I need to find a few things out."

Henry nodded.

Finn adjusted his sleeve and squirmed in his chair.

"I'm aware of how your father died, …….. I was on the train which……. " his voice trailed off, not knowing how he should complete the sentence.

Henry looked expressionless, and Finn continued.

"I was on the train which hit your father."

"The train didn't hit my father, he threw himself in front of it."

"I'm sorry," said Finn. He nodded and found the whole thing more difficult than he expected.

"I'm the one who found your father's head…….. and now…….. and now, I live in his house."

"It's your house now," said Henry trying hard not to show emotion.

It should have come as a shock to Henry when Finn told him he'd been on the train which killed his father, even more so that he'd been the one who discovered Robert Buxton's head. But after hearing what Finn told him he didn't appear surprised.

Henry considered the others who'd lived at 11a who had taken their lives and more importantly, the connections between them.

Robert Buxton sold his car to David Gosling. David killed himself when he lived at 11a before Robert. More importantly, Gosling used the car he'd bought from Buxton to commit suicide. He'd died of carbon monoxide poisoning.

Before Gosling lived at 11a, it had belonged to Shaun and Janet Morrison who'd both died after Shaun drove their car into Bitterwell Lake. Gosling was a member of the police diving team searching the lake and had been the one to find their bodies in the car.

Henry shuddered at the thought of Finn's connection to his father's suicide and became overcome with sadness.

"What is it you want to talk about?" asked Henry.
Finn wriggled in the chair again and then continued.
"Do you have any idea why your father took his life?"
Henry shook his head.
"Do you know whether he was depressed, or anxious about anything?"
Henry stood up.
"My father and I spoke little towards the end….. we grew apart, even though we lived so close to each other."
Finn looked at the table and ran his finger over the ring.
"I wanted to speak to you because odd things are happening in the house and I wondered whether your father ever mentioned anything to you."
"I don't believe so, what odd things?"
Finn shuffled awkwardly.
"We've seen things. Myself, my wife and our daughter. We've seen ghosts."
"Ghosts?" snorted Henry.
Finn nodded.
"What kind of ghosts?"
Finn told him about William and Rosie's pictures.
"And there's something else," added Finn, "on the anniversary of your father's death he visited my daughter."
Henry became animated.
"That's enough. I've told you I don't know why my father killed himself, and now I want you to leave," said Henry standing up.
"Please, Mr. Buxton, I haven't finished."
Finn saw anger in Henry's face, but was determined to continue.
"My daughter said a man came to her as she drew in the kitchen. She said he had paper stuck to his face. It turns out she had described a man with a paper bag over his head."
Finn paused and looked at Henry who was rooted to the spot.
"Don't forget, I saw your father when he died and I know he had a bag over his head when he jumped in front of the train."
"Did 'this ghost' of my father speak to your daughter?"
Finn nodded.
"She didn't understand what he was saying, because of the bag ……. But they drew a picture together."
Henry looked at him with his head to one side.
"What kind of picture?"
"It was more patterns than a picture, circular patterns. This seems to be a theme with the ghosts who visit our house."
Henry was silent and in deep thought. The colour drained from his face. He looked at Finn nervously.
"Patterns you say?"

Finn nodded.
"Wait there."
Finn watched Henry leave the room. He could hear him in the dining room shuffling and opening drawers. He returned with a box file which he dropped on the table with a thud.
"Take a look," said Henry stepping back.
Finn opened the box and saw it was full of A4 paper.
"What's this?"
"I hope you can tell me."
Finn took a handful of sheets and placed them on the table. He looked at the patterns. Each one was like another although they were all slightly different.
"Where did you get these?"
"They were stuck to the walls and ceiling of my father's study."
"His study?"
"The small room upstairs in your house."
"That's my son's bedroom," said Finn under his breath.
Henry disappeared again and left Finn to search through the box of paper. He returned with an envelope.
"And there's this," said Henry handing the envelope to Finn.
"What is it?"
"He had it on him when he killed himself."
"Is it a note?"
"Just open it."
Finn opened the envelope, pulled out three sheets of paper and laid them on the table. His pulse quickened, and he perspired as he recognised the patterns. They were the same as Rosie drew under the guidance of both William and Robert Buxton's ghosts. He saw the third sheet was blank. The two patterns had a tick alongside.
Henry walked to the window with his back to Finn. Finn compared the two patterns Robert Buxton had drawn to the two on his ring.
The same thought Finn.
"Do you mind if I borrow these?" asked Finn waving the three sheets from the envelope in his hand.
Henry shrugged his shoulders with a look of indifference.
"Have them, and the box file. They're of no use to me."
He watched Finn hold the sheets with the patterns in one hand and the blank sheet in the other. His eyes darted from one sheet to the other. He became absorbed by them.
"Do they mean something?" asked Henry.
Finn didn't answer. Robert Buxton's drawings made something stir within. Even though they were same as the patterns on the ring, and to his daughter's

drawings, holding the versions drawn by Henry's father awoke something deep inside. Something so familiar, yet so very distant.

He placed the two sheets with the patterns on the table to one side and stared at the blank page.

He lay it on the table and flattened it with his hand. The blank sheet called to him, it summoned him to use his mind's eye and fill in the blank. He looked at the sheet and a new pattern developed before his eyes. A swirling mass of colour faded in from nowhere. There different shades and hues spinning and interacting with each other. It was like looking upon the eye of a hurricane. The colours gyrated and danced with one another until the different shades fused together and created the most vibrant red Finn had ever seen. It was so bright he covered his eyes with the back of his hand. He sensed warmth which radiated from the pattern. The warmth intensified into a heat that forced him to move away from the paper.

Henry watched Finn cover his eyes and screw up his face as if he was too close to a fire.

"Can you see it?" said Finn turning his head away from the paper.

Henry looked at the paper.

"Can I see what?"

Finn didn't answer. He became too engrossed with what was happening.

Wisps of grey smoke spiralled up from the corner of the paper just before the sheet ignited in front of his eyes.

"What the fuck?" snapped Finn jumping back in shock, whilst watching the paper crumple and burn on the table. A blue flame enveloped it turning it to smouldering ash.

Henry watched with a look of apathy.

"I think it's time you left," said Henry, who had been unaffected by what Finn had just seen.

"But what just happened?" demanded Finn.

"Nothing happened, other than you acting like a mad man which is why it's time for you to leave. Take what you need and go."

Finn looked back to the table and to the third sheet of paper. It was intact. No burn marks, no patterns, not a single thing other than the crease from where it had been folded and placed in Robert Buxton's envelope.

He rubbed his eyes and looked again.

"Please Mr. Maynard, take these papers and leave."

Finn stood up and stared at the paper in front of him.

"This is all I need," he said picking up the mysterious blank sheet. He folded it and placed it in his pocket.

Finn left Henry's house leaving paper tumbling from the box file and strewn across the floor.

Henry cursed and bent forward to scoop up the hundreds of sheets of paper. He placed them on the table and squared them up so they would fit back into the box file. He laid his hand on the table where the third sheet had been and quickly recoiled as a pain shot through the palm of his hand.

"Yowch!" exclaimed Henry, rubbing his hand with his finger. The table was hot. He shook his head, not being able to comprehend what happened. The varnish on the table was sticky as if something scalding had been placed on it.

He went to the kitchen and ran cold water over his hand. After the pain subsided he returned to the table.

"Shit! The table's ruined," he muttered whilst looking at the varnish which had bubbled. Then, he noticed something in the wood. He took his reading glasses from his pocket and bent forward to inspect it.

"How on earth did that get there?"

He moved closer and couldn't believe what he was looking at.

In front of him, embossed into the wood where the varnish had bubbled, was a faint circular pattern, just like the patterns drawn by his father. He grabbed the two sheets his father had with him on the day he'd died and compared them with the one in the wood. They were similar, but not the same.

Again, he looked at the two sheets on which his father had drawn the patterns, each with a tick below. He glanced back to what was etched into the table.

And then he saw it.

Beneath the imprinted pattern burnt into the table was a tiny scratch. Henry looked again. But it wasn't just a scratch, it was something else. He adjusted his glasses to get a better view and as he did he followed it with the nail on his forefinger.

It took a few seconds to sink in before he realised what it was.

It was a tick. Beneath the circular pattern was a tick.

"What the…..?" muttered Henry Buxton as he huffed air through his cheeks.

Chapter 37

Gabriel Butler settled into what had been Kieran Tempest's favourite chair. He'd turned it so it faced the window in the lounge allowing him a perfect view of 11a, the house his 'short lived' company had built thirty years earlier.

With his feet resting on Linda's footstall, a copy of George Eliot's Middlemarch in one hand and a Carlito Fuente cigar in the other he waited for the show to begin.

It could happen today, tomorrow, or in the next six months.
Gabriel Butler was a patient man, who this time had waited over seventy years for what was going to happen. Waiting a little longer wouldn't hurt.

And then the fireworks would really begin.

Chapter 38

Late November

"The taxi will be at your place by ten am, make sure you're ready," said Chloe Grant.

Ian Tomlinson asked Chloe to book a taxi to collect Finn and take him to the airport. Finn was leaving for Washington for a three day visit to close the Goldman deal he'd been negotiating.

"Remind me Chloe, what time's the flight?"

"Jeepers Finn, I've told you. You're boarding the plane at four thirty this afternoon."

"Yeah, sure, sorry I forgot."

Since the episode at Henry Buxton's house, Finn had become preoccupied by the blank sheet. He'd been staring at it, willing the strange colours to return like at Henry's.

He put down his phone and checked the time. It was just past nine, just under an hour until the taxi was due.

Sophie was away. She'd decided to stay at her parents with the children whilst Finn was in America as she didn't want to be alone in the house at night because of the strange things that had happened. She knew it would be hard work looking after both children on her own for three days and appreciated her parents helping out with childcare. Finn wasn't much use these days, but at least when he was around he did a few menial tasks.

Finn wandered around the house killing time and waited for the taxi.

He sat at the table in the kitchen and pulled out the blank sheet of paper, placed it flat on the table and stared at it. He knew it shouldn't be blank and there should be a pattern on it, like the two on his ring. Now he understood what Robert Buxton had been determined to achieve. Buxton knew of the two patterns on Finn's ring and sketched them on separate sheets of A4, but he'd not been able to come up with a third pattern.

Finn imagined Robert Buxton labouring over hundreds of sheets of paper until he'd been driven mad with frustration trying to work out the two patterns. He'd cracked after many attempts. He imagined Buxton staring at the third sheet with no idea what the third pattern should be. Finn also became obsessed with the patterns without understanding their meaning.

Buxton had done the hard work of figuring the first two patterns. Finn knew this because of the drawings his daughter had done which matched Robert Buxton's, and they also matched the face of his ring. Finn had no idea of the pattern on the third sheet. He didn't stop to question why there should be a third pattern, he instinctively knew that there was one.

Finn jumped up, strolled to the printer in the lounge, grabbed a handful of A4 paper and took them back to the kitchen. He pulled a red pen from his jacket pocket and worked on the third pattern. He was getting nowhere fast. Every attempt at a pattern was wrong. He wrote an 'X' under each failed attempted and dropped it to the floor. He became lost in what he was doing and hadn't noticed the time which ticked closer to ten.

Finn was a great freehand artist, but better at creating images using the computer. He grabbed his laptop from the hall which lay next to his suitcase ready for the trip to the States. He plugged it into the mains in the lounge and fired it up. He loaded Corel Painter, the software he used to create freehand art, and stared at a blank document. With his finger hovering over the mouse he became overcome by the same feeling he'd experienced when he had been at Henry's. But this time it was different. He didn't see an image appear in front of him, this time he felt the image stirring from within.

He clicked 'red' from the digital pallet and selected a fine nib pen and waited.

Finn was right handed. He couldn't write, draw or barely hold a pen in his left hand, but something repeatedly made a nerve twitch in the middle finger of his left hand. He moved closer to the computer screen and watched a single red pixel appear on the top right corner of the blank document. A minute later another pixel appeared, and this time it was in the middle of the screen. A few seconds later another appeared at the bottom.

What's happening? thought Finn as pixel after pixel appeared on the screen.

He was so engrossed with what was happening he hadn't noticed it was his finger that was tapping the mouse and making each pixel appear one by one. His middle finger on his left hand, the one on which he wore the ring, gently nudged and clicked the mouse making each pixel materialise on the screen.

It was almost ten o'clock, Finn was in a stupor and became fixated by the screen. Each time a new pixel appeared he became lured further into a trance like state.

Just after ten a taxi beeped its horn, but Finn didn't hear. He became more and more engrossed as a pattern emerged on the screen.

The impatient taxi driver beeped again and strained his neck to look out of the passenger window to see if anyone came to the door. He cursed, got out and walked along the garden path, looking at the barren garden as he made his way to the front door.

Angrily, he rapped on the door and rang the bell.

Finn continued to become entranced by what materialised in front of him. His eyes were almost shut and were tiny slits, causing his vision to blur. He couldn't hear the taxi driver banging on the door and calling through the letter box.

After five minutes the driver gave up and sped away.

Subconsciously Finn continued to tap away with his finger on the mouse and the image continued to develop. He was becoming tired and lethargic and his head dropped. He rubbed his forehead with his right hand as he carried on clicking the mouse with his left. He rested his head on his right hand and drifted into a semiconscious state as his middle left finger clicked away creating the random image on the screen.

An hour had past and Finn was in the same position adding pixel after pixel to the image unfolding before him. His eyes were closed and he rocked back and forth. The hypnotic lull of his rocking lured him into a light sleep in which a strange and vivid dream manifested in his subconscious.

He was upon a black horse galloping through the countryside on a cold day. He could feel the rush of frosty air across his face as the steed continued to race through fields and lanes. He was not alone. Behind him were other riders dressed to keep warm against the winter morning. The sun rose behind them and the western sky showed the last of the night stars. Venus was ahead of the sun in the east and shone like a beacon.

The excited dogs were somewhere in the distance. He followed the baying of the hounds.

Finn and the riders passed a small building in a rocky field. He glanced at it as he sped past. The building was familiar. He continued toward the hounds.

Finn and the riders slowed their horses when they had reached the dogs yapping and howling in a canine dither.

"What are your intentions?" asked one rider who was an ugly short man with a menacing tattoo across his face.

"We must go back, we've missed something," replied Finn in a voice which did not belong to him.

The ugly man with the tattoo climbed from his horse and teased the dogs with a section of torn cloth. The dogs became excited and jumped up at the man.

"Get back on your horse Mr. Morris and follow me," shouted Finn and made his way back towards the east.

Morris and the other riders followed Finn, and the dogs followed the riders.

Five minutes later Finn saw the building as he neared the top of a small hill. He slowed down and waved to the riders to do the same. The dogs charged past Finn and Morris who cautiously made their way to the stone building.

"I think you've found her," said Mr. Morris.

The riders trotted their horses to the building and dismounted.

Finn watched Morris light a torch and make his way to the building, followed by the other men.

Finn stood alongside his horse and lit a briar pipe.

"She's in here, tell Drake we've found her," shouted Morris.

Finn snuffed out his pipe, placed it in his pocket and made his way to the building. He stopped outside, thanked Mr. Morris and waited a few seconds before stepping into the building.

His eyes became accustomed to the dimness of the small building when he heard a strange sound in the corner. The sound increased, it was a niggling repetitive tune that wouldn't go away. The building faded and was replaced by a red pattern on a glaring white background. Finn rubbed his face and gazed at the laptop.

He came out of the strange dream, blinked his eyes and gawped at the screen.

"Did I do that?"

He pushed back the chair, stood up and glared at the computer.

"No, no no!" he shouted.

He placed the cursor beneath the red circular pattern and put a cross below it, then slammed the lid.

The niggling tune started again. He looked at his phone next to the computer and saw he had missed a call. Finn grabbed the phone and threw it across the room.

He fell to the settee, curled up in a ball and thought of the dream. He looked at the ring and rubbed it with his finger. Thoughts of his journey to the States eluded him. He hadn't heard the taxi driver knocking and he'd missed a call from Tomlinson's secretary.

She'd received a call from the taxi company who'd told her that their driver wasn't able to collect Finn and she was worried about him.

Finn switched his attention to the pattern which should have been on the blank sheet of paper found on Robert Buxton when he'd jumped in front of the train.

He stood up, lurched back to the laptop and lifted the lid. He looked at the pattern and hit delete.

And then it started again.

He became lured by the blank document and subconsciously clicked one pixel at a time. A new image appeared on the screen and just as before, he became sleepy.

The dream he'd had before repeated from the start. Just as before, he chased through the countryside with the sound of the howling dogs ahead of him. Behind him were Mr. Morris and his disparate gang endeavouring to keep up. He ended up at the same small stone building in the field to be advised by Morris that inside was the woman for whom he'd been searching.

Finn entered, and this time the dream didn't abruptly end.

In the corner sat a young woman in her early twenties. She was tired and scared. Finn stepped closer while Morris stood behind holding a burning torch.

Finn took a breath and spoke in a voice which sounded familiar.

"Hello Alice, I've been looking for you……..what have you done with my children?"

The trembling girl didn't speak. Finn knelt beside her and spoke again.

"Alice, I'd really like to know what you've done with my children. Please tell me where they are."

"They're not your children," replied the young woman.

Finn moved closer and put his mouth to her ear.

"This will be my final time of asking. Think carefully before you answer. What have you done with my children?"

"I won't tell you. They're somewhere you'll never know. I may be young, but I'm not stupid. I know your secret and I know you're not their father."

"You know nothing!" shouted Finn.

"I know enough to make sure you never see those children again."

"Very well," said Finn. His voice became calm as he stood over her.

Finn noticed the girl looking at the ring on his finger. He had an urge to kill her, but didn't know why. He was about to order Mr. Morris to deal with her when a notion occurred to him.

He turned back to the girl who covered her face with her hand expecting him to hit her.

"Why are you interested in this ring? Tell me what you know about it?"

The woman looked at him without speaking.

Finn repeated the question in calm, almost reassuring voice.

"Tell me what you know about this ring?" he said whilst watching the rubies sparkle in the light of Mr. Morris' flaming torch.

"Why are you even asking?"

"Because I need you to tell me. I want to hear it from you."
"It's your obsession. Don't worry, I've worked it out. I know why you took William and Louisa after their mother died after giving birth. I know why you want them and that's why I'm making sure you'll never see them again."
"Tell me about my obsession, why do I want the two children so badly?"
"But it's not only them you want is it? Even if you get your hands on them, your search still isn't over."
Finn looked at her with a puzzled expression.
"Why not? Why is my search not over?"
"Don't play games with me Alexander. Either let me go, or kill me...... the choice is yours."
Finn looked at her.
"Alexander? Why do you call me Alexander?"
Morris looked with concern.
"Is something the matter?"
Finn ignored Morris.
"Don't play games with me. You're an evil man. Either kill me or let me go," said the girl in a brave voice.
"She's not going to talk" said Finn. "Mr. Morris, do your worst."

Finn stepped out of the building to the sounds of muffled screams as Joseph Morris kicked the defenceless but brave young girl.

He awoke from the dream to the sound of Sophie calling his name. The door wouldn't open because Finn deadlocked it the night before.
"Finn, Finn can you hear me? Are you in there?"
Her voice became clearer as she bellowed through the letter box.
"Finn, are you okay?"
He was confused. He glanced at the clock on his laptop and couldn't believe the time.
Finn rubbed his eyes, looked at the laptop and saw something amazing. A pattern, like the ones on his ring and that Rosie had drawn. It was also very much like the drawings that Henry Buxton had shown him in his house.

Although similar, it was so very different. He had a feeling that the image staring back had something to do with the 'new' Finn Maynard, and the strange things happening in his house.

Sophie called his name, but it didn't register. He was lost in his own world and continued to stare at the screen. He knew this was what drove Robert Buxton to take his life. This was the third pattern that Buxton had been trying to draw. The pattern that caused him to lose his mind. Now Finn had it. It belonged to him. Beneath the pattern he drew a red tick, saved the file and closed the lid.

Sophie was beside herself with worry. Ian Tomlinson had phoned and told her that Finn hadn't answered the door when the taxi driver had called. Tomlinson had called several times but Finn hadn't answered. He had called Sophie a quarter of an hour ago, and Sophie had rushed round to check he was okay.

Through the letter box she could see his suitcase in the hallway so assumed he must be in the house. She screamed his name as loud as she could.

Finn looked up. Her shrill voice registered with him.

"Not now bitch," he whispered to himself.

He crawled along the floor, popped his head around the lounge door and looked along the hall.

His eyes met with hers and he ducked back into the lounge.

"Finn, what's happening? Why're you still here?"

He sat on the floor in the lounge with his back against the wall. She'd asked a good question. Why was he still here? He had no idea. He'd no recollection of the taxi driver and couldn't remember what had happened that morning. He could vaguely recall the dream, and the pattern on the laptop had become a distant memory.

He knew something important had just happened, but couldn't remember what.

"Finn, what are you doing in there?"

One thing of which he was sure, his infuriating wife had nothing to do with whatever was happening to him.

The pattern on his laptop popped back into his mind's eye.

He crawled back to his computer and lifted the lid. The thing whirred back into life showing the red pattern he'd just subconsciously finished drawing.

As soon as he saw it his memory of the dream became clear. He felt strong and powerful. His moment of insecurity had passed.

"Leave me alone bitch," shouted Finn along the hall.

Sophie heard him holler and was shocked by the words he'd yelled.

"Finn, open the door, please speak to me."

"Fuck off!"

"Finn…… please come to the door."

"Which bits of 'fuck' and 'off' don't you understand?" snarled Finn.

Sophie cried. She didn't understand what had happened to the man she loved.

"Why are you still here?" bellowed Finn.

"Because I love you and I'm worried about you."

'Because I love you and I'm worried about you' spun around his mind.

For a moment he felt vulnerable. His love for Sophie returned. He was going to unlock it when he heard a voice. The same voice he'd heard coming from himself when he'd seen the vision of Alice Donaldson in his bathroom and it was the voice he'd spoken in the dream.

'Maynard you little shit. Step back from the door, stay focussed. This is too important to fuck up.'

Sophie waited outside and Finn turned the lock. The door opened, and he looked her in the eye.

The voice had brought the 'new Finn' back after his brief lapse.

He looked at Sophie, but didn't see the woman he used to love. Instead he saw a parasite. He saw a scrounger. To him she was nothing but a freeloader who had been living off his hard earned money. She didn't work, she stayed home looking after the sorry excuses she had for children. She didn't do anything of benefit to him.

"I'll tell you this once. Fuck off. Get away from my house. I don't want you here."

Sophie was beside herself and couldn't understand what was happening.

"What have I done to upset you so much?" she asked through her tears.

"You're pathetic," said Finn shaking his head.

"But what's happening to you Finn? I don't understand."

"Forget about Finn, he's gone. He's dead."

She stopped crying, swallowed hard and looked at him.

"So you're telling me you're not Finn. You're not Finn Maynard, the man I married and have two wonderful children with?"

"Shut up and go."

She knew she was getting nowhere. He was having some kind of breakdown and she worried he would become violent.

Sophie turned around to leave, then stopped, turned back and asked him a question.

"If you're not Finn, then tell me who the hell you are?"

He looked at her with an air of puzzlement. She'd floored him.

He thought of the dream. He recalled chasing through the countryside on horseback and the young woman in the stone farm building who spoke to him of his children. He remembered what she'd said. She told him 'They're not your children'.

It had made little sense, but one thing was beginning to connect with him, which was the person he'd been in the dream. It was like nothing before. In the dream he'd been unstoppable and untouchable. He was wealthy, important, and a man who had great influence over others. He'd felt strong and confident until he'd confronted the young woman Alice. There was something about her, something she said that he didn't understand. It was about the ring. She knew why the ring was important. She'd said the ring was his obsession and she'd also talked about the children, William and Louisa, and that he'd taken them from their mother. She'd referred to him as Alexander. Finn shut his eyes and gripped the door.

Alexander.... Alexander.... Alexander, he thought as the name circled his mind. And then it came to him.

"I said, if you're not Finn, tell me who you are?" repeated Sophie with her hands on her hips and a look of defiance in her eye.

"Who am I?" asked Finn. "You really don't know me do you?"

"No, right now, I can honestly say I've no idea who you are."

"My name is Alexander. Alexander Drake. I'm busy, so fuck off and leave me alone."

She was about to speak, but she knew it was pointless.

"I said fu......," said Finn, but was interrupted by Sophie.

"Don't worry Finn, or Alexander, or whoever the hell you're supposed to be. I'm leaving you. You won't be seeing me again."

He smirked and slammed the door.

Gabriel Butler watched and grinned from the porch of Kieran Tempest's house.

"Welcome back Alexander my friend. It's been a long long time."

Chapter 39

He still found it hard to believe. Even months after Gabriel Butler had transferred over one and a three quarter million pounds to his account, Kieran Tempest would spend hours staring at his bank balance, which was just over one and a quarter million, as the Tempest's had just purchased a five-bedroom house at a shade under half a million pounds.

"It's ready sir, it's yours to drive away."

Kieran looked up. He'd been contemplating his newly found wealth and became lost in his own little world.

"I'm sorry, pardon?" said Kieran.

"Your new car, it's on the forecourt and here're the keys, it's ready to go sir," repeated the salesman.

Kieran took the keys, thanked him and followed the salesman to the forecourt where the red Porsche 911 Carrera was waiting for him.

The salesman's voice faded into the distance as Kieran walked around the car. He was stunned by the beauty of the thing as it reflected the afternoon sun.

It wasn't for him, it was an early birthday present for Linda. He knew she'd love the car, but he knew she'd love something else about it even more. The registration plate. HE11 BDG. Both he and his wife were huge Beatles fans. They'd first met at a Beatles convention in Liverpool thirty years earlier. Their favourite Beatles song was Hey Bulldog, which was why he'd chosen the personalised number plate for her new car. HE11 BDG was the closest he could find to Hey Bulldog. He knew she'd love it.

After over twenty years of patiently waiting and reporting the comings and goings of the strange house in Whitcombe Fields Road to Gabriel Butler, Kieran had become a rich man. He'd walked away from his job and was living a life of leisure.

He felt no guilt over how he'd earned the money and he'd never believed the eccentric billionaire's prediction of what would happen.

Even though Butler's prophesy of the spate of suicides had turned out to be true, Tempest found it hard to believe the old man when he'd told him of the consequences of Kieran's involvement. The event the crazy old man described seemed too 'earth shattering' to happen. But Tempest was taking no chances, and he'd shipped out as soon as he could. The sight of the raven perched in the garden of 11a, the day he'd pulled away in the hired transit van, had been the sign that hinted that maybe everything Butler had predicted would happen.

Chapter 40

Sophie had been crying for the past two days. Her daughter didn't understand why mummy was so upset and why daddy wasn't looking after things.

Grace put her arms around Sophie. She had been trying to console her daughter since yesterday, but there seemed nothing she could do to end her flood of tears. Tending to Jack was something which distracted her from what was happening.

"Wait until I get my hands on that bastard," cursed Sophie's father. He'd never seen his daughter so upset.

Grace threw him a look.

"Not now John."

Grace tried to comprehend what was going on, but Sophie's description of what happened between her and Finn on their doorstep was conveyed through a mass of unstoppable tears and Grace wasn't sure what had happened between them.

Finn was suffering a mental breakdown, and was showing signs of having a dual personality. He needed professional help.

At last Sophie's tears subsided. Her face was red and puffy. Grace handed her a glass of water.

"Are you ready to talk?" asked Grace.

Sophie put down the glass, wiped her eyes and nodded.

Over an hour later she'd told her mother of how Finn had changed in such a short space of time. She'd described how almost overnight he'd transformed from the fun loving father and husband dedicated to nothing else but his family into a self-centred, money oriented bully, who had no time for anyone other than himself. She explained what had happened when she'd called at their house after receiving the call from Tomlinson's secretary.

"It all seemed to have begun around the time he cut himself," said Sophie.

"Did you ever find out what happened?"

Sophie shook her head.

"He's changed so quickly. He decided not to get his hair cut, and I've never seen it grow so fast. It seems like every day it grows another quarter of an inch. I mean it mum, he's changing not just mentally, but also physically. It's like he's a different person."

Grace understood what she meant. She'd seen him a few days earlier and hardly recognised him.

"You're welcome to stay with us until this is over."

Sophie hadn't mentioned the other things that had been happening in her house. She'd told her parents nothing of the visits from William, or the ghost of Robert Buxton and Rosie's strange drawings. She'd not wanted to worry them and now didn't seem the best time to mention it. Her mother had experienced enough supernatural nonsense with great grandmother Elizabeth, so the last thing she wanted her mother to know was that Rosie spoke with the dead, like Elizabeth had done.

"So, Finn acted differently after he'd cut his face" asked her father.

Sophie sat back and thought. She gazed at the ceiling and cast her mind back.

"No, it was before then. It was about the time he wore that awful ring."

"You mean the one that looks like it fell out of a Christmas cracker?" added John.

Sophie nodded.

"I wish it was from a cracker, I would have thrown it out. Do you know that thing is solid gold, 18 carat and it's covered in tiny rubies?"

John blew air through his cheeks.

"Wow, no I didn't. Where did he get it?"

Sophie told them the story of how he'd got it after Jack was born. John listened as she told him about the mystery antique shop.

"I'm not suggesting Finn's been lying to you Sophie, but your mother and I have lived around here for over forty years and I can assure you there has never been an antique shop on the high street."

Sophie shrugged her shoulders and wiped her eyes.

"I can only tell you what he told me. He seemed sincere at the time." She took another sip of water and continued. "He didn't wear it until recently, and I'm certain he changed the evening he put it on. He's not taken it off since."

Grace hugged her again.

"Mum, dad……. what am I going to do? I love Finn, and I want the man I married to come back. I want us to be happy like we were before."

"Perhaps he's having a midlife crisis?" suggested John, who was trying to be helpful. Grace shot him another glance and John lowered his head.

"I wish it was as simple as that dad. Shall I tell you what I think?" said Sophie looking to her mother, and then to her father.

"I think he's haunted."

Sophie hadn't wanted to bother her parents with the odd things that happened in her home, and what she'd said just slipped out.

"Haunted? By what?" blurted her father.

"By …… by, I don't know," stuttered Sophie. She wiped her eyes and continued.

"It's like something is haunting him from the inside. A spirit or something from the past. Oh, I'm not sure what I'm saying. All I know is that the person I saw on my doorstep yesterday wasn't my husband."

John stood up and turned to Sophie.

"I think the best thing you can do right now is give him some space. Let him work through whatever is happening. If it carries on for more than a few days you should seek professional medical advice. If he becomes violent towards you, make sure you involve the police. Don't deal with it on your own. Remember, we're here to help you."

She reached for her father's hand and squeezed it.

"I know dad, thank you. I appreciate it, I really do."

John's intentions had been good. But it would take more than a loving family to help Finn Maynard through what was about to happen to him.

Chapter 41

1st December

Ruth Jackson smiled at Gabriel Butler as he crossed the road from Kieran's old house. She did a double take when he opened Finn Maynard's garden gate and strolled up to his front door.

Her curiosity was getting the better of her.

Do these two know each other? she thought as she peered from behind her hydrangea.

Ruth ducked down when she heard Butler rapping on Finn's door.

She'd not seen the confrontation Sophie had had with her husband the other day and knew nothing of what happened when Finn told his wife he was Alexander Drake.

It took several attempts at rousing Finn before the door opened.

"Yes!" said Finn in an abrupt tone.

"Hello Finn, my name is Gabriel Butler, I've just moved in across the road and I need to make your acquaintance."

Finn viewed him with suspicion and didn't speak.

Butler offered his hand, but Finn declined to shake it.

"I see you have the ring. It's beautiful don't you think?"

Finn raised his hand and looked at it.

"What do you know about it?" asked Finn warily.

"There's a lot of things I know about what's been happening to you Mr. Maynard, or should I say Mr. Drake?"

"Carry on," replied Finn, wanting to know more.

"Would you be kind enough to invite me in? We have a lot to discuss."

He hesitated, but warmed to Butler's smile. Something about the man seemed familiar and Finn sensed he was someone he should trust, someone who was on his side.

Butler looked toward the sky, shielded his eyes against the sun and looked up at the raven which had appeared and circled the rooftops.

"Ah, I see our friend is in town," said Butler motioning towards the bird.

Finn took a few steps forward, stood alongside Butler on the garden path and watched the huge black bird as it soared out of view.

"It's beautiful," said Finn.

After a few seconds of awkward silence Finn invited Butler in.

Ruth Jackson popped her head up from behind the leafy hydrangea just as Finn's door closed.

She'd heard their conversation and was bursting with curiosity. She was desperate to tell someone what she had just witnessed, but knew she should keep this to herself. She was dying to know what was happening in her road.

Who was this stranger with the Rolls Royce and why had he moved into Tempest's house? He seemed to know Finn, but it was obvious that Finn wasn't sure who Gabriel Butler was. And why on earth would he refer to Finn as Mr. Drake? Was Finn Maynard hiding something?

Ruth Jackson was damn sure she would make it her business to find out.

Chapter 42

Heather was frustrated. It had been over a week since she'd seen and spoken with Charles Nash in the graveyard of St Michael on the Mount Without. Nash told her the same thing her great grandmother had said, that she'd been chosen for something big. Nash said that she was his protector and he needed protection from the worst possible evil imaginable and what was going to happen had begun. He said the wheels were in motion and nothing could stop them.

She rolled over in her bed and sighed. Heather couldn't concentrate on anything other than the strange things happening to her.

These ghosts were playing games with her. She was certain that Elizabeth and Charles were real and not her imagination.

Heather rolled over and looked up at the stone head. Nash told her she didn't need a channel to speak with him, she only required belief.

"I believe in you Charles, I've seen you, I've spoken with you. I definitely believe. Give me a clue, a snippet. Please, I need to know what this is about."

Heather glanced at the clock and sighed again. It was after two am. Lately Heather had been sighing a lot. The only person she'd told of the strange things was her sister. She was relieved when Sophie said she'd believed her about the visitation from Elizabeth and the voice of Nash. Heather had not spoken to her since and had told no one about seeing him in the graveyard.

Heather was playing a waiting game. Waiting for something big to happen. She'd been watching the news over the last few days in case there was any clue of impending doom which could be linked to what Nash hinted at when he referred to the 'worst possible evil'. Was Nash talking of a natural disaster such as an earthquake or a tsunami? Or was he referring to something crashing from heavens? Maybe a meteor strike. If so, how on earth could she stop such a thing?

"The worst possible evil?" she whispered to herself.

Earthquakes, tsunamis and meteor strikes are deadly, but they aren't evil, they are natural things. Evil is a predetermined act. Something that someone does with intent. Such as an evil dictator.

She pondered over history's evil leaders. The obvious culprits flit around her mind. Hitler, Pol Pot, Saddam Hussein. Heather thought she would have more chance of stopping an earthquake, tsunami or a meteor strike than an evil dictator.

The stress of what had been happening was affecting her. Heather had no appetite, and had to force herself to eat. Normally she didn't drink very much, but recently she'd drink a bottle of wine in an evening. Drinking wasn't doing what it should. Instead of calming her nerves, she became morose when intoxicated and her mind worked harder than when sober trying to work everything out.

Even though it was December, the night was unseasonably warm. It didn't help that she'd forgotten to turn off the central heating and on top of everything else, her hot bedroom was another reason she found it hard to sleep. The window was open, and she appreciated the waft of gentle breeze which filtered its way through and cooled her hot skin.

Heather had finished a bottle of wine before she'd gone to bed and now she was thirsty. The alcohol dehydrated her. She got out of bed for a glass of water. She stood in her bedroom and looked at Charlie with his permanent grin etched upon his stupid stone face.

"Come on mate, give me a clue. You need to help me out," said Heather, then made her way to the kitchen.

The instant Heather set foot in the hallway she felt cold. It hit her like an icy blast. She shivered and took a step back into her bedroom where she appreciated the balmy heat. She was confused. She put her arm out into the hall and goose bumps made the hairs on her skin stand up. Heather was tired and a little bit drunk, but not enough to imagine the change in temperature. Thirst ravaged her and she craved a cool glass of water, but it was far too cold to walk to the kitchen in just her pyjamas.

She grabbed her jeans from the floor and slipped them on. In her wardrobe she found a jumper.

She made her way to kitchen at the end of the hall. For every step she took, the temperature dropped a degree.

The kitchen door was shut. Heather pushed on the handle and was shocked by how cold it felt. The iciness stung her skin.

What on earth is happening?

The door swung open, and she was hit by such a blast of icy air, it made her hallway feel positively clement. Her small kitchen was as cold as the outdoors on a winter's evening.

She flicked the light switch, and instead of the white harsh radiance of the fluorescent light, the kitchen became lit by a dim orange glow which danced around the room.

But it wasn't her kitchen. She had walked into a shed, or an out-building. She shuddered as the cold permeated her jeans and jumper. Her bare feet tingled against the stone floor and hurt as small pieces of stone and grit stuck to her soles. Her eyes got used to the dim light, and as they did she saw two figures in the corner. She rubbed her eyes.

Could this be a sign from Charles?

She took another step closer.

The orange light which illuminated the stone building was coming from behind her. She turned around, but couldn't see its source. It was as if someone behind her held an oil lamp, or something which emitted a naked flame.

She looked at the two figures who were a few feet in front of her. They were talking, but she couldn't hear their words. She knew it was only a vision and was not scared in the slightest. She stepped forward and knelt to the level of the one sitting on the floor. Heather looked at the young woman. Her clothes suggested she was not from the 21st century. She appeared afraid, with her back against the hard stone wall of the building.

Heather instinctively moved back as the other figure swiped the young woman across the face with a riding glove. The other figure was male with his back to Heather so she couldn't see his face. She took another step back. Even though she was sure he was an apparition, he scared her, and she didn't want to get too close.

She watched them speak and was frustrated because she couldn't hear what they were saying. She watched the woman's lips and tried to work out what she was saying. Heather was behind the man and knew by his stance and his body language that he was perplexed.

He climbed to his feet, turned and faced the door. Heather gasped and placed her hand over her mouth when she saw his face.

"No!" she whispered. She couldn't understand why it was him.

He looked right through her. She watched his mouth move as he spoke and this time she heard his words.

"She's not going to talk. Mr. Morris, do your worst."

It was his face, but it wasn't his voice.

He passed through her. She turned as he left the building.

What the hell does this mean?

The man was her brother-in-law, Finn Maynard.

After Finn left the building a short ugly man holding a burning torch entered and stood over the woman.

Heather was horrified and rooted to the spot as the ugly man relentlessly and repeatedly kicked the defenceless woman.

Heather could hear her voice. She flinched as the woman screamed.

The short man, Morris, grabbed a lamp hanging from the beam and smashed it to the ground beside her. Oil splashed across the floor and onto the woman's clothes.

"You really should have told Mr. Drake where his children are," grunted Morris.

The woman looked at him and with a voice which conveyed both defiance and confidence, told him they were not his children.

Heather knew what was coming next, but she felt compelled to watch.

Morris dropped the flaming torch and took two steps back as the oil ignited and flames raced towards the helpless woman. He stood for a few seconds and watched her body thrash from side to side as the flames engulfed her. Heather watched the fire illuminate his grim face. She wasn't sure if she saw him smirk as the woman's life drew to a dreadful close. He raised his hands and warmed them against the fire which consumed the building. Morris turned and headed for the door, passing through the space which Heather occupied. The heat of the flames was punctuated by the chill of Morris passing through her.

The woman writhed with agony. Her eyes met with Heather's and gazed at her with a sad and tired look.

She can see me, she can actually see me.

The woman relaxed as if she accepted her circumstances and was at peace. And then she spoke.

"Heather, I'm sorry that you have to see this. I'm sorry that you witnessed my horrible death. I can assure you it happened a long long time ago and since then, I have found happiness because I did the right thing. I needed you to see what you are up against. You need to prepare yourself for the worst possible evil."

"Who are you?" asked Heather.

"My name was Alice, Alice Donaldson. And I died whilst doing my best to keep two special and extraordinary children from that man."

"Children? What children? And that man? He's Finn Maynard, my brother-in-law."

Alice shook her head. "It may have looked like someone you know, but I can assure you it isn't."

The heat became too much for Heather to bear. The smoke was getting to her. She turned to the door, longing for the cool air of the hallway from where she'd entered the strange stone building. She pulled at the door, but it wouldn't open. It wasn't her kitchen door, but the dilapidated wooden door of the farm building in which Alice was losing her fight with death. A smouldering wooden beam fell from above, trapping her behind the door.

The smoke took Heather's breath. Each gasp for air choked her. Over the crackling sound of the flames she could make out a repetitive thud. Her eyes stung, and she tried to focus on the door.

Heather phased in and out of awareness. The smoke and heat robbed her of consciousness.

The last thing she saw before she closed her eyes was the door crashing down and two tall figures wearing yellow helmets and a masks.

Chapter 43

Gabriel Butler left Finn's house just after three am. He'd spent the last nine hours explaining to a very confused, and at times angry Finn Maynard what was happening around him. Occasionally during the long meeting, Butler talked to his old friend Alexander Drake, and Drake spoke with Joseph Morris, but for most of the time Butler was trying to reason with Maynard and found it hard to pull Drake through Maynard's strong willed personality.

When Finn opened the door a stranger confronted him. But as soon as Butler mentioned the ring and referred to the raven as it flew above the rooftops, Finn connected with him. And as the initial short-lived connection happened, he saw a different person. Gone was the tall debonair gentleman sporting a Panama hat, and instead stood a short, squat, ugly man with a blue ink tattoo across his cheek. When he smiled Finn was shocked by his lack of teeth. As hideous as the man appeared, Finn warmed to him. There was something about him that gave him an overwhelming feeling of confidence, almost as if they could be brothers. He resisted the urge to throw his arms around the man and hug him. Instead, he'd invited the visitor into his home.

Finn closed the door and faced the stranger. The short ugly man with the tattoo was no longer there and instead stood the tall silver haired man from across the road.

"Take a seat in your lounge, I'll make us both a drink. What's your poison? Coffee or tea?"

Finn didn't answer. He sat in his lounge and tried to make sense of what was happening.

Butler stood in Finn's kitchen and watched the kettle come to the boil. Beneath the kitchen table lay a scattering of upturned sheets of paper. He closed his eyes and sensed the surrounding atmosphere. His long search was nearly over. He could almost smell the decay of the children's bodies as they lay over ten feet below. He'd taken a big chance when his short-lived construction company bought the land and built 11a Whitcombe Fields Road in the early eighties. It had been a leap of faith. But now, as he stood over the well in which lay the two hundred-year-old skeletons of William and Louisa, he was certain he'd been right. This was the reason he existed.

Butler placed the mug of tea on the table next to Finn and looked at his expressionless face. Part of him felt sorry for the pathetic man and part of him appreciated the strange transition he was experiencing. He understood that Finn was going through a period of confusion and doubt. He'd quickly transformed from the person he used to be to who he was now. Most of Finn

Maynard's original character no longer existed, other than brief lapses when he fleetingly reverted to the man he once was...... the man who would do anything for his family. But now, the Finn Maynard who perched uneasily on the settee was mostly a confident and outspoken man who would think nothing of treading over his fellow men to achieve his personal goals. Butler's first job was to rid Finn of the wretched vulnerable man he used to be, and make sure the new Maynard was here to stay. And after, he would work hard at transforming Maynard into his old friend and associate Alexander Drake. Then the fun would begin.

Butler had been close to giving up over the past thirty years as each male who'd lived in 11a proved not to be the chosen one, despite the connection by way of their suicides.

Each male who'd lived in that house needed to have connected by way of their death to the next occupant of the home.

Butler's wait was over. Finn Maynard was the one. Although, in fairness to those before him, Finn had had a head start. He'd seen Buxton's drawings of the first two patterns which had been confirmed as correct because they matched his ring, and the drawings made by his daughter. But, he had done what none of those before him had achieved. He'd been able to work out the mysterious third pattern. Finn wasn't aware it was he who'd drawn it, he had no memory of doing so. He'd subconsciously clicked away on his computer mouse whilst in a deep trance like state, when he should have been in a taxi on his way to the airport.

But it hadn't just been Finn, Buxton, Gosling and Morrison. There were two hundred years of men obsessed by figuring the patterns. Everyone had been chosen by either the present day Butler, or one of his earlier incarnations, and each had been a victim of their own self-inflicted demise.

"What's going through your mind? I expect you have many questions for me?" said Butler.

Finn looked up.

"As a matter of fact I do. I have one big fat question for you. What the fuck is going on?"

"Well, I guess that is the sixty four thousand dollar question isn't it? And it's one which I can't answer, well at least not in full, and not to you."

Finn looked at Butler with complete bewilderment.

"What's that supposed to mean."

Butler sighed and shook his head.

"Do you remember the person you were recently?"

"I don't follow you."

"It wasn't very long ago you were a typical family man with no great ambition. And now look at you. You were about to bag a deal in States for your company."

Finn sat bolt upright.

"Shit, the Goldman account in Washington." He checked his watch, "I should be there right now."

Finn stood up and became erratic, pacing around the lounge.

"I need to get to the States."

Butler raised his hands and gently lowered them, signalling Finn to calm down and take a breath.

"Don't worry, I'm sure Tomlinson will find a way of covering your ass."

"How do you know Tomlinson?" asked Finn suspiciously.

"As I said when you opened the door, there are many things about you which I know. I've been keeping an eye on you. I've been doing my homework. You see Mr. Maynard, you're like an investment. I've invested a fair bit of money and an awful lot of time in you."

Finn was agitated. He wanted answers, and he wouldn't be pissed around by a pensioner wearing a ludicrous hat.

"I'm going to count to three, and if you don't start talking I'll pick you up by your throat and throw you out of my home."

Butler stared at him and appeared completely nonplussed.

Finn took two paces towards Butler and started to count.

"One, two, three……"

On the third count he raised his hand to strike the elderly man, only to be taken by surprise by Butler's lightening reactions and overpowering strength.

Finn lay crumpled on the floor.

"Don't fuck with me Maynard. You've no idea who or what you're dealing with."

Finn rubbed his head and looked at Butler.

"Now get up, sit over there and drink you tea."

Finn did as he was told.

Butler unbuttoned the top of his shirt and showed a gold medallion.

"It looks familiar doesn't it!" said Butler.

Finn squinted his eyes.

Butler took a couple of paces closer.

"It's the same as my ring, it has the same two patterns," answered Finn in a weary voice.

"That's right. There are only four pieces of jewellery with these patterns. The ring you wear, this around my neck and two other medallions identical to mine."

Butler looked at his medallion as he held it in the palm of his hand. Finn watched him transfixed by the two ruby red circular patterns.

"They're archetypa," said Butler

Finn looked at him with a frown.

"We refer to them as archetypa, not patterns."

"We? Who are we?"

"Questions, questions, questions, Mr. Maynard. You are so full of questions. But I guess you have every right."

Butler sat opposite Finn and picked up his drink.

"Why don't you start by telling me a few things? I'd like to know what's been happening to you over the past few months," said Butler.

Finn nodded.

"Okay, but before I do, tell me about you. Who are you, I mean who are you really?"

Butler nodded.

"I've told you who I am, but in case you've forgotten within the last ten minutes, my name is Gabriel Butler and my company built this house."

"Drake-Butler," whispered Finn as he recalled the conversation he'd had with Kieran Tempest.

"Yes, Drake-Butler. That was my construction company. We didn't last long. In fact we only built one house," said Butler gesturing with his hand to suggest he was referring to Finn's home.

"You went out of your way to build this house?"

Butler nodded

"So you are aware of the things that happened on this plot when the original builders were constructing here, and I assume you also know of the suicides of those who lived here before me?"

Butler nodded again.

"And Mr. Maynard, I know that you were on the train that separated Robert Buxton's head from his body."

Finn rubbed his face. He had many questions but didn't know where to begin. He knew that Butler wouldn't be answering many of them today.

"Now, tell me what's been happening to you. I reckon you have your own story to tell," said Butler.

Finn let out a long sigh after he'd explained how he came by the ring, his daughter's drawings, the ghost of Robert Buxton and the young boy, William, he'd seen in the kitchen. He didn't mention the vision of the young woman in the bathroom. He kept that story close to his chest.

"One thing I'd like to know, which has been plaguing me for almost a year, …… how did I come by this?" asked Finn as he outstretched the middle finger of his left hand to show the ring.

"It's my understanding the owner of an antique shop on the High Street gave it to you. I believe it was a gift."

"But I seem to be the only one who remembers that shop. I've asked around town and no one can recall it ever being there."

"Oh it was there. The reason no one else saw it was because they're weren't tuned in like you," explained Butler.

"Tuned in?"

"Think of it like a radio signal. Do you remember when you had to tune in a radio by twiddling a little knob?"

Finn nodded apprehensively.

"Well think of it this way. When you visited the antique shop, you were a little 'out of tune' with the world. It was like you were between two radio stations. Imagine being able to hear Radio Three fairly clearly, but you can also hear a ghost of another radio station. If that happened, what would you do?"

"I'd turn the tuning dial, to get rid of the other station."

"Correct! And what happened to you on that day was a little like being tuned in between two radio stations, but instead of two stations, you were tuned between two very close universes."

"Like parallel universes?"

"Yes, compare it to what you know of parallel universes, if it makes it easier for you."

Finn nodded, but wasn't sure where Butler was heading.

"You see, the antique shop was there, but only for you. The shop was out of phase with everyone else, so only you could call in that day."

"What of the shopkeeper, was he real?"

"Yes, and he still is. He's my good friend Mr. Snow. He's another who has one of these," said Butler as he gestured to the medallion around his neck.

"So whatever is happening is some kind of set up, some kind of conspiracy."

"Oh, Mr. Maynard, conspiracy is such a nasty word. Think of it not as a conspiracy. Think of it more that we are pleased to have you aboard. There's something you have which my friends and I need."

Before Finn could open his mouth, Butler raised his hands to silence him.

"Let me show you something."

Butler pulled his wallet from his pocket and shuffled through a large wad of money. He muttered and cursed until he found what he was looking for.

He handed over a small picture which was a copy of an old oil painting.

Finn held the picture and took a while to understand.

"Familiar isn't it?" said Butler.

"It's me, where did you get it?"

"It isn't you. It's a copy of a painting almost two hundred years old."

Finn stood up and walked to the mirror in the lounge. He looked at the picture, then his reflection and back to the picture. He ran his finger along the scar on his face and looked at the scar on the cheek of the man in the painting. His chiselled jawbone was almost identical to Finn's. Finn had only recently discovered he had such a handsome appearance since he'd joined the gym and had trimmed his body by losing almost two stone. Finn's long dark hair with a streak of grey above his temple matched the image of the man.

"Are you saying that this isn't me?" asked Finn.

"Come come Mr. Maynard. You're an intelligent man, I'm sure you can work out who this is. I heard you refer to him earlier this week when speaking with your wife."

Finn thought hard about what happened. He struggled to remember.

Butler would have liked to help Finn remember the conversation he had with Sophie, but knew it was up to Finn to work it out for himself.

Slowly Finn recalled her calling through the letter box. She had been concerned for his wellbeing. He remembered how the sight of her repelled him. He'd been irritated by her being there. The clouds fogging his memory lifted and the recollection of their heated conversation became clearer. He remembered standing on the door step telling her he wasn't Finn. He recalled what she'd said

'If you're not Finn, then tell me who you are?'

He looked at the picture and concentrated. Then he remembered what he'd said.

'My name is Alexander. Alexander Drake. Now fuck off ....'

"This is Alexander Drake!" said Finn in an agitated tone of voice.

"Bingo!" said Butler accompanied by a slow patronising handclap.

"And he must be the father of William and Louisa, the children my daughter talks about."

"Wow, Finn. You're cooking on gas now."

Finn slouched on the settee and stared at the picture. He thought of the incident in the bathroom with the young girl who'd spoken of Drake's children. The more he thought, the wearier he became.

Butler was happy for Finn to take a rest. The evening had taken the wind out of the confused man's sails. Butler grinned as Finn's head dropped and he began to snore. He lit a cigar and watched the blue grey smoke fill the room. He chuckled as Finn twitched and fidgeted whilst he slept.

I wonder what strange dreams are filling your head right now? thought Butler.

Just over an hour later Finn stirred. Butler sat upright and straightened his collar.

Finn's eyes opened and he looked at Butler.

"Wakey wakey young man."

It took Finn a few seconds to remember what had happened before he'd fallen asleep.

Butler gave him a few minutes to come around and then he spoke.

"You've something for me, something I'd like to see."

Finn looked at him blankly.

"I've something for you?" he replied sounding vague.

"Yes. You have the third archetypon. You have two of them on your ring, and now you have the third."

Finn sounded groggy.

"Archetypon?"

"Yes, the third pattern. I know you've worked it out, otherwise I wouldn't be here talking with you."

"I remember working on patterns, but I don't recall…….."

Finn didn't finish what he was saying. He watched Butler jump up and move to the door of the lounge.

"Don't worry, I may have found it," said Butler, remembering the messy pile of A4 paper on the floor under the kitchen table.

Butler knelt beneath the table, scooped up the sheets of paper, turned them over and lay them on the kitchen table.

"This isn't right," he muttered to himself.

Each sheet had an attempt of the third archetypon, and each attempt had a cross. Just as Robert Buxton, David Gosling, Shaun Morrison and the others before them had done.

He stormed back to the lounge and dropped the papers on the floor.

"What's the meaning of this?" shouted Butler.

"Meaning of what?" asked Finn.

"These, they're wrong. You've not worked out the third archetypon."

Finn looked at the papers. He could vaguely recall working at the kitchen table. The past few days seemed as if he'd been in a morphine haze. His memory was clouded and muddled, only remembering brief snippets of what had taken place.

Butler was certain that Finn had worked out the elusive archetypon, the proof had been when he'd heard him refer to himself as Alexander Drake during the argument with his wife two days earlier. That could have only happened after Finn had seen it.

References to Drake, Alice Donaldson, William and Louisa would have infiltrated his mind from time to time, but to announce to Sophie that he was Alexander Drake could only have happened once he'd worked out the archetypon.

"Do you have another one, one without a cross? There must be one with a tick. Think man, think."

Finn felt like a schoolboy being intimated by the headmaster. He was confused and couldn't understand what he was supposed to do.

"Come on, think ……… concentrate. There must be one with a tick!"

"One with a tick," whispered Finn.

He closed his eyes. Suddenly the image of a pattern drawn in red flashed before him. He focussed with all his might and then he saw it again, and this time he caught a glance of the tick.

"Yes, I see it, I can see it in my mind."

"In your mind? It's no good there. We need it here, in front of us," demanded Butler in a raised voice.

"It's not on paper." said Finn.

"What do you mean, not on paper?"

"Shush, I'm trying to remember."

Butler became agitated and paced around the room. Finn raised his hand gesturing him to keep still.

"Let me concentrate, keep still, you're interrupting my thoughts."

Finn opened his eyes and glanced around the room, and then he saw it.

It had being lying there untouched since he'd put it down two days ago.

"Of course," he muttered.

He lurched over to the laptop, picked it up and lifted the lid.

Butler stood alongside Finn as he held the computer. The thing clicked and whirred into life.

The computer prompted Finn for his password and he stared at the incandescent screen.

"Bloody log onto the thing," insisted Butler.

Finn's mind was blank. He couldn't recall the password and stood shaking his head.

"My password, what's my password?"

"Is it your wife's name, or your daughter's?" shouted Butler.

Finn said nothing. He blocked out the sound of Butler's voice which geared up a notch every time he spoke.

Finn remembered receiving the laptop as a Christmas present from Sophie and he could recall setting a password that was topical. It had been a week after Christmas until he'd got the thing out of its box and set it up. His fuddled memory did him no favours.

"New Year's Day!" exclaimed Finn.

"What?"

"I set this thing up on New Year's Day!"

"Okay, try 112006," suggested Butler.

Finn shook his head.

"How about January06?"

Finn said nothing.

The two men stood in silence. Butler's patience wore thin, he bit his lip as Finn did his best to remember.

He recalled Rosie showing him the stone face she'd painted with Heather on New Year's Day.

He sat down, rested the computer on his lap and typed.

c h a r l i e 2 0 0 6

The little icon on the screen spun. Butler looked at Finn's face, lit by the pale glow from the laptop.

"Any luck?"

Finn didn't answer.

Butler watched the white glow reflecting in Finn's face change to red. Finn's pupils dilated as he gazed at the screen.

Butler took a pace forward, sat alongside Finn and looked at the screen. The radiance of what he saw was breath taking. He took the computer from Finn and placed it on his lap. A smile spread across his face as he gazed at what was in front of him. He ran his finger over the LCD screen in the spiral direction of the pattern. Years of searching were over. The old man swallowed hard as he struggled to hide his emotions. And then he spoke.

"Mr. Maynard you've done it, you've discovered the third archetypon."

Chapter 44

"You're a very lucky lady," said Doctor Newton as she examined Heather lying in the hospital bed. "Another few minutes and the smoke would have killed you," she added in a matter-of-fact tone of voice.

Heather's neighbour had called 999 after she'd seen smoke coming from the ground floor flat. The firefighters were breaking the door down within minutes. If it hadn't been for her neighbour, Heather would have died.

"What do you remember?" asked Grace, who sat beside her daughter holding her hand.

Heather had no intention of telling anyone what happened in the early hours of the morning. The memory of the young woman being physically and verbally abused by her brother-in-law and then kicked and set on fire by the other man were the first things she'd remembered when she'd regained consciousness in the hospital a few hours earlier.

"You're lucky the whole building didn't go up in flames," added her mother.

There would be an investigation to discover what had caused the fire, but the firemen were almost certain it had been due to a faulty gas oven. Heather was happy to go along with whatever the investigation found if it meant she didn't have to explain what really happened.

"You can stay with us until the insurance sorts out the mess in your flat. I reckon your place will stink of smoke for months," said her father.

Heather turned away from her parents and sighed.

She blocked out her parent's wittering voices and thought of Alice and what she'd said. She'd referred to Finn when she'd told her 'although the man who she saw resembled someone she knew, it wasn't that person'.

It's definitely my sister's husband, thought Heather.

The young woman told Heather her name was Alice Donaldson and she'd died whilst protecting two children from the man. The man who Heather was certain was Finn.

She visualised him in her mind's eye. He even had the same scar where Finn cut himself. There was no doubt in her mind.

"You have to leave now, visiting time's over," said the nurse pulling open the curtains around Heather's bed.

Grace kissed Heather on the forehead and told her they'd visit her again soon.

"Don't worry, we'll make room in our home for when you're discharged," said her father.

"But how? You've already got Sophie and the kids staying with you."

"We'll sort something," said Grace.

Heather watched her parents make their way out of the hospital and tutted to herself as her father searched his pockets for cigarettes.

The nurse was busy at her bedside.
"Put your finger in here please," asked the nurse as she prepared to measure her blood pressure.
Heather held out her hand whilst the nurse attached the monitor to her finger.
"One hundred and twenty over eighty, not bad," said the nurse removing the clip from Heather's finger.
Heather looked at the nurse and gave her a weak smile. She looked again and couldn't believe who stood next to her.
"Alice Donaldson," whispered Heather.
"Heather, please listen and listen carefully, I can't speak for long. What happened last night was real. But that man wasn't Finn. He's one of the men from whom you need to protect Charles Nash. He's coming back, and he needs Nash, and it's up to you to make sure he doesn't find him."
Although what was happening was surreal and unbelievable, Heather had experienced so many strange things over the last few months she accepted that Alice was real and talking to her. She'd also learnt that she needed to ask questions and demand answers.
"If not Finn, then who was it?"
"Alexander Drake. He died one hundred and seventy four years ago and was evil. His spirit is infiltrating your brother-in-law and will use him to do his work."
Heather blew air through her cheeks as she digested what Alice told her.
"And the children, what of them? You said something about keeping them from him?"
"Louisa and William, they're brother and sister. They're not his biological children. He took them on as his own after their mother was murdered."
"Murdered by Drake?" asked Heather.
"More than likely, but it wasn't proved."
A doctor made his way along the ward and Alice ducked down and attempted to look busy. When he'd passed she continued in a hushed voice.
"I discovered something on the eve of the children's fifth birthday, and after what I'd found out I had no choice other than to get them out of the house as soon as possible. I had no plan, I just took them and ran."
"What did you discover, what was Drake planning?"
"A sacrifice."
"He would have killed the two children?"
Alice nodded.
"Not just Drake, there were three others."
"But why?"
"It would have been a ritual. An offering which had it happened would've resulted in something so hideous I don't even want to contemplate it."

"But why those children?"
"They held a secret."
"What could they know, they were only children for God's sake?"
"It's not what they knew, it's what they had."
"Sorry, you've lost me, what could two five year olds have that would be worth killing them for?"
"It was a birthmark, they both had a mark on the back of their heads. But it wasn't just a blemish or a nevus, it was a pattern as if it had been carved into their bone. You could even see it through the thin skin covering their skulls."
"What would have happened if the sacrifice had gone ahead? What kind of evil are you talking of, and why I am supposed to protect Nash?"
The doctor walked back along the ward and Alice ducked again and pretended to adjust the sheets on Heather's bed.
When the doctor had gone Heather repeated the question in a hushed tone.
"Tell me about the sacrifice?"
"I beg your pardon?"
"The sacrifice, why would Drake do that?"
The nurse looked up with a worried expression and Heather saw that she was no longer Alice.
Heather let out a long sigh, apologised and explained that she felt confused.
"You need more rest Heather, you've had a nasty experience and your mind is mixed up at the moment," said the nurse plumping up the pillows.
Heather lay on her side and thought of what happened. She was convinced she wasn't losing her mind.
There was something of which she was certain. The next time, if there was to be a next time, that she spoke with either Alice Donaldson or Charles Nash, she wouldn't let them slip away until she'd found out exactly what was going on.

Chapter 45

"Don't worry, you'll soon get the hang of it," said Kieran through the window of the Porsche he'd bought for Linda.

Linda had been driving the high performance car around the empty car park for the past hour and a half.

"I had no idea how hard these things are to drive," said Linda as she gripped the wheel and looked over to her husband. "It's so different to the Mondeo."

"This car's a totally different beast, you're bound to find it strange at first. Don't give up, you'll be fine, I promise."

Linda wasn't sure it was a good idea for her to have such a powerful car. She was a nervous driver at the best of times. She'd appreciated her husband's good intentions when he'd surprised her with the keys to the gleaming red car, and she had to admit the surge of excitement at the time was overwhelming. She loved the registration plate HE11 BDG and thought it was a nice touch. But now, after a few attempts at driving, she thought she'd be better sticking with her eight year old Ford.

"This thing makes me nervous and I'm not sure how safe I'd be on the road."

"Well, it's too late to take it back now, and I'd lose a fortune if I sold it," said Kieran in a frustrated tone.

"Surely you'd get your money back if you sold it second hand, it's less than a week old."

"I've lost thousands just driving out of the showroom."

"Okay, I'll try to get used to it, but if not, I'd prefer not to have it," said Linda with a sigh.

Kieran looked grouchy.

"It's not as if we're poor!" said Linda. "And if you want my opinion, this millionaire malarkey is not what it's cracked up to be."

"What's that supposed to mean?"

"Oh, I don't know. Maybe it's the way you earned the money."

"Well, It's not as if I'd made it overnight."

"I don't trust Gabriel Butler. He's got his claws into you. He says 'jump' and you say 'how high'?"

"It's not like that at all."

"Really? You've been watching that house for over twenty years. And like a little arse licker you've been telling him of the comings and goings like 'a snake in the grass', ready to strike and report back to Butler the moment there was something new to squeal to him about."

"Linda, you make me sound as if I'm a criminal."

"All I'm saying is that he's paid you an awful lot of money to do very little, and I won't be surprised if he'll be back wanting more from you."

What Linda said had put him in a terrible mood. But deep down he knew she was right.

"Okay, move over, I'm driving this bloody thing back home," said Kieran opening the driver's door with a look of thunder on his face.

Chapter 46

Butler wiped a tear from his eye with one hand and gripped the sheet of paper with the other. What he held in his hand was something he'd been waiting for all of his life. And before his life, he'd been waiting for it for fifty-two years when he'd been Jonathon Trafford, forty-one years as Benjamin Stride and before Stride, as the original evil Joseph Morris.

Butler had asked Finn to print five copies of the third and all-important archetypon.

Having the archetypon in front of him wasn't the end of his search, it was only the beginning. There was plenty more to do.

"I know you're out there somewhere Mathias you little shit," said Butler under his breath. "Why couldn't you have just drowned when I dumped you in the pond like any normal kid would have done?"

He sighed, stood up, walked over to window and looked across to Finn Maynard's house.

"Don't worry, I'll flush out the bitch who's looking out for you this time around, and when I do, she'll wish she'd never been born."

Chapter 47

After considering her parent's offer, Heather accepted. She had little choice. Most of her friends didn't have enough room. Those who did where married with children, which made things awkward.

It would be weeks, or maybe months until she could go back to her flat. The fire in the kitchen had caused a lot of damage, not only to Heather's, but also the property above.

After being discharged from hospital she'd called to the fire damaged flat to collect a few things to take to her parents. The first thing Heather noticed was the bitter acrid smell left in the wake of the fire. She took none of her clothes, they were unwearable because of the pungent odour. She hoped the insurance would pay for a new wardrobe of clothes. She grabbed her laptop, a few books and DVDs which had not been damaged. She walked past her bedroom and saw Charlie staring at her from the bookshelf.

"I suppose you'd better come too," she said reaching up for the heavy stone head.

She cradled it in her arms and thought that something about if seemed different.

"Why are you so cold?" whispered Heather.

The stone had always emanated warmth as if it had an inner core heating it. Now it was icy to the touch.

Her father waited outside with the engine running as she locked up the flat. She made her way to the car with two plastic bags and Charlie.

Heather was greeted at the door of her parent's house by Grace, Sophie, Rosie and Jack. Grace and Sophie flung their arms around her, Rosie hopped up and down with excitement and Jack stared up from the floor with a look of indifference. John huffed as he carried his daughter's things from the car.

"It'll be a squeeze," said Grace, "but if you don't mind sharing a room with your sister and Jack, things should be fine."

"It will be like old times, having you two girls back in the house," said John with a smile.

Heather sat next to Sophie while their parents were in the kitchen.

"Sorry I didn't have time to visit you in hospital, and I'm sorry about what happened to your flat," said Sophie with a look of sadness.

"Don't worry about it, you've got enough on your own plate, let alone to be overly concerned about me."

The two sisters hugged and tears welled in their eyes.

"So what's happening with you and Finn, are things improving?" asked Heather.

Sophie burst into tears and Heather felt awful for saying the wrong thing.

Sophie wiped her eyes, looked at her sister and feigned a smile.

"I don't know what's happening to him. He's lost it, he really has. I've been back once since the episode on the garden path to collect a few of the children's things to bring here."

Heather put her arms around her.

"Mum and dad haven't told me much. What happened on the garden path?" asked Heather.

"It was awful. You should have heard what he said. He called me 'pathetic' and told me to 'fuck off'. You know Finn, it's not like him at all. I'm so worried for him. I'm sure he's having a breakdown and I can't be near him to help."

Heather held her and kissed the top of her head.

"He said 'forget about Finn, he's gone. He's dead,'" said Sophie fighting back tears.

"I asked him if he wasn't Finn, then who was he. Do you know what he said next?"

Sophie broke down in tears and couldn't continue.

"Shush," said Heather, "we needn't discuss it now, we can talk about it later. I'll be here for you."

Heather spent the rest of the day calling her insurance company to organise what would happen after the fire.

By nine o'clock the sisters were too tired to stay up and headed for bed. Sophie had been staying in her parent's spare double room with Jack, while Rosie had been sleeping in the small box room. Heather would share the double bed with her sister until her flat was repaired and ready for her to return.

Heather lay next to her sister in the quiet bedroom. The only sound was Jack snoring.

"I see you've brought that stone head with you," said Sophie.

Heather nodded.

"Don't tell Rosie, it freaks her out," she added.

Sophie turned and faced her sister.

"Does the head still speak to you?"

"If you mean Charles Nash, then no, I've not heard from him for a while."

"How about Elizabeth?"

Heather shook her head.

"Heather, did you really hear and see these things, or do you think it may have been, well you know......?" Sophie's voice trailed off. She chose her words carefully, but it was hard to not accuse her sister of being crazy.

"I don't blame you for thinking I'm mad sis, but I can assure you I really spoke with the dead. It's not something I want, it just happens."

"You'd told me you're supposed to be looking out for Charles Nash, and you needed each other. Have you found out anything else about what that's supposed to mean?"

Heather swallowed hard.

"Sophie, I'm about to tell you something, and I can assure you I haven't made this up. I've not heard from Elizabeth or Charles, but I have spoken with someone else. I'll tell you, as long as you promise you won't tell mum and dad. They've got enough to worry about with you and Finn, I don't want them worrying about me."

"Okay," said Sophie warily, "I promise."

"The fire in my flat, it wasn't caused by a faulty gas cooker. That will probably be what the report says, but it's not what happened."

Sophie looked at her intently without speaking.

"I'll not go through every detail, but the fire was caused by a vision."

"A vision like Elizabeth?"

"Not quite. When I saw Elizabeth, she stood in my flat and spoke to me. This was different."

Heather told Sophie of the young woman in the stone building arguing with a man.

"Why a stone building?"

Heather shook her head.

"I've no idea. I went to the kitchen and I saw them, but it wasn't my kitchen, it was an outbuilding, like a barn."

"Why were they arguing?"

"That's not important. What scared me was the man. It was your Finn!"

Sophie frowned.

"It was him in every detail, even the scar on his face and that grey hair across his temple."

"And you're certain it wasn't a dream?"

Heather nodded.

Sophie said nothing, she stared at the ceiling.

"What's on your mind?"

Sophie didn't answer, she continued to look blankly into space.

After an awkward silence that seemed to last forever, Sophie turned to her sister.

"I have a confession."

Heather didn't speak, which urged Sophie to continue.

"You're not the only one who's been seeing ghosts."

Heather lifted her head from the pillow as her ears pricked up.

"There're things happening in my house too."

"What things? Why didn't you mention this before?"

"I wanted to keep it to myself, but now I need to talk."

Sophie told her about Rosie's imaginary friend, who in the end, wasn't so imaginary after all.

"And there's another thing, when we saw the apparition of the little boy, I smelt the same odour you described."

"Fresh rain?" asked Heather.

Sophie nodded and sighed.

"And there's something else. A year to the day Finn was on that train……..."

"The one that killed the old man?" interrupted Heather.

Sophie nodded and continued. "A year to the day, Rosie saw a man in her bedroom and we're sure it was Robert Buxton, the man who died under the train."

Heather huffed air through her cheeks.

"This must be more than a coincidence. Do you think this is what's affecting Finn?"

"I think so."

"Sophie, this whole thing is getting out of control. We need to save Finn before he does something stupid."

Sophie hadn't told her sister of the run of suicides that had happened to those who'd lived in the house before, but it had been playing on her mind since Finn had told her that he was Alexander Drake. The day he'd announced Finn was dead, and he was someone else.

"Okay, tomorrow we'll go round to your place and speak with Finn, We'll try to reason with him, and perhaps dad could come too. He could provide moral support."

Sophie nodded, but was becoming tired and crotchety.

Heather was desperate to tell Sophie about what happened in the hospital when Alice Donaldson had appeared at her bedside. She was itching to tell her of Drake and the two children he'd planned on sacrificing over two hundred years ago.

But Heather said nothing. She looked at her sister who had fallen asleep.

The poor woman has heard enough for one night, thought Heather, *I'll tell her about Alexander Drake another time.*

Heather had no way of knowing how intertwined their lives had become.

Chapter 48

A knock at the door brought Finn out of a light slumber. He cursed, rolled off the settee and landed on the floor. He walked to the lounge window and saw Gabriel Butler at the door. Their eyes met and Butler greeted Finn with a smile.

"What the fuck does he want?" muttered Finn as he turned and walked to the front door.

"Hello young man, I thought we should carry on from where we left off last night."

Finn sighed and let Butler in.

"Besides, I expect you're hungry. I bet you've not eaten in days."

Butler held a carrier bag.

"What's in there?" asked Finn.

"Leave it to me, I'll cook us a hearty breakfast."

Finn slumped in a chair, stared out of the window at the hawthorn tree, and soon the smell of bacon and eggs wafted from the kitchen. His stomach gurgled. He couldn't remember the last time he had eaten.

He wandered into the kitchen just as Butler scooped an egg from the frying pan. Finn had to admit, the food looked and smelt fantastic.

Neither of them spoke as they ate at the kitchen table. He hadn't realised how hungry he was.

After they'd finished Finn sat back in his chair and announced he could eat another breakfast. Butler smiled, took the plates and placed them in the sink.

"Tell me Finn. What does this room mean to you?"

"Do you mean the kitchen?"

Butler nodded.

"It's just a kitchen, and nothing more," said Finn with the shrug of his shoulders.

"Really?" said Butler. "Have you not seen anything unusual?"

Finn knew Butler was referring to William and Louisa.

"Remember last night, the third archetypon?"

Finn nodded.

"And Alexander Drake, do you also remember that?"

Finn nodded again. He could vaguely remember.

"Finish your coffee and come with me. I have a surprise for you."

They crossed the road and got into Butler's Rolls Royce. Butler reversed onto the road and caught sight of Ruth Jackson from the corner of his eye, peering at him from her window.

Five minutes later they waited at the electric gates which slowly opened. He drove onto the gravel forecourt of the beautiful house and pulled up outside a large oak door. He glanced at Finn who admired the house through the car window.

"Shall we?" said Butler as he opened the car door.

Finn warily followed him. He stopped and surveyed the area. The building was huge, and the garden had been beautifully manicured.

"Is this your home?" asked Finn.

"It's where I normally live, and technically it's my home. But I like to think I'm just looking after it for someone."

"Who?"

"An old friend."

Butler unlocked the door and gestured at Finn to enter.

The instant he set foot in the hallway he felt it. He shuddered as familiarity hit him square between the eyes. Slowly he walked around the hall. He recognised each of the doors and knew the rooms behind them. He looked up and recognised the ornate plaster ceiling.

"What's happening, why is this place so familiar?" said Finn.

Butler smiled. "Take your time, just let it sink in."

Even the smell of the building was familiar. The sound of his feet on the wooden floor echoed along the hall. Finn closed his eyes and touched the newel post at the bottom of the stairs. He could hear the sound of children playing and their footsteps as they ran past him and up the stairs. He opened his eyes, expecting to see them, but there was no one there other than Butler.

Just being there evoked distant memories. He could recall lots of people busying themselves around the house. Maids carrying food from the kitchen to the dining room and familiar faces came and went.

"What is this place?" he whispered.

He walked upstairs and inspected the five bedrooms and three bathrooms.

Butler watched as Finn went from room to room, hoping to find an answer to why the place meant so much to him.

In his mind's eye he saw another room. A dark room, with no windows, lit by candles.

He made his way back downstairs and opened each of the doors along the hallway. He needed to find the dark room.

Butler looked from the stairs as Finn randomly flitted from room to room like a man who'd lost something.

His heart pounded, and he tried to recall where the dark room was. He stood in silence and placed his hand to his head and concentrated on the strange and distant memories which were surfacing to the forefront of his mind.

"Is something bothering you?" asked Butler in a slightly patronising tone of voice.

He didn't answer. He placed his hand against the wall and tapped with his fingers. The touch of the wall against his fingertips stirred another memory. He walked along the hall with his eyes closed, tapping the wall as he went.

He's getting it, thought Butler as he watched the frustrated and confused man work out what was going on around him.

Finn stopped. The feel of the wall at the end of the hallway seemed different. It had a hollow sound as he tapped it. He opened his eyes and looked at a wood clad partition.

"What's behind here?" demanded Finn.

"Open it," suggested Butler.

Finn couldn't find a way to open what appeared to be a door. Most of the downstairs hallway had been decorated in flock wallpaper, apart from the far end where Finn stood. The last twenty foot of the wall was clad with rustic oak. The wood sounded solid and dense as he knocked and tapped at it, but the sound had changed when he'd got to the end of the hall.

He stood rooted to the floor and tried to recall why this part of the hall seemed so important. He ran his hand up and down the vertical oak timbers.

He jumped back as one of the timbers moved as he touched it, and as it did, what appeared to be a hidden door opened an inch inwards. Finn pushed against the door which creaked and swung open.

A damp and mouldy smell arose from a dark staircase behind the door.

"You may need this," suggested Butler holding a small torch.

Finn peered through darkness and into a basement. He carefully made his way down wooden steps which groaned beneath his feet.

The torch wasn't casting enough light to be of much use. Finn caught sight of a few shadowy forms. He continued to shine the torch around the basement and Butler made his way behind him.

And then he saw it.

At first Finn thought he was seeing things. He took a step closer and shone the torch at it.

"Woah!"

He'd seen it before, but very much smaller. Butler had shown him a smaller version when he called to his house yesterday.

Butler entered the basement and struck a match.

"There's no electricity in here. No one's been in here for over one hundred and fifty years."

Butler lit candles which were placed around the cold and dusty room. The flickering yellow light cast an eerie glow as shadows danced from side to side.

Finn gawped at the painting hanging from the wall and shone the torch at the face of the man in the portrait.

"It's the same picture you showed me the other day, the one from your wallet."

Butler nodded.

The strange things that had been happening had affected his memory. Everything he tried to recall was vague and without clarity as if they had happened in a distant dream.

He looked at the image of the man and was drawn to the scar on his face. There wasn't much about Finn that was different to the man in the painting, other than his nose was a little wider and his brow heavier set.

"Do you remember who I told you he is?" asked Butler.

Finn nodded.

"Alexander Drake."

"Take a look at this," said Butler as he walked to the middle of the basement.

A discoloured sheet covered a circular table.

Butler removed the sheet to show the table swathed in a blue velvet cloth which overhung the table by about three feet.

Finn walked around the table and the first thing that struck him were the two red circular patterns etched into the fabric of the cover overhanging the table.

"The two archetypons," said Finn.

"Archetypa, the plural is archetypa."

"The two archetypa," repeated Finn comparing them to his ring.

"And this should have been embossed here," said Butler as he held the third archetypon which Finn had discovered the other day, and pointed to the other side of the cover.

"Unfortunately time wasn't on our side to have this added to that beautiful cover, it would have finished it nicely," said Butler in a light hearted voice. "And had we added it to the cover way back then, we wouldn't have been in the predicament we are now. But since you've worked so hard and have found the third one, we can move forward and complete what we should have finished just over two hundred years ago."

On the table were three ornate carved wooden boxes. On the top of each box lay a blue cushion. Each cushion was stitched with a pentagram.

The instant Finn saw the cushions he knew what they were.

"Do you remember now?" asked Butler.

Finn ran his finger over the table and nodded.

"This was my home."

"It still is, I've just been looking after it for you."

Finn looked at Butler but he was no longer there. In his place stood a short man, with a blue ink tattoo across his cheek.

"Joseph Morris!" said Finn and stared in disbelief.

"Alexander my friend, welcome home."

Morris pulled up a chair and Drake sat down. His legs shook as he took on board what was happening.

"Joseph. You've done it, you've really done it," said Drake.

Morris flashed a toothless smile.

"And which poor bastard has had to put up with me infiltrating their life?" asked Drake.

"Finn Maynard." replied Morris and handed him an old mirror from the corner of the basement.

Drake took the mirror, wiped away the dust and looked at his reflection. The dim candle made it difficult to see his face in detail, but there was enough light for him make out the uncanny resemblance to when he was alive in the nineteenth century.

"He's rather handsome," whispered Drake.

Morris smiled and took back the mirror.

"It's taken a long time to find the right one. But there's no mistake, Maynard is our man. He's the one who worked out the third archetypon."

Morris handed the paper to Drake.

"So with this you will be able to find Mathias, providing he's still out there somewhere," said Drake.

"Don't worry Alexander, he's out there. And since I've had the third archetypon I've picked up a few vibrations. It's already drawing me to him."

"If you hadn't fucked up in the first place we wouldn't be where we are now," said Drake in a raised voice.

Joseph Morris dropped his head and took a step back.

"I know, and now I'm aware of how stupid I was. I panicked and I should have remained calm. After it was obvious William and Louisa were dead and after I'd killed Alice I thought we no longer needed Mathias. I thought everything had been ruined."

"So you dumped him in the village pond!"

"But as soon as I realised we may still need the boy I went back. I looked for his body, but it wasn't there. Alexander, there's no way he could have survived. He was five years old, and that pond was frozen. I'd dropped him through the ice, he disappeared under the water."

Drake shook his head.

"Well, whatever happened he'd gone. Whether he'd crawled out, was saved or was pulled out dead, he wasn't there when you went back...... and therein lies the problem."

"But with the third archetypon I'll find him."

"What month is it?" asked Drake.

"December."

"Well Mr. Morris, you have weeks, maybe only days."

Morris nodded.

"You've got your work cut out too Alexander."

"I know. Do you know exactly where they are?"
"They're beneath Maynard's house."
"How can you be certain?"
"Alexander, I'm sorry I fucked up with Mathias, and I'll put things right, but you need to believe me when I say how hard I've worked to find those kids and I can pinpoint where they are."
"But the problem is that when I leave this old house, Finn Maynard will return, and to him I will be nothing but an echo. I'll be a vague memory rattling around the corridors of his confused mind."
"You'd be surprised how easy he is to manipulate. Don't forget, he's the only one who worked this out," said Morris holding the third archetypon.
"Okay, we'd better get to work. Take me back to his house and I'll get started."
The two old friends climbed the stairs and left the basement.
"What about Donaldson, the nanny?" asked Drake.
"She's still around in one form or another," replied Morris.
"Don't underestimate that woman. She's trouble."

Drake stood next to the Rolls Royce and Morris loaded a bag of tools into the boot.
Even though he was only twenty yards from his house Drake was becoming confused. Morris' appearance morphed between the short squat man and the tall handsome pensioner and the memory of his conversation with Morris five minutes earlier was fading.
"Okay Mr. Maynard, it's time I took you back to your house. You've got an awful lot to do."

Chapter 49

Heather sat alone in her parent's house. Sophie had gone out with Jack, Rosie was at school and John and Grace were at the cinema.

She lay on the bed and contemplated what Alice Donaldson told her in the hospital. Frustration consumed her. She'd had enough of 'peekaboo' ghosts who had a habit of materialising, tempting her with snippets of information and then vanishing back to wherever they came. She needed to understand what it meant when she'd been told she was Charles Nash's 'protector'.

Alice Donaldson mentioned a sacrifice which would have happened had she not taken the two children from Alexander Drake. What the hell did she mean? A sacrifice? Heather conjured up images of ancient rituals and the scenes she'd expect in a Hammer Horror movie. Heather desperately wanted to speak with either Alice, Nash, Elizabeth or the mysterious old lady in the heavy winter coat she'd seen in the graveyard, when she'd experienced what Elizabeth referred to as 'a happening'.

She remembered Elizabeth telling her how she'd used a channel to contact those who'd passed over, and that the channel that worked for her was a small cross which hung from a chain around her neck. Charlie, the stone head, was the only thing Heather considered as a channel. Even though Nash told her all she needed was belief and a channel wasn't necessary.

"I guess there's no harm in trying," whispered Heather as she rolled off the bed and reached beneath for the head.

She placed it on the duvet and knelt down so she was opposite the grotesque face and staring into its eyes.

She wasn't fussy about who she spoke with, whether it be Elizabeth, Charles, Alice or the old lady. As long as one of them gave her the answers she desperately needed.

She placed her hands on Charlie's head and closed her eyes.

Nothing.

She tried again and this time she pleaded for help.

"If any of you can hear me please let me know. Alice, you've told me so much, but I need to learn more. And Charles, if you need protection, please tell me what I need to do. You're already dead, so in God's name what do you need protecting from? I don't understand."

She paused for a second and thought of her great grandmother.

"Elizabeth, please. We're flesh and blood, please do your best to guide me. I'm so lost and need your help……. Please!"

Heather dropped to the bed, her hands still gripping the stone

The head felt different. She'd noticed it yesterday when she'd taken it from her flat. It was cold to the touch, as if it was dead.

She stared at the ugly head and considered the strange things that had happened.

Why me? Why am I so special you chose me for such an epic task, and one which I know nothing about?

She sat on the bed and lugged it on to her lap.

"Somebody please speak to me!"

There was no reply. Then she became struck with a notion.

Other than the visit from her great grandmother and the first time she'd known of Charles Nash, all the really odd stuff had happened since Charlie had been on the scene.

"Maybe this your fault?" she said looking at the head.

"How can I trust you? How can I be sure you're not the evil one?"

If Nash was correct, and she didn't need a channel, was there any reason to keep Charlie? The ugly thing scared her and wasn't making contact with any of the four spirits any easier.

She sighed and decided what to do with it.

"Sorry Charlie old boy, it's time for you to go."

She bundled the head into a carrier bag and carried it downstairs.

"Let's go for a ride."

She left the house and made her way to the bus stop and hopped aboard the bus which took her to Clifton. She got off the bus at Durdham Downs and walked to the Clifton Suspension Bridge intending to throw the thing over the side and watch it plunge seventy five metres to the muddy water flowing below.

What Heather had in mind would not go according to plan.

Chapter 50

Linda Tempest was late for an appointment with the beautician. Since she and her husband had become millionaires, she had decided to spend some money on herself.

She looked older than she should and hoped that a meeting with one of Bristol's top beauticians would suggest a few pointers to shave a few years off her tired face.

She closed the door of their new five-bedroom house and hurried to the Mondeo which stood on the drive.

The red Porsche Kieran had bought her had been in the garage for the past ten days. The car was far too powerful, and she didn't feel confident behind the wheel.

She jumped into her trusty Ford and turned the key.

'Click'.

She tried again.

'Click'.

And again.

'Click, click, click, click'.

"Shit! The battery's dead," she cursed under her breath.

She looked at her watch. There wasn't enough time to call a taxi and she hated travelling on buses. She wasn't going to cancel the appointment.

She looked at the garage door and huffed air through her cheeks.

This will be a baptism of fire, she thought as she contemplated driving the Porsche.

She opened the garage and saw the gleaming car with the top down. She'd owned it for less than two weeks and it only had thirty-five miles on the clock. She had to admit, it was a beautiful looking thing.

Reluctantly she got in and started the car. The throaty engine made her shudder as it echoed around the garage.

She put it into gear and slowly lifted the clutch. Gently, she inched it forward and out of the drive.

"Be confident Linda, for God's sake it's only a car," she told herself out loud.

She did her best to ease it onto the road, but found it difficult not to let the thing run away with her. Luckily there was nothing coming either way, and she headed along the tree lined road ahead of her.

A man on the pavement sniggered and watched the terrified woman gripping the steering wheel with all her might.

Her appointment was in Clifton, and from the direction she was coming, the quickest route would be a quick jaunt over the Clifton Suspension Bridge.

She became more used to the car, but still lacked confidence as she cautiously drove towards the bridge.

She pulled up at the toll booth, tossed the coins into the basket and waited for the barrier to rise.

She lifted the clutch and the car jerked forward. She looked to her right and saw the city and the River Avon flowing below. She didn't like heights at the best of times and having the responsibility of getting the Porsche to the other side and being two hundred and forty-five feet above the water was too much for her.

The car lurched across the bridge, veering from left to right, nearly scuffing the safety barriers which separated pedestrians from cars.

Eventually, she crossed the bridge. She stared at her white knuckles as they clenched the steering wheel. She let out a sigh and continued her journey to Clifton.

Chapter 51

The red car took Heather by surprise as it headed towards her. She jumped to her left just before it mounted the kerb, missing her by only a few inches. As she leapt clear of the Porsche, she instinctively lifted her arms, and in doing so lifted the carrier bag, which ripped causing Charlie to drop onto the bonnet and roll to the ground, leaving an ugly dent in the beautiful body work of the car.

Heather dropped to the floor, twisting her ankle as she fell.

Linda shut off the engine and jumped out.

"My God, are you okay?"

Heather didn't answer, she was too shocked to speak.

Linda gasped at the damage then caught sight of the stone head on the road. The instant her eyes met with the dent she knew the woman had dropped the rock onto her car.

Kieran will kill me, she thought whilst staring at the dent and the scraped paintwork.

Her attitude changed in a heartbeat and she went into defensive mode.

"Do you know how much this Porsche is worth? It's virtually brand new. This will cost a fortune to repair."

Heather paid little attention as she rubbed the side of her ankle.

"I want your name and address young lady as I'll be sending you the bill."

Heather came to her senses and stared at the red-faced woman who was fuming with rage.

"What are you talking about? You ran me off the pavement. You're a bloody lunatic."

"And you threw that bloody rock at my car."

A heated argument followed and a group of people laughed at the two women brawling in the road.

"I'm taking this as evidence," said Linda stooping down and picking up Charlie.

"No, you leave that alone, you've no right to take it," shouted Heather.

Linda held the stone head and gawped at the painted face.

"What the fuck is it?"

"Give it back," shouted Heather.

Linda became mesmerised by the thing. She felt how warm it was in her palms. After a few seconds it was too hot to hold.

"What the hell is this thing?" she shouted and dropped it onto the passenger seat.

"It's none of your business. Give it back."

"This is evidence!"

"Evidence of what?"

"Evidence you used this thing to wreck my car. My husband will kill me, and it's your fault."

"Never mind your husband killing you, you very nearly drove into me."

Linda saw a policeman approaching in the near distance.

"You're lucky I don't report you," said Linda jumping back into the car.

"Oi! Where are you going?" called Heather as Linda started the engine. Linda didn't answer.

Heather watched the Porsche speed away with Charlie in the front. She shook her head and watched the policeman approach, pulling his notebook from his pocket.

Chapter 52

Gabriel Butler checked the time. It was only eight thirty in the morning. He knew Finn would be exhausted after yesterday.

Finn wasn't coping well with what was happening. He wasn't eating and his personal hygiene left a lot to be desired.

Since he'd discovered the third archetypon he'd been living a hazy existence between waking and sleeping. The transformation into Alexander Drake hit him for six.

Now he was back at Whitcombe Fields Road, Butler guessed Finn would be groggy and disoriented. But time was running out. There was little time until the next window of opportunity to recreate what should have happened on the 14th December 1804.

At nine 'o clock, Butler marched across the road and banged on Finn's door carrying a tool bag and a pick axe.

Finn looked weary as he opened the door.

"Oh, it's you," said Finn rubbing his eyes.

"Can I come in, please?" asked Butler pushing past Finn and dropping the bag and axe on the floor.

"What are those for?" asked Finn.

"All in good time. But first, have a wash." replied Butler with his hand over his mouth to block out Finn's body odour.

Finn obediently did as he was told and slumped upstairs to the bathroom. Butler made coffee in the kitchen.

Ten minutes later Finn returned looking brighter. He wore the same clothes he'd had on for almost a week.

They drank coffee at the kitchen table.

"What do you remember of yesterday?" asked Butler.

"Not very much."

"Do you remember the big house yesterday?"

With a frown, Finn nodded.

"Do you remember going inside?"

Finn gazed into the middle distance and nodded again.

"The big house? Yeah, I remember the big house."

"But do you remember the basement?"

Finn concentrated and shook his head.

This was what Butler had expected. Finn's memories of Drake wouldn't last long. It would take time to draw the spirit of his old friend Alexander from Finn. It was something which must be done, otherwise the hard work over the past two-hundred years would be wasted.

"Yesterday I asked you whether this kitchen meant something to you. Does it stir any memories, does it make you think of anyone or something specific?"

Like yesterday, Finn knew Butler was referring to the ghosts of William and Louisa.

"Stand next to me," said Butler.

Finn reluctantly got up and stood next to Gabriel.

Butler closed his eyes and could sense the bodies of the children beneath his feet. He could feel the fear they experienced the day Alice Donaldson took them from their home. Their sadness overwhelmed him.

"Finn, take my hand."

"Why?"

"Just do it!"

Finn held Butler's hand.

"Now close your eyes and concentrate."

Finn shut his eyes.

Butler channelled the emotions and pain of the two children. Finn winced as he experienced the same sorrow and anguish racing through the core of Gabriel Butler.

Finn pulled his hand away.

"The children, they're here, they're with us now," said Finn.

"It's your job to get them out of there. Relieve them of their pain and sorrow, they need to be free," said Butler.

"But they're dead, I can't free them."

"Are you sure?"

He recalled seeing the vision of William the day he played with Rosie. He remembered how sad he looked. William said his sister was too scared to come out and play.

"They need your help Finn, it's up to you."

"I can't do it, I just can't do it."

"Why? All you need to do is dig. I can assure you that you'll find them."

Finn shook his head.

"What would it take?" asked Butler.

"What do you mean?" replied Finn in a tired voice.

"I'm talking about money, how much?"

Butler was appealing to Finn's mercenary side, which lately had waned because of the strange things happening to him.

"I'll tell you what Mr. Maynard, I'll give you fifty thousand pounds in cash if you break your way through the foundations of your house and find the bodies of those children."

The easy money tempted him.

"All I have to do is dig for their skeletons?"

Butler nodded.
"I'll do it for one hundred thousand."
"I'll give you seventy five and not a penny more."
They shook hands on it and Butler noticed a sparkle in Finn's eye.
"When do I start?" asked Finn.
"There's no time like the present."

Butler stood back and Finn moved the kitchen table to one side. He pulled up the vinyl flooring and used Butler's the crowbar to yank up the floor boards.

From the hallway he watched as Finn wrenched the boards out of their place and discard them to the side of the kitchen as if he was possessed.

Butler knew that in order for his scheme to work, Finn had to be the one to find the children, although by the time he'd reached the bodies he would no longer be Finn. Alexander Drake would have completely taken over.

Butler had no intention of paying him. By the time he discovered the bodies, Finn would no longer exist.

Butler leant against the kitchen door and considered what he had to do. Even though he possessed the archetypon, he had no idea where to look for the body of Mathias Morris.

Chapter 53

"What were you thinking you stupid woman? Do you have any idea how much it will cost to repair?" shouted Kieran.

"I don't know why you're getting so mad, it's not as if we can't afford it," snapped Linda.

When she'd returned home after running Heather off the road, Linda put the Porsche back in the garage, closed the door and wondered what to do next.

She'd spent the evening fretting and pacing around the house worrying about how her husband would react when she told him of the accident.

Eventually she'd plucked up courage and explained what had happened.

"So what you're telling me is that the woman who you almost drove into, threw the rock at the car?" asked Kieran whilst stroking his chin.

"More or less," replied Linda.

"You need to find her, we need to get to her pay for the damage. Why didn't you get her address?"

Linda was aware she didn't have a leg to stand on. The accident was her fault and Heather accidently dropped Charlie on the bonnet when she'd jumped out of the way.

Linda didn't know Heather was Sophie Maynard's sister. Although Heather visited her sister many times neither Linda nor Kieran had ever seen her in Whitcombe Fields Road.

"Is that the rock the woman threw at the car?" said Kieran pointing to Charlie and asking the obvious.

Linda nodded.

She leaned in and picked up the head to show Kieran.

"Ouch!" exclaimed Linda.

"What now?" snapped her husband.

"It's hot, I mean red hot," she replied blowing on her hands.

Kieran pushed passed her and touched it.

"What do you mean, 'hot'? The thing's stone cold."

"Stone cold, is that meant to be a joke?"

"Check it for yourself, it's not hot in the slightest."

He placed it in her palms.

"Ow, it's burning!" said Linda tossing it back in the car.

Kieran turned to walk away.

"Don't piss around. Find the woman who damaged the car. I'll make her pay," he said, and left Linda alone in the garage.

"What are you?" said Linda to Charlie.

Was it an accident that Charlie fell into the hands of Linda Tempest? Or was it part of the grand scheme of things?

Chapter 54

"So you got rid of Charlie?" said Sophie gripping her mug of coffee in the lounge of their parents' house.

Heather nodded.

"I regret it now, but you need to understand that yesterday I'd had all I could take. I'm not sure whether you understand the things that have happened, and to be honest Sophie, I don't care. But the fact of the matter is the strange things that have occurred have happened since Rosie and I painted that rock."

Heather took a sip of coffee, wiped a tear and continued to tell her sister what happened the day before.

"I'd decided to get rid of the head because I'm certain it's behind what's been going on."

Sophie said nothing. She wanted her sister to get everything off her chest. She had enough of her own problems to contend with, but needed to be there for Heather during what appeared to be a breakdown and obsession with speaking with the dead.

"I've not told you this, but since Rosie and I created Charlie, the stone emanated warmth, as if it was alive. Sometimes I really believed it was. But when I took it from my flat to bring it here, the warmth had gone, as if Charlie had died."

"So you threw the rock off the Suspension Bridge?" asked Sophie.

"That was my plan until the crazy woman in the sports car nearly drove into me. We ended up rowing, and she drove off taking Charlie with her."

Sophie reached over and took her sister's hand.

"I'm sorry to bother you with everything that's been going on in my life, but I need to tell someone. I don't want to bother mum and dad, and you're the only person I can talk to."

Heather felt Sophie squeeze her hand. She couldn't blame Sophie for not believing her. She had no proof to back up what she'd been telling her.

"The most infuriating thing about these ghosts, is none of them tell me what's happening. Even Elizabeth seems to play games with me. They only give me snippets of information and tell me how important I am and that I've been chosen to protect someone who's dead from a terrible evil……., and also something about a sacrificial ritual with children."

What Heather didn't fully appreciate was how hard it was for Elizabeth, Charles, Alice and the old lady in the graveyard to materialise. It drained them of their energy just to stand before her and it took considerably more to communicate with her. It was as equally frustrating for the ghosts as it was for Heather.

Sophie shuddered. Her sister was coming out with macabre talk of evil and sacrifices. Heather needed professional help and counselling. She was going along with her story while doing her best not to sound patronising.

"Do you think you need to stop the sacrifice of children?"

"I don't know, I mean I guess so. I only get to hear part of the story before the ghosts disappear. Although, there's something of which I'm certain, the children who Alice told me were to be sacrificed, died long ago."

"Alice, who's Alice?" asked Sophie.

"Alice Donaldson, a ghost who visited me the other day in the hospital."

Heather had Sophie's attention.

"Alice Donaldson, did you say Alice Donaldson?"

Heather nodded.

Sophie trembled, let go of her sister's hand and stood up.

She recalled the night Finn had been talking to himself in the bathroom. It was when he'd really changed and become more out of character than ever before. He'd told her he'd been talking to someone called Alice Donaldson. He'd mentioned children. Something about them not being his children.

Suddenly her attitude towards her sister changed. She paced around the room and remembered Rosie's imaginary friends. Her friends who were perhaps not so imaginary.

"Heather, what did Alice Donaldson say about the children?"

"They were brother and sister. She'd helped them escape on their fifth birthday."

"Escape from who?"

"Their father, although he wasn't their father."

Sophie cast her mind back to Rosie's picture. The picture of kids in the well, a burning woman, and children in a handcart chased by dogs. She remembered Rosie told her the woman in the fire was Alice and she was their nanny.

Sophie rubbed her forehead and swallowed hard as the enormity of the situation sank in.

She turned to Heather, and in a hushed and wavering voice she spoke.

"Heather, the children……… their names………., I know their names."

Heather stared at her sister, whose pallor changed to a light shade of grey.

The silence seemed to last forever as Heather waited for her to speak. She watched Sophie's lips tremble as she formed the words she was about to say.

"The children……., William……., William and Louisa. Their names are William and Louisa aren't they?"

Heather nodded and flinched as Sophie's coffee mug smashed to the floor after dropping from her hand.

Chapter 55

Ruth Jackson awoke to a thud. She rubbed her eyes and checked the clock. It wasn't even seven thirty.

And then another thud. And another, followed by another.

Thud – thud – thud – thud.

Slow and regular as a pendulum. A thud so loud that her bed shuddered and her window rattled.

She got up, threw on her dressing gown and peered from the window overlooking her back garden. She couldn't see where the noise was coming from.

Thud – thud – thud – thud.

She marched out of the room, across the landing to the front bedroom overlooking the road. She'd expected to see council workmen digging, but there was no one there.

It continued.

Thud – thud – thud – thud.

Ruth wasn't a morning person. Since she'd retired, one of her luxuries was hours of uninterrupted sleep. She normally woke around nine, so to be wrenched from slumber at such an unreasonable hour angered her.

Downstairs it was even louder.

Thud – thud – thud – thud.

Her hands clenched the kitchen worktop as the floorboards juddered.

And then it stopped.

She relaxed her grip as the tension in her body lessened. She waited in anticipation for the sound to continue, but it didn't.

"Thank God that's finished."

She poured cereal into a bowl, threw on a splash of milk and took it to the lounge. She was about to put the spoon in her mouth when she heard voices.

Peering out of the window she saw the top of Gabriel Butler's head above the fence.

"What's going on," she muttered.

“Good morning Finn, I can hear from across the road that you’ve started early this morning. Good man!”

Finn stood at the door. His hands and face where filthy and he had an old T-shirt wrapped around his head to keep his hair away from his eyes.

“May I come in and inspect your work?”

Finn opened the door and Butler followed him into the kitchen.

“You have been busy. You should open the back door, it’s warm in here.”

He did as Butler suggested.

The cool air of the early morning was good.

Butler surveyed the kitchen.

Floorboards were removed and lay in the hallway. Finn had left enough boards remaining to allow him to walk around the edge of the kitchen.

He had cut and removed the rafters which had supported the floorboards. Luckily there were no gas or water pipes beneath, which had given him space in which to work.

He'd started to break through the concrete foundations, but made little headway as the concrete was hard work. He had over a metre to get through before he’d make it to the hard-core below, and once he had cleared it, his job of finding the bodies would begin.

Ruth returned to her kitchen and wondered what was happening. Strange noises early in the morning and neighbours knocking at such an unearthly hour. Her inquisitive mind was getting the better of her.

She took her empty breakfast bowl to the kitchen and placed it on the work surface. She stopped in her tracks and cocked her head to one side.

Voices. She could hear voices. It was Finn and Butler talking in Finn's back garden.

She opened the kitchen door and strained to listen.

She tiptoed into the garden and ducked behind the fence which separated their gardens.

“You’ve made good progress,” said Butler.

Finn nodded.

“Once you’re through the concrete and the shit below, you’ll be down to the clay and the rock. Compared to what you’re digging through today, it should be easy work.”

“It’d better be! How deep will I have to dig?” asked Finn.

“That's anyone’s guess, they've been there over two hundred years.”

Finn cursed under his breath

"Don't forget young man, I'm paying you seventy-five thousand pounds. Even if you take days or even weeks, it's good money for little work," snapped Butler.

Finn nodded again, wiped his forehead and stepped into the garden. The air was damp, and it felt good against his hot skin.

Ruth ducked even further below the fence when she heard his footsteps on the gravel.

"What happens if I find them?" asked Finn.

"It's not if you find them Mr. Maynard, it's when you find them."

"Okay, so what happens when I find them?"

Butler stared at him with a look of pure evil.

"I want you to come and get me as soon as you find the bodies. And you need to be careful. When you find their skulls you mustn't damage them, and I mean not even a scratch. I need them in perfect condition. If you make so much as a mark on them, you won't be paid a penny. Do you understand?"

"Okay, okay I get it," said Finn shaking his head.

"What about their bones? Don't you want their skeletons?"

"No. You can throw them to the dogs. It's just the children's skulls I need, and the sooner the better, so I suggest you stop talking and dig."

Deep down Finn knew where he'd discover the bones. He'd find them in a well right below his house. Just where his daughter's drawing had depicted them to be.

Ruth Jackson huddled behind the fence with her hand over her mouth. Her heart beat loudly in her head and her body shook. She couldn't believe what they'd said.

She considered what to do next. Ruth knew she should call the police. But something deep inside urged her to wait it out. Intrigue and curiosity gnawed at her and she was desperate to know why the elegant and dashing mysterious man needed the skulls of two-hundred-year-old bodies buried beneath her next door neighbour's house.

Chapter 56

Sophie found it hard to take on board what her sister had told her the night before.

They had talked in hushed tones until the early hours. Heather had told her everything that happened since the first encounter with Charles Nash until the recent apparition of Alice Donaldson in the hospital.

Sophie had listened with disbelief when she'd heard of the resemblance of the man in Heather's vision to Finn and shuddered when he'd ordered Alice to be killed by Morris.

What scared her the most was Finn's connection with what was happening. She needed to find out his association with Alexander Drake's past life. According to Alice, Drake's spirit had infiltrated Finn, which explained the changes in her husband.

Heather was equally shocked when Sophie told her what she knew of William and Louisa, and that Alice had been burnt alive because she'd seen it in her daughter's drawing.

"Heather you need to speak with these spirits and find out what's happening," demanded Sophie.

"Good God, I've tried, I really have tried! I'm telling you, it's not as easy as calling them up. They speak when they're ready."

"Well, you can tell them I need to know what's happening to my husband and I need to know now!"

After a pause, Heather spoke.

"The thing is, I may have lost it."

"Lost it! Lost what?"

"The ability to speak with them. I noticed the other day when I felt how cold Charlie was. I'm sure he *was* the link I needed to talk with them."

"Do you really think this is all down to Charlie?"

"No, not entirely, but I think it helped me make contact. It's as Elizabeth told me, I needed a channel to speak with the dead, despite Charles Nash saying that all I needed was to believe."

"And do you?"

Heather nodded.

"Tell me again what Elizabeth told you when she said you were the chosen one?"

"That I'd been blessed with the veil of tears."

"That's right! You have this gift and you must use it."

"But I'm not sure I am the one. Elizabeth told me that my connection with the afterlife was much stronger than hers, which is why I'd been chosen, but I don't think it's true. I don't feel it. I'm nowhere near as in touch with the dead as Elizabeth was."

Sophie sighed.

"Okay, okay….. but in the meantime Finn is having a breakdown and is barricading himself in our house. I need to help him, and I need your help too."

Heather nodded.

"I understand," replied Heather in a despondent tone.

"It's ten o'clock, Rosie's in class and we can leave Jack with mum and dad. We need to go now," said Sophie.

"Dad should be there too, in case Finn gets violent."

"No," replied Sophie. "I don't want mum and dad involved, at least not right now."

Sophie grabbed her keys, kissed Jack and handed him to her mother.

"Where are you going?" asked Grace.

"Sister stuff," replied Heather and gave her mother a hug.

Chapter 57

It was midday and Ruth Jackson's mind worked overtime. She was intrigued and excited by what was happening in her road. She'd watched Gabriel Butler return to Kieran and Linda's old house and was desperately thinking of a reason to speak with him and find out what was going on.

As hard as she tried, she couldn't think of a reasonable excuse to knock on his door. Or maybe she could?

She lifted the lid of her slow cooker and sniffed the beef stew which had been cooking overnight.

"That's one way to get to a man," she whispered as she took a spoon from the kitchen drawer and tasted the food.

And, of course there may be another way, she thought to herself.

She walked upstairs to the bathroom, turned on the taps and ran a bath. She slipped off her dressing gown and looked at her naked body in the mirror.

"Not bad for an old 'un," she whispered as she admired herself.

The long bath soothed her and gave her time to think of what she would say to Butler. She needed a reason to start a conversation, find out more about him and what on earth was going on in her neighbour's house.

She climbed out, dried herself and looked through her wardrobe to find something nice to wear.

What the hell am I doing?

She hadn't had the company of a man since her husband had died, which was too many years ago. The thought of inviting herself over to the handsome stranger's place excited her. He was in his seventies, good looking and judging by the car he drove, she guessed he was a man of class. She wanted to find out what was happening in Whitcombe Fields Road, and she planned to have a little fun whilst finding out. She was ten years younger than Butler and confident her female charm would help get the answers.

After she'd dressed and applied a little subtle makeup, she picked up the pot from the slow cooker and took it to the hall. She placed it on the floor, had another check of her face in the mirror, took a deep breath and left the house with the gorgeous smelling stew.

Ruth stood outside Butler's home. She was as nervous as a school kid and giddy with excitement as she knocked on the door.

"Hello Ruth, what a pleasure to see you."

Ruth blushed and smiled. When she smiled, her face lit up. It wasn't very often that she did these days, but when she smiled, she radiated a beauty difficult to ignore.

"What do we have here? It smells wonderful. That's not for me is it?"

Ruth smiled again, and began to spin a web of white lies.

"I expected a friend for lunch, but she had to cancel at the eleventh hour. I didn't fancy eating alone and wondered if you would want to share this with me?"

He leaned in and lifted the lid from the pot.

"It looks gorgeous, please come in."

Butler opened the door wide to let Ruth in and she carried the pot to the kitchen.

"Shall we have a glass of wine to go with your wonderful cooking?"

Ruth looked around the Tempest's home. She'd not been there for several years, but recognised paintings and furniture from last time she'd been there.

My God, something really did make them leave in a rush, thought Ruth as she looked around. She recalled the day Kieran and Linda took off in a small transit van. Most of their furniture had been left.

"I'll lay the table," said Butler.

Ruth made herself busy and served the food.

The two of them ate and to begin with, the silence was a little awkward until Butler broke the ice.

"You're a wonderful cook. I'm honoured that you considered sharing this with me."

"It's my pleasure Mr. Butler."

"Please call me Gabriel."

Ruth smiled and lit the room.

Now it was Butler who blushed.

"Tell me Gabriel. What brings you to Whitcombe Fields Road?"

"I'm in between properties and I needed a place to stay until I find somewhere new. You see, I'm downsizing," lied Butler. "I'd heard that this place had become available as a short lease, so I took it," he added.

"Did you know the people who lived here before?"

"No. I understand they were a married couple. I was told their names, but I don't remember."

"They'd lived in the road for years, and one day they just left," said Ruth.

"Is that a fact? Well, as I said, I'm just leasing the house for a short time, and then I'll be gone."

"That's a shame. It's nice having you in the street. You add a touch of class."

Butler smiled and took a sip of wine.

"So tell me about you," asked Butler.

"There's not very much to tell. My husband and I moved into this road just after we married. It's the only house I've owned."

"Did you buy your house when it was new?"

"Yes. My husband and I are the only ones to live in it."

"You've been here a long time. I expect you've seen many people come and go."

Ruth detected a slight edge to his voice. She wondered whether he referred to the suicides in 11a.

"There have been a few over the years."

Butler had to be careful around women. He knew somewhere nearby Alice Donaldson would keep a watchful eye on things. Like Alexander Drake had done with Finn, her spirit would have infiltrated another woman, as it had done many times over the past two hundred years.

He needed to be cautious. That 'goody two shoes bitch' Donaldson would be ready to stop what he, Drake and the others had been preparing for what seemed an eternity. He had to be vigilant as he was so close to bringing together the three elements needed to make their vision become a reality.

"Would you like another glass of wine?" asked Butler with a smile which could charm its way into any woman's heart.

Ruth passed her glass and smiled.

"What line of business were you in?" asked Ruth.

"Oh, many things over the years. I've been lucky enough to be successful in business and now I can afford a few of the finer things life offers."

"Like six months in Whitcombe Fields Road," joked Ruth.

She saw a look in his eye that told her she'd said the wrong thing.

"Well, let's just say my money is tied up in other things, and I made a sensible economic decision to rent somewhere like this," said Butler gesturing to the house.

Ruth became nervous as she geared herself up to ask the question which had been on her mind. After all, it was the reason she'd knocked on his door.

"Gabriel, would you mind if I asked you another question?

"Be my guest."

"This morning I heard you and Finn talking."

Butler raised an eyebrow and Ruth paused. The look in his eye made her edgy. She touched the stem of her wine glass and continued.

"I heard you and Finn talking about digging for two hundred-year-old skeletons, and I'm curious……. well, more intrigued, to know what you were looking for."

Butler smiled. His old charm had returned, and it put her at ease.

"You're intrigued and I completely understand. You have every right to ask what's happening in your neighbour's house."

He emptied the last of the wine into Ruth's glass and continued.

"One of the many careers I've had, and one which remains a passion in my years of retirement is archaeology."

"You were an archaeologist?"

"That's right. Many years ago I studied archaeology at university and after graduating it became my career and I loved it. But things changed. I became involved in business and archaeology took a back seat for far too long. Now I'm retired I have spare time on my hands, and it's something I've become interested in doing again."

Ruth became captivated.

"But why this road?"

"Ruth, can you keep a secret?"

She nodded

"There is a legend which says two hundred years ago, two children were murdered. Their bodies were dumped somewhere on farmland in this area and have never been found."

"Farmland, here?"

"Yes, farmland. Are you aware why this road is called Whitcombe Fields?"

Ruth shook her head.

"James Whitcombe owned a huge farm, as did his family before him, and this road used to be Whitcombe's farm land. It had been a huge field for thousands of years, until recent times when it was sold, developed and turned into what we have here today."

"Wow! I didn't know that," replied Ruth.

"So why are you so interested in finding the children's skeletons?" she added.

"They were family."

"Family? Wow!"

"That's right," replied Butler. He looked to the ceiling and appeared to be counting.

"They were my great, great, great auntie and uncle."

"They were brother and sister? That's so sad. How old were they?"

"They died on their fifth birthday."

"They were twins? That's awful."

Butler didn't answer.

"I can see why you are so interested in finding them."

"So Ruth, I thought it'd be nice to give them a proper burial, providing Finn can find them."

"Why is Finn searching, why aren't you digging, or using a team of professionals?"

"That's a very good question." Butler was becoming irritated by her questions.

Could this be Alice Donaldson? he thought to himself.

"After years of research I've identified that the best place to search for their bodies is beneath Finn's house. I approached him and asked whether I could excavate beneath his home. As you can imagine, he wasn't happy. I offered him an awful lot of money for the inconvenience and he agreed on the condition that if anyone would dig beneath his house it must be him."

"But why?"

Butler shrugged his shoulders.

Ruth accepted Butler's story and was pleased that she had found out what was going on.

The wine had made her a little drunk, and it wasn't even one o'clock in the afternoon.

"Ruth, your cooking is amazing, and I would love to do this again."

Ruth blushed. She'd blushed a lot since being with Gabriel Butler and was falling for his charms.

"Would you like more wine? I've another bottle in the fridge?"

"No thank you Gabriel, I'd better not."

"Are you sure?" asked Butler, with a look which made it difficult for her to refuse.

"Oh okay, maybe a small glass……. and no more."

Butler smiled and went to get another bottle.

For the first time in years Ruth was excited. Something about Butler was alluring. Just being with him made her feel forty years younger. She felt as silly as a teenager. She hoped he felt the same towards her.

Ruth moved to the settee and Butler walked in with a new bottle of wine. He sat next to her and poured her a glass.

"Woah! That's too much," giggled Ruth.

Butler leaned closer and passed her the glass. His expensive aftershave smelt wonderful. He looked and smelt fantastic. Just sitting next him made her tremble with excitement.

She placed her glass on the floor and kissed him on the side of his face.

"Ruth!" said Butler with a smile.

She kissed him again. And again.

Butler did nothing. He sat alongside her and sipped his wine while Ruth continued to kiss his face and neck.

"Perhaps we should go upstairs?" said Butler.

Ruth didn't answer. She was unbuttoning his shirt which caused him to spill wine on his chest.

She ripped open his shirt and kissed his chest, tasting the white wine as it trickled down.

Butler sat motionless with no expression on his face.

He stood up, walked to the hall and climbed the stairs. Ruth eagerly followed. He opened the door to what had been Kieran and Linda's bedroom and before it was fully open, Ruth pushed passed him and took off her dress.

She lay on the bed with her arms outstretched. Butler obliged and walked over to her.

Twenty minutes later Ruth lay still. She was exhausted. She couldn't recall sex ever being so good. Not from her husband or any of the men she'd met before him. Her whole body shook.

Butler looked at her from the side.

Gabriel Butler didn't care for her. He didn't even find her particularly attractive. He did what he did because he needed to be close to her. Close enough to learn what was going on within her. He needed to know whether deep inside of Ruth was the life-force of Alice Donaldson.

Butler was confused. He couldn't make her out.

As the euphoria passed, Ruth lay on her back and stared at the ceiling. Suddenly, from nowhere a thought struck her. Something he'd said earlier made little sense.

"Gabriel, may I ask you something?"

Butler nodded.

"The two children you're looking for, you said they're your relations."

"That's right, like I said I'm their great, great, great nephew, on their father's side."

"And when you find them you want to bury them properly."

"Yes, once DNA proves we're related I will."

Ruth lay in silence and recalled what Butler had said to Finn.

"But why do you only need their skulls?"

"I beg your pardon?"

"You told Finn that you only wanted the children's skulls and not the whole skeletons. Why would you say that if you'd told me you wanted the children to have a proper burial?"

"Oh Ruth, my dear Ruth, or perhaps I should say Alice?"

She looked at him in puzzlement.

"Alice, who's Alice?"

"I wish I could say I'm sorry for what I'm about to do, but to be honest, I'm not."

Ruth didn't understand. Confusion turned to terror as Butler grabbed a pillow and pushed it over her face. He climbed on top of her and pinned her down with his large frame.

She struggled and kicked. The more she struggled, the harder Butler pushed on the pillow. Her muffled cries became quieter and her struggling ceased.

At sixty two years old, Ruth Ella Jackson was dead.

Butler lay on his back and sighed.

Butler was certain Alice Donaldson would be back soon, but hopefully not before he had the skulls of William and Louisa Drake, and equally important, the skull of Mathias Morris.

He smiled, closed his eyes and listened to the dull and distant thud – thud – thud – thud, coming from Finn Maynard's kitchen.

Chapter 58

It was a minute after two when Heather and Sophie arrived at the house.

Sophie had only been away for a few days, but her road seemed different, as though she'd not been there for years.

She passed Ruth's house, and half expected to find her twitching from behind her curtains and keeping a close eye on what was happening in the road. She was relieved that she wasn't there.

She put the key in the lock and expected Finn to have deadlocked the thing from the inside so was surprised when it swung open.

The door opened and she retched at the stale stench of sweat and unwashed clothes. There was another odour, although not as strong, the smell of soil.

Finn had been breaking through the concrete and had smashed through to the hardcore just before two o'clock. His arms and back ached, and his hands blistered. Wearily he'd made his way upstairs and dropped to the bed. He was asleep before his head hit the pillow.

The sisters entered the house. Heather almost tripped over Finn's suitcase which had been there since the aborted trip to the States. Sophie frowned when she saw a pile of wooden planks near the kitchen door. The lounge was a complete mess. Dishes strewn over the floor and a pile of clothes in the corner. The dining room was in a similar state of disarray.

There was no sign of Finn.

"Maybe he's out?" whispered Heather.

"Maybe. I'll check upstairs," said Sophie.

She quietly made her way upstairs while Heather snooped around downstairs looking for any clues as to what he'd been doing.

She walked back to the hall and to the kitchen. The door was ajar. She pushed it open to be met by the huge hole in the floor.

"What the fuck is this?"

Most of the floorboards had been removed. She tiptoed to the hole and peered in. The concrete beneath the floor had been smashed and removed. The back door was open and rubble was discarded in the garden.

She turned and ran to the bottom of the stairs.

"Sophie, Sophie come here."

Sophie stopped just as she was about to open the bedroom door.

"What is it?"

"The kitchen, it's smashed up."

Sophie hurried down the stairs to the kitchen. She held her hand over her mouth when she saw the state of the floor.

"What in God's name is he doing?"

Heather shook her head.

Sophie couldn't believe what she saw. Instead of floorboards there was a three feet deep and six feet wide hole.

She jumped down to the edge of the hole and knocked over a large black bucket which Finn had been using to clear the rubble.

"Hand me a torch, there should be one in that drawer," said Sophie pointing to the corner of the kitchen.

Heather tossed her the small Maglite.

She climbed into the hole which came up to her waist. Crouching she shone the light.

"What there?" asked Heather.

"Nothing, it's just a huge hole. What the fucking hell is he doing?"

Heather offered her hand and helped Sophie out. She rubbed dust from her trousers and sleeves.

"He's gone bloody insane," said Sophie.

"What are you doing here?"

The sisters turned around and saw Finn. He looked awful.

"Finn!" shouted Sophie.

She ran to him and threw her arms around him. He didn't move or speak. He just stood in the doorway staring at the hole.

"We're so worried about you. What's happening?"

Finn pushed past Sophie and stood over the hole.

"What are you doing?"

"I'm digging a hole."

Finn spoke with a lifeless and monosyllabic voice.

"But why, what are you digging for?"

"I'm decorating the kitchen," he replied with a false smile which made him look insane.

"Finn, please stop. Tell me what's happening to you."

"Nothing's happening. So please fuck off so I can carry on with my work."

Tears rolled down Sophie's cheeks.

Finn bent forward, picked up the pickaxe and raised it above his head.

"Leave her alone!" shouted Heather.

"Don't be so stupid woman. I'll not hurt anyone."

He jumped into the hole and continued breaking up hardcore.

"Come on, let's leave him to it. There's nothing we can do, and I don't trust him with that pickaxe," said Heather.

"Finn, speak to me," pleaded Sophie.

He stopped, looked his wife in the eye and demanded that she left the house.

"Sophie, we have to get out. We need to get help."

She pulled her sister's arm and Sophie backed out of the kitchen.

The two of them stood in the front garden. Heather did her best to console Sophie whose head was in her hands.

"What's happening in there?" said Heather.

Sophie wiped her eyes and stood in silence. She cast her mind back to the picture Rosie drew with Alice in the burning building and the other awful things.

"I know what he's doing," said Sophie.

Heather looked at her sister and waited for her to speak.

"He's digging for the bodies,……….. the bodies of William and Louisa Drake."

Chapter 59

Finn deadlocked the front door and returned to the kitchen refreshed after a brief rest.

He took the pickaxe, jumped into the hole, held it above his head and brought it down with a thud onto the hardcore.

The instant the pick contacted the ground a surge of electricity raced through his body. He shuddered and dropped the pick.

He bent forward, grabbed it and held it over his head for a second time. A spark glinted as it cracked through a lump of hardcore, splitting it in two. Again, a surge of power. This time he wasn't surprised. The shock left him reinvigorated and stronger than before.

He swung the pick again, and again. Each time he broke through the hardcore he felt sharper and more focussed on what he had to achieve.

He stopped to catch his breath. In the space of a few minutes he'd reduced several large lumps of rock into tiny fragments.

After he'd composed himself he grabbed the pickaxe and was ready to start again.

The pick came crashing down on the rock and everything around him changed.

He was no longer in the hole, but in the cellar illuminated by candles. In the middle of the room stood the circular table covered with a blue velvet cloth. Patterns adorned the cloth which matched the two on his ring.

On the table lay two wooden boxes, on which were cushions. On each of the cushions lay an infant's skull. On the back of the skulls were circular patterns which were slightly different. He looked at the ring on his finger. The light from the candles reflected in the rubies and gold. Although the light was dim he could see the patterns were identical to those on the skulls.

Beneath the table was another wooden box which also had a cushion on it.

Finn put his hand out to touch a skull, but before his finger made contact he found himself back in the kitchen and up to his waist in the hole. He dropped the pick and, with his hand, shielded his eyes from the bright sunlight streaming in through the back door.

A voice came from behind.

"Maynard, keep digging and don't stop until you find the bones."

He looked around but saw no one.

Then he heard it again.

"Don't stop. With every strike of that pick, you will become stronger."

Finn continued to hack away at the hardcore and dumped the smashed rocks in the garden. The pain in his arms and back became unbearable.

Every time the pick struck a rock, a little part of him became possessed by the life-force of Alexander Drake. It was Drake's essence that pushed Finn to continue, despite every muscle in his body pleading for him to stop.

Chapter 60

Gabriel Butler looked down upon the body of Ruth Jackson as it lay contorted on the bed. She'd been dead for just over three hours and her outstretched arm was rigid.

He'd killed her as he was almost certain that Alice Donaldson's spirit was guiding her. Ruth asked too many questions and Butler couldn't take any chances.

Alice proved herself to be an indomitable and resolute nemesis. She'd been the one who'd stopped the wicked and evil ceremonial ritual that Alexander Drake, Joseph Morris, Rupert Snow and Albert Cromwell intended to carry out on December 14th 1804.

During the past two-hundred years she'd been lying in wait to obstruct any attempts of the vile ritual.

Her benevolent spirit guided chosen mortals to obstruct the evil plan.

Likewise, Joseph Morris had always been around in one form or another to make sure the invocation to summon Azazel would happen.

But he couldn't do it alone. He needed Drake, Snow and Cromwell. And importantly, he needed the children.

He had relentlessly searched for the bodies of William and Louisa, but never had he got so near as he was today.

But he also needed Mathias. The infant he'd thrown in the frozen lake on the day the ritual should have happened. He'd assumed because Alice hid William and Louisa and put an end to the sacrifice, there would be no need for Mathias. How wrong he had been.

Now Finn was close to finding the skulls, Butler had never been more certain that this time it really would happen. On the 14th December Azazel would stand before them.

He, Drake, Snow and Cromwell would sit at the right hand of the King of the Devils.

But before the ceremony could happen he needed to find the body of the missing infant Mathias. He also needed to ensure Drake, Snow and Cromwell were with him.

Drake wasn't a problem. Soon, Finn Maynard would no longer exist. The closer Maynard came to the skulls, the more Alexander Drake would take over. The instant Maynard touched the skulls would be the tipping point. His body would exist, but it would be a host for Drake's life force.

Rupert Snow was already on board. He'd lured Maynard to the antique shop and given him the ring.

Albert Cromwell was the problem. Without him, the ritual couldn't go ahead.

There was plenty of work to do.

Butler pulled Ruth's body from the bed and dragged it across the floor to the top of the stairs. He held her by her ankles and pulled her step by step down the stairs, hauled her to the utility room, dumped her into the chest freezer and slammed the lid.

Killing Ruth Jackson wouldn't stop Alice Donaldson, but hopefully it would buy time before she returned in the next incarnation.

Chapter 61

Sophie slammed the phone on the bed.

"Bloody police, a fat lot of good they are!"

"What did they say?" asked Heather.

"They asked whether I was at risk, or if Finn possessed a weapon blah, blah, blah. I told them what was happening to him, but because neither me nor the kids are at risk they're not making it a priority."

"So are they sending anyone?"

"They said they would, but I'm not sure when. They're not treating it as an emergency."

"I suppose we should consider things from the police's point of view, if he's not a risk to anyone, then he's not at the top of their list."

"IF HE'S NOT A RISK TO ANYONE?" shouted Sophie. "He's a risk to himself. I'm sure he'll end up dead. Every man who'd lived in that house killed himself, and Finn's heading the same way for sure," she added.

Heather shrugged her shoulders.

"Maybe we should go back and ask a few of your neighbours to keep an eye on things and tell you if anything happens, or if the police arrive," suggested Heather.

"We've not got to know any of our neighbours other than the Tempest's, but they've moved out. We do know Ruth next door in number 11, but let's say things are a little frosty between us right now."

Sophie paused and let out a large stress induced sigh.

"I guess we should just wait to find out what the police say," she added sounding defeatist.

"Fingers crossed he'll be referred to Social Services, and he'll get counselling," said Heather.

Sophie nodded.

"I guess this is what it's all about, it's his mental health. He's having a massive breakdown, and he needs help. Maybe I shouldn't have called the police, perhaps I should have called his doctor."

Sophie looked at her sister as she stared towards the middle distance. She considered the recent events and how they were both embroiled.

"Heather, have you had any recent visits from any of the ghosts?"

"Don't call them ghosts, that's not what they are," snapped Heather.

"What are they then?"

"I'm not certain, but I don't consider them ghosts. It's not like they're dead, it's as if they're..........," she paused as she thought of the best way to describe Charles Nash, Alice Donaldson and Elizabeth, "it's as if they're alive, but living on a different plain. They're living on a surreal abstract plain."

Sophie struggled to understand what her sister was saying.

"But, no. I've not seen any of 'the ghosts' since I was in hospital," she added.

"You should find a way of speaking with them again, you should try to rekindle whatever it was you had," said Sophie with an air of desperation. "Social Services or counsellors won't get to the bottom of what's going on in Finn's head, we need to hear it from the ghosts of Christmas past," she added.

Heather huffed.

"I can't just make them appear! Elizabeth says I'm blessed with an extra special gift, the veil of tears, but to be honest with you, she's wrong, and Charles and Alice are wrong. I've nothing special to offer."

"You must have a gift. How else would you have known of Alice and the two children?"

Heather shrugged and looked nonchalantly at her sister.

"Would you like to hear what I think?" asked Heather.

Sophie looked up, the strain of what was happening reflected in the lines across her forehead.

"We have to get him out of that house."

"Well that'll not happen anytime soon. He's wielding a pickaxe, and he's losing his mind. How do you expect us to get him out?"

"We'll get help. I'll ask Mark and Hugh from work to come with us, they're built like two brick shit houses and they don't scare easy."

Heather was right. It was what lay beneath the house that affected Finn, and the further from that place he was the better.

But it would take more than two burly rugby players to drag Finn Maynard from his home.

Chapter 62

With every strike of the pick he became mentally stronger.

Finn had been through a rollercoaster of emotions and personality swings over the past few months.

The once 'family man' had briefly turned into a self-centred person, whose only consideration was for himself. He'd alienated his wife, and his daughter couldn't understand why daddy had stopped loving her. Jack was too young to understand.

After discovering the elusive third archetypon, he'd become a confused and vulnerable man. His brain was muddled, and he lived in a chaotic existence somewhere between Finn Maynard and Alexander Drake. Drake's overpowering character had been taking over. The transition between the two personalities had been gradual and as Finn evolved into Drake he'd found solace in Gabriel Butler.

He had cleared the hardcore and was making good progress breaking through clay and stone beneath the foundations of his house. The hole was becoming deep. Finn had used floorboards to shore the sides to prevent them from falling in and burying him alive. He used a ladder to climb in and out of the hole.

He stopped digging and admired his work.

"Not bad, not bad at all," he whispered to himself.

He deserved a well-earned drink. He climbed from the hole and grabbed a glass of water. It felt good as it hit his dry and dusty throat. He stretched his arms and rubbed his shoulders. In a strange way the pain felt good. He strolled to the lounge, leaving muddy footprints behind him and stood by the window. He watched a young police officer walk up the path. Their eyes met as the policeman knocked on his door.

Gabriel Butler opened his door to take a black bag of waste to the wheelie bin when he saw the officer knocking on Finn's door.

Shit, he's checking up on the Jackson woman, he thought as he watched Finn open the door.

She'd been dead less than twenty-four hours and Butler thought it odd that someone reported her missing so soon. It wasn't as if she was a person people would particularly miss.

He'd intended to haul the body to the boot of his Silver Cloud and dispose of her that evening. Everything was coming together and the last thing he wanted was the police snooping around. Although, all they would do at this stage is make general enquiries. They wouldn't be searching his house for a body.

Butler didn’t care either way whether he went to prison. He’d been inside several times over the past two hundred years and conditions today were much better compared to what they were in the nineteenth century. But what he didn’t want was to delay the next opportunity to attempt the ritual.

Finn reluctantly opened the door to the police officer. Finn's dishevelled and dirty appearance shocked the young policeman. The ugly scar on his face made him appear menacing.

“How can I help you?”

“Are you Finn Maynard?" asked the officer.

Finn thought for a second, he wasn’t sure who he was anymore.

“I believe I am,” replied Finn.

The officer sighed.

“Do you mind if I come in? I have some questions for you.”

Finn shrugged his shoulders, nodded and pulled the door open wide to let him in.

The officer was hit by the stale stench and the complete disarray of Finn's house. Uninvited, he entered the lounge, sat on the corner of the settee and pulled his notebook from his pocket.

“We’ve had a call from your wife sir, Sophie Maynard, I understand that there are issues between the two of you and she’s put a call in as she’s concerned about your well-being.”

Finn didn’t answer.

“Don’t worry sir, you’re not in any trouble, as far as we’re aware you’ve not broken any laws, but it would be prudent to make sure everything is okay.”

“Everything’s just fine officer.”

“I understand that you’ve not been into work for over a week, nor have you contacted your employer.” The officer checked his notebook. "SOS Graphics, sir?"

The name SOS Graphics sounded familiar to Finn.

“Sorry officer, I remember little.”

“You don’t remember who you work for?”

Finn didn’t answer.

“Your wife has told us that you're digging a hole beneath your house.”

“Uh huh,” said Finn slowly nodding.

“Why?”

“Why not?” replied Finn, “It’s something to do.”

“Can I take a look please?”

The officer was on his feet before Finn replied.

He didn’t need to be told where the hole was, he followed Finn’s dirty footprints on the carpet which led to the kitchen.

"What the hell?" whispered the officer as he peered into the hole.

Finn stood behind the officer. Drake's persona was fighting to get through. Drake mustn't let the officer stop the search for William and Louisa. Under Drake's command, Finn picked up a spade and was going to strike the young officer on the back of his head. Finn looked at the spade. He had no recollection of picking it up. He looked at the officer crouching and surveying the hole. He placed the spade back on the floor. Enough of Finn's judgment remained to know right from wrong.

"This shaft is as deep as I'm tall," said the officer.

Finn nodded.

The officer was right. It was no longer just a hole. What Finn had dug was so deep it had become a shaft, propped up with wooden boards to stop it from collapsing in on itself.

"What's it for?"

Drake took over and answered the officer's question.

"Treasure."

"I beg your pardon?" asked the officer.

"Roman coins," added Finn. "It's my belief that if I carry on I will find one of the biggest hoards of Roman coins ever found in the West Country."

"How can you be so sure?"

"I've been undertaking years of research. It's something I've been searching for all of my adult life. I couldn't believe it when I worked out that the most likely place to find them was under my home."

The officer looked at him disbelievingly.

"So you've searched all your life for treasure, and it just happens to be under your home?"

"I know, it's incredible isn't it!...... I've not broken any laws have I?"

"Not that I'm aware of, but I'm not certain if what you are doing is safe. You could interfere with the foundations of this house. I'm no expert, but I suggest that you seek advice from a professional."

"You're right officer. I'll get on it right away."

Drake's instinct prevented what would have been a disaster. He was sure the officer didn't believe him, but it would put him off the scent for the time being.

Drake's persona diminished and Finn's came to the forefront.

"Let's go back to the lounge" said the officer.

Butler paced up and down. He was agitated and desperate to know what was happening. The policeman had been there for half an hour. Surely it shouldn't take that long to ask a few questions about a missing person?

And then he realised.

"Shit! The hole."

Butler considered what must be going through the police officer's mind. He would surely link the report of Ruth Jackson with what appeared to be a shallow grave being dug beneath Finn's kitchen.

"This is just fucking great!" cursed Butler.

Butler had to intervene. He was certain that Finn would be arrested.

A missing woman, and the next door neighbour found digging a hole beneath his house, pondered Butler, *the police would put two and two together and make five.*

There was no way that Finn/Drake could stop digging now. And it had to be Drake who found the bodies, and no one else, otherwise the ritual couldn't go ahead on the 14th December.

"Why should things be so fucking complicated?" he whispered.

Butler needed to go to Finn's and intervene. Even though Butler had Ruth's body in the chest freezer, he couldn't risk Finn being pulled in for questioning by the police. He was taking a big chance, and he had to be careful not to raise the suspicions of the police officer.

He crossed the road and rapped on the door. Through the window he could see the police officer taking notes as Finn sat on the settee looking vacant. Finn stood up when he saw Butler at the door.

"It's my neighbour, I'll find out what he wants." said Finn.

The officer nodded and sighed.

He watched Finn traipse to the door, looking like a vagrant.

"Hello Finn mate, I thought I'd check up on you. See how you're getting on, can I come in?"

"I don't know. There's a policeman here."

"The police, what in heaven's name do they want?"

"I'm not too sure, they're not happy with the hole."

Butler frowned and put his fingers to his lips to shush Finn from saying anything else.

Butler followed him to the lounge where the officer was waiting.

"Oh, hello, I hope I'm not interrupting," said Butler.

"May I ask who you are?" asked the officer.

"My name's Gabriel Butler, I live across the road, Finn and I are friends," he lowered his voice and continued in a whisper, "to be honest, I'm concerned, he's been having a tough time of it these past few weeks and I've come over to check he's okay."

The officer nodded.

"Well Mr. Maynard, we're done here. Would you mind if I had a quick word with your friend?"

Finn nodded.

The officer gestured to Butler to follow him to the hall.

"I understand Mr. Maynard has been having family issues, and it appears he's having a breakdown."

Butler nodded.

"His wife left him and took the children. It's become complicated, and he's not taking it well."

The officer looked thoughtful.

"In my report I'll suggest that he receives counselling."

"I'm already on it. Finn may not have told you, but I've arranged for a home visit. Someone from Social Services will visit him during the next few days."

"No, he didn't mention it."

"It doesn't surprise me, he's become very confused lately, it's very sad."

"How do you know Mr. Maynard?"

"Oh, Finn and I go back a long time," lied Butler, "is this why you've visited him today?"

"Yes, his wife is concerned and asked us to pay a visit."

The officer paused and then spoke in an even more hushed tone.

"What's with the hole, he told me he's digging for treasure?"

"I know, he told me that too, I don't know what's happening. I'm sure a counsellor can help."

"I'm worried about the kitchen falling in on itself, have you seen how deep it is?"

"I have, and luckily I was in the building trade before I retired, so I can assure you his house is safe, providing he digs no deeper."

"He's lucky to have you as a friend," said the officer.

Butler smiled and shook his hand.

"I'll note what you've told me in my report."

"Yes officer, you do that. And if you need to speak with me, you'll find me in the house across the road," said Butler pointing to the other side of Whitcombe Fields Road.

Butler saw the officer to the door and promised to keep an eye on Finn. He closed the door and let out an almighty sigh.

He turned to see Finn in the hallway with a vacant look upon his face.

"I can't do this anymore," said Finn.

"You can, you're almost there, you can't stop now. Think of the money and what you can do with the seventy five thousand pounds I'm paying you."

"I'm tired and I ache," complained Finn.

"Come with me," said Butler as he took him by the arm and led him towards the kitchen.

With every step Finn took towards the kitchen, Drake became more prominent. Butler guided him to the edge of the hole and the two of them peered in. Drake's character overpowered Finn's diminishing spirit. Butler noticed the muscles in Finn's arm tense as they looked at the hole. Finn climbed down. The instant his feet stepped from the ladder he called to Butler who was looking from above.

"Joseph, pass me the pick and be quick."

Butler smiled when he referred to him as 'Joseph'.

"Good work Alexander, you must be close."

Alexander Drake looked up at his old friend Joseph Morris and smiled as Morris handed him the pick.

"I am close Joseph, I'm very close indeed. I can almost smell those little bastards beneath my feet."

Chapter 63

"I can assure you I don't know anyone called Gabriel Butler," protested Sophie.

"He told me he's been friends with your husband for a long time," said the police officer.

Sophie was confused and looked perplexed.

"He said he lives in the house across the road," he added.

"That house belongs to Kieran and Linda Tempest, but they've moved out. They did a moonlight flit, they just upped sticks and went."

The officer noted what Sophie said.

"The thing is Mrs. Maynard, your husband has broken no laws, there's nothing he can be arrested for, and all I can do is refer him to Social Services and that is already in hand."

"ALREADY IN HAND!" shouted Sophie.

"Yes, Mr. Butler is taking care of things."

"I'm telling you, neither Finn, nor I, know Gabriel Butler."

Sophie stood up, stormed to the other side of her parents' lounge and faced the officer with her arms folded.

"So you're telling me that although my husband has made a complete 360 degree turn in personality, he no longer seems to remember who he is, has thrown me out of the house and is digging a cavern beneath our house, there's nothing the police can do."

"It's hardly a cavern, it's a hole," replied the officer.

"That's not the point, and you know it."

"As I've previously mentioned, Gabriel Butler has contacted Social Services and has arranged a home visit from a counsellor."

"WE DON'T KNOW GABRIEL BUTLER!" shouted Sophie.

She turned away and placed her hands against her temples to calm herself.

"Sorry, but you may as well go, you are neither use nor ornament."

The officer stood up and placed his notebook in his pocket.

"I'll investigate Gabriel Butler and see whether we have any information on record," said the officer in a sheepish tone of voice.

"Yes, you do that," snapped Sophie as she almost bundled the police officer out of the house, closing the door behind him.

Heather sat in the corner.

"We have to get Finn out of there," said Sophie.

"I'll speak with Mark and Hugh from work, the big guys I told you about. They'll have no trouble convincing him to leave."

“Call them now, Finn needs to be out of that place as soon as possible. I’m worried that he'll go the same way as the others."

Just after six pm, Hugh Black and Mark Cook pulled up outside Finn and Sophie’s house in Hugh’s transit van. Heather and Sophie were sitting on a couple of bean bags in the back.

Both Hugh and Mark were well over six feet tall and both played rugby for Clifton Old Boys. Most of the time they were two gentle giants unless someone or something had upset them. If that were to happen, there would be trouble with a capital ‘T’.

Butler watched with curiosity from his lounge window as Sophie knocked on the door. He wondered who the other young woman and large men were.

Sophie rapped again - no answer. She grabbed her keys and luckily Finn hadn’t deadlocked the door from the inside. Sophie entered, followed by Heather, Mark and Hugh.

Finn wasn’t in the lounge or dining room, so Sophie went to the kitchen expecting to find him in the hole. He wasn’t there either. She was shocked to see how deep it had become since the last time she’d seen it.

She made her way back to the hall where the others were waiting for her.

“He’s not here,” whispered Sophie shrugging her shoulders.

Heather put her fingers to her lips and shushed her sister as the sound of running water came from upstairs.

“He must be in the bathroom,” whispered Heather.

Sophie ushered Heather and the two giants into the lounge and waited for her husband at the bottom of the stairs.

Finn made his way down, and at first he didn’t notice his wife waiting in the hall.

She was shocked at how vague and worn he looked.

His eyes met with hers. He said nothing, pushed past her and made his way back to the kitchen.

“Finn, you need to get out, please come with me.”

He didn’t answer and continued to make his way to the hole.

“Don’t go to the kitchen, come with me, you must leave.”

There was no response.

It was time to involve Mark and Hugh.

Butler strode across the road. Again he had to intervene. Whatever Sophie was doing needed to be stopped.

The door was ajar, he pushed it open and stepped inside. Finn stood by the kitchen door and Mark and Hugh gripped his arms.

"What do you think you're doing?" boomed Butler.

"We're getting him out of here," replied Hugh in a confident voice which made it clear he wouldn't be intimidated by the elderly man.

"Under whose authority?" demanded Butler.

"Mine!" said Sophie stepping into the hallway.

Sophie looked at the tall old man with grey hair.

"I suppose you must be Gabriel Butler," said Sophie.

"Hello Sophie, it's a pleasure to finally meet you," replied Butler in a suave and charming tone.

"Boys, don't listen to this man, get Finn out of here," demanded Sophie.

Hugh and Mark walked Finn along the hallway. He didn't put up a fight and sluggishly allowed them to walk him towards the front door.

Butler stepped between Finn, Mark, Hugh and the door.

"Let go of him!" demanded Butler.

Hugh and Mark ignored him and continued to walk Finn out of the house.

Butler stood nose to nose with Hugh, who was similar in height. Hugh had the advantage as he was fifteen stone of well-toned muscle. Butler was small framed at just over 12 stone.

"I'll ask one more time. Let go of him and step aside," said Butler in a calm and authoritative tone.

Hugh grinned and continued to push pass Butler whilst holding Finn by his arm. Mark was on the other side gripping Finn's other arm.

And then it happened.

Sophie could not believe her eyes. In a heartbeat, the old man grabbed Hugh's arm and twisted so he'd broken it and the ulna protruded through his skin.

Hugh dropped to the floor and howled as the pain made him feel ill.

Mark couldn't believe what he'd seen. A man who appeared to be in his seventies, had broken his best friend's arm and had hardly touched him. He relaxed his grip on Finn's arm and took a step back.

"Now, unless you would like the same thing to happen to you, I suggest you let go of my friend."

Mark pulled Finn towards him and replaced his hand on Finn's arm.

"Come no closer," said Mark. His voice hinted an air of nervousness.

Before Mark could react, Butler darted forward, grabbed the back of his head and rammed it into the newel posts of the stairs. His head broke clean through a post, rendering him unconscious.

Butler turned to Sophie.

"Young lady, don't be deceived by my appearance, you can see what I am capable of. I suggest you and your friend leave and don't, under any circumstances, involve anyone else."

"I'm not giving up that easily," said Sophie trying her best to not show fear.

Butler raised an eyebrow.

"Let me put it this way. You've seen what's just happened to Tweedledum and Tweedledee. Wouldn't it be a shame if something happened to your beautiful children."

"Don't you lay a finger on them," demanded Sophie.

"Oh, I'm sure I won't, unless you continue to snoop around and get in the way of things."

Sophie took Butler's advice. She looked at Hugh, who rocked back and forth while he gripped his broken arm. She glanced towards Mark, who was out for the count and had a severe cut to the top of his head. She called to Heather who had been in the lounge and was trembling with fear.

Heather stepped into the hall and for the first time she set eyes upon Gabriel Butler.

But she didn't see the tall silver haired man that Sophie, Mark and Hugh had seen. Instead she looked at a short, squat, ugly man with a blue ink tattoo on his cheek and a mouthful of rotten teeth.

"My God," whispered Heather into her sister's ear. "That's the man who killed Alice Donaldson."

"What do you mean," replied Sophie in a confused tone.

"He's not Gabriel Butler, his name is Joseph Morris, and he's the one who murdered Alice Donaldson…….., we need to get out of here now."

He cackled a menacingly deep laugh and watched the two women leave the house and hurriedly make their way along Whitcombe Fields Road.

"I'll deal with them later," he said to himself. He turned to Finn slumped in the doorway to the kitchen.

"Come on Mr. Drake, the party's finished. It's time to return to work."

Chapter 64

"What do you mean 'it's cold'," snapped Linda Tempest.

"Because it's a cold lump of rock," replied Kieran.

He held the head and examined the painted face.

Linda placed her hand next to her husband's on the rock and shook her head.

"What's the matter with you, it feels as if it's been in an oven!"

"Not to me it doesn't."

She sighed, took the stone head with an oven glove and cautiously placed it on the floor. Kieran eyed her with suspicion.

"Butler called this morning," announced Kieran.

He was nervous about telling Linda because she didn't trust the man.

She glared at him.

"I guessed it wouldn't be the last we'd hear from him. What does he want?"

"He has a job for me."

"I hope you said no."

"I didn't, he told me it'd be worth our while. He's talking about a million for an evening's work this month. It's the last thing he wants me to do for him."

"A million, for an evening's work in December? What does he expect you to do? Be Father fuckin' Christmas for the night?" snapped Linda.

"He didn't say, he told me about the money. I mean a million for an evening's work, I couldn't say no."

"Kieran, we don't need any more money, we have more than we'll ever need and I don't trust the man. And to be honest, I was happier before we were wealthy."

Kieran attempted to speak, but Linda interrupted him.

"I've told you before. He's got his claws into you. He thinks he has you under his control and you need to prove him wrong. Tell him you're not interested."

"But you know what he's like, it's difficult to say no."

"Which is why you need to stand your ground and tell him no."

Kieran knew she was right.

"Admit it, weird shit was happening in our old road, and Butler wanted to find out everything. Like who lived in that house, who died there and how they'd died. And that stuff you had to confirm about the connections between those who'd killed themselves."

Linda stood up and circled the room.

"And what about that bloody bird, that huge crow or whatever it was."

"It's a raven."

"Whatever the hell the thing is, it freaks me out."

"Butler predicted it would turn up when the right person moved into that house, and he was correct," said Kieran.

"Which is why you must have nothing further to do with him. I'm telling you, he's trouble, and I reckon he's evil."

Everything Linda said was right. He should say 'no' to Butler, but just couldn't. Linda had hit the nail on the head when she'd said Gabriel Butler 'had his claws in him'.

"I promise, this will be the last job I do for him," said Kieran.

Linda crossed her arms, shook her head and didn't speak. She didn't need to. Her body language made it clear she'd had enough of Butler.

Butler had promised Kieran one million pounds. But there wasn't enough money in the world to pay for the task Butler had in mind.

Chapter 65

Butler bundled Hugh Black and Mark Cook into the transit van and assured them if he ever came across them again, or should they contact the police, he would kill them. They knew he wasn't kidding, and what scared them about the threatening and intimidating old man, he was more than capable of carrying out his promise.

He'd guided Finn back to the kitchen, and just as before, the closer Finn got to the hole, the more prominent Drake became.

An hour later, Joseph Morris sat in the corner of the kitchen reading Middlemarch, making observations of the story in his notebook whilst listening to the clank of the pickaxe against the rubble. The sound of Drake digging stopped and Morris looked up as he hauled out another bucket of rubble to be dumped.

He emptied the stones and soil in the garden which looked like a bomb site, returned to the kitchen and sat down next to Morris.

"You're still reading that crap," said Drake.

Morris smiled and put the book down.

"Haven't you something else to do, whilst I'm sweating my balls off digging that hole?" added Drake.

Morris sighed.

"All in good time. Don't worry I'm confident I'll find Mathias. Azazel will guide me as he has for the past two hundred years."

"Well, don't be too confident. If it wasn't for you dumping the kid in the pond, we wouldn't be here today wondering where the hell we should look for his body."

Morris raised his hand.

"It's going to be fine. Just leave Mathias to me."

"What about Albert Cromwell? He needs to be with us too."

"I know, I know. That's something I've already taken care of."

Drake took a swig of water and climbed back into the hole, whilst Morris settled back in a chair and continued reading his book.

Drake was like a machine. He was relentless and it was astonishing how much rubble and soil he'd cleared in the past few hours.

When Finn began digging, his work was sluggish and half-hearted. His only motivation had been the money Butler offered. Finn didn't know he wouldn't receive a penny from Butler, nor did he know that within a matter of days Finn Maynard would no longer exist. The deeper the hole became, and the closer he came to the well, the more Alexander Drake's life force crept up and infiltrated him. Memories of Sophie, Rosie and Jack became lost in the swirling ocean of Drake's evil mind. Recollections of the time when he had last walked the earth just under two hundred years ago became clear and vivid, as if they were yesterday.

The sound of the pickaxe against the soil changed. Instead of the dull thud and the cracking of stone, Drake heard a hollow clunk. He stopped and took a breath. In the cramped confines of the hole, he lifted the pick and plunged it down again.

He heard it again. Drake put down the pick and stamped on the ground. He detected a slight movement.

"Joseph, throw me the spade, I've found something."

Morris jumped up and ran to the edge of the hole.

"What is it?"

"I'm not sure, just pass me the spade."

Morris dropped the spade which Drake caught by the handle.

"Get me a torch."

Drake scraped away at the soil and rocks with the spade until he came across something flat and smooth. He knelt down and in the confined space he scratched at the soil with his fingers.

"What is it?" repeated Morris.

Drake didn't answer, he continued to clear away the soil with his hands. His beating heart was in his mouth as shards of grit cut into the tips of his fingers.

Morris waited impatiently for Drake to say something, but couldn't wait any longer.

"Alexander, what is it, what's down there?"

"It's wood. I've found what appears to be a large plank of wood," said Drake shining the torch.

He rapped on it with his knuckles and listened.

"It's hollow."

When Alexander Drake had been alive he'd been a man who'd rarely let his emotions show, but it was obvious by the tone of his voice he was tense with anticipation.

"Be careful Alexander, the wood's probably rotten and may not take your weight."

"It's fairly sturdy, I'm okay."

Drake continued to clear the remaining soil until the plank was completely exposed. He was unable to lift it as part of the plank disappeared beneath the wall of soil that was shored up with floorboards. With the spade he dug into the soil which covered the unexposed section of the plank. Morris paced up and down the kitchen like an expectant father waiting for the birth of a child. He peered down, but all he saw was the top of Drake's head as he dug at the wall of soil and rock. He sighed, sat down, continued to read his copy of Middlemarch and scribbled annotations in his notebook.

Drake ascended the ladder with the final bucket of rubble which he emptied in the garden. He looked to the sky and high above the trees he made out the familiar silhouette of the raven.

"Hello my old friend," he whispered as the bird soared.

Back in the hole Drake cleared enough soil and rock to expose the edge of the plank. He put the spade to one side, dropped to his knees and attempted to lift the plank. He teetered on the solid section of soil whilst trying to lift it, but the confined space made it impossible.

"Joseph, I'm almost through, but I can't lift the blasted plank, have you brought something I can use as a lever?"

Morris shuffled around in the tool bag and found a crowbar. He tossed it to Drake and heard a thud as it hit the plank.

"Careful!" shouted Drake angrily.

He jammed the crowbar beneath the plank and put his weight behind it. The wood groaned as it moved for the first time in two-hundred years. Drake tried again, and the plank lifted a quarter of an inch, but as soon as he pulled the crowbar out, it dropped back into position.

He grabbed the spade and put it next to him. Again, he used the crowbar to lift the plank, and again he lifted it a quarter of an inch. He picked up the spade and slid the blade in the gap under the plank. He pushed the spade as far as it would go and when he could push it no more, he lifted the shaft of the spade and levered the wood. He lifted the plank eight inches. Using the crowbar, he propped up the plank, so it remained in position.

He slid his hand under the plank and felt something cold and rough like the top of a grid. He picked up the torch, got down as low as possible, and shone the torch beneath the plank. Drake was just able to squeeze himself low enough to peer below.

And then he saw it.

The plank covered a rusting metal grille, and Drake saw below the grille was a shaft. He climbed back to his feet and wiped his forehead. He was about to call to Morris, but waited until he'd removed the plank and was able see what was there.

Drake had two choices. He could either try to lift and remove the plank which would be difficult in the confined space, or he could use the pickaxe to smash the plank into smaller pieces. The plank was two inches thick, and would take a long time to break down.

Drake rested against the floorboards supporting the wall and considered what to do. He wondered whether there was an easier and quicker way to shift the plank. He wasn't able to cut through it. He didn't have enough room, and the metal grille beneath would make it impossible to use a saw. He sighed and decided to smash the plank into pieces.

Drake spat on his hands, gripped the shaft of the pick firmly, lifted it then brought it down upon the plank. The pick sliced into the wood. The point of the pickaxe jammed into the plank. He cursed as he tried to pull it out, but it was stuck fast. He placed a foot on the plank and tugged at the pick, but it wouldn't budge, it was stuck.

He thought about what he should do next.

Morris waited impatiently above and wondered what was happening.

Drake checked whether the pickaxe could be used as a handle to lift the slab of wood. He yanked on the shaft of the pick and the plank moved.

For a third time, he used the crowbar to raise the plank and again, rammed the blade of the spade beneath the gap. With all his strength, he levered the shaft of the pickaxe towards him and the huge and hefty plank shifted. His movements were limited by the lack of space around him.

The raven which had been circling the house for the past hour, swooped and landed in the garden. It hopped into the kitchen, stopped at the hole, cocked its head to one side and watched Drake struggling below. Suddenly, as if it had been agitated by something, it flapped and cawed. Morris watched it jump down the hole and land on Drake's shoulder. Drake was briefly taken aback as he felt the talons of the bird dig into his skin, like small hooks gripping his shoulder. He made out the form of the large bird in the darkness of the hole. The raven tightened its grip on Drake's shoulder who winced as the claws dug in.

Suddenly Drake became energised as if he had the strength of half a dozen men. The raven flapped its wings and dug its talons even further into Drakes skin, jabbing into the bone of his clavicle.

He pulled with all his strength and lifted the plank from where it had remained untouched since 1804. He raised it vertically and propped the plank against the wall with the pickaxe still in place. Drake saw the metal grille by his feet.

He exhaled and his body ached. The raven released its grip and flew up and out of the hole. Drake had to remove the plank and the tools before he continued his search for the bodies.

Morris watched in awe as the raven flew from the hole and landed in the kitchen, followed by Drake climbing the ladder dragging the spade behind him.

"Take this," demanded Drake, hauling the spade from the hole.

Drake descended and ascended three more times until he'd taken away the plank and tools, giving him enough room to continue.

Back in the darkness of the hole he shone the torch between the gaps in the metal grille. The torch didn't cast enough light for him to see what was below. Drake sighed and considered what he should do next.

"Joseph, I need a length of string."

Morris scurried around the shell of the kitchen, opening and closing drawers and cupboards until he found a bundle of green twine, which he tossed to Drake.

Drake wrapped the twine around the end of the torch and tied a knot. He heaved at the grille until he was able slide the torch beneath it and into the cavern. Slowly, he lowered the torch, and the light created mysterious shadows. The lower the torch went, the more he was able to make out.

And then he saw something. He pulled the torch back a few inches and waited for it to stop swinging. He squinted his eyes and could make out a yellowish white object. The torch wasn't as bright as he would have liked it to be. He pressed his face against the grille and strained to see what was below. He became accustomed to the darkness and as he did he made out other similar coloured objects. His heart pounded in his chest as he continued to make out what was down there.

They're bones, they're definitely bones, and they're small, he thought as the enormity of what he was looking at hit him. *They're infants' bones.*

Morris perched at the edge of the hole as Drake climbed the ladder.

"We'll, don't keep me waiting any longer," said Morris as Drake stepped from the ladder and rubbed dirt from his sleeves.

A menacing smile spanned Drake's face.

"Joseph, I think I've found William and Louisa."

Chapter 66

"That man's pure evil," said Heather.

"Which one, Butler or Morris?" asked her sister.

"Both, I mean, they're the same person," replied Heather as she nervously sat on the bed.

Sophie didn't understand.

"I can only tell you what I saw, and there wasn't a short ugly man with tattoos," said Sophie.

"And I didn't see the person you did. Don't you understand? This is part of Drake's plan, or maybe it's Joseph Morris who's behind this."

Sophie said nothing and recalled how the old man had broken Hugh's arm and smashed Mark through the stairs in less than a heartbeat. It was as if he had supernatural powers.

"Okay Heather, what do we do now?"

Heather didn't answer. A tremendous feeling of fear overcame her.

Rosie ran into the bedroom and was distraught.

"Mummy, mummy, William and Louisa are in trouble, they're scared, you need to help them."

"Okay Rosie, take a breath and tell me again."

"I was playing in my room and William came in, and he said his daddy took him and Louisa away," sobbed Rosie.

Heather turned to her sister. They knew what one another were thinking, but Heather spoke first.

"Drake and Morris. They've found the children."

Chapter 67

Drake removed the heavy metal grille, hauled it up the ladder and droppe‹ it next to Morris.

"I'm going back."

"And remember, we only need their skulls," said Morris.

Drake descended and teetered at the edge. Morris lowered another ladder for Drake to use to climb into the well.

Drake placed the three metre ladder into the well which was deeper than the ladder by three inches, so Drake was unable see where the top of the ladder was without peering over the edge. With the torch in his mouth, he got on his knees, carefully edged backwards, extended one leg into the well and searched for the top of the ladder with the tip of his toe. He let out a breath when his foot engaged with the top rung.

In life, Alexander Drake hated heights, and he was no different now.

Slowly, he descended. Drake found it easier once his hands held the rails and soon he stood on the rocky floor of the dried up well.

He looked up and saw Morris peering from above. Morris seemed an awfully long way up.

Drake shone the torch around the well and the dim light picked out two small skeletons tied to a length of rope. He leant forward, picked up one of the skulls, turned it over and looked at the back of the cranium. Even in the faint and shadowy light he made out the pattern on the skull. He ran his fingers over the strange outline which had been with the child since birth.

Drake trembled with excitement. He'd been waiting for this day since 1804, and now he had the skull in his hand he wasn't sure how to deal with his emotions.

He placed it at the bottom of the ladder and shone the torch at the other skull, and as he did he saw something that took him by surprise.

The skeleton fingers of the tiny hand gripped something. He took a step closer and bent forward. The hand clutched a child's toy. He reached and pulled it from the bones. It was a pink bear.

"What the fu……"

Drake read the writing on the label.

'To Rosie, my favourite granddaughter.'

The tiny part of Finn Maynard that remained came charging to the forefront. He held the bear in his hand and trembled.

Rosie gave Amy, her favourite bear, to William for him to pass on to Louisa. Drake had pulled the toy from the remains of the little girl's hand and the instant he took it, Finn was almost back to his old self. Memories of his daughter evoked by the bear were too powerful, even for the overwhelming command of Alexander Drake to contend with.

He stood in darkness and thought of his wife, daughter and son.

Oh my God, what have I done?

He shuddered and looked at the tiny bodies by his feet.

His thoughts were jumbled, but he recalled Sophie telling him that Rosie gave Amy bear to Louisa, the sister of the ghost who'd appeared in their kitchen. He also remembered Gabriel Butler offering him a ridiculous sum of money to dig beneath his kitchen and find two bodies.

He gripped the bear to his chest. He was desperate to be with his family.

Butler looked down from above.

"Alexander, what's keeping you my old friend?"

Finn stood motionless and assessed the situation. He knew the name Alexander, but couldn't place its significance.

Joseph Morris became impatient.

"Drake, answer me, what's the holdup?"

Drake…. Alexander….. shit, Alexander Drake, he thinks I'm Alexander Drake, thought Finn.

He wasn't sure who Alexander Drake was, but enough dim memories fogged his mind to associate the name with 'Gabriel Butler' for Finn to know it was important. He winced at the pain in his hands after digging the shaft which towered above him. Whatever had been happening needed to stop. The vital connection made by the bear to Rosie was enough to give him the strength of mind he required to overcome what was happening to him.

"I'm on my way up," called Finn.

Morris detected something different in Drake's tone. He assumed it was tiredness and thought nothing else of it.

Finn shoved the bear in his pocket and climbed the ladder. Having it close allowed him to focus on his family and his love for them.

He ascended the well and stood at the bottom of the hole. Butler's head loomed from above.

"Where are the skulls?" called Butler.

"I'll go back for them in a minute, I need to come up for air," replied Finn.

"We don't have time, go back and bring me the skulls."

"I will, just let me get a breath of fresh air, a glass of water and I'll go back."

Morris sighed.

Finn climbed from the hole and up to the kitchen. He was taken aback by the surrounding devastation.

Did I do that?

He grabbed a glass, ran the tap and wondered what to do next. He needed to get out at once.

Morris watched his old friend drink the water from a pint glass. Someth about him wasn't right. Why hadn't Drake brought the skulls up with him? I didn't make sense.

Suddenly, in a lame try at creating a diversion, Finn threw the glass of water in Butler's face and darted for the front door, but before he even made it to the hall, Butler blocked his exit from the house. Finn turned and ran to the back door, but before he'd a chance to barely move Butler stood in the doorway between the kitchen and the garden. He turned again back to the hall, but Butler stood facing him, nose to nose.

Finn was stunned by Butler's speed, as if he was in two places at the same time.

Butler couldn't work out what had happened to Drake, but he knew it was Maynard facing him and not Alexander.

"Going somewhere?" asked Butler in a patronising tone.

"Yeah, out of here," replied Finn.

Butler didn't want to exhort too much force upon Maynard, he mustn't risk harming him. He needed him to return to the state of Alexander Drake and get back to the well to get the skulls.

"Finn, what are you thinking of, don't forget the money, you'll be a rich man, just go back down and get those skulls."

"You can take your cash and shove it."

"But why the sudden change of heart?" asked Butler in an imploring tone.

"Because of this," replied Finn holding the bear to Butler's face.

Butler shook his head. He couldn't understand the connection.

"It's my daughter's, and I found it in the clutches of the dead child. I must get it back to her. I need to be with my family."

Butler didn't understand how it got there, but knew it had been the catalyst which sparked Finn Maynard's sudden return.

"Let me see it," asked Butler in a gentle tone of voice.

"Oh, no you don't," replied Finn.

The next thing Finn saw was the bear in Butler's hands. With unbelievable lightning speed he had grabbed it from Finn's clutches and held it above his head.

Finn wobbled and felt lightheaded. He was about to fall to the floor, but Butler caught him before he hit the ground.

Butler held Finn's limp frame tightly in his grip. He placed the palm of his hand against Finn's forehead and chanted.

"Hic en spiritum, sed non incorpore, evokare lemures de mortuis, decretum espugnare, De Angelus Balberith, en inferno inremeablis."

Butler trembled as he quickly recited the next four repetitious lines.

"Wa ta na siam, wa ta na siam, wa ta na siam. wa ta na siam"

Drake opened his eyes and looked at Joseph Morris whose brow was wet with perspiration.

"What happened?" asked Drake.

"Nothing to worry about, I'd lost you for a second, but now you're back. Please continue with your work."

Morris smiled as Drake unsteadily walked back to the kitchen and disappeared back down the hole to retrieve the skulls.

Chapter 68

"What the hell are we supposed to do?" said Sophie.

Heather had no idea. She'd received no guidance from Nash, Elizabeth or Alice in a long time. It was as if they'd upped and gone away before they had explained what on earth was happening.

"If only I could speak with Elizabeth, she would know what to do," replied Heather.

"Speak to her then, get her to help us."

"How many more times?" snapped Heather angrily. "I can't, I've lost the ability. I should never have let Charlie go. I'm sure it was because of him I could contact them all so easily."

She looked at her sister and tears welled in her eyes.

"Elizabeth said she used a silver cross around her neck. That was her channel, it was her means to make contacting the dead easier."

Sophie stood in silence and cast her mind back.

"Do you remember the cross? Could you describe it?" asked Sophie.

Although Heather hadn't seen the cross since the last time she was with her great grandmother in hospital, she could recall it hanging around Elizabeth's neck as she lay on her deathbed.

"It was small, no bigger than the top of my middle finger, and it had a tiny figurine of Christ," replied Heather.

"Wait there," said Sophie, and she left the bedroom.

"Where's mummy going?" asked Rosie in a frightened voice. She'd been sitting on the edge of the bed listening to the adult's conversation.

Heather didn't answer as she stroked Rosie's hair.

A few minutes later Sophie returned with a small blue box and handed it to Heather.

"Take a look in there."

Heather tentatively removed the lid and huffed air through her cheeks when she saw the small silver cross and the tiny statuette of Jesus, with arms outstretched.

"This was Elizabeth's, where did you find it?" asked Heather.

"I remembered coming across it in Mum and Dad's bedroom when I was small. Nan had handed it down to mum and before that Elizabeth must have passed it to Nan."

"It's beautiful," said Heather removing it from the box and holding it by the delicate silver chain.

"I don't know why mum's never worn it," said Sophie.

"I do," replied Heather, "because she wanted nothing to do with Elizabeth's gift. She probably worried that if she wore it, she'd end up speaking with the dead as Elizabeth did."

She ran her finger over the tiny silver effigy of Jesus and then stood up, walked to the mirror and put the necklace on.

She turned to face Sophie who was sniffing the air.

"It's that smell," said Sophie, "the same in the kitchen when William appeared."

Heather knew what she meant. It was the same smell Heather had noticed when she'd seen Elizabeth and Charles Nash.

She turned back around to face the mirror and jolted when she saw Elizabeth standing between her and the glass.

The heat emanating from the apparition was intense and Heather took two steps back.

"I'm sorry we've not spoken for a while, but something's been stopping us from seeing each other," said the vision of Elizabeth.

Heather stood with her mouth open and gaped in awe at what had materialised in front of her.

Sophie watched her sister staring into the middle distance.

"I thought you'd given up on me," said Heather.

"No, not at all, never."

"What was stopping you?"

Elizabeth shook her head and looked despondent.

"I'd prefer not tell you, but what's important is that you stop what Drake, Morris and the others are planning to do."

"They're planning a ceremony aren't they, and they need the skulls of the children buried beneath Sophie's house," said Heather, not asking, but stating a fact.

Elizabeth nodded.

"Do you remember the old lady in the churchyard?" asked Elizabeth.

Heather nodded.

"Her name was Hermione, and Alice Donaldson had been guiding her for nearly one hundred years and it was her duty to protect Charles Nash and prevent Drake and his gang from doing what they intended. But now she's passed away, and now Alice is guiding you, or she was, until she was prevented by the force driving Drake and Morris."

"The force driving Drake and Morris?" repeated Heather, "you mean the Devil?"

Elizabeth nodded.

"I don't think Alice can help you anymore, she's not strong enough to compete with the evil that Drake and his gang have in mind."

"You mean the sacrifice, I need to stop the sacrifice."

"Yes, but it's not a sacrifice. It's an offering to the devil, or Azazel as Drake and Morris refer to it."

"But why those skulls, why are the skulls of William and Louisa Drake so important."

"Because they carry the mark of the Beast."

"Do you mean 666?"

"I only wish I did. The three sixes are nonsense, they never existed."

"But they're in the Bible, I've read it for myself."

"Yes, they are in the Bible that you and hundreds of millions of others have read, but that doesn't mean to say that what the Bible states is entirely factual."

Heather looked puzzled. "But why not?"

"We've all read the King James version," said Elizabeth.

Heather nodded.

"Eight members of the Church of England completed the King James version in sixteen-eleven," said Elizabeth.

"I'm aware of that, they'd translated it into English," said Heather.

"Are you sure? There were, and still are, no original texts of the Bible to translate. The oldest manuscripts which exist were many many years after the last apostle died. There are thousands of old manuscripts and none are alike."

Heather listened intently.

"But even with these ancient manuscripts, the translators used none of them. Instead, they butchered earlier translations and created a version of which their king would approve."

"So you're telling me the Bible is made up?" asked Heather.

"No, not at all, it's just not entirely correct."

"How correct is it?"

"Well, let me put it this way. Many modern day Christians believe in a Bible written in the seventeenth century, from sixteenth century translations of thousands and thousands of copies of fourth century scrolls, many of which were contradictory and which claim to be copies of lost letters written in the first century."

"How can you be sure?" queried Heather.

"Don't forget, I'm privy to 'inside information'," replied Elizabeth pointing upward with a smile.

"So the mark of the Devil isn't three sixes."

"No, the only similarity is that there are three marks, like the three sixes I suppose. But the original and true mark of the Devil is carried through the bloodline."

"Whose bloodline?"

"The Devil's. The Beast would have laid with William and Louisa's mother to ensure she carried on the bloodline and his mark."

"But what about the third mark, William and Louisa are twins, they're brother and sister. You mentioned the third mark of the Beast. Where would that be?"

"I don't know and luckily neither does Morris or Drake, but Morris won't let anything stop him until he finds it and he's running out of time."

Heather looked at Elizabeth and tried to take on board what she was saying.

"So the Devil fathered William and Louisa, did he father another child by another woman?" asked Heather.

"No, the mother was the same person. She would have given birth to all three at the same time."

"So, William and Louisa are two of triplets," stated Heather.

"Correct. Drake, Morris and their associates have no way of completing the offering unless they have the three marks of the Beast. The two skulls alone are useless to them."

"Why are they intent on making an offering of the three skulls?" asked Heather.

"Because it will create the worse evil known to mankind. It will give Azazel, the King of Devils, the power to walk among mankind and to carry out his evil."

Heather swallowed hard. Why had she been chosen to stop such an immense happening? Why wasn't a senior church person chosen? Why a lowly young woman who hadn't set foot in a church for years?

"The Beast has been here in recent times, and has always been defeated by good," added Elizabeth.

Heather was stunned.

"You mean the Devil has walked the earth, in my living memory?"

Elizabeth nodded, "do the names Hitler, Saddam and Attila the Hun ring any bells?"

Heather gasped.

"And I'm expected to stop the next in line?"

"No, you're expected to prevent him from ever happening to begin with."

Heather paused for reflection as she took on board the momentous task set before her. She took a breath and looked at Elizabeth who was fading.

"So it's my job to make sure Drake and Morris don't find the Third Skull!"

Chapter 69

Drake placed both skulls on the kitchen table next to the pink bear he'd found in the well. A smug look crossed his face.

The raven hopped excitedly in the doorway.

Morris bent forward and pulled them towards him. With one in each hand he examined the archetypa.

"I'd never thought I'd see the day," said Morris, who found it difficult not to show his emotions. "They're beautiful."

"Joseph, I've kept my side of the bargain, I've retrieved the skulls, and now it's your turn to find Mathias'. I need not remind you, but without it, all of this has been futile," said Drake motioning to the skulls and the hole under the kitchen floor.

Morris ignored him. He replaced the skulls on the table and picked up the bear, examined it and read what was on the label, 'To Rosie, my favourite granddaughter'.

"How did that get down there?"

"I don't know, but keep it out of my sight. I don't want a repeat of what just happened," replied Drake.

Morris pushed it to the side of the table.

"So what's your plan Joseph? You seem pretty laid back about the whole thing. We're days away from our goal and you're walking around with your thumb up your ass, while you should be searching for Mathias."

Morris stood up and walked over to Drake. The short, rotund man grabbed him by the collar and threw him to the floor with such force, a shock wave ripped through his body.

"What's that supposed to mean, I've been walking around with my thumb up my ass?" snarled Morris as he stood with his foot pressed hard against Drake's chest.

"Don't intimidate me! I'm the one who's been single handedly digging that hole, whilst you've been reading your stupid book."

Morris exerted more pressure with the sole of his foot.

"Okay my friend, let me take this opportunity to remind you of a few things, which may just overshadow my mistake of losing Mathias."

Drake braced himself for a lecture from Morris.

"First, there's the small fact that you lost not one, but two of the children in your charge, and that somehow you were cheated by a young woman barely out of her teens, who, by the force of 'bloody good', has become our nemesis for the past two hundred years. And second, whilst you've been relaxing between earth and hell, I've been the one who's spent every day searching for the kids you'd lost. I've kept your soul alive and have brought you back from the dead more times than I care to remember. So Alexander, I think digging that hole is little compared to the shit I've had to endure these past two centuries, wouldn't you agree?"

Drake nodded silently.

"Okay," replied Drake in a pitiful tone, "what's next?"

Morris removed his foot from Drake's chest and stepped back.

"What's next? I'll tell you what's next. You need to back fill that hole and leave the rest to me."

He sat back on a kitchen chair, picked up Middlemarch and continued reading from where he'd left off.

Drake huffed, got up from the floor and held his hand against his chest. He was irate with Morris and his obsession about that stupid book.

Chapter 70

The sisters lay in the bed they'd shared since the fire in Heather's flat. It had been over an hour since Elizabeth's visitation and Heather still quivered with shock.

"You're telling me you couldn't see her?" asked Heather.

"No, but I knew she was there. I could smell dampness and I could feel her heat. I don't doubt you for an instant," replied Sophie.

"Could you hear what we were talking about?"

"Yes, but only from your side. What did she say?"

"She's put me in the picture, and now I know what's going on."

Heather told her sister of the ritual to raise the Devil and Morris and Drake's need to find the missing third skull.

"So there were three children,……. triplets, and only two of them are beneath my house. Why not all three?"

"I'm not sure, but after what Rosie said earlier, it's my reckoning that Drake and Morris have found William and Louisa, so they're two thirds of the way there."

Heather stared at the ceiling and contemplated the whole bizarre situation.

"I understand why I need to stop Drake and Morris from finding the third skull, but what I still don't grasp is what Charles Nash has to do with it. Why would Nash need protecting? He's dead."

"Didn't Elizabeth give you even the slightest idea?"

"No, although she mentioned the old lady I saw in the graveyard was my predecessor, she's the one who'd been protecting Nash before me, and guided by Alice Donaldson."

An idea pinged into Sophie's head. She turned and looked to her sister.

"Why don't you try to speak with the lady in the graveyard, maybe she can tell you what's so important about Charles Nash?"

Heather shook her head and Sophie sensed her sister's frustration. Sophie just didn't seem to understand how difficult it was to connect with the dead.

"I'm sorry, I'm just trying to help," sighed Sophie.

Heather lay still and thought of what Sophie had suggested. She recalled what Elizabeth had told her when she had first materialised in her flat. She said that she used the cross as a channel to speak with the dead. Heather had assumed that the stone head would have been the channel to enable her to speak with Charles Nash and any of the other spirits who had been communicating with her, but it hadn't proved to be effective. She touched the cross and thought.

I wonder?

Heather jumped out of bed and pulled her jeans on.

"What are you doing?" asked Sophie.

"I'm going out."
"Where, it's ten thirty?"
"I'm off to speak with the old lady."

It was just after eleven on a cold December night when Heather pushed open the gate to the graveyard of St Michael on the Mount Without, where it had all begun sixteen months earlier.

She pulled her coat around her to keep away the chill of the night and made her way to Charles Nash's gravestone. It had been a long time since Heather had been to the graveyard, and Nash's grave had become overgrown with weeds. The orange glow of a nearby street light made it just possible for Heather to see the gravestone. She knelt on the damp ground and pulled away a handful of weeds.

After a few minutes she stopped. Her fingers stung with cold. She'd cleared a bundle of weeds and grass and the gravestone looked better. She reached inside her coat, touched the cross around her neck and closed her eyes.

She recalled the time she spoke with the old lady. As Heather recollected the brief conversation with her she became uncertain whether it had actually happened. It was the night she'd been taken to Frenchay Hospital after being discovered by a passing policeman. The doctors where treating her for exposure due to the cold. But did that ever happen? She recalled how she awoke back in her own bed the following morning with grass and soil on her feet. Elizabeth had spoken to her and explained what took place was 'a happening'. 'A midpoint between a dream and reality'.

Heather shuddered as the cold air permeated through her thick winter coat. She closed her eyes and began.

"Hermione, we've spoken before. My name is Heather and I've been chosen to protect Charles Nash. I'm aware of William and Louisa, and that I need to prevent Alexander Drake and Joseph Morris from finding the skull of the other child. But I don't understand why I need to protect Charles. Please guide me, I really need help."

Heather dropped to the floor, lay across Nash's gravestone and sobbed.

"Please, I can't do this on my own. I need help to understand what I have to do."

She lay face down upon the stone and put her head in her arms as if she was on her bed with her head on the pillow, and as she did so she became aware of an overwhelming sense of tranquillity. For the first since she could remember Heather felt relaxed. Every tense muscle in her body loosened.

The night became mild as if she became enveloped in a radiant warmth. Heather sat up, looked at the church wall and watched her shadow as it danced on the stone of the ancient building.

She didn't understand why her shadow was so well-defined, the street light alone wasn't bright enough to cast enough light to create such a distinct shadow. She turned around, and met with the image of a beautiful young woman. The woman cast an enchanting incandescent glow. Heather looked at her face. Her kind eyes looked familiar.

And then she spoke.

"Hello Heather,"

Heather backed up towards the wall of the church.

"Don't be scared, I heard you call for help."

Heather focussed on her face, then she remembered where she'd seen her before. It was the old lady.

"You're Hermione aren't you? And Alice guided you."

"Alice has guided both of us," replied the ghost of the young woman.

"But why did she guide you, why were you chosen?"

"I was Hermione Nash."

"Nash, you're related to Charles?"

"He was my grandfather."

Heather took time to appreciate the enormity of the situation.

"So you knew Charles?"

Hermione shook her head.

"He died a young man, long before I was born."

Heather glanced at the faded inscription on his grave.

Born ----ber 1- --99
Died September 6 1839

"How old was he?" whispered Heather.

"Thirty-nine years old," said Hermione.

Heather knew Hermione wouldn't stay for long. She needed to take advantage of what she understood would be a brief meeting and find out as much as she could about Charles Nash and what he needed protecting from.

"From what does Charles need protection?"

"Not what, it's who he needs protecting from. There are four malignant echoes from the past determined to use my grandfather and involve him in something awful."

"What do you mean by echoes?"

"Spirits, ghosts, like myself and Elizabeth. But unlike Elizabeth and me, they are fuelled by pure evil."

"Do these spirits have names?"

"Rupert Snow, Albert Cromwell……."

The first two names meant nothing. Hermione continued.

"……. Alexander Drake and Joseph Morris."

"There's four of them? I thought I was only up against Drake and Morris."

"Drake and Morris are the two who walk amongst the living. Snow exists, but he's not of this world and Cromwell, well Cromwell is the most evil of the four and he is the lynchpin which holds their evil plan together. Without him, the others have no power."

Heather was more confused than before. It seemed the task set for her was insurmountable. How was she ever going to stop such wicked souls from carrying out their evil work?

"So I have to stop Cromwell and protect Charles?"

"I don't think anyone or anything will stop Cromwell, he's too powerful. But he needs Morris to resurrect him."

Her mind swirled as she tried to keep up.

"But why does your grandfather need protecting?"

"He has something they need. He holds a secret."

"But he's dead, why can't Drake or Morris get what they want from him in the afterlife, or wherever you go?" pleaded Heather.

"Please make sure they don't get him."

Hermione's image became hazy.

"By any way you can," she added.

Heather ran towards Hermione to stop her from disappearing, but recoiled when she came into contact with the space in which the fading image occupied. The heat was like an oven.

Hermione had gone. All that remained in her wake was the buzz of static, the familiar smell of ozone and the fading heat of her aura.

Heather was more despondent than ever. She had been so close to getting the answers.

It was definitely Drake and Morris from whom Nash needed protection. But what did the malevolent ghouls want from him?

In two days' time, Heather would find out.

Chapter 71

Joseph Morris poured over the well-thumbed copy of George Elliott's Middlemarch. He'd been reading it yearly since his fourth incarnation.

In the mid-nineteenth century, Morris had taken over the body of Bristolian shopkeeper Alistair Grant. One night in eighteen seventy four, he'd woken after a vivid dream where Azazel, the King of Devils, had spoken to him.

'Morris, if you want to find out what happened to that brat Mathias, then the answer is in the seven hundred and forty third hour of the third month.'

Morris had been certain that Azazel had spoken with him and spent over a year pondering what the message had meant. He was sure the message from Azazel wasn't a dream, but was a clue which would lead him to the remains of Mathias, and he would never forget the date he'd received it. As far as Morris was concerned, Azazel had contacted him. It plagued him constantly and each day he tried to understand what it could mean.

The following year a friend introduced him to Elliot's book. He turned to the inside cover and saw that the date of publication happened to be the same day he'd heard from Azazel.

The seven hundred and forty third hour of the third month could only mean the middle of March. Middlemarch. He'd read the book repeatedly for one hundred and thirty years and would not give up until the book told him where to find the bones of Mathias.

Morris made thousands of notes with scribbled ideas, based upon what he thought may have been clues to where he would find the boy. There were hundreds of different permutations of calculations he'd worked out based upon page and chapter numbers. He'd read pages and cross referenced them with other pages hoping to find a cypher within the text of the story. The clues he thought he'd discovered had led him up and down the UK, around most of Europe and North America. Over the years he'd desecrated the graves of hundreds of young children hoping to find Mathias.

And now, two days before the ritual, he was nowhere nearer finding the answer.

He lay on the settee in Finn's house, dropped the book to the floor and let out a despondent sigh. He could hear Drake in the kitchen back filling the hole.

Morris wondered whether the last two hundred years had been a complete waste of time. Maybe the boy's body *had* disappeared a long time ago and his remains turned to dust. Morris felt downcast. The work to find William and Louisa had paid off, so why should it be so difficult to find Mathias?

Drake adopted William and Louisa, and Morris took charge of Mathias minutes after the children were born. After which, he and Drake killed their mother and dumped her body in a shallow grave. Nobody missed the homeless woman who yielded the three children which carried the lifeblood of the Devil.

The children were innocent vessels of evil.

In their five short years, Drake and Morris ensured the children had everything they wanted. A good home, food, toys and in William and Louisa's circumstances, the love of Alice Donaldson, whom they'd considered the closest person to a mother.

Neither William nor Louisa had met, nor known of Mathias. Since their birth, Morris and Drake needed to make sure the three would never occupy the same space, until they were ready to be sacrificed as an offering to Azazel.

Even though the children died over two centuries ago, the secret they held was as important now as it was when they were alive.

Morris and Drake, along with Rupert Snow and Albert Cromwell were pure evil and had no reservations about their intentions.

Morris considered his situation. Two days until the offering and he was desperate.

He stood up and walked over to Finn's printer in the corner of the lounge. There were several copies of the third archetypon which lay in a neat pile. Morris picked up a sheet of A4 and looked at the pattern which Finn produced subconsciously under the guidance of Azazel. Morris held it up to the light and ran his fingers over the strange pagan like form.

"If Mathias wasn't out there somewhere, then why would Azazel have given me this?" said Morris under his breath.

He lit a Carlito Fuente and strolled into the kitchen.

Drake was feverishly back filling the hole. He stopped when he saw Morris enter the kitchen.

"Has your book told you where to dig?" asked Drake in a patronising tone.

Morris shook his head and examined the archetypon.

"I thought not," grunted Drake.

Together with finding Mathias, something else urgently needed Morris' attention. The ritual not only required the three skulls, it also needed Albert Cromwell who was key to the success of the sacrament.

Morris exhaled, picked up the phone and made arrangements to bring Cromwell back from the dead.

Chapter 72

"That was Butler wasn't it?" asked Linda with a stern look.

Kieran sat down, placed the phone on the table and looked at his wife awkwardly.

"It was, but he sounded different."

"Why?"

"I don't know, it was him, but he sounded……… different."

"What did he want?" snapped Linda.

"He rang with details of where and when to meet."

"But I told you to say 'no'."

"Listen Linda," barked Kieran, "Gabriel Butler is a powerful and persuasive man, and he's someone to whom you don't say 'no'."

Linda huffed air through her cheeks.

"I just don't trust the man. Did he tell you what you're supposed to do?"

"No, he only said I need to be at his mansion on the fourteenth at five o'clock."

"The fourteenth of December? You're aware what happened on that date two years ago aren't you?"

Kieran nodded.

"It's the second anniversary of Buxton's suicide," he replied sheepishly.

Linda stood with her arms folded and a look on her face which made Kieran shudder.

"Kieran, you're a fucking fool. I'm not asking you, I'm telling you don't go or else you'll end up dead. Butler's evil and whatever he's got in store, you're his whipping boy and he's using you. You're doing this for the money, but I'm sure you won't be around by the end of the night to see a penny of what he's promising."

"Listen to yourself, what's got into you? Don't be so stupid. Never doubt the man and his promises. He's wealthy and has paid for this," said Kieran in a raised voice waving his hands around the room.

"He gave you a shitload of money for twenty years of obligation. You watched that house in Whitcombe Fields Road and told him of the ins and outs of what happened there dutifully without a break. Now he reckons he'll give you almost the same amount of cash for one evening's work. It doesn't make sense!"

"I'm going, and that's the end of it. You can do whatever you want, but you're not stopping me."

Linda's opinion of Butler had changed. When she and her husband first met him, she considered him an eccentric billionaire who had a strange interest in the house across the road. They got to know him, and although he could be peculiar, they liked him.

As time went on, Butler asked more questions of the comings and goings in 11a and many of his questions were strange. By the time Finn Maynard and his family moved in, he had Kieran reporting on what was happening there almost daily.

She'd put up with his unusual requests because of his promise of a huge 'thank you', of one and three quarter million pounds. He was true to his word and paid the inordinate sum as soon as Finn told Kieran he'd been on the train which killed Robert Buxton, and he'd seen the body. This is what Butler needed to know and had been specific about when he'd told Kieran that Finn Maynard must tell him of Robert Buxton's suicide of his own will. Kieran mustn't have coaxed the information out of him.

Neither Linda nor Kieran understood why Butler's demands were so specific. They didn't know that each adult male who lived at 11a Whitcombe Fields Road ended up there for a reason. And that reason was to confirm the whereabouts of the remains of William and Louisa, and to also work out the pattern of third archetypon, which would aid Butler in finding the body of Mathias Morris.

Shaun Morrison, who had been the first to have been lured to live in the house by Butler proved to be useless, even though Azazel assured Butler that he'd been the one. David Gosling was next to live there. Again, he'd been unable to provide the information Butler needed. His suicide happened in a car purchased from Robert Buxton, who was next to live in 11a. Buxton had been so close to confirming where the bodies of William and Louisa lay, after he subconsciously worked out the archetypa which matched their skulls. But he'd not been able to work out the third archetypon, which matched Mathias'. Madness set in and he'd hurled himself in front of the train which carried Finn home from the meeting in Cardiff that fateful day in December two thousand and four. Finn was next to move in and when he'd successfully, under the guidance of Azazel, worked out third archetypon, he'd proved to Butler that he was most definitely the 'chosen one'.

Linda and Kieran didn't understand why Butler had such an interest in what went on in that house, and neither of them particularly cared as the lure of the money he'd promised outweighed whatever plans the odd billionaire had in mind.

But Linda's attitude towards Butler had altered. Now she viewed him as a wicked malevolent man who was planning something evil. She could pinpoint exactly when her attitude changed.

It had changed since she'd gained the mysterious stone head.

Chapter 73

"So what do you suggest we do?" asked Sophie.
"I've no idea," replied Heather shrugging her shoulders.
She turned and looked at the darkness of the evening sky from the bedroom window.
"I can't say what Drake and Morris want with Charles Nash, but I know when he needs my protection."
Sophie walked over to the window and stood next to her sister.
"The fourteenth of December by any chance?" asked Sophie.
Heather nodded.
"This started the day Finn discovered Robert Buxton's head on the railway line."
Sophie nodded, took her sister's hand and squeezed it.
"A year later Buxton's ghost was in Rosie's room, and ever since then these hideous things have been happening to my Finn."
A tear rolled down her cheek.
"Heather, do you think I'll ever get him back?"
Heather held onto her hand and nodded.
"I'm sure we will."
Sophie knew her sister wasn't speaking the truth and was as unsure of what was happening as she was.
She cleared her throat and let go of Heather's hand.
"Well, I guess there's only one thing we can do," said Sophie.
Heather looked from the window and turned to her sister.
"We'll go to Nash's grave on the fourteenth and wait."
"And what if Morris and Drake turn up, there's no way the two of us can stop them, you saw what Morris did to Hugh and Mark," said Heather nervously.
"Wasn't that Butler?"
"I've said before, they're one and the same."

They spent the next hour working on their plan, but ultimately realised they didn't have one, other than waiting at the grave. They had no idea when Butler and Drake would arrive, so they agreed that they should be at the church of St Michael on the Mount Without at the stroke of midnight and wait until something happened.
"Maybe we should bring dad with us?" said Sophie.
"No, we mustn't tell mum and dad what's happening. We need to keep this to ourselves. Anyway, what's the point? If Mark and Hugh couldn't help us I can't see what good dad would be."
Sophie nodded dejectedly.
"There's someone I'd like to have had with us," added Heather.

"Who?" said Sophie as she looked towards her sister curiously.
"Charlie," said Heather with a pained expression.
"I wish Charlie could be with us. He'd tell me what to do."

Chapter 74

Morris watched Drake replace the last floorboard after spending the day back-filling the hole.

He placed the spade and the pickaxe in the hall and blew out a long sigh.

Drake was filthy, his hands blistered, and he hadn't been near a sink in days.

"Put those tools in the back of my car then tidy yourself up," said Morris.

Drake's body ached, but mentally he was as sharp as a tack. The ritual was less than twenty-four hours away and there was plenty to do. Not to mention the small matter of finding Mathias.

Drake clumped down the stairs after having a quick wash and a change of clothes. He still looked a mess. His hair was unkempt, and he needed a shave.

Morris tutted.

"That'll do, but make sure you smarten yourself up for tomorrow."

Drake ignored his comment and Morris slipped the copy of the third archetypon in a brown envelope and placed it in his pocket.

"We need to get over to the mansion and prepare the basement for tomorrow evening," said Morris.

"Joseph, is there any point? Unless you find Mathias, what we've achieved is futile. And what's happening with Cromwell? Even if you find Mathias, we need Albert."

"Don't concern yourself with Cromwell, I've taken care of things. Don't worry about Rupert Snow either, he's at the mansion."

Drake couldn't understand why Morris appeared so calm. But despite appearing composed on the outside, Morris was a bundle of nerves. He didn't know where to find Mathias. He'd torn up Middlemarch and scattered the pages over the floor in anger after wasting over one hundred and thirty years reading the wretched thing. Morris had been searching for clues that just weren't there. He'd given in to the notion that Azazel hadn't spoken to him, and what happened that night way back in eighteen seventy four was nothing more than a dream which he'd interpreted as the word of the Devil.

"The seven hundred and forty third hour of the third month," muttered Morris.

With less than a day until the ceremony, Morris craved Demonic intervention. Fortunately for him, he wouldn't need to wait very much longer.

"Alexander, get the skulls from the kitchen and let's get out of here," said Morris.

"What about that thing?" said Drake pointing to Rosie's bear he'd found with the skeletons.

“Don’t you get near that thing, I’ll take it and destroy it,” said Morris scooping it from the kitchen table and ramming it into his pocket.

The two men got into the Rolls Royce, left Whitcombe Fields Road and made their way to the mansion where Drake had lived in the nineteenth century. The same building in which Morris, under the façade of billionaire Gabriel Butler, had lived for the past fifty years.

The black Silver Cloud turned the corner and headed towards the gates. Drake smiled when he saw the frail man in the black overcoat standing on the pavement.

“It’s Snow,” said Drake breathlessly, “he’s here.”

Rupert Snow waved as the car pulled up to the gates. He walked over to Drake’s side and waited as he lowered the window.

“Rupert my dear friend. How are you? I’ve not seen you in centuries.”

Snow smiled and glimpsed the ring he’d given Finn in the antique shop last year.

“I’m absolutely fine Alexander. It’s wonderful to see you again.”

“Okay, okay, there’ll be time to catch up later, but right now there are preparations to be made,” said Morris interrupting the two old friends.

Morris hit the remote and the huge metal gates slowly opened. Snow walked behind the car as it quietly coasted along the gravel drive.

Drake climbed from the car and looked in awe at the house. He had no recollection of being there earlier that week. He ran his fingers along the stone work. Suddenly, memories of living there and being one of Bristol's most influential men came rushing back.

Morris watched from the car. He didn’t have time to let Drake reminisce, but allowed him a few minutes to take on board what was happening to him.

Drake looked up at the building. Not much of the mansion had changed since he’d lived there. He turned and looked through the gate.
He remembered the fields and lanes that had surrounded it back in the eighteen hundreds'. He was grateful to Joseph Morris, who'd been looking after the place in one form or another since Drake died in eighteen forty one.

"What are your intentions?" said Morris as he climbed from the car.

Drake came around from his dreamlike state.

"My intentions?" asked Drake quizzically.

"If it's alright with you and Mr. Snow, I'd like to get things started and I'd like you to come too."

Morris unlocked the door and stood in the great hallway. He turned to face Drake, whose memories were flooding back.

"Alexander, haven't you forgotten something?" asked Morris.

Drake looked at Morris blankly and shook his head.

"The skulls, they're in the car."

Drake stepped outside and returned with them.
Snow took a step closer and inspected the patterns on each skull.
"I'd never thought I'd see the day. Can I hold them?"
Drake deftly passed the skulls to Snow who held them with care. He marvelled at the 'pagan like' patterns.
"Sent from the Devil himself," he said under his breath, and then returned them to Drake.
"Okay you two, there'll be time for that later. We must go to the basement and prepare, there's plenty of work to do."

Morris opened the hidden door and descended the rickety stairs. Snow and Drake were close behind.
"What about the other skull?" whispered Snow.
"He doesn't have it," replied Drake.
Morris stopped, turned to face them and threw them an icy glare.

Drake lit the candles while Snow and Morris retrieved the ceremonial costumes from the tall wardrobe at the back of the basement.
"They look as fine as they did two hundred years ago," remarked Snow as he ran his fingers over his attire. He admired the blue and silver cloak. The gold pentagram looked resplendent as it shimmered in the candlelight.
Drake placed the skulls in a box in the corner. He walked over to the table in the centre of the basement and removed the cloth which had protected it since the three men were last together.
The three wooden boxes with ornate carvings were equally spaced upon the table. On each box lay a blue cushion with an emblem of a pentagram. He removed the cushions and opened each box which contained a small pewter saucer.
"Rupert, please could you pass me the blood?"
Snow replaced the costumes in the wardrobe and took a silver container from a shelf below the portrait of Alexander Drake. He looked at the picture which was painted when Drake had been in his thirties. In the painting he wore a beautiful fitted tailcoat over a starched white shirt with a chin high neck and an ornate cravat which at the time was de rigueur. On the breast of the tailcoat was the Drake family crest. Snow glanced at the man standing at the table. The likeness was uncanny. He handed the container to Drake.
Drake sprinkled dry animal blood in each of the pewter saucers and closed the lids of the boxes.
Snow and Morris hauled a heavy wooden chair from beside the wardrobe and placed it in front of the circular table
The three men spent the next few hours hanging emblem embossed tapestries from the walls and made final preparations for the following day.

By ten o'clock everything was ready. They ascended the stairs and left the basement. Morris was hot. He walked to the front door, opened it and let the cold winter air chill his skin. He took half a dozen steps along the driveway and rested against the bonnet of the Rolls Royce.

Morris reached into his trouser pocket and took out the envelope in which was the copy of the third archetypon which matched the pattern on the back of Mathias' skull. He studied it in the bright glow of the security light which had turned on when he'd set foot on the driveway.

The sound of a bird cawing distracted him as it circled overhead. Morris looked upwards but saw nothing in the dark sky. He heard it again, and this time it was louder. The raven swooped from eves of the mansion and settled alongside Morris on the bonnet of his car.

"Get your claws off my car," laughed Morris as he tickled the bird's head. The raven gurgled, hopped from the car and strutted across the gravel drive.

"How on earth am I going to find the little bastard," muttered Morris as he looked at the pattern on the A4 sheet of paper.

The raven gurgled.

Morris was tired. He rubbed his eyes, folded the paper and was about to place it in his pocket when the raven hopped up and snatched the paper from Morris' hand with its beak. It looked at Morris and cocked its head to one side.

"Give that back," demanded Morris.

The bird strutted away from him with the folded paper in its bill. Morris cautiously took two steps towards the raven who hopped and strutted further away.

"Don't play games, I need that."

The raven sprung into the air and flew away.

"Come back you little shit."

The raven soared over Morris' head and landed on the roof of the car. Morris shuffled towards the bird, mindful not to scare it. Just as he could reach out and grab it, the bird jumped down to the drive and hopped towards the gate before taking off again. It circled the driveway and landed on the gate. It stared at Morris as if it was taunting him to climb the gate. Morris gingerly walked over, stopped at the gate and looked up at the bird. The raven flew from the gate to a street lamp across the road. Morris hit the green button on a control panel behind the hedge, and the gate slowly opened. He stepped out of the driveway, onto the pavement and walked towards the street lamp. The raven watched him with the paper still in its beak. Morris got to the streetlight, but the bird flew off and landed on the next lamp.

"It wants me to follow," muttered Morris.

He turned on his heels and ran back to the mansion.

"Alexander, Rupert… quick, come outside."

Drake and Snow ran along the hall to find an agitated and excited Morris.

"The raven, he wants me to follow him. I think he'll take me to Mathias."

The men glanced at one another with a look of doubt.

"Listen, we need to follow the bird. It has the picture of the archetypon in its beak and it's waiting for me in the street."

Drake shrugged his shoulders and turned to Snow.

"We've nothing to lose," said Snow.

Butler opened the door of the Rolls Royce.

"Quickly, get in. We mustn't lose the bird."

The black car purred as it passed through the gateway and onto the road. Snow wound down the window and craned his neck to see the bird.

"Joseph is right, the raven has something in its beak."

"It's the archetypon," said Morris.

The car approached the street lamp, and the bird took off, flew to the end of the road and stopped at a 'T' junction. Morris drove towards the bird which took off again and flew to the left, towards the city and stopped on the roof of a bus shelter.

Drake couldn't believe his eyes. "Morris is right. The bird is leading us somewhere."

"What did I tell you?" grinned Morris. "It's taking us to Mathias."

He turned to Drake and Snow.

"The raven is leading us to the third skull."

Chapter 75

"What did you tell mum and dad?" asked Sophie.

"That we were invited to a Christmas party, I told mum it was to do with work."

"And they believed you?"

"I think so, and they're happy to look after Jack and Rosie if we're back late in the morning."

"Jesus Heather, how long to you expect us to be out?"

Heather shrugged her shoulders.

Tears welled in Sophie's eyes.

"I'm scared, I mean really scared. What the hell are we doing?"

Heather stood up and tried her best to sound confident.

"First, we're getting your husband back, and secondly……..," Heather's voice trailed off, and she swallowed hard.

"And secondly we're stopping the Devil from walking the earth," said Sophie finishing her sister's sentence for her.

Neither of them could believe what was happening. Had Heather really been given the responsibility of stopping the Devil? She wished it had been a dream from which she would soon awake.

"Shouldn't we take something with us?" asked Sophie.

"Like what?"

"I don't know. Maybe a wooden stake and a cross?"

"It's not a bloody vampire we're stopping, it's the Devil."

"Although I guess these may come in handy," said Heather as she picked up two torches.

"It'll be very dark and very cold, we have to make sure we'll be warm."

The two young women put on winter coats and warm hats. Sophie pulled two pairs of gloves from a drawer and handed a pair to her sister.

At eleven twenty-five they left the house and made their way to St Michael on the Mount Without.

Half an hour later they parked at the bottom of the St Michael's Hill. The church was silhouetted against low cloud which had an orange glow cast by the streetlights below.

"Shall we?" said Heather and nervously looked at her sister.

They climbed the steep steps leading to the church and stopped when they reached the fence enclosing the graveyard.

"It's different," exclaimed Heather.

"Why?"

"It's always an overgrown mess. Normally, Charles Nash's grave is the only one that can be seen. The others are hidden by brambles."

"I guess someone from the council has been busy tidying up?" suggested Sophie.

Heather pushed the gate which creaked as it opened and pointed to Nash's grave.

"It's that one."

"What's the time?" asked Sophie.

"Shit, I don't know. I don't have my watch."

The Great George Bell struck twelve in the nearby tower of the Wills Memorial Building which answered Sophie's question.

"Okay, I guess it's now or never."

There wasn't a soul around and the sisters huddled together, crouched against the wall of the church.

Heather looked at the other gravestones.

"I had no idea there were so many graves in this churchyard."

She stood up and walked to Nash's grave. Next to it was another which was equally weathered and worn. She shone her torch on it, but the inscription was even more faded than the one on Nash's.

Heather turned round when she heard Sophie talking quietly to herself.

"What are you doing?"

Sophie didn't answer, she continued to speak in a hushed tone. After a few seconds she stopped.

"I was praying, maybe you should do the same."

"Perhaps we should have brought a Bible with us," suggested Heather.

She reached beneath her coat and touched Elizabeth's cross which hung around her neck.

"I have a bad feeling about tonight," said Sophie. "I've seen what that man Butler is capable of, and we don't stand a chance," she added.

"Don't forget about Drake, somewhere deep within is Finn. Perhaps you can appeal to him and get him on our side?"

Heather held the cross between her thumb and forefinger.

"Something tells me we'll be okay," said Heather trying to appear optimistic.

Heather remembered what Elizabeth had told her on the night she appeared in her bedroom.

'Heather, you're blessed with the veil of tears. Few have been chosen and you're the lucky one who has. Be brave, good is on your side. Believe in good, always believe in good.'

"How can you be sure?" replied Sophie.

"Because God is with us, we must believe and have faith."

"I hope you're right."

Just as Sophie spoke, a huge black bird landed on the rails surrounding the graveyard.

The sisters watched it hop along the railings. It was as black as the night was dark. They could barely make it out.

"What's that crow doing?" said Sophie.

"That's too big for a crow, it's a raven….. and look, it has something in its beak."

Sophie turned to her sister.

"A raven, are you sure?"

"Definitely, it's a raven."

Sophie cast her mind back to the day she, Finn and Rosie moved into their house. The day Rosie had been scared by a huge bird she'd seen in her bedroom. No one other than Rosie had seen it, although there was a pile of black feathers and the form of a bird which had crashed into the bedroom window from the inside.

"This must be a sign," said Sophie.

"What kind of sign?"

"I'm not sure, but we had a raven in the house, the one that scared Rosie."

Heather said nothing as the bird jumped from the railing and strutted towards Nash's grave. It stopped at the grave and cocked its head.

"It's holding something in its beak," said Sophie.

Heather squinted her eyes. "It's a piece of paper."

Sophie 'shushed' her sister.

"What was that?"

"Car doors," replied Heather in a whisper.

"Listen, there're footsteps, someone's coming this way."

"Not someone, there's more than one person," said Heather.

They stood up, scurried from the grave and ducked around the other side of the church.

Morris, Snow and Drake trudged up the steep steps to the graveyard.

"I hate churches," said Drake, "stupid Christian do gooders."

"Don't worry my friends. After today, everything will be different," said Morris with a grin.

Snow was the first to see the raven who strutted excitedly between two gravestones. The paper with the archetypon was still in its beak.

"Over there, look, the raven."

"What did I tell you?" said Morris, sounding smug.

The three men approached the bird which clucked as they came closer. Drake put his arm out and the bird jumped up and landed on his shoulder. Morris put his hand out toward the raven who dropped the paper in his palm. Morris unfolded it and shone a torch at the archetypon.

"Gentleman, shall we?" said Morris gesturing at the gravestones.

"Is one of these graves Mathias'?" asked Drake.

"Yes, Azazel has given us a sign, the bird has led us to the grave."

The raven jumped down and hopped between Nash's grave and the one next to it.

"But which one?" said Snow, "Neither of them have a name, the inscriptions are weathered away."

"It can't be that one, Mathias was five when I dumped him in the pond, whoever is buried there died many years later," said Morris, pointing to Nash's gravestone.

Drake stepped forward and placed a foot on the grave next to Nash's. He knelt forward and pressed his hand against the slab of stone, and as he did, a surge of electricity raced through his body. Snow and Morris looked as Drake was thrown backwards by an invisible force. He lay on his back in a pile of decomposed leaves.

"What just happened," said Drake, rubbing the palm of his hand.

"I think you've found Mathias' grave," said Morris with a glint in his eye. "Alexander, please go with Rupert and get the tools from the boot."

Morris tossed the car keys to Snow, and the two men made their way back to the Rolls Royce.

Morris waited alone and contemplated the enormity of what was about to happen. He looked at the grave and envisaged Mathias' skull lying in the casket below. He shuddered in the cold of the winter air, blew on his hands to warm them up and then pushed them into his pockets. In his right pocket he felt something soft. He pulled out the toy bear that Drake found in the well. The bear that almost brought Finn back. The stupid toy that had very nearly put an end to everything that he, Drake, Snow and Cromwell had set out to achieve. He tossed it towards the far wall of the church. It landed and bounced out of view and around the corner.

Sophie and Heather watched the three men from the corner of the churchyard and had gone unnoticed.

The bear landed at Sophie's feet.

"What the hell?" she muttered under her breath and leant forward to pick it up.

"What is it?" whispered Heather.

Sophie didn't answer. She turned the bear over and inspected it.

"No, it can't be."

She ducked further away from Morris, around the corner and to the furthest side of the graveyard. She pulled the torch from her pocket and shone it on the bear.

"It's Rosie's."

She turned it over and read the label hanging from the back.

'To Rosie, my favourite granddaughter'.

She remembered Rosie saying she'd given Amy bear to William so he could let Louisa have it.

How the hell did it get here? she thought to herself.
Heather crept over.
"What is it?"
"It's Rosie's bear. Mum gave it to her a few years ago."
"Shush," said Sophie, "they're coming back."

Drake and Snow hauled the heavy canvas bag of tools up the steps and into the graveyard.
"Okay, let's get a move on," said Morris unzipping the tool bag and pulling out a crowbar.
"Come on, give me a hand."

Heather and Sophie peered under the cover of darkness as the three men worked to remove the tombstone.
"That's not Nash's grave," whispered Heather.
"Whose is it?"
"I've no idea, but they're digging up the wrong body."
"Shouldn't we be trying to stop them?"
"No, not if they're not interfering with Nash. Besides, I don't think we could stop them, we've seen what Morris can do."
Sophie and Heather still saw two completely different people when they viewed the same man. Heather saw the short ugly man with the tattooed face, whilst Sophie saw the tall, silver haired distinguished gentleman. It didn't matter how he appeared, both sisters regarded what they saw as pure evil.

The three men found it easier than expected to lever the heavy stone on to its side and lower it to the ground several feet away from the grave it had marked for the past one hundred and sixty six years.
"I don't have a good feeling," said Drake.
"What are you sensing Alexander?" asked Snow.
"Something isn't right."
The raven continued to strut excitedly from Nash's grave to the patch of soil which had been covered by the other gravestone.
"Come on men, let's put our backs into it. If we work as a team, we'll reach the coffin in a couple of hours," said Morris whilst handing out spades.
Heather and Sophie huddled against each other to keep warm whilst the evil men dug into the ground.
For every shovel full of soil Drake removed he became wearier. He wasn't tired physically, but was drained mentally.
An hour later Drake could dig no more.
"Sorry Joseph, I need a break."
"Not now Alexander, we're nearly there."

Drake couldn't hear Morris' voice. He was overcome by a high pitched ringing and his vision became blurred. He staggered and dropped to his feet.

Snow put down his spade and checked on Drake.

"He's unconscious."

"Okay, leave him. We'll worry about him later. We need to work harder. It's just you and me."

The only sounds were the steady repetitive thud of spades, and the wheezes as Snow and Morris continued to excavate their way to the coffin. Other than Morris, Snow and Drake there was no one else around, apart from the two scared sisters crouching behind the corner wall of the church.

"What was that?" said Snow as his spade hit something solid.

Snow beat the blade of his spade downwards and each time both men heard the dull thud of the spade against wood.

They spent the next fifteen minutes clearing the last of the soil from the lid of the coffin.

"That's it," spluttered Morris, "We're there, get the crowbar."

Snow lugged himself out of the hole which was nearly as deep as he was tall, and threw the crowbar to Morris, nearly hitting him on the head.

"Careful you clumsy bastard," joked Morris.

Morris found it difficult in the confined space to wrench open the lid. He dug his feet into the soil with his legs astride the coffin and jammed the crowbar into the head end of the casket. The wood was old and rotten. Morris hacked at the lid until it came away from the coffin.

"Rupert, go to the tool bag and get me the rope."

Snow did as Morris asked and dropped the fifteen foot length of rope to him. Morris passed the rope under the end of the lid he'd wrenched from the coffin and tied a knot.

"Catch this," shouted Morris and threw the other end of the rope out of the hole to Snow. Morris climbed out of the hole and instructed Snow to stand with him at the foot end of the grave. They held the rope and after the count of three pulled with all their strength.

The sound of splintering wood tore through the still night air as the lid became detached from the coffin.

Snow dragged the lid from the hole and Morris shone his torch into the casket.

He shook his head in disbelief.

Rupert Snow peered over Morris' shoulder and gawked at the remains in the coffin. Both men recognised the faded clothes shrouding the skeleton.

"Joseph, I have to say, he's the last person I expected to find tonight."

Chapter 76

Linda lay in the double bed alone. She'd placed the stone head on Kieran's pillow and felt the heat radiate from it.

She'd had a huge row with her husband because of the evening's work he'd agreed to do for Gabriel Butler. Kieran was ordered to sleep in the guest bedroom. Linda was fuming with him. Although she was tired to the core, she couldn't sleep. She stared at the head and wondered where it came from. And who the girl was who'd dropped it on the bonnet of the car?

At just after three am she fell into a light sleep which brought her no rest. Her sleep was plagued with awful dreams of disaster, death and fire as she rolled from side to side in bed.

Had she been awake she may have noticed a tear roll from the eye of the stone head and land upon the pillow.

Chapter 77

Rupert Snow sipped whisky from a hipflask which Morris had the foresight to bring with him.

Drake stirred as he regained consciousness.

"Are you going to tell him or shall I?" asked Snow.

"I'll do it," replied Morris.

"Hang on, won't we have a paradox on our hands?"

Morris looked at him and shook his head.

Drake sat up and shivered.

"Have a sip of this," said Morris offering his hipflask.

Drake took a large gulp and shuddered as the whisky hit the back of his throat.

"How are you my friend?"

Drake looked around recalling where he was.

"I've been better, I must have fainted."

He stared through the darkness and saw the pile of earth and the coffin lid.

"Did you find Mathias?"

"No, it's not Mathias' grave," said Snow.

Drake looked dejected. Morris offered his hand and helped him to his feet. Drake walked to the edge and peered into the grave. He sensed an air of awkwardness as Snow shuffled uneasily by his side.

"Who is it?" asked Drake.

Morris passed him the torch. Drake shone the light on the skeleton. And then he saw it.

"Fuck!"

Drake saw his family crest on the tailcoat which adorned the skeleton. The same tailcoat he wore when he posed for the picture hung in the basement of his home.

"Shit, is that me?"

"Sorry Alexander, this has come as quite a shock to us," said Morris.

He sat beside the grave and peered back down.

He couldn't believe that he was looking at his own skeleton.

Shit! That's really me down there, he thought as he recognised his boots. He shuddered and became nauseous.

After a few minutes he composed himself and turned to Morris

"My feet are facing east. They gave me a bloody Christian burial. Why did they bury me in a church?"

"I don't suppose many people were aware you worshipped the devil. It wouldn't have been great for business if they had."

Drake recalled how in life he kept his beliefs private, only sharing them with a few close friends, which included Snow and Morris. He had been a successful and influential entrepreneur and understood if his business associates had known of his preoccupation with the Devil, it would have seriously affected commerce.

"But why bury me here, why so far from where I lived?"

"Look at the name of this place, St Michaels on the Mount Without'," said Snow pointing the sign above the entrance.

"It's because it was originally outside of the walls of the city," he added.

"What difference would that have made?"

"If I remember correctly, you'd upset many people," said Snow with a grin, "and in particular, you fell out of favour with the mayor of Bristol, John Kerle Haberfield."

Drake smirked, he recalled upsetting many people towards the end of his life.

"Yes, I was a bastard, wasn't I!"

"It wouldn't surprise me if the reason you're buried here was because the city disowned you," grinned Snow, "this is only conjecture, as both myself and Mr Morris had died a few years before you, and neither of us have any idea what happened."

"So, if we don't have Mathias' skull, what are we supposed to do next?" asked Drake, who was still shaken by what he'd seen.

Morris was going to speak when the raven reappeared and became extremely animated. It jumped back and forth between the coffin lid and Nash's grave. The bird settled on Nash's gravestone and scratched with its talons and scraped its beak over the stone.

"It's still trying to tell us something," said Snow.

"Yeah, it's saying the two of you have dug the wrong grave," grunted Drake.

No one answered.

"Okay, we're out of time. I hope the bird's got it right this time. Let's start work again."

Snow groaned.

Sophie and Heather watched from the corner of the church. They had no idea what the men were saying and weren't aware of Drake's skeleton. When Heather saw Morris plunge the crowbar under Nash's gravestone she let out an audible gasp, then clasped her hand over her mouth.

"What was that?" said Morris, stopping what he was doing.

"It came from over there," replied Drake, pointing towards the sisters.

Heather and Sophie had nowhere to hide. They backed away, but were trapped against the railings surrounding the graveyard.

Morris turned the corner and shone his torch.

“Hello, who do we have here?”
He took several steps closer and knelt in front of the two young women who were crouched and cowering together.
Sophie squinted as he aimed the torch at her face.
“We've met before, you’re Finn Maynard’s wife…… and who’s this pretty young thing?”
The sisters didn’t answer.
“Mr. Drake and Mr. Snow will take you somewhere comfortable.”
Snow took Sophie by her arm and Drake took Heather. Sophie felt a chill as Snow’s hand brushed her skin. He was colder than the evening air, as if he had no blood in his veins. Heather found it hard to comprehend she was so close to her brother-in-law without him knowing who she was. She had to remind herself that it was Alexander Drake and not Finn.
Snow and Drake marched them to the other side of the graveyard, forced them to sit and tied them to the railings. Morris tied a scarf tightly around their mouths to stop them from calling for help.
“I guess one of you was sent to stop us by that bitch Alice Donaldson,” said Morrison with a snarl.
Heather watched the men walk to Nash’s gravestone. She struggled to free herself but couldn’t and resigned to the fact she’d failed.
The men raised the heavy stone and she pondered what on earth she could have done to protect Nash? How could she have been expected to stop them from desecrating the grave? She struggled to understand what they wanted with Nash. It was the skull of William and Louisa’s brother they needed, not Charles Nash’s.

“I still don’t understand how this can be Mathias’ grave. Whoever is buried here died in eighteen thirty nine, that’s thirty-four years after Mathias died,” said Morris.
“But how can you be sure he died?” said Drake.
“Listen I’ve told you. I dumped him through the ice of a frozen pond. There was no way he could have survived, he was only five for fuck’s sake.”
“But when you went back to retrieve him He Wasn't There,” shouted Drake.
“HE DIED I TELL YOU,” snapped Morris.
“In that case, why are we wasting our time excavating this bloody grave,” said Snow.
The raven became agitated again and hopped back and forth across Nash’s grave.
“Because the bird’s telling us something. It knows something we don’t. So let’s stop talking and keep digging,” said Morris.

Snowflakes fell as the men continued to dig. Heather watched knowing she had to intervene. She needed to tell them they were digging the wrong grave as this may stop them from getting to Nash. She'd heard their conversation. If it was a boy called Mathias they were looking for, then they should dig elsewhere.

Heather needed to talk with them. She struggled and tried to shout, but the scarf muffled her voice. Her arms were tied behind her back and her hands secured to the railings. She stamped her feet, but the men were making too much noise digging down to Nash's coffin to notice her.

Morris stopped and took a sip from his hipflask. He handed it to Drake, who dropped his spade and took the flask. Heather tried to gain their attention again. She wriggled and stamped her feet until she caught Drake and Morris' eye.

"Someone excited," joked Drake, handing the flask back to Morris.

Morris slipped it back into his pocket and walked over to the women. He knelt to Heather's level.

"Is something troubling you?" he asked in a patronising tone.

Heather nodded.

"This had better be important," he said and undid the scarf and removed it from her mouth.

"You're digging the wrong grave," said Heather breathlessly.

"And how would you know?"

"Because Alice has sent me, and I know things. And I'm certain that's not the right grave."

Morris cocked his head to one side and didn't speak, which urged Heather to continue.

"You're digging for a boy right? A boy called Mathias? I can assure you the grave doesn't belong to anyone called Mathias."

"Okay, you have my attention. Tell me, to whom does it belong?"

Heather considered what she was doing. The whole thing was absurd. The boy Mathias was who they wanted. Why in Heaven's name did she need to protect Nash? She decided to tell them to whom the grave belonged. She hoped that by telling them, they would stop the excavation of Nash's grave.

"The grave belongs to Charles Nash."

"Who?" said Morris shaking his head.

"Charles Nash. I've no idea who he is, but that's who's buried there."

Morris could tell by the desperate look in her eyes she was telling the truth.

He turned to Drake and Snow, who were by the side of Nash's grave.

"It appears Mathias isn't buried here, the grave belongs to a man called Charles Nash. Does that name mean anything to you?"

They shook their heads.

"She's lying," shouted Snow.

Morris shook his head and turned back to Heather.
"Is this what Alice Donaldson told you?"
Heather didn't answer.
"Speak!" shouted Morris.
"I can assure you there is no one by the name of Mathias in that grave. It's a man called Charles Nash, and that's all I can tell you."
Morris walked back to the others.
"She's not lying, I can read her like a book. Time is running out, we need to decide what to do. We either stop what we're doing, or we keep digging and see what surprise Charles Nash has in store for us."
Snow thought hard about the name Nash. It sounded familiar, but he couldn't recall why he knew it.
"We're wasting our time," grunted Drake.
"Mr Snow, what's your opinion?" asked Morris.
He didn't answer. He was trying to remember why the name Nash was familiar. And then it came to him. He turned to the two men.
"Do either of you recall that 'do good' Baptist minister?"
"You mean the one who was always swanning around the community sticking his nose into everyone's business?" said Drake.
"Yeah, that's the one," said Snow, nodding his head, "he was Reverend Paul Nash."
"Did he have any family, any offspring?" asked Morris.
"I don't think so, but I'm not certain. I know little of him, but I am aware he had a wife."
"Maybe he had a brother?" suggested Drake.
The men pondered what to do. Should they carry on digging, or give up now and use the final hours leading up to the ceremony to search elsewhere for Mathias? They were fresh out of ideas. Morris had nowhere else to look.
The raven interrupted them, it perched on the headstone of a nearby grave and frantically croaked and gurgled. It flew from the grave and landed on the spade thrust into the soil by Snow.
It became even more agitated, hopped from the spade and strutted across the earth which covered Nash's grave.
"We should continue digging," said Snow as the bird vied for their attention.
"Rupert's right," said Drake, "the bird led us here from the other side of the city. It's even taken us to my grave, and although I feel a pang of reluctance, I agree we should keep digging."

The three men agreed that they should continue to dig the grave and hope for the best.
Heather dropped her head in sorrow. She had tried her best which was all she could do. She felt useless and helpless.

Heather had let Charles and everyone else down.

It was just after six when they broke through to the coffin. The morning was as dark as midnight. Heather and Sophie were shivering, even though Morris had thrown a blanket over them.

Snow, Morris and Drake stood on the edge of the hole and took a breath.

"Good work," said Morris as he put his arms around the shoulders of his colleagues.

"Do you mind if I rest up for a few minutes?" said Snow. "I need to keep my energy levels up for tonight."

They stood in silence and finished the last of the whisky.

Heather squeezed Sophie's hand. Neither of them knew what to expect, and the suspense of watching Drake, Snow and Morris doing nothing was killing them.

"Shall we?" said Morris placing the empty hipflask in his pocket.

Drake and Morris climbed back into the hole and worked to remove the lid.

"Open you bastard," cursed Drake as he jammed the crowbar beneath the lid.

Drake's coffin had opened almost effortlessly, but Nash's casket wasn't giving up its secrets so easily.

"We'll have to wrench those nails out," said Morris resting against the side of the hole with his feet astride the head end of the casket.

"Rupert, look in the tool bag, there should be a claw hammer." shouted Morris.

Snow found the hammer and lowered it to him.

Morris dropped to his knees and used the claw end of the hammer to prise the rusty nails. It was a laborious and time-consuming job punctuated by huffs and curses from Morris.

Ten minutes later Morris had removed enough nails to enable Drake to jam the crowbar under the lid and wrench it away from the box.

Drake helped Morris pull the up lid and stand it on its end. Snow reached forward, took the lid, pulled it out of the hole and dropped it to the ground. He cursed as a splinter stuck into his hand.

"Okay gentlemen, let's see what we have here. Alexander, please be kind enough to pass me the torch," said Morris.

Drake passed the torch. Snow looked from above and waited with eager anticipation as Morris fumbled with the torch.

The light flashed intermittently and then produced a dim yellow light.

"The bloody batteries are dying," said Morris whilst giving the side of the torch a whack with the palm of his hand.

The torch had been on for hours and was nearly out of juice.

Snow, Morris and Drake stood over the grave, looked down and made out the bones of an adult wearing perished clothes.

"Okay, we need to empty everything from the coffin and take it with us. It's too dark to see anything," said Morris.

"Take everything?" asked Drake.

"Yes, everything, including the last scrap of clothing. If there *is* a clue we need to examine everything thoroughly. Let's dump it in a bag and get it back to the house."

It was half-past six and the early risers were wearily making their way to work. Drake heard a bus chugging up St Michael's Hill beyond the graveyard.

"Come on, we have little time," said Morris.

They bundled the contents of the coffin into a black bin liner.

"What about them?" said Snow, pointing to the women huddled together and tied to the railings.

"Bring them with us," replied Morris.

Snow carried Nash's remains to the car and placed them in the boot, whilst Drake and Morris undid the ropes and helped Sophie and Heather to their feet.

"You're coming with us," snapped Morris as both women stretched their tired arms and legs.

Drake marched Sophie and Heather down the steps, away from the church and to the Rolls Royce.

Morris opened the rear door, and with no resistance the women climbed in. They were tired and exhausted and had no strength to fight. The car was warm and inviting, and the seats were comfortable compared to where they'd been tied for the past six hours. Snow sat in the front passenger seat and Drake sat in the back next to Sophie. She glanced at the man whom she used to consider to be her husband and wondered what was going on inside his mind.

Morris parked outside the house. Drake and Snow guided the women from the car, whilst Morris retrieved the bag of bones from the boot. Heather looked at the huge house with tired eyes. She was confused, weary and close to tears. Sophie took her hand and tried to give the impression she was cool and confident as they walked to the door.

Butler's large house was warm, which was something for which the sisters were grateful.

"Take them to the basement," demanded Morris.

Drake led the way to the concealed entrance, opened the door and escorted the sisters down the rickety stairs. He lit candles and ordered the women to sit in the corner.

Drake climbed the stairs and left them alone in the basement.

"I'm sorry I've got you involved in this," said Heather.

"You didn't get me involved, I've been mixed up in this shit from the start."

Sophie stopped talking and gasped as she saw the painting hanging from the wall.

"Bloody hell, take a look at that, it's Finn."

Heather followed her eyes.

"No, that's Drake, the man your husband has become."

Morris and Snow waited in the study for Drake.

"Let's clear the table, and empty the bag," said Morris.

He and Snow moved books and newspapers from the large table and placed them on the floor, just as Drake entered the room.

"Okay," said Morris, untying the knot in the top of the black plastic bag.

Snow and Drake watched with expectation as Morris turned the bag upside down and emptied the bones and rotten fabric onto the table.

"What are we looking for?" asked Snow.

"I don't know. A clue? Maybe a map? Something that can lead us to Mathias' skull," replied Morris.

They shuffled the bones around the table and searched through the pockets of the brittle and mouldy clothing which turned to dust as soon as it was touched.

After five minutes Drake let out a sigh.

"There's nothing here. It's just bones and old cloth," he remarked.

Morris didn't hear Drake. He wanted to speak, but couldn't because his mouth had become too dry. It was staring him in the face and neither he, nor the others, had seen it. They'd been too busy looking through the tiny fragments of bone and rummaging through Nash's clothes to see what was in front of them.

Drake and Snow watched Morris saunter to the far end of the table. He trembled as he picked it up. He carried it to the centre of the room where a light hung from the high ceiling. His heart was in his mouth as he ran his fingers over the fragile artefact.

And then he spoke.

"Mr Drake, Mr Snow…….. I believe we have what we've been looking for. We've found the third skull."

Chapter 78

'Police are investigating the desecration of two graves in a church near the centre of Bristol.

The police were called just after seven am by a pedestrian who passed the church on her way to work.

St Michael on the Mount Without, which closed its doors over twenty years ago, has had two graves severely damaged. One grave was robbed of the body, whilst the body in the other grave remains intact.

At this early stage in their enquiries, the police do not know to whom the graves belong. Both are very old, and one is dated 1839. Police suspect that either one, or both of the graves may have contained something of value.

Police have cordoned off the area and are asking the public to stay away whilst they are carrying out their investigations.

The Police are appealing to anyone who may be able to help with their enquiries'

Linda switched off Sky news and glanced at the clock. It was ten am, and she felt tired after a poor night's sleep. She wasn't looking forward to speaking with Kieran after the row they'd had the previous evening.

The news report she'd just watched sent a chill down her spine. The thought of grave robbers in the twenty-first century made her uneasy.

Kieran entered the lounge wearing his dressing gown, grunted 'good morning', and went to the kitchen.

He returned with coffee for each of them and hoped she'd accept the drink as a peace offering.

"Are we speaking?" asked Kieran.

"That depends, doesn't it," replied Linda staring at the blank television.

He sighed and returned to the kitchen. He leaned against the work surface and thought of their 'heated words'.

Linda was right. They didn't need Butler's money, they had more in the bank than they could ever spend. Kieran's problem was that saying 'no' to Gabriel Butler wasn't easy. He was manipulative and always got what he wanted. Kieran had known of others who'd not toed the line and had regretted their decision.

He looked up as Linda entered the kitchen. She placed her coffee on the kitchen worktop and kissed the side of his face.

"I've got such a bad feeling about this evening. Please don't go, I'm begging you."

"What can I do? I have to go. You were right when you said that 'Butler had his claws in me', because he has."

Linda saw he was scared.

"I promise, I'll be careful. I'll do whatever he wants me to do, and then I'll get out of there and come straight home."

Kieran's phone interrupted them. He pulled it from his dressing gown pocket and took the call in the lounge. Two minutes later he came back with the phone in his hand.

"That was Gabriel. I have to be at his place at six."

Linda lowered her head. She had given up. A tear formed in her eye and made its way down her cheek. There was nothing more she could say to change Kieran's mind.

She brushed past him and went back to the bedroom.

Linda lay on the bed, turned to her side and looked at the stone head on the pillow beside her. It faced the ceiling and had been next to her during the night. From the side she looked at its manic 'drawn on' eyes and creepy grin.

"I don't know what the fuck you're smiling about," she said under her breath.

The head flipped on to its side as if someone had rolled it over. It stared into her eyes and radiated the strange heat.

Then she heard the voice of an elderly woman.

"Help me Linda."

Chapter 79

"It's definitely Mathias, there's no doubt," said Morris after he'd compared the pattern on the back of the skull to the third archetypon that the raven had carried in its beak to the church.

"But that skull belongs to an adult," said Drake," you were sure the kid died in the pond."

"Well, I was wrong. Somehow or another he either escaped the pond, or was rescued and grew to be an adult."

"I hate to say 'I told you so'," said Drake in a borderline patronising tone of voice.

"Okay ladies, let's not fight. We have the third skull and that's what's important," said Snow.

"May I?" asked Drake, reaching out his hand.

Morris passed the skull to Drake who took his time to marvel at it.

"I find it more than a little odd to know that it's been lying next to my dead body for all those years."

"I wouldn't let it worry you Alexander. Let's put it down to coincidence."

"It's so much bigger than the infants' skulls, do you reckon it'll be okay?" asked Snow.

"I don't see why not, it's the archetypons that matter. Providing they correspond everything should be fine."

Drake admired the skull.

"It's amazing. Let's take it to the basement with the others."

"No, no you can't. The three skulls mustn't be together until the ceremony. That's the whole point of keeping Mathias away from his brother and sister when they were alive."

"May I raise a practical question?" asked Snow.

Morris looked up.

"What shall we do with the women?"

"Kill them," blurted Drake.

"No, no, let's not be too hasty, they may be of use," said Morris thoughtfully

"To whom?"

"To Azazel. He's not experienced the gratification of flesh since he impregnated the triplet's mother. I'm sure he'd welcome the pleasure of their company."

"How thoughtful of you," smiled Snow.

"But what shall we do with them after Azazel has finished with them?"

"I'm not sure. By that time Azazel will be among us and we can leave the big decisions to him."

Both Snow and Drake grinned menacingly.

Sophie and Heather were terrified.

Sophie had been studying the portrait of Alexander Drake and found it impossible to contemplate that it wasn't her husband.

"But it has to be Finn. Look at the scar on his cheek and that grey wisp of hair over his temple, it's exactly like him."

"No Sophie, it's the other way around. Finn is exactly like Drake. Finn hasn't always looked like that," said Heather pointing at the painting.

She was right. Until recently he had been a little overweight, wore his hair short, and he didn't have the scar. But ever since he'd gained the ring from the antique shop he'd completely changed. And now, by means of a force Sophie didn't understand, he'd metamorphosed into the man in the portrait which had been painted over one hundred and fifty years ago.

Heather shuddered and looked around the basement. It had been decked out in the way she expected a cheap B movie horror film would have been. Tapestries adorned the walls with demonic images.

Sophie recognised the patterns embroidered on the blue cloth which covered the circular table in front of her.

"Those patterns are the same as the ones on Finn's ring. And they're the same ones Rosie drew."

Heather didn't answer. She was considering what would happen next, and whether she still had a chance to protect Charles Nash from Morris and the others.

The basement was cold. Sophie thrust her hands into her pockets to keep them warm. She felt something in her right-hand pocket and pulled it out.

"It's Amy! I've no idea how Butler or Morris, or whoever that man is supposed to be, got his hands on it. It went missing and Rosie said she'd given it to William to give to his sister."

Sophie looked at Heather.

"So where are your guiding spirits now when we need them?" asked Sophie.

Heather was going to answer, but the sound of a creaking door interrupted her. The dimly lit basement became illuminated by light pouring in from the top of the staircase. Sophie rammed the bear back in her pocket.

Drake descended the stairs followed by Snow. Drake carried a tray on which were two plates with bread and butter.

"I hope you're making yourselves at home," sneered Drake. He placed the tray on the floor in front of the women.

"You two must be hungry," said Snow, following behind with two glasses of water.

"What do you intend to do with us?" asked Heather.

The men didn't answer. Sophie saw a smirk on Drake's face.

"Finn, don't you remember who I am?" said Sophie.

"I'm aware of who you are, and I'm grateful to your husband for loaning me this," said Drake waving his hand over his body. "It's a pity he won't be getting it back."

He turned to walk towards the stairs.

She knew her husband existed somewhere within the body that Drake had commandeered. She needed to find a way of getting him back.

"Don't you remember our children, Rosie and Jack?"

Drake stopped in his tracks, turned around and looked at Sophie.

"Rosie….., Jack?" he said with a puzzled look as if deep within, something stirred.

"Yes, our children, don't you remember them?"

Sophie watched a smile appear on his face.

"Of course, Rosie and Jack, our children."

Sophie's heart pounded hard as she looked at the man standing over her. His facial expression gave her the impression she had connected with Finn.

He knelt to her level. He was so close she could feel his breath against her skin.

"Sorry, I've never fucking heard of them," said Drake shaking his head and laughing.

Drake got to his feet and turned towards the door.

"Eat your food, you two need to keep your strength up."

He and Snow left the basement, pulling the door shut behind them.

"So I guess this is it," said Sophie after Drake and Snow had gone.

Heather didn't answer.

"I'll never see my children again."

She sobbed and thought about her children. She considered her parents. They would be beside themselves with worry not knowing where she and Heather were. All she wanted was to hold her children close and feel their skin against hers.

She cast her mind back to when the estate agent showed her around the house in Whitcombe Fields Road for the very first time and how Heather became ill after walking into the kitchen. She should have guessed back then that something was wrong. She wished she'd taken Ruth Jackson's advice and got out of the house as soon as she'd been told of the suicides.

The land on which the house had been built was sour, and it had carried Drake's evil secret for two centuries.

For the past two hundred years, other than the hawthorn tree, not a flower or plant grew, not a creature burrowed, or bird sang. Snowflakes didn't settle and raindrops evaporated the instant they fell upon the barren soil. Men became ill and death always followed those who spent too much time on the desolate strip of land above the well.

The bodies of those two innocent children, who carried the mark of the devil, cast a spell on the land above them.

Heather considered those she'd let down. Charles Nash, Alice Donaldson and her great grandmother Elizabeth. Most of all she'd let down Sophie and her family.

Elizabeth told her she'd been blessed with the 'veil of tears', and that she'd been the chosen one. As far as Heather was concerned she had been useless. Why was she considered so special? Maybe Elizabeth had been wrong all along? What if a mistake had been made? Heather never considered any great gift had been bestowed upon her. She didn't think that her character was strong enough to deal with such things.

She wallowed in self-doubt and negativity, when a wave of warmth passed over her. From somewhere deep within her came a surge of positivity. It was as if something had enveloped her in a cloud of love and support.

"I think everything will work out," whispered Heather, squeezing her sister's hand.

"I wish I was as positive as you."

"I feel someone or something's watching over us. I reckon we've a guardian angel."

"I hope you're right, I really hope you're right."

Sophie looked at the tray of bread and butter.

"Is that the best they could offer, bread and butter and a glass of water?"

"We should eat it. Like he said, we need to keep our strength up."

Drake and Snow went back to the study as Morris scooped away the pile of bones and fabric into the black plastic bag.

"We need none of this shit. One of you get rid of it and leave no trace."

Snow took Mathias Morris' remains and drove the Rolls Royce to the council recycling centre, where he dropped them in the landfill section along with thousands of other black bags full of household waste.

"No one will find you here, my elusive friend," said Snow as the bag plunged into the skip.

Back at the house Drake and Morris were contemplating the long road they'd travelled to get to where they were today.

"Joseph, I have to say, I never thought you'd do it. We have all three skulls and just in time……., but I hate to bring up one small point…….., we don't have Albert Cromwell."

"Don't worry about Cromwell, I've told you before. I have everything in hand."

"Really? We have less than ten hours before the rite and there's no sign of him. I've not seen him since eighteen hundred and four, and I'm getting more than a little concerned."

"Alexander, when I say don't worry, I mean don't worry! He will be here. You have my word."

Drake didn't know what Morris had planned. He was a man of few words. He hated being left in the dark, but had no other choice than to trust him.

"We should try to escape," said Sophie.

"There's little chance of that. We've seen what Morris can do, he'd snap us like a twig if he caught us."

"But we're not even tied up, we should at least give it a go."

"Part of me wants to get out of here, and part of me wants to stay. Tonight the men intend to raise the Devil, and I believe they will do it. Maybe I've let Charles Nash down, but perhaps I can stop Drake, Morris and the other man from carrying out their plan."

Sophie slumped against the wall. She had to stay with her sister. If there was just a hint of a chance she could get her husband back, then she needed to stay in the basement and help Heather.

"By what means could we stop them?" asked Sophie.

"I've no idea. But Elizabeth said I have a gift and I believe her. I've spoken with dead people and seen incredible things these past few months. Maybe I really have been blessed with something to stop these men from bringing the Devil from Hell to Earth."

"I hope you're right."

Snow returned and joined Drake and Morris in the study.

"What do we do now?" asked Snow.

"Nothing other than patiently wait. We've done all we can," replied Morris.

Drake wanted to know Morris' plan regarding Cromwell. Cromwell was as crucial to raising Azazel as the three skulls, and yet there was no sign of him and Morris didn't appear concerned.

Morris poured a small whisky for himself, Snow and Drake.

"Let's raise a glass and salute our achievements. Each of us have played an important role in getting to where we are today."

Morris lifted his glass and smiled at the others.

"To us."

Drake and Snow raised their glasses and in unison said 'to us'.

Morris replaced his glass on the table.

"After today we will live in a world where the devil walks amongst us in physical form and we should take a little time to consider the consequences of this fact."

"He will infiltrate his way into every living soul and will overpower anyone or anything that tries to stop him." said Drake.

"And what of us? Consider the powers he will bestow upon us. He has already made us immortal, just imagine how formidable we will be when sitting at the right hand of Azazel," added Snow.

"People have a misguided understanding that the world is a bad place. Just wait and see what they think of it after today," laughed Morris.

The three men spent the rest of the morning and afternoon contemplating their future and the future of mankind. They were confident that there was nothing to stop them. Alice Donaldson hadn't prevented them from finding the skulls of Azazel's children, and Morris' plan to bring Cromwell back to the fold had been instigated days ago.

All they needed was patience. There was under five hours until the ceremony. It would be the longest five hours the men would know.

Heather and Sophie didn't know the time or how long they'd been in the basement.

They were tired and scared. Sophie thought of her children and Heather was beside herself with anxiety.

All of a sudden, the atmosphere changed. Sophie sniffed the air and sensed something was going to happen.

"It's that smell, you're about to have a visitor," said Sophie.

She was right. Seconds later Charles Nash stood in front of them, but only Heather could see him.

"It's Nash," said Heather under her breath.

"Heather, I'm sorry you and your sister have been put through this. But we were certain you were the chosen one and could have defeated Morris and his men."

"Well, it looks as though you're wrong," said Heather in an angry tone.

Nash lowered his head.

"Can you at least put me out of my misery and tell me what Morris, Drake and Snow want from you?"

Nash nodded sadly.

"When I was alive, I carried a secret with me. Something only a few people knew of."

Sophie looked at the expression on her sister's face and listened to the one sided conversation taking place next to her.

"Memories of my childhood are blurred. I had no mother, and I was brought up by a man called Joseph Morris. He treated me well and I remember being happy. Until one cold and dark day he took me from the house. He didn't speak, but I recall he was angry about something. I have a memory of falling through a frozen pond, but after that I knew nothing of Joseph Morris, or what happened after the pond. It was as though my life started over again. I grew up a troubled child who lived under the roof of a Baptist minister called Reverend Paul Nash and his wife Sarah. Reverend Nash and his wife were protective towards me. I gained a new identity and became Charles Samuel Nash. He named me after his father."

"So Morris was your father. What was your name when you lived with him?"

"Mathias.... My name was Mathias Morris," replied Nash.

"You said you carried a secret."

"It was something I couldn't see, but Reverend Nash and Sarah told me of a strange mark on the back of my head embedded deep into the bone of my skull. I could make it out if I ran my fingers over it, so I knew it was there."

"That must have been frightening."

"It was, but I didn't know until I was eleven. He told me how he and Sarah rescued me from the pond. They'd been out walking and saw the shadowy figure of Morris dumping something into the frozen water. That something was me. The Reverend had known that Morris was an evil man and that he associated with other bad people, including the unscrupulous businessman Alexander Drake. He risked his life to save me. I nearly died, and if it wasn't for Reverend Nash, I would have."

Things were making sense, but Heather was angry that none of what Nash told her had been relayed to her before by either him, Alice or Elizabeth.

"When did you discover what Joseph Morris wanted from you?"

"After I'd died. I lost my life in a riding accident in my late thirties, and since my life ended I've never entered the Kingdom of Heaven because of the secret I hold. If Morris raises the Devil, I will go to Hell, through no fault of my own."

"So you've been at a midpoint between Heaven and Hell since eighteen thirty nine, that's over one hundred and sixty years."

Nash nodded.

"Believe me, one hundred and sixty years is a very long time when you're locked in a halfway house."

"So, when was everything revealed to you? When did you find out what Morris' and Drake's intentions were, and what they still had in store for you?"

"Alice Donaldson told me everything. She is also in limbo, and is in the same position as me. She's never entered Heaven, and like me will go to Hell should Drake succeed. Alice has told me of William and Louisa, my brother and sister, and how between the three of us we hold something deadly to mankind."

Heather swallowed hard and shuddered as Nash continued to speak.

"I've spent a long time watching over those two scared children. Unlike Alice and me, they've never been released from the grasp of mortality. They've continued an existence of purgatory in that well. And like Alice and me, their fate depends upon the success of Morris in raising the Devil this evening."

Heather saw a tear in the ghost's eye.

"You're not the first to be chosen to protect me from Morris. Before you, my granddaughter Hermione was there for me. She tended to my grave weekly and vigilantly watched over me. She did so without grievance for seventy-six years ever since she was a young lady. She'd devoted her life to me and in doing so never had one for herself. She'd never married and raised a family, instead she waited in readiness to stop Morris from finding me."

Heather lowered her head. She considered herself useless and pathetic. Nash was waning.

"We saw Morris take your bones from your coffin, and before he did, he found the body of Alexander Drake lying in the grave alongside yours. Why would that be?"

"We were buried in the church of St Michael for a reason. St. Michael defeated Satan twice. First when he ejected Satan from Paradise and secondly in the final battle of the end of times. But that won't be the final battle if Morris succeeds. Drake and I are considered the adversary of good. Drake, because of his association with Morris, Snow and Cromwell and their intentions to bring the Devil to this world, and myself because I carry the mark of Satan. We were buried alongside each other not by chance, but by divine intervention so that St. Michael could stop us from raising the Devil and allowing him the opportunity to walk among mankind."

The door to the basement creaked open. Heather looked up and her blood ran cold as she looked towards the stairs.

"They're coming and I must go. You still have a chance to stop them. Please Heather, do whatever you can."

And with that, the ghost of Charles Samuel Nash faded away.

Chapter 80

Linda remained in her bed for the rest of the day. The head scared her, but she kept it next to her on the pillow. There was something about it that lured her.

She'd drifted in and out of sleep. The most horrific thoughts and images had troubled her as she lay in a half sleep. She'd visions of her husband tied up and bound as Butler beat him to within an inch of his life.

Then she saw death and destruction on a scale of unbelievable proportions. She'd foreseen streets of cities in darkness and thousands of scared and hungry souls existing in a living hell as around them everything turned to rubble. She saw the aftermath of an event as horrendous as the wake of Hiroshima after the bomb fell, but the destruction was on a worldwide scale.

Linda woke from her dreams and sat up when she heard the front door slam. The clock on the bedside table told her it was twenty minutes to six. From the window she watched Kieran get in his car, pull off the driveway and head away in the darkness to Butler's house. He hadn't even said goodbye.

She had a horrible feeling she would never see her husband again.

She sat on the edge of the bed and remembered the voice of the elderly lady she'd heard earlier in the day.

'Help me Linda.'

Had she dreamt it, or had it been real? Whether she'd imagined it or not, it scared her.

The head was hotter. Using a shoe which had been on the floor beside the bed, she rolled it on its side and saw a scorch mark on the pillow.

"Just what's your story?" she whispered as she knelt down and looked at the painted face.

She was alone and had no one to whom she could turn. She was groggy and bleary-eyed after spending the day in bed, so she decided to make some strong coffee to help pull her out of the fog.

From the kitchen she called Kieran's mobile, but he didn't pick up. It was ten past six and he would be at Gabriel Butler's house by now. She suspected he was being briefed by Butler to do whatever it was he wanted him for.

If she did nothing to stop her husband, she knew she would live to regret it. She had an awful feeling about Butler and knew she needed to get her husband out of there. But how, what could she do?

Drinking the coffee made her more awake. She returned to the bedroom and again considered how alone she was.

Linda looked at the head and noticed it had moved. Before she'd left the bedroom to make coffee she'd placed it on its side and saw how it had scorched the pillow. But it was back where it was before, facing towards the ceiling.

The caffeine raced through her veins and she became alert. She looked it square in the eyes and asked a question.

"What the fuck are you?"

Of its own accord it rolled to one side and then back to where it originally lay.

Linda jumped back as it stared towards the ceiling.

Again, she heard an elderly woman's voice.

"Please Linda, help me stop them."

Chapter 81

Drake descended the staircase just as Nash faded.

"Who were you talking to?"

"No one,……… I mean I was talking to my sister," replied Heather.

Snow followed behind with the rope he and Drake had used to tie them to the railings earlier that day.

"Something momentous will happen tonight, and we can't have either of you getting in the way. We know one of you has been sent to stop us under the guidance of Alice Donaldson and we're not taking any chances."

Snow pulled a knife from his pocket and passed it to Drake.

"No, please don't hurt us," cried Sophie.

Drake paused for a second, smirked and cut the long rope in two.

"You, stand up and walk over there," snapped Drake pointing to the other side of the basement.

Sophie reluctantly got to her feet and cowered as she did as he commanded. She had to keep reminding herself that he was not her husband.

Snow stood over Heather while Drake secured Sophie to a chair. He pulled the same scarf from his pocket he'd used to gag her in the graveyard and tied it around her mouth. When she was securely tied he walked over to Heather and secured her with the other half of the rope and gagged her with a scarf. The sisters shuddered with fear as they faced each other from either side of the basement.

Morris clumped down the stairs and saw the women were securely tied.

"Good work," said Morris checking the time. "We've just over an hour."

Snow was going to speak when the doorbell rang.

"Excuse me gentleman, I'm expecting a visitor," said Morris. He turned and left the basement.

Kieran pulled his coat around him against the cold December chill and waited for Butler to open the door.

"Good evening Mr. Tempest, it's wonderful to see you again. Please come in, let me take your coat," said Butler gesturing to Kieran to come into house.

Kieran handed him his coat and Butler hung it from a coat stand in the hallway.

"Follow me to the study. I'll get you a drink and we'll talk about your little job."

Kieran was uneasy. What kind of 'little job' paid one million for an evening's work?

"Please take a seat. What would you like to drink? Maybe a brandy to warm you up on this cold night."

Kieran nodded warily.

"Gabriel, what is it you would like me to do for you?"

"Not an awful lot. I'd like you to meet a few friends of mine. We're having a celebration, and I'd like you to make up the numbers. Unfortunately we're a man short," said Butler with his back to Kieran. He poured the brandy and added a tiny amount of chloral hydrate.

"What sort of celebration?"

"Don't be concerned. We'll discuss the finer details later," said Butler handing the brandy to Kieran.

Butler had poured one for himself and watched Kieran take a sip.

Kieran felt odd. He looked at Butler who appeared blurry.

"Tell me about the celebration?" repeated Kieran whilst slurring his words.

"Think of it as a fancy dress party, where you won't be coming as Kieran Tempest, you'll be someone else for the night."

He found it hard to concentrate as the drug took hold of him.

"Tonight, you will become a good friend of mine by the name of Albert Cromwell," laughed Butler as he watched Kieran's head roll from side to side.

Joseph Morris put his hand under Kieran's chin and lifted his head up. He opened his eye lids with his thumbs and looked at his eyes. Kieran was out for the count.

He hauled him over his shoulder and carried him from the study to the top of the staircase leading to the basement.

The women were terrified. Heather watched Morris carry the stranger over his shoulder and down the stairs, whilst Sophie saw it was Butler who carried the man.

He lowered him to the floor and Sophie realised who the man was.

Shit, it's Kieran Tempest.

Butler turned to Sophie and threw her a sinister grin.

"I think it's time for you to see me as I really am."

Butler muttered a few inaudible words and before Sophie's eyes changed from the tall handsome gentleman, to the short ugly man with missing teeth and a blue tattoo on one side of his face.

Sophie gasped beneath the gag.

Morris ordered Drake and Snow to lift Kieran and sit him at the table.

"Gentlemen, prepare to be reacquainted with our old friend Mr. Cromwell," said Morris as the two men lowered Kieran onto a chair.

Morris waved Drake and Snow to one side and stood over Kieran. He knelt to his level and placed his hand against his forehead.

Quietly he chanted.

"Hic en spiritum, sed non incorpore, evokare lemures de mortuis, decretum espugnare, De Angelus Balberith, en inferno inremeablis."

He chanted a second time, and a little louder.

"Hic en spiritum, sed non incorpore, evokare lemures de mortuis, decretum espugnare, De Angelus Balberith, en inferno inremeablis."

And a third, and louder still.

"Hic en spiritum, sed non incorpore, evokare lemures de mortuis, decretum espugnare, De Angelus Balberith, en inferno inremeablis."

And a final time.

"Hic en spiritum, sed non incorpore, evokare lemures de mortuis, decretum espugnare, De Angelus Balberith, en inferno inremeablis."

Then Morris chanted in a voice so loud, it made the flames of the candles flicker as if a breeze had blown over them.

"Wa ta na siam, wa ta na siam, wa ta na siam. wa ta na siam"

"Wa ta na siam, wa ta na siam, wa ta na siam. wa ta na siam"

"Wa ta na siam, wa ta na siam, wa ta na siam. wa ta na siam"

"Wa ta na siam, wa ta na siam, wa ta na siam. wa ta na siam"

Morris took a step back and wiped his brow. Sophie watched in astonishment. A few minutes earlier he had appeared tall and distinguished, now he was a different person. He chanted in what sounded like Latin to a man who used to live across the road from her.

Is this really happening?

Morris looked exhausted. He had beads of perspiration on his brow and his hands were trembling.

He took a step closer to the man in the chair and put his mouth to his ear.

"Albert, can you hear me?"

Morris tried again.

"Albert, it's Joseph Morris, can you hear me?"

The man in the chair stirred.

Morris ran his hand across the man's forehead and his eyes opened.

"Albert, is that you?"

The man frowned, squinted his eyes and surveyed the room. He looked at the portrait of Drake, and then over to Alexander who stood to his right.

"Albert, is that you?" asked Drake.

He didn't answer.

He looked at Morris and his lips pursed as a faint smile appeared on his face.

Bartholomew Snow took a step forward.

"Albert, do you know who I am?" asked Snow.

He attempted to stand up, but found it hard. Morris got to him before his legs gave way.

"Take it steady old friend, take it steady."

"I can do this," said the man. He placed his hands on the table and struggled to stand for a second time.

He pulled himself to his feet and held onto the side of the chair. He glanced at the women sitting and gagged either side of the basement.

Without speaking, and on unsteady feet, he walked around the room. Again, he looked at the portrait and compared the likeness to Drake. He nodded with approval.

Albert Cromwell took in the tapestries which hung from the wall and ran his fingers over them.

He made his way to the centre of the basement, stopped at the table and admired the patterns on the cloth.

Cromwell turned to Morris and spoke.

"Is this what I think it is? Is it really happening?"

Morris nodded.

"Yes Albert, this is really happening."

Albert Cromwell walked towards Morris and put his arms around him.

"Thank you Joseph, you've worked hard and you've done well."

Morris, Drake and Snow watched in awe as Cromwell continued to walk around the room. His legs became steadier, and he ambled to the bottom of the staircase.

"Are we in the basement of Drake's house?"

The others nodded in unison.

"What year is it?"

"Two thousand and six," replied Morris.

"Two thousand and six!" said Cromwell before letting out a whistle signifying his astonishment.

"What's the date?"

"December the fourteenth," said Morris.

"So we're doing it tonight?"

Morris nodded.

Drake, Snow and Morris revered the man as if he were royalty. They almost stood to attention.

"But the children, what about Mathias, William and the girl?"

"They're dead," replied Drake.

"But we have the skulls," interrupted Morris.

"I see," said Cromwell nodding thoughtfully.

"Is there anything we can do for you Albert, is there anything you need?" asked Drake.

"I don't think so."

Cromwell looked at a clock on the shelf below the portrait of Drake.

"Gentlemen, it's time to get things underway."

Chapter 82

Linda cursed as she attempted to lift the head from the pillow. It had always emitted a little warmth, but lately it had become much hotter and now it was too hot to touch. It was as searing as a saucepan on a hob.

She opened a drawer and rustled through it looking for something in which she could wrap the head and protect her hands from being burnt. She pulled out a double electric blanket. She rolled the head onto the blanket and picked it up.

She carried it downstairs to the kitchen where she found a grocery bag which was large enough to accommodate the head and the electric blanket. Linda pulled on a coat, grabbed the keys to the Porsche and disappeared into the night with the head.

Chapter 83

Sophie and Heather watched in astonishment as the four men adorned themselves in the most ridiculous attire. Morris, Drake and Snow wore identical blue and silver cloaks which had a gold pentagram embroidered on the back. Cromwell's cloak was different. His was gold, and unlike the other three, it bore no pentagram. Sophie couldn't believe it was happening. It was so stereotypical of the classic depiction of Devil worshipping she'd seen in cheap films it seemed almost comical. It wouldn't surprise her if Christopher Lee entered the basement and took charge of the ceremony.

Snow positioned the three ornately carved wooden boxes on the table. He measured and checked the distance between each box was the same. He placed them in such a way that all three internal angles were sixty degrees, so the boxes formed an equilateral triangle.

On each of the boxes he placed a blue cushion embroidered with a pentagram.

Heather was helpless to intervene. She'd never been religious, but if there was a time to pray that time was now. With the gag over her mouth she said the only prayer she could remember from start to finish. The Lord's Prayer.

"Our Father, who art in heaven, Hallowed be thy Name. Thy Kingdom come. Thy will be done in Earth as it is in Heaven. Give us this day our daily bread. And forgive us our trespasses,…………….."

Although she was gagged, the four men heard her mumbling beneath the scarf. They stopped what they were doing, looked at her and listened. Even though the words were barely audible, Cromwell knew what she was saying. He marched over to her and struck her across the face. Heather let out a muffled scream as he slapped the side of her cheek.

"Don't you ever say those words in my presence."

Her face throbbed and she tasted blood in her mouth.

"Okay gentlemen, let's continue," said Cromwell.

"Mr. Snow, align the first two skulls and Mr. Morris, I would be indebted to you if you could bring me the third skull."

Morris nodded, bowed to Cromwell and left the basement to get Nash's skull from the study.

"Mr. Drake, please make sure that all doors and windows in this house are open, and when you return please make sure you leave the door to this basement wide open."

Drake looked at Cromwell quizzically and Cromwell rolled his eyes.

"The house needs to be open to allow Azazel to enter."

Drake nodded and darted up the stairs, dashed to every room opening every window letting in the icy chill of the night. He opened the two doors at the rear of the house and finally unlocked the large front door and wedged it open with the coat stand from which Kieran's coat hung. He stared up at the cloudless sky and saw the form of the raven silhouetted against the backdrop of stars as it soared beyond the roof.

In the basement the candles flickered as a cold breeze blew.

Until recently Heather assumed that Alexander Drake gave the orders and commanded the situation. The visions she'd seen of him demanding Alice Donaldson to reveal where the children were and ultimately ordering Joseph Morris to kill her gave her the impression he was the leader. But since she'd seen Morris with his sadistic and heartlessly aggressive attitude towards everyone, including at times even with Snow and Drake, she felt it was he who was in charge. But now she'd seen Albert Cromwell ordering Snow, Drake and Morris and how they did exactly as he instructed, she now understood that it was he who ran the show.

Snow had placed the infants' skulls on the cushions on top of two of the wooden boxes. He had made sure they followed the same sixty-degree angle as the boxes. The skulls partially faced each other.

Drake hurriedly returned to the basement, taking two steps at time with his blue cloak trailing.

"Thank you Mr Drake and thank you Mr. Snow. When Joseph returns with the third skull and it's correctly aligned we will begin the ritual to raise Azazel."

Whilst Cromwell waited for Morris he took the time to inspect William and Louisa's skulls. He bent forward as close as he could get without touching them and marvelled at the intricate patterns.

"It's really happening this time isn't it Albert?" said Snow whilst watching his old friend study the detail of the archetypon.

"Yes Bartholomew, everything's in place, we're all together and today would have been the triplet's birthday."

Snow smiled.

Morris returned to the basement carrying Charles Nash's skull under one arm and holding a large and ancient book under the other.

"I almost forgot this," said Morris, placing the book on the table. Next to the book he placed the skull.

"You disappoint me Mr. Morris, I thought you would have the entire contents of that book embedded in your memory," said Cromwell with a faint hint of a smile.

"I'm sorry, but the last time I needed to read from this was over two hundred years ago. Even my memory isn't that good."

"No matter," said Cromwell. "When you are ready, and in your own time I would like you to align the third skull."

Morris nodded.

"Gentlemen, after Mr. Morris has aligned the skull, and the ceremony has begun, there will be no turning back. I am required by Azazel, the King of Devils, to ask that those who are responsible for his renaissance are willing to proceed."

One by one, Snow, Morris and Drake confirmed that they were happy for the ceremony to go ahead.

Sophie struggled to free herself from the rope, but the knot was tied so she could barely move her wrists. Cromwell watched as she squirmed against the chair. Briefly their eyes met and just for a second she thought she saw a look of recognition in his eye. Maybe there was just a little part of Kieran Tempest to which she could appeal to stop this from happening. Cromwell looked the other way.

Morris opened the antiquated book and thumbed through until he'd found the page he needed. He laid it open to the page he required and placed a heavy leather book mark to stop the pages from rustling in the breeze which blew through the open basement door. He studied the words on the page and memorised them.

He closed his eyes, recited the words in his mind and then turned to Cromwell.

"Albert, I am going to align Mathias' skull, after which everything will be complete and we will be ready to summon Azazel," said Morris.

Cromwell nodded.

"Albert, please sit."

Cromwell lowered himself on to the chair by the circular table. In front of him was one of the three carved wooden boxes on which lay the blue embroidered cushion. The other two cushioned boxes each had an infant's skull placed upon them.

Morris picked up the skull and placed it on the cushion in front of Cromwell with the back of the cranium facing him. He aligned each skull to an angle of sixty-degrees so they partially faced each other.

He slowly walked around to the other side of the table and faced Cromwell.

The room was deadly still, and all eyes were on Morris as he stood at the table between William and Louisa's skulls. He raised his arms, took in a large breath of air and began the spell to summon Azazel.

"Bagabi laccia bachabe Lamca cahi achababe Karrelyios Lamaci lameci Bachalyas Cabaheagy sabalyos Baryolas Lagoz athia cabyolas Samahaic et famiyolas Harrahya."

Chapter 84

Linda drove like a fool. Adrenaline pumped through her and her fear of being behind the wheel of the Porsche subsided. On the seat beside her lay the stone head wrapped in the electric blanket. The head generated so much heat she could smell the fabric of the blanket slowly scorching.

She hadn't been to Gabriel Butler's house in years and found it difficult to remember where he lived. The streets were dark, and she wasn't familiar with the neighbourhood, even though it was less than a mile from where she used to live in Whitcombe Fields Road.

She spent fifteen minutes driving in and out of cul de sacs and coming to dead ends.

Eventually she found Butler's road and recognised his huge house surrounded by tall hedges and a large electric gate across the driveway. She spotted Kieran's car.

Linda stepped out of the car and tugged at the locked gates. She considered buzzing the intercom, but decided against it. She needed to find another way in.

Linda returned to the car, sat on the bonnet and considered her options.

A shadow moved across the road against the orange glow cast by a streetlight. She looked up and noticed a huge black bird fly over Butler's gates. The bird circled the drive and landed on the roof of his Rolls Royce.

"The raven," muttered Linda beneath her breath.

She recalled her husband's words the day they'd hurriedly left their last home, when the raven circled Finn Maynard's house.

'It's the bird, its Drake's raven, it's gonna happen sooner than I thought.'

Something about the bird had scared her husband, and here it was again, but this time it hung around Butler's house. She'd only seen a raven once, which was at the Tower of London. She'd never seen one near her home in Bristol before and she was sure it was the same bird that had worried Kieran.

The bird took off, flew towards the end of the Butler's road, turned and headed straight for her. She ducked just as it flew above her head. It turned when it reached the far end of the road and headed back towards her. This time the bird flew lower and Linda slammed herself onto the tarmac to avoid it crashing into her. It squawked as it flew over her and made another turn. Linda jumped to her feet, unlocked the car and got in just as the raven flew over the Porsche.

She watched from the car as the bird settled again on Butler's gates. She trembled as the bird stared at her.

"What do you want from me you little shit?"

The raven flew from the gate and landed for a second time on the Rolls Royce. It appeared to be agitated and strutting along the top of the car. Its talons didn't grip the shiny metal roof, and it slipped and tottered.

Linda wondered what the hell was up with the bird. The thing was acting crazy.

The bird flew into the darkness. Linda lowered the window and strained her eyes to see where it had gone. In the distance she heard a faint cawing which became louder quickly. She wound up the window as the bird passed above her car at an incredible speed. She gawped in astonishment as it headed for the house without slowing.

"My god, that thing will kill itself," she said to herself as it sped towards the front of the house.

The bird showed no sign of slowing as it approached. It picked up speed the closer it came to the house.

And then it disappeared.

There was no noise. She'd expected a thud or a squawk as it rammed into the house.

Linda jumped out of the Porsche and ran to the gates.

She strained her eyes and saw that the front door was wide open.

The bird had soared through the doorway of the house.

"What the hell?"

She didn't know why, but she had a hunch the bird was significant. The bird had bothered Kieran the day they'd seen it in Whitcombe Fields Road and here it was again acting strangely.

She looked at the hedges which surrounded the house. They were twelve feet high, topped with barbed wire with no way of getting over. The place was like a fortress.

She knew her husband was in grave danger and she needed to get to him.

She paced along the road and scoured the perimeter of the house for a way in.

Linda noticed something from the corner of her eye. She stopped in her tracks and was rooted to the ground. Something ran in front of her and disappeared into the hedge. She took two steps closer and then yelped as a fox bolted from a small hole in the hedge. After she'd taken a few seconds to compose herself, she got on her knees and saw the damage to the bottom of the hedge. Linda assumed a family of foxes had caused it. She was a petite lady and could squeeze her head and shoulders into the hedge. Sharp twigs and sticks scratched her face as she forced her way through to the centre of the hedge which was around four feet thick. She pushed against the twigs and leaves and followed the route made by the foxes. At last she fought her way through and pushed her head to other side of the hedge into Butler's garden. She'd broken her fingernails and was covered in cuts. Linda was about to haul herself into Butler's garden when she heard the voice of the elderly lady.

"Linda, go back and get the head."

Chapter 85

"Bagabi laccia bachabe Lamca cahi achababe Karrelyios Lamaci lameci Bachalyas Cabaheagy sabalyos Baryolas Lagoz athia cabyolas Samahaic et famiyolas Harrahya," chanted Joseph Morris with his eyes closed and his arms raised in front of him.

Heather looked on in total disbelief. Were Morris and his gang really summoning the Devil?

Morris continued the mantra.

"Bagabi laccia bachabe Lamca cahi achababe Karrelyios Lamaci lameci Bachalyas Cabaheagy sabalyos Baryolas Lagoz athia cabyolas Samahaic et famiyolas Harrahya."

Morris repeated the chant of sacred words three times and then lowered his arms.

Sophie and Heather saw something they couldn't believe was possible.

Black light.

A glow of black light materialized over the table. Tension in the basement grew and even the flames from the candles were drawn to the strange black light. It was a glowing cloud of darkness. The black light emanated a smell like sulphur and emitted a deep drone which sounded like a rumble of distant thunder.

The rumbling drone intensified and hurt Heather's ears and the black light pained her eyes.

Sophie squealed as something brushed past her face and a second later Heather felt the same thing. They looked up and saw the raven circling the basement. It barely missed the walls and continued to circuit the room. Heather tried to push back in the chair to dodge the bird. The raven flew faster, and the drone got louder. Drake, Snow and Morris stood motionless and Cromwell sat with his eyes closed. The bird continued to pick up speed and was flying in smaller circles as it came closer to the centre of the basement. The drone became unbearable, and the sisters wanted to put their hands over their ears to block it out.

Cromwell stood up, raised his arms and released a primal cry which was only just audible over the increasing drone from the strange black light. The bird flew nearer to the middle of the room and closer to the table.

Sophie shook with fear.

The bird made its final circuit and as it did the cloud of black light expanded, engulfed the raven and then vanished taking the bird with it.

The room was silent. The rumbling stopped the instant the light disappeared and Cromwell had stopped screaming.

Heather looked around the room. She wondered whether if it was over. Did the men just summon the Devil?

And if so, what would happen next?

Chapter 86

Linda looked around. The voice came from behind the hedge.
"Go back and get the head."
"Who's there?" called Linda.
No one answered.
She wasn't scared, she knew whoever spoke was trying to help.
"Who is it, who's there?"
"Go back to the car."

Linda scurried through the hedge backwards and winced with pain as the twigs and branches cut her face.

She backed out of the hedge, stood up and saw an old lady wearing a heavy black coat buttoned to her neck. The lady stood by Linda's car with something in her arms. Linda crossed the road.

"Who are you? Are you the person who's been speaking to me?"

The lady smiled. She had a kind face.

She held the electric blanket in which was wrapped the stone head.

"How did you get that? I'd locked the car."

"My name is Hermione. Take this to the house. Find your way to the basement. You need to go now."

Hermione passed the blanket to Linda. The heat from the head radiated through the fabric.

"What should I do?" asked Linda.

The woman had gone.

She was dumbstruck. She wondered what on earth she'd just seen. She questioned whether it had been a ghost. Strange things were happening, and she was more concerned than ever for her husband. She wanted him to be back home with her. She would have to worry about the ghostly lady later. She had to rescue her husband from whatever Butler had in mind for him.

She ran back to the hedge, ducked down and made her way through the hole. She emerged through the other side with the head, stood up and brushed leaves from her coat. With the head tucked under her arm, she made her way to the house. Slowly she crept into the large hallway.

The basement, Hermione said I need to find the basement, thought Linda.

Warily she tiptoed along the hall as quietly as possible.

Which way is the basement?

She tried each of the doors along the hall. None of them opened to a basement. She got to the end of the hall and noticed part of the wood clad wall appeared to be open.

This must be a secret door.

Linda pushed the door open, saw the wooden staircase and made out the wavering glow of the candles from below. She held the head against her chest and felt the heat permeate through the blanket.

She took a deep breath and placed her right foot on the top stair.

In the basement silence prevailed.

After screeching at the top of his voice, Cromwell lowered his arms. Heather looked at his eyes. They were different. The sclerae of his eyes, which should be white, were as black as coal, giving his pupils no definition. She turned and faced the other way.

Morris began a new mantra which started in a tiny whisper.

"Anil nathrach, ortha bhis is beatha, do chal danaimh."

And again, but a little louder.

"Anil nathrach, ortha bhis is beatha, do chal danaimh."

And louder again.

"Anil nathrach, ortha bhis is beatha, do chal danaimh."

Sophie saw the black light again, but this time it was different. The light appeared from an eye socket of one of the infant's skulls as an obscure murky beam which slowly inched its way towards the third skull. It reminded her of a snake slithering through the air. It reached the left eye socket of Mathias' skull and quickly emerged from the right one. It picked up speed and continued towards the other infant's skull where it entered through the left eye socket. Sophie waited in anticipation for it to come out of the right one, but it didn't, at least not straight away. Then, with a high-pitched whine it shot from the right socket and joined up with the left eye socket of the first skull making a perfect equilateral triangle. The black light pulsated and the low drone returned whilst the high-pitched whine diminished.

The drone became louder than before and Heather squirmed as it shook her to the core. As the sound increased the temperature in the basement became warmer.

At the top of the stairs Linda heard the drone. It sounded like an old gas-fired furnace. She smelt something odd which reminded her of spent matches.

She took another step down the stairs.

What the hell's happening in there? She thought, as she cautiously took another step.

The old staircase creaked. She didn't need to worry about anyone hearing it, the noise from the basement drowned it out.

She reached the bottom of the stairs and poked her head around the corner and noticed how hot the basement was. The heat hadn't risen up the stairs to the hall, it remained at the bottom of the stairs. She tightened her grip on the stone head and pulled it against her chest.

The basement was lit by candles, and it took Linda a few seconds for her eyes to adjust to the light. She saw the circular table surrounded by four men. She placed her hand over her mouth when her eyes met with Finn Maynard. He, like the other two men who were standing, wore a blue and silver cloak with a gold pentagram. Another man sat and wore a gold coloured cloak with his back towards her. She couldn't see Gabriel Butler in the room, so assumed it was him in the chair.

Linda gasped when she saw Sophie tied with a gag over her mouth. The young woman looked ashen with fear. She saw Heather on the other side. Linda recognised Heather as the woman who she'd nearly run over with the Porsche, the same woman who'd dropped the stone head on the car.

What the hell is she doing here?

Her eyes became more accustomed to the dimly lit room, and she spotted the infants' skulls on the table with the strange black beams of light pulsating from the eye sockets. She couldn't see Mathias' skull because it was obscured by the man in the chair. The throbbing drone beat in her ears and she became disoriented. She took a breath of sulphurous air and slowly advanced into the basement. She was scared, but had an inner confidence which drove her to find her husband.

The drone felt like a drill through her head. She trembled as she walked towards the table and was astonished to see that none of the men had noticed her. They were transfixed by the light coming from the skulls. Then she saw the larger adult skull.

"What in God's name is happening here," she whispered. Linda needn't have bothered whispering. She may as well have shouted at the top of her lungs and still no one would have heard her over the drone which had become so loud, it made the floor of the basement shake.

She took another pace forward and felt her knees buckle when she saw who was sitting in the chair.

"Kieran," she called.

He took no notice.

She looked at his eyes, they looked horrible. They were as dark as the December night sky.

"Kieran, what are they doing to you?"

Her eyes darted around the basement and she wondered why Gabriel Butler wasn't there. She turned and stared at Sophie, who looked terrified and had been watching Linda from the moment she'd entered the basement. Her eyes pleaded with Linda.

Then everything changed.

The drone stopped and the black light beaming from the eyes of the skulls vanished.

Everything became quiet.

Fear overcame Linda. She stood a few feet from the men, and yet they didn't see her. She was rooted to the spot, like a rabbit in headlights and was so scared she couldn't move or think properly.

Then something brought her to her senses.

Mathias' skull began to pulse like a beating heart. Linda watched Finn and the other two men standing around the table transfixed by the throbbing skull. She looked at her husband and his ghastly dark eyes. He seemed lifeless and stared into space like a waxwork dummy.

For the first time she noticed the archetypon on the back of Mathias' skull as it continued to throb. The skull looked like jelly. She couldn't comprehend what was happening. The throbbing skull became translucent and she could see a spinning whirlpool of black light inside.

The room was silent and all she could hear was her heart beating in her head.

Suddenly a beam of black light blazed from the archetypon on the back of the third skull and contacted Kieran's face. He jolted in the chair, but otherwise remained motionless. The black light crackled as it flickered. Then one of the men spoke.

"It's happening," whispered Morris, "this is the moment we've been waiting for. Gentlemen, prepare to stand in the presence of Azazel, the King of Devils."

Linda watched her husband. His body arched forward as the light emanating from the skull pulled him in.

The three men were so engrossed by what was happening, they still hadn't noticed Linda on their peripheral.

Kieran's face contorted, and he continued to be pulled towards the skull.

Linda watched in horror as her husband's appearance changed in front of her eyes. His jawbone was widening, his temple became more prominent and his darkened eyes became wider apart. He was metamorphosing into someone else. Someone hideous.

She remembered what the tattooed man said.

'Prepare to stand in the presence of Azazel, the King of Devils.'

Then it occurred to her what was happening. Finn Maynard and the other two men were using her husband to summon the devil, and her husband was becoming the devil, or as the man had just said, 'Azazel, the King of Devils'.

Her eyes darted between Sophie and Heather as if she sought guidance from them.

Her husband's face continued to change, and she barely recognised him.

She needed to concentrate. What could she do to save him?

Come on Linda, think, use your head.

And then it came to her.

I must use my head.

Linda stepped back out of view of Finn and the other two men, kneeled on the floor and unrolled the blanket which she'd been holding tightly to her chest. The scorching hot stone head rolled from the blanket and onto the floor. She hurriedly laid the blanket out flat and crawled on her knees to pick up the stone. It was too hot to touch with her bare hands. Linda looked around, but found nothing with which she could pick it up. She spat on her hands and nudged the head with her palms, wincing as the stone burned her skin. It was like touching a scalding hot dish straight from the oven.
Linda climbed to her feet and rolled the head with the sole of her shoe until it lay in the middle of the blanket.

She leant forward and picket up two corners of the blanket, took two paces forward and picked up the other two corners and lifted the head from the floor.

She gripped it with both hands so she was as close to the stone head as possible, hauled the blanket over her head, lunged unceremoniously towards the table and brought the stone head in the blanket crashing down upon Mathias' skull.

The skull cracked into two pieces. One half dropped from the cushion and slid across the table and the other half bounced to the floor.

Morris made a swipe at Linda, but was surprised to find he had little strength as he staggered towards her.

Linda saw him coming and jumped out of his way. She moved towards the half of Mathias' skull on the floor and crushed it with her foot. Morris fell to his knees and stumbled across the floor. He reached for her leg, and she effortlessly kicked him in his eye with the toe of her shoe.

She heard a thud and saw Kieran had fallen forward face down onto the table. She turned and was about to make her way to him, but was stopped by Morris who had grabbed hold of her ankle, causing her to lose her balance. Linda fell forward and hit her chin on the edge of the table. As she fell she grappled for the side of the table, pulling the blue velvet cloth which covered it. She rolled over holding onto the cover just as Morris lunged at her. She held the blue cover in front of her face, catching Morris as he fell towards her. Linda rolled him to one side in the cover and was surprised at how little resistance the funny little man put up. It was like pushing away a child. She clambered to her feet, picked up the stone which was still scorching hot. She tolerated the burning to the palms of her hands before sending it crashing down upon Morris who flailed beneath the cover. Then he lay still.

Linda surveyed the basement. Finn Maynard looked around with a dumbstruck expression. She couldn't see the other man. He seemed to have disappeared. The blue and silver cloak he'd been wearing lay crumpled on the floor. Linda weighed up the situation. She was sure she'd single-handedly brought down the short squat man with the tattooed face, Finn looked disoriented and appeared harmless enough, and there was no sign of the other man apart than the cloak he wore. Linda couldn't be certain but was sure he hadn't escaped up the stairs.

She made a beeline for her husband who lay face down on the table, pulled away the hood of the gold cloak and saw the back of his head as he lay slumped upon the table. Linda held her breath and closed her eyes and moved to lift his head, not sure if she wanted to see his face after experiencing how it had contorted whilst being blasted by the black light which had flashed from the back of the skull.

Slowly, she lifted his head and heard him breathe erratically as though something was blocking his airway. She turned his head, dreading what she expected to see.

She let out a huge gasp when she saw he looked normal. His eyes were tightly closed, and he was definitely breathing.

"Thank God," she murmured.

Linda looked up. She heard muffled shouts and screams coming from either side of the basement. It was Heather and Sophie vying for her attention. She jumped up, scurried to Sophie, untied her from the chair and removed the scarf from over her mouth. Sophie stretched her aching limbs and rubbed her wrists before going over to Heather and freeing her.

As soon as she'd released her sister she ran to Finn, who ambled around the basement as if he was sleepwalking.

"Finn, Finn its Sophie."

He turned around with the hood of the cloak obscuring his eyes. She bent forward to look at his face beneath the hood.

"Fin, speak to me."

Heather came over and hugged her sister.

"He doesn't know who I am," sobbed Sophie.

"Give him time, let him come around slowly," replied Heather.

Linda shook Kieran.

"Wake up, please open your eyes and say something."

Kieran lifted his head from the table and opened his eyes. The blackness which had engulfed them had faded and his sclerae were a faint grey colour.

"It's okay, it's over," said Linda whilst holding her confused and disorientated husband.

She pulled him close and hugged him.

"What's happened to Snow?" asked Heather surveying the room.

"I've no idea, I didn't see him leave. But I'm not worrying about him, I'm concerned for Finn," replied Sophie.

Heather walked over to the cloak Snow had been wearing and nudged it with her toe.

She scanned the room and the aftermath of the event. Heather saw what was left of Mathias' skull lying crushed on the floor. She picked up a piece, examined the pattern on the back, dropped it back to the floor and crushed it with her heel. The two infant's skulls lay next to each other near Charlie, the stone head.

"Well Charlie, you've come in handy after all," she said and then bent forward to pick up the head.

She turned to the two skulls, pushed them with her foot so they lay next to each other, lifted Charlie as high as she could and then brought him crashing down upon both skulls shattering them into dozens of pieces.

"What about him?" said Linda, pointing to Morris who lay motionless concealed by the cloak.

"What about him?" replied Heather.

"We should check him, make sure he won't cause any further trouble."

Heather and Linda bent forward to turn him over when Heather realised who Linda was.

"Hang on, you're the woman who nearly ran me over, you drove off with Charlie."

"Charlie?"

"Charlie, he's the stone head that bounced onto the bonnet of your car. I was on my way to the Suspension Bridge. I was going to throw him into the river."

"Well it's a bloody good job you didn't. If it hadn't been for 'Charlie', I doubt whether I would have been able to stop what was happening here tonight," smiled Linda

The two women went to grab Morris' side so they could roll him onto his back, but were bemused when they found there was nothing beneath the cloak for them to grip. Heather whipped away the cloak and beneath it was nothing. Just as Albert Snow had appeared to disappear, Joseph Morris had also vanished into thin air.

Sophie pulled at her husband's hand and pleaded with him.

"Finn, it's me, Sophie, don't you know who I am?"

He moved his head and looked at her with a distant look in his eye. Sophie reached out and pulled down the hood of the cloak which partially covered his face.

Sophie put her hand into her pocket for a tissue to wipe her eyes and found something large and soft. She pulled it out, it was Rosie's pink bear. She took a few seconds to look at it and was going to hold it to her breast when Finn raised his hand.

He reached for the bear and with a trembling hand took it from her.

She heard him whisper, almost inaudibly beneath his breath.

"Rosie."

"That's right, it belongs to your daughter Rosie," said Sophie.

"My daughter?"

Finn was still confused and disoriented, but the pink bear stirred something deep within him.

"Rosie's your daughter and you have a son called Jack. Rosie's five and Jack's one." Sophie paused and then continued, "my name's Sophie and I'm your wife."

Finn had difficulty understanding what was going on around him. Sophie touched his hand and felt the ring on his finger given to him by Albert Snow. She lifted his hand and looked at the ghastly thing. It made her shudder. Everything went wrong the day he put it on. She gave it a tug and was surprised at how easily it came off. She threw it to the floor and watched it bounce and settle on the cloak which Snow had been wearing.

Sophie and Heather watched in astonishment. The ring dissolved before their eyes, burning a hole in the cloak. Within a few seconds the cloak caught fire and burnt so ferociously that in under a minute it was reduced to smouldering ash and the ring had disappeared. Nothing near the cloak had been burnt, the flames hadn't even left a scorch mark on the floor.

Finn blinked and looked around. By removing the ring Sophie had broken the strange spell that had taken over her husband. He looked at her with a quizzical expression.

"Sophie?"

She smiled and threw her arms around him. He hugged her and kissed her neck. Suddenly he stopped and staggered towards the table. Heather grabbed a chair and placed it behind him just in time.

"I'm dizzy, where are we?"

"All in good time, all in good time my darling," said Sophie with a smile as she knelt to his level and placed her hand on his knee.

She turned to Linda sitting with Kieran and looked at her with a sombre face.

"You knew about this. What kind of people are you. You're devil worshippers."

"No, it's not how it looks," said Linda. She took a pause and continued. "I don't think it's over, there's another man we need to stop, someone who's behind all of this."

"Who?" asked Sophie.

"Gabriel Butler. He asked Kieran to come here tonight. Butler offered Kieran ridiculous money for an evening's work, and now I know why. He had no intention of paying him, and if I hadn't stopped this tonight, I would have lost my husband to the Devil."

"Butler's gone," said Sophie.

"Why, what happened? Where did he go?"

Sophie pointed to the cloak which Joseph Morris had been wearing.

"That was Butler, he's gone, he's no more."

Linda frowned. "That wasn't Gabriel Butler."

"Believe us, it was Butler," said Heather.

"That wasn't Gabriel, you must be mistaken."

"Sorry Linda, it's difficult to understand, you must believe me……. that was Butler."

Linda looked bewildered and shook her head.

"But how can…………?" said Linda, her voice trailed away, comprehending what she'd been told.

She removed the gold cloak from Kieran, tossed it onto the floor and helped him to his feet.

"If you ladies don't mind, I'd like to take my husband home."

Kieran was unsteady as Linda helped him to his feet. She walked him to the stairs, and he hobbled like an old man.

"What's happening?" shouted Sophie pointing to the gold cloak which Linda had thrown down.

It lunged back and forth across the basement floor.

"There's something underneath it," said Heather, who made her way towards the cloak as it twisted and turned.

"Be careful," said Sophie.

Heather hesitantly reached for the cloak, lifted it and screamed as the raven flew at her.

"Get that bird," shouted Sophie.

But it was too late. The raven flew out of the basement. Heather trembled with fright.

"It's okay, it's gone," said Linda.

Sophie led her husband to the stairs. He was weak, but could walk. Kieran and Linda followed behind. Kieran hadn't spoken a word since he came round. Linda looked at him and gave him a weary smile and saw the whites of his eyes had returned.

Heather waited for the others to leave before it was her turn. Apart from the creaking of the old stairs, the basement was silent.

Then she heard a voice.

"Heather, you did well."

She looked around to see Elizabeth standing before her with a beaming smile.

"Elizabeth!" Heather went to hug her, but stopped when Elizabeth raised her hand.

"Don't get too close, don't forget I'll burn you."

Heather took a step back when she felt heat radiate from the vision.

"But I didn't stop it, it was Linda, the other woman."

"I suppose things didn't happen quite as we'd expected, but if it hadn't been for you, then Morris, Drake, Snow and Cromwell would have summoned the Devil this evening."

"But I didn't protect Charles Nash, I was only partly responsible for what Linda did tonight. She smashed his skull."

"And that's what protected Nash from them. Without his skull they've no need for him."

"So is he okay?"

"He will be, and so will his brother and sister. They will be happy now. They will move on."

Elizabeth paused and smiled.

"Those men, they've gone now haven't they? They can't harm us anymore," asked Heather.

"Unfortunately not, they will be back, but hopefully not for a long time, and when they do it will be someone else's job to stop them and not yours."

"That bird, it signified the Devil didn't it."

"No Heather, the raven didn't signify the Devil……….. it was the Devil, and like Morris, Snow, Drake and Butler, it will return."

The image of Elizabeth faded, and as it did Heather could just make out her final words before she vanished altogether.

"Heather, remember, you did okay."

Then she was no more.

She stood on her own in silence and contemplated what Elizabeth had just told her and the events of the evening.

Another voice brought her out of her thoughts. This time it was Sophie.

"Heather, hurry and get out of there, we're waiting for you."

She took one last look around the basement and gazed at the smashed skulls on the floor. The room dimmed as the candles quickly burnt out one by one.

"Wait for me, I'm coming," called Heather breathlessly and ran up the stairs.

She slammed the secret door to the basement and heard it click as it locked.

She threw her arms around Sophie and Finn, and looked over Sophie's shoulder to Linda and Kieran.

"Come on, let's go home."

They slowly lumbered their way along the hall and out of the door.

The crunch of the gravel beneath their feet felt good.

Somewhere in the distance they heard the caw of the raven as it soared high in the dark December evening sky.

"What a hideous night,……… did that really happen?" said Sophie.

Heather nodded.

"I'm just glad it's over. I'm desperate to see my children," added Sophie.

Heather turned to her sister with a solemn look and touched her hand.

"This thing will never be over."

The End

Epilogue

After many months Finn Maynard made a steady recovery from the events leading up to the 14th December 2006. He had no recollection of ever being Alexander Drake.

In February 2007, for the first time, plants began to grow in the front and back gardens of 11a. A small crop of narcissus and crocus grew by the front gate and by early summer grass was growing, even though neither Finn nor Sophie had sowed any seeds.

Finn and Sophie decided to move away from Whitcombe Fields Road and bought a new property in the summer of 2007.

Also in February Heather returned to her flat, but like Finn and Sophie, in Whitcombe Fields Road, she couldn't bear to live there and moved out the following summer.

Finn left SOS Graphics and doesn't keep in contact with his old work colleague Sally.

Linda Tempest felt partly responsible for what had happened to the Maynard family and insisted that Kieran pay for the damage that had been done to 11a. Kieran paid for the repairs to the foundations and a brand new kitchen.

Ruth Jackson's body was found by police investigating her disappearance. She was discovered where Butler had dumped her in the chest freezer in Kieran's old house. Both Kieran and Finn were principle suspects, as at the time Kieran still owned the property and police were aware Finn had been digging beneath his kitchen. Police suspected Finn had been digging a hole to hide her body.

During their investigations, police inspected the hole in the Maynard's kitchen. They didn't find the remains of William and Louisa which had inexplicably disappeared. Finn had no recollection of the skeletons he had been digging for.

After forensic DNA testing, both Finn and Kieran were no longer suspects in Ruth's murder enquiry. The police turned their attention to Gabriel Butler who was known to be living in the property after Kieran and Linda had moved.

Police are still searching for Butler. His Rolls Royce Silver Cloud was found in the driveway of his empty mansion. In the basement police found the crushed remains of two infants' skulls and one adult's. They also found a strange painted stone head. One of the investigating officers said the stone head felt warm.

Forensic evidence dated the skulls between one-hundred and fifty to two-hundred years old and also confirmed that they were related.

Charles Nash, William and Louisa no longer live in purgatory and have moved on to find happiness.

Kieran suffered a nervous breakdown in early 2007. He made good recovery, but always looks over his shoulder and is never lets his guard down. He became paranoid and expects Gabriel Butler to return at any time.

Heather and Sophie are haunted by what happened that night in the basement and are plagued by nightmares.

Occasionally Heather hears the caw of a raven, although she has never seen one since that night in December 2006.
Heather never heard from Alice Donaldson, her great grandmother Elizabeth, or Charles and Hermione Nash again.

There is one thing of which Heather is certain.

Azazel will return

A Message from the Author

A personal note from Andrew M Stafford

Hello,

Thank you for reading The Third Skull. I'm grateful that you've chosen it and have taken the time to read it.

I am a relatively new author. If you would like to contact me with your thoughts on this story, you can email me at andy@andystaffordbooks.co.uk

If you did enjoy it, I would be grateful if you would leave a review on Amazon telling other visitors to the site what you thought of The Third Skull. Positive reviews can really help new authors succeed and could help others decide whether or not to purchase a book.

It is easy to write a review and can be done by going to the Amazon page where you purchased the book and scroll down to where it says **'Customer Reviews: Write a customer review'**.

You may like to visit my website at:

andystaffordbooks.co.uk

Visit my Facebook page.at

www.facebook.com/AndrewMartinStafford

Follow me on Twitter @worksovart

My very best wishes

Andy Stafford

Other books by Andrew M Stafford

The Hill: A Paranormal Murder Mystery Thriller

'The Hill reveals the world for what it is; a place where the impossible is real, and the dead speak with the living'

What if you were murdered? And what if by supernatural intervention you are given the chance to help the police find your killer? This is what happened to rookie police officer Ben Walker after he and his new girlfriend, Liz Mason became victims of a callous and brutal attack by Daniel Boyd, a grudge bearing drop out, and his gang.

Ben's body lay alongside Liz, who was unconscious and barely alive at the bottom of Mill Tut, a Bronze aged burial mound in the beautiful Badock's Wood in Bristol.

DCI Markland Garraway, who at the last moment is brought in to lead the investigation into Ben's murder has a reputation of being a maverick detective who thinks outside the box.

The mystical powers of the ancient burial mound begin to influence Garraway's attitude towards the case and soon he is alienated by his colleagues. Mill Tut, or The Hill as Garraway refers to it, opens up a Pandora's Box of supernatural happenings which infiltrate his waking and sleeping life, creating a host of mental demons which the Scottish detective must learn to deal with.

Daniel Boyd has fled Bristol to evade capture for the crime he has committed. To those who know him, he's vanished off the face of the earth. But can he escape the mystical powers of The Hill?

The power of The Hill does not only affect Garraway. It reaches out to many, including Christopher Jameson, who was born at the precise moment Ben's life ended.

The Hill reveals to Garraway and the others who are affected by its influence, the world for what it is; a place where the impossible is real, and the dead speak with the living.

What people are saying about **The Hill**

Reviews of the Omnibus edition of The Hill from Amazon UK (Containing both Book One and Book Two).

5.0 out of 5 stars **Wow** 2 August 2015

What a fantastic book. I have been reading books for 50+ years and never ever have I come across anything like this one. I just had to keep reading and reading. The plot was unlike anything I have ever encountered. Very well thought out and even believable. I was constantly asking myself if the story could be based on truth it was so convincing. I find it hard to believe this was the author's first book.

The spelling was very good and the grammar (apart from 2 or 3 mistakes) was excellent far better than most books I buy on Kindle I sincerely hope there will be further books from this author.

Give yourself a pat on the back Andrew you deserve it.

5.0 out of 5 stars **Best book I've read on kindle,** 21 April 2015

I loved this book, I felt as though I was there with the characters. Full of suspense and would love to see it made into a film. Can't wait for more by this author. Well done Andrew Stafford.

5.0 out of 5 stars **Superb!** 19 April 2015

This is a truly excellent book and a page turner from start to finish. It has a gripping plot and holds the attention all the way through. I can thoroughly recommend it as an excellent read.

5.0 out of 5 stars **would make good viewing,** 12 April 2015

Can't wait for his next book. Why don't they make films or TV dramas, would make good viewing

5.0 out of 5 stars **A truly amazing read best book I've read by far** 7 April 2015

A truly amazing read best book I've read by far and I read a lot. A fantastic story of which you feel every emotion cannot rate it highly enough truly brilliant

5.0 out of 5 stars **I loved this book and couldn't put it down,** 28 Mar. 2015

I loved this book and couldn't put it down. .would make a fabulous mini series or film.. highly recommend.

HOW TO BUY THE HILL

Purchase The Hill: A Paranormal Murder Mystery Thriller. (Omnibus Edition containing both Book One and Book Two) from your Amazon store at the following link

www.lrd.to/7gRNgpOsag

Or available for Free as an e-book.

The Hill - Ben's Story **(Book One).** A Paranormal Murder Mystery Thriller.
(50% of the Omnibus edition) for free from your Amazon store at the following link

www. lrd.to/Hill-Bens

If you enjoy **Book One** (Ben's Story), you can purchase **Book Two** (Carla's Story).

Andrew M Stafford

Printed in Great Britain
by Amazon